DOCTORS
AND
WIVES

DOCTORS AND WIVES

A NOVEL BY

Ann Pinchot

 ARBOR HOUSE *New York*

To my friends of the
Stamford Medical Society

CHAPTER 1

Karen awoke, flushed and trembling, after the most erotic dream.

Delos was involved. At least she thought it was Delos—his powerful body, the quirk of his splendid mouth. He was making love to her, the way he had the first time they were together ("Relax, darling, don't be afraid. I'll take care of you, promise. . . ."). And then, as she felt her body yield, felt herself go loose and wet in readiness for him, his image dissolved in a kind of mist, and then, though the next lover holding her so tightly was still passionate, still insistent, he had a gentleness lacking in Delos. . . . He was Peter.

Why? Why had Delos faded and taken on Peter's shape?

The question puzzled her as she emerged from sleep, opening her eyes to a morning that promised April at its loveliest. She took a deep breath, lifting her rounded breasts, the rose-beige nipples still erect.

Our needs, she recalled reading somewhere, *first show themselves on a dream level.*

That being true, how could she tell which of them meant more to her, Delos or Peter?

Wasn't it strange that she had met both men through the Arnold Lukases?

Arnold Lukas was the patriarch of the German Jewish family that had owned politically powerful newspapers and magazines in Berlin, among them *Das Plakat*. With the help of American friends like Karen's grandmother, Sarah Wickersham, the family had managed to smuggle part of their vast fortune out of Germany before the Holocaust. In Manhattan they invested in a small, struggling radio station that in time blossomed into the Third Network, the least popular but most politically responsible of the major television broadcasters.

Mady Lukas, the granddaughter, had been in Karen's class at Bennington, her best friend there. Which was how Karen got her first job after college at the Third Network.

It was the elder Arnold Lukas who discovered Karen's interest in broadcasting, when he took both girls to lunch at the Plaza. With characteristic generosity, he offered to arrange for her to meet the personnel head.

"I wish Mady had your interest and enthusiasm," he added, smiling wistfully at his granddaughter.

"I'm not interested in a career," Mady retorted. "Right now I'm interested in love and marriage and I don't mind which comes first, just as long as I have both."

Mady was a perfect specimen of the German *Mädchen:* strong bones, a well-shaped head, wide-spaced amber eyes, thick chestnut hair. But she was one hundred percent Jewish—as she quickly reminded anyone who was interested. She went to Europe right after graduation, to seek out members of her displaced family in Antwerp, Brussels and London.

Karen went to work for the Third Network, starting as a receptionist on the fifth floor. She didn't remain there long.

She did well. She had the unconscious assurance of tradition and money. She was gracious and helpful to visitors. The top brass inspected her closely—as they did all the new "girls"—and approved. These men were all lean, body-conscious, three martinis for lunch executives. They were a cool, calculating, self-centered lot, and they rated the women who worked for them, grading them on looks, charm, amiability—"the slave-girl syndrome," as one of the young women described it to Karen. "They don't bother with the girls in the downstairs typing pool, they want the cream of the crop."

Since Karen was the new one, the others were watching her, trying to discover which man would stake out his claim.

Nobody expected it would be Delos Burke. Not after all the problems he was rumored to be having with his wife.

At various times nearly all the pretty young television women had been in love with Delos. At first he was an urbane, elegant man, both on camera and off, who stirred his TV audiences with his sense of history. He had tremendous visual appeal; though not good-looking in the traditional sense, he was handsome in a rough-hewn, flagrantly masculine way. The look, Karen thought, of a Black Irish pirate, with a shock of coarse dark hair, intense black eyes under heavy brows, the nose slightly crooked as though broken in a fight. And his smile, which had knocked her over with its sudden spontaneity. It was like a caress, that smile . . .

He had a unique presence and the voice to go with it. Old Mr. Lukas had the highest regard for Delos; he was important to the network. Few anchormen inspired such respect, such awe. And in women he inspired something more. . . .

He had known many women, some of them in the hermetically sealed world of the very rich, where he was an intriguing and mysterious cypher, some of them young women who worked at the network. But he made no secret of the fact that he was married. His wife, Karen gleaned from various sources, was a charming woman in her forties, whom he called "mother."

When Karen first met Delos he was just back from Sweden, where he had gone to film a documentary. Mr. Lukas was so pleased with it, that he assigned Delos a series of evening profiles on people in the limelight. He would temporarily give up his duties as anchorman for the six o'clock news to concentrate on his series, which would follow the six o'clock report in an effort to keep viewers tuned in.

A flurry of gossip accompanied Delos's return. The grapevine said he'd had a fling with one of Sweden's great models. He was back sooner than expected. There were whispers about his wife; nothing out in the open, just speculation. . . .

Karen never dreamed he would notice her, hadn't even wanted

him to, not at first. Her experiences with college dating had not prepared her for a man like Delos . . .

The first weeks Delos merely nodded pleasantly to her as he stepped out of the elevator. Then, one morning, he stopped at her desk.

"You're Sarah Wickersham's granddaughter," he said.

How could he have known, unless he had gone through her job application?

"Yes," she said, shy but with a touch of pride.

"She's a remarkable woman. Second only to the late Eleanor Roosevelt . . ."

"My grandmother and Mrs. Roosevelt were friends."

"I'd like to meet your grandmother one day. I knew Mrs. Roosevelt when she was at the United Nations." He tilted his rough dark head. "We might have something in common."

It started in August when he was making plans for his profile series. He offered her the job as his girl Friday and she accepted, torn between trepidation and joy. She was flattered; she found him immensely attractive; she felt herself trembling in his presence. She tried to hide it from him but suspected he was wise to her and that his effect on her amused him. She was disconcerted to feel his gaze on her, a glint of Irish humor in his eyes.

She didn't know how to deal with her impulses, these wayward new feelings. She had found even adolescent petting vaguely frightening. So she stifled her desire, afraid that if she let go the result would be something wild, passionate; something she wasn't ready for and might regret.

If she had similar fears about Delos's feelings, he assuaged them. For one thing, he kept her so busy the next month that she had no time for reflection. He was shaping up his schedule for tapings and her job included making contact with the people he wanted to interview, reading enough about them to give him material to enliven his interviews. Not the routine stuff, but little-known and authentic "giblets," as they were called in the trade. He liked to spring surprises on the more stuffy personalities. He made enemies and friends; he was curious, he prodded, he questioned—and his Nielsen rating went up. Mike Wallace, move over . . .

He was a perfectionist in his way, never pleased with what he'd produced, and before a taping he was so energized that afterwards it took a generous amount of vodka to settle him down. He had a house in Westport, which he seldom had time to visit and where his wife lived most comfortably with her dogs and horses. Karen saw a photograph of her on Delos's desk—a slender woman in a riding habit, her dark hair pulled severely off her face, a faint brooding expression in her eyes, her mobile mouth barely smiling. It was an enigmatic face, Karen thought.

He never spoke of his wife; if he called her or accepted calls from her, it was never in Karen's presence. He maintained a small apartment in Manhattan, on the west side off Central Park, where a number of men kept efficiency apartments for their own use—or to lend friends who met their current girl friends for a "matinee."

It seemed inevitable that Delos would make love to her. They often worked late, not at the studio but in his apartment. Here she saw another side of Delos Burke, relaxed after a few drinks and much more approachable. After they were finished going over plans for future tapings, he liked to sit back in an easy chair, or stretch out on the studio couch and talk. Under the influence of a drink he often rambled in a casual way, as if free associating. She learned about his youth in the northwest; his father had been a logger who was killed in an accident when he was floating logs down a river to a sawmill. Delos was a self-made man, worked his way through college. But through travel and friendships with the right people, he had acquired a finish that together with the suggestion of a certain primitive sensuality made him very engaging to women.

The women in the office made book as to how long it would take Delos to make Karen his mistress. "That's the perk for working so hard for him. Delos always rewards his current choice."

Perhaps she should feel vulnerable when they discussed Delos; perhaps it was not only jealousy but pity for his latest conquest. By now, however, she was committed to him. Her doubts about commitment to a married man, at the beginning, had made her uncertain, but Delos's skill as a lover brought to life all her submerged sexual feelings. A good teacher, he was enchanted by her response, by the openness of her passion. The fact that these emotions were new to her gave them an added charm. He told her sometimes, as they lay together on the narrow daybed, their bodies entwined, that he had never felt anything like this before; that she brought back his youth, his energy, even his dreams, and he would be forever grateful to her.

Karen too was grateful. To Delos, for awakening her. To whatever had kept her from going all the way in college, when most of her friends were losing their virginity—if they hadn't already done so in high school. "There's a sexual revolution going on," they teased her, "you'll miss it." Karen smiled and assured them she was only waiting for the right man. She knew she wouldn't find him among the Ivy League types who came to the Bennington mixers or the brothers of classmates she sometimes dated. For Karen the first time had to be special—and with Delos it was . . .

It was certainly unlike an affair with a boy her own age and background. There was enough potential danger in the situation—his wife, Karen's family—to add zest and something more, a kind of storybook romance, which she, in her innocence, allowed to deepen and dominate her life. Fortunately her parents were both occupied with their own lives and not aware of her trancelike state. If her mother commented several times that she looked awfully thin, Karen blamed it on the demands of her job.

The women in the office were put out because she had never confided her experiences to them. They discussed the men they were sleeping with, shared notes about male behavior like good housewives sharing recipes, but if someone mentioned Delos, Karen would get up quietly from the women's lounge and disappear.

My God, the girls said, is she riding for a fall.

And the fall had come. . . .

It happened very simply. She was working in Delos's apartment one afternoon, reviewing a book by a former member of the White House staff who was critical of the new administration. Delos would analyze the critique and compare it in his next profile to the country's disenchantment with an earlier president.

He was clever about the sequences of his profiles. He'd follow a laudatory one with a stark documentary, showing all the warts . . .

She paused at her typewriter as a key clicked in the lock. It was too early for Delos, but who else could it be? She always had a tray waiting for him; vodka, ice, Perrier, cheese and Carr's table water biscuits. She noticed that recently he tended to get high too quickly if he drank without eating something first.

She left the typewriter, moved to the door, intending to embrace him at the entry as she always did. Then, with a drink at his elbow, he would go over the messages, mail and some of the documentary material he sometimes interspersed with the day's news. He'd leave for the studio while she waited in the apartment, tuning in to the station, watching with pride, then waiting eagerly for his return, for the hours they would spend together . . .

The door opened. A woman stepped over the threshold.

Karen froze. They stood facing each other for a moment. She knew that the woman in the blue Givenchy suit, the fine lizard handbag and pumps, the carefully made-up face that showed, nevertheless, a map of strain and misery, was Delos Burke's wife.

"You're the new one?" The woman's voice was cool, dispassionate, as though she were thinking aloud. "He's showing good taste this time. He doesn't always, you know."

Good God, Karen thought. What am I supposed to say—Thank you, Won't you sit down, Can I fix you a drink? She wanted to turn and run. Guilt flooded through her, guilt and remorse. She had hurt this woman—his wife.

She had never thought of it before, not like this. There'd been a brief flickering of the moral sense, some long-forgotten minister's voice from childhood warning, "Thou shalt not commit adultery." Adultery—ugly word. She had stifled it in her conscience, protested. It wasn't adultery—*she* wasn't married, wasn't betraying anyone. And Delos? Whatever he did seemed right, and if it wasn't right it was good—a higher notch on the new scale of ethics that Karen was quickly developing. Besides, from what Delos implied, his wife was beyond being hurt. Karen had seized on the merest hint, imagined (invented?) a lover in the country for the charming Mrs. Burke, a European-style marriage. That exotic Mediterranean face—how easy to create an appropriate setting for it.

Except it wasn't true, Karen realized now, as she stood facing her. The woman's cool exterior was slowly dissolving: those tragic eyes blinking, the mascara blurring, the face crumbling beneath the Georgette Klinger mask, the flared nostrils and taut lips quivering. The woman was in pain . . .

"Let me tell you something that you should know," Delos's wife said, her voice hoarse yet oddly mechanical. "When he and I took our vows, it was with the understanding that only death would part us." The thin lips twisted in a wry smile. "That's how it was for our generation—we weren't as liberated as yours."

Karen was silent.

She went on: "After our first years, after he became so well known that the women wouldn't leave him alone—not that he ever discouraged them . . . But it was more than I could bear. I tried to kill myself. But I did a bad job of it and I spent a year in a sanitarium getting myself together. And now, it's started all over again . . . Only this time I won't be so foolish. This time *I* will kill *him*."

She's being melodramatic to scare me off, Karen thought. But some instinct warned her. The depth of such passion, voiced so quietly, was a source of danger. Like a volcano, it might erupt . . .

"You look like a nice person," Delos's wife continued. "Too nice for this." Her gaze took in the daybed, the cocktail tray.

Karen began to bristle, then felt herself go limp. She had no right to get angry. Delos's wife was not the evil woman she had imagined her to be; she could hardly resent her now. She found her voice, or a feeble imitation of it. "I'm sorry—"

The woman cut her off. "Don't be. Just get out of our lives, before you get hurt. This could get rather unpleasant, you know." She paused, as if waiting for Karen to react to the veiled threat, but Karen was mute, paralyzed.

Delos's wife went on. "I suggest you give up your job at the network, make yourself unavailable to my husband. Leave him to me."

She turned on her heel and walked out. Quietly.

At the doorway she collided with Delos, who was coming in. Karen, immobilized by the event and the speed with which it had happened, noticed the strangest thing . . . how beautiful they looked together, both tall, dark, intense; how they must have loved each other at one time . . . how she must love him still . . .

"Introductions are not necessary, Delos—we understand each other perfectly. I'll simply repeat to you what I told her. The next time the headlines won't say: 'Anchorman's Wife Tries to Commit Suicide'. Do you know what it will be? 'Anchorman Shot by Wife'."

Delos tried to grab her arm but she escaped him and ran down the stairs.

Karen wondered if everything that had just happened were real. But one look at Delos's face assured her that it was.

"You've got to understand, Karen—I'm not in love with her," Delos said.

"She's in love with you."

"She's obsessed, which is not the same thing."

The room seemed suddenly unfamiliar. She thought wildly, What am I doing here? She walked back to her typewriter, pulled the sheet of paper out of the carriage, laid it on the desk. Her movements were mechanical, mindless.

Delos had closed the door and was leaning against it, never taking his glance from her tense body. His thick brows came together over the bridge of his nose; his eyes were searching, as though her behavior would give him a clue to the future. But there was no future . . .

She opened the closet door, where her blazer hung among his suits. She returned to the desk and took out her handbag, putting the long leather strap over her shoulder. She was pale but she looked composed. But she felt as though she were going to be sick.

"Karen—" he had her by the arm and wouldn't let go. His grip was powerful and unyielding. "She's done this before . . ."

Karen could not control herself. She burst out: "It's cruel to put her through this. My God . . . that face . . ."

"I support her," he said grimly. "She has everything she needs or wants. She has a good life in the country . . ."

"Which leaves you free, I suppose. And there's always a woman ready to fall into your arms—like I did!"

"There have been others, sure." His voice was so persuasive; the assured baritone that made him so appealing on television. "But they never meant much to me. You're different, darling, and you know it."

She tried not to melt when he called her darling.

"Look, Karen, I'll go out this weekend and have a talk with her. Maybe I can work something out."

"What do you mean?"

"I won't let you go, baby. I can't let you go."

All she could think was that her first love, the love on which she'd built her dreams, was morally shabby. Yet as she struggled to break away from him, she realized that he could have many women and yet he wanted her; he was even willing to try to arrange something with his wife because it was Karen he wanted.

"I could never go to bed with you again. She'd be there with us."

She pulled free of him.

"I'm quitting. As your girl Friday, as your girl in the sack. I'm sure you'll have no trouble finding a replacement."

She kept herself together until she was down on the street and hailed a cab. Once inside, she broke down and cried all the way home.

The telegram she sent the network the following morning simply said that she was leaving her job. For the next three days Delos called her home constantly. She hung up on him. Several of the women she worked with also telephoned her and she was able to reply truthfully that she was in bed with a virus infection.

Delos didn't give up easily. He wrote her several letters; she read them all and answered none of them. She was disconsolate. What hurt so much was the knowledge that she had been swept away by his reputation, his stature. She had been so proud to be a part of his stimulating life.

I was such an idiot, she thought.

She wasn't aware of it, but this was a therapeutic time for her; it was as important to mourn the death of love as the death of life. She stayed home most of the time in her parents' townhouse on East Sixty-third Street. Fortunately her parents were busy and accepted her story about losing her job. Another job? She wasn't ready yet, couldn't face the world again. But with the coming of winter she began to emerge from her cocoon.

Sometimes she visited her grandmother, Sarah Wickersham, in the lovely old brownstone off Lexington Avenue, just a couple of blocks from her parents' house. The gracious old lady, whom Karen adored, was still alert and dynamic, still absorbed in her projects. She put Karen to work addressing and stuffing envelopes and typing letters about the state of the world to the editor of the New York *Times*.

"Are you going to Hobe Sound for Thanksgiving?" Grandmother Wickersham asked.

"I hadn't thought about it."

"I may stay here until Christmas. Would you like to join me?"

"I'll think about it, grandmother."

"Karen, I don't intend to pry. But you look unhappy. Is there anything I can do to help?"

"Not really. But thank you."

When she left, she put her arms around her grandmother's erect shoulders and kissed her on the cheek. When Grandmother Wickersham held her close it was comforting. And comfort was what she craved more than anything.

It came from an unexpected source.

"Karen, it's Mady Lukas. I'm back!" The voice on the other end of the telephone was exuberant. "I checked out all my European roots and they were nice, but there was not a husbandly candidate among them."

Karen heard herself laugh, responding to Mady, who promptly invited her up to her family's country place in Belfort, Connecticut, for the weekend. "I'm dying to tell you about the men I met. What about you, Karen?"

"I'm betwixt and between . . ."

"Good. My brother Eric will be there with some medical genius he's met . . ."

Mady's call had brightened her day; she looked forward to the weekend. When the Lukas Cadillac came for her, old Mr. Lukas was bundled up in the front seat beside the chauffeur, and Mady and Eric greeted her warmly in the rear of the car. Karen knew Eric casually when she and Mady were at Bennington and he was at Dartmouth. He seemed more German than the others in the family; very proper, very precise.

Yet to her surprise, he was working on his doctoral thesis. While doing research in Belfort—which was easy, since he could spend time working out of their country house—he had met a young doctor at the hospital, Peter Norris. Enormously interesting, Eric said, very all-American. He'd be coming up Sunday to spend the afternoon.

When Peter arrived Sunday at noon, Eric greeted him warmly and brought him into the library where the girls and Mrs. Lukas were having sherry. Karen would always remember her first impression of Dr. Peter Norris. He looked like he spent a lot of time outdoors; his face was windburned and tan. By contrast his hair was sunstreaked and light, falling over his forehead and behind his aviator glasses. His blue eyes were bright. He wore a beat-up suede jacket, a white turtleneck sweater and gray flannel slacks. He seemed very much in command of himself, Karen thought as they shook hands. And he looked kind; his smile was warm, friendly, with just a quirk of his sandy eyebrows, as though he were sharing a joke with her.

Perhaps because his looks were so typically American, evoking the vast wheat fields, fertile farmland and great rivers of the Midwest, she felt immediately at ease with him. She also felt a certain chemical attraction. Peter presented a sharp contrast to Delos, who was also lean but with more of a dancer's grace. Delos was striking, with that blend of Greek and Irish genes, but she'd always had a sixth sense about him. There was something violent, perhaps even sinister, in his character; a suggestion of danger, of sexual challenge. Peter was a completely different type, but his rugged healthy good looks, his fresh, open face aroused feelings in Karen that were disturbingly sensual. She wanted to run her fingers through his tousled blond hair, touch the smooth hollow of his cheek . . .

After lunch they went for a walk along the trails of the estate. The day was cold, with a feeling of snow in the air. But they walked for three miles, returning to the library flushed and full of high spirits. Mr. Lukas had gone to his room for a nap. They drank mulled cider and ate fresh donuts. Peter, Mady and Karen sat on the long comfortable sofa in front of the fireplace, and Eric sat on a soft white shag rug near the fire, warming his legs.

Peter talked about Wisconsin and the earlier generation of the pioneers who had settled the farms. He talked about his grandfather, a horse-and-buggy doctor, his father, a Ford Model-T doctor, and about the continuity of the small town and the changes. He talked about his boyhood and the kind of wholesome small town life he and his brothers enjoyed, about his pre-med days on scholarship and his medical education at Yale.

Karen was mesmerized by Peter, how different their backgrounds were. I'll probably never see him again, she thought after he left.

But she did.

Mady, who considered herself a born Jewish matchmaker, saw to it that whenever Peter came up to the Belfort house on a Sunday afternoon, Karen was invited. The four of them went skating on the pond below the house, or walked through the frozen lanes, or just sat around, talking.

In February Mady went to Palm Beach; Eric returned to the Lukases' New York apartment to do more research at the public library, and Karen and Peter met in New York whenever he was off duty.

One evening Peter met her parents. They were impressed with him, especially her father, who concurred with Peter's ideas about nationalized medicine. Her mother enjoyed talking to him because he seemed to know a good deal about trees and plants, and he explained that his mother had a small greenhouse that he and his brothers had built so she could have some fresh growing greens in the icy winter months.

One Sunday in March, when her parents were in Palm Beach for a week between her father's Washington duties, Karen invited Peter back to the house. Otto and Verna, the live-in help, were off for the afternoon, so they were alone on a bitterly cold day. It happened naturally, as she had intended it to happen. In her own bed, where she'd dreamed her adolescent fantasies and cried over Delos, she and Peter made love for the first time.

He was hesitant about taking her to bed here, and she was touched by his sensitivity. She was the seducer and he was aware of it, even seemed to be excited by it. He knew all about the human body, yet he seemed rather tentative with hers, she thought with a secret smile. But once she slid between the cool sheets and held out her arms to him, he covered her body with his and pressed against her with a fierceness and authority that excited her.

He was not like Delos. Even with her limited experience she could sense a host of subtle differences in them as lovers. Delos had been with so many women before, and the wealth of his experience had attuned him to all the possible differences in women's bodies, women's needs. He had been sensitive to Karen's virginity, had been patient and tender with her. But despite what he claimed was a special feeling for her, there had been a kind of jadedness about his lovemaking: he had been, above all, a master technician, who had needed to please her to gratify his ego as well as to satisfy her. He desired her, yes, but he had desired so many women before her, had fulfilled his desire in so many ways that Karen was afraid he would grow bored with the simplicity of their lovemaking, would try to introduce her to practices that went against her nature. He had tested her once, asking casually if she'd like to try a *menage à trois* with another woman. He had been very drunk—they were at a party—and after one look at Karen's white face he had dropped the suggestion, but it had given her a glimmering of the chasm between them . . .

With Peter things were more equal. She was not the first woman he had slept with, nor even the second or third, but he did not seem to have the consciousness of himself as a lover that Delos had. At times she and Peter were almost like children, romping playfully together, until Peter would seem to be overcome by his desire for her, would assert himself, though still with a gentleness that Delos, she was sure, would never have been capable of. Delos had always seduced her, but with Peter she felt they were seducing each other, deliciously absorbed in each other's bodies as if both were discovering sex for the first time. There was a Romeo and Juliet quality about their intimacy, which was important to Karen for emotional reasons as well as physical ones. If she didn't make it with Peter, she risked drifting into another affair with an older, sophisticated man like Delos, risked becoming like the older women at the network, who boasted with a trace of sadness that they were women of the world.

As their need for each other increased, as the days between their meetings grew unbearable with longing, she asked, What were they going to do?

She had unburdened herself of the story of her affair with Delos. Somehow it seemed unfair to keep anything from Peter, who was so honest and straightforward. She suspected that the confession hurt him—there he was probably divided in his feelings as a doctor, who understood, and a man, who felt primitive jealousy.

"We could try it," he answered, looking directly at her. "We could live together in Belfort, and if it works out, if we're right for each other, if you really feel—"

"Feel what?" she asked.

"Feel that our relationship is not a second choice, that you're not on the rebound. That we can make it together."

"Let's try," she whispered.

It never occurred to her that, in a different way, Peter's life was as

15

tension-producing and as difficult as Delos's, that there were separations and temptations, that nearly every female patient was in love with her doctor when he was as attractive as Peter. Or that the life of a physician's mate wasn't all security and safety and oneness and the total commitment that she so ardently craved.

Perhaps she had entered the arrangement because Delos was going to South America with his wife. The paper had carried a picture of them at the airport on the personalities page opposite Liz Smith's column.

She had taken the news calmly, not revealing either to the woman who telephoned her or any of her other friends from the network that she had any particular interest in the movements of Delos Burke. She had never confided the affair to any of the women at the network; in retrospect she wondered if that had been a mistake. Surely those chic, sophisticated ladies knew more about Delos than the coffee break chatter suggested. Suppose she had been warned? Suppose one of the older women had taken her aside and said, "Look, he's handing you a line." Would she have listened? Probably not. She had been a willing, gullible victim. She had been in love.

CHAPTER II

Well, it's over, Karen told herself now, as she stored away the last traces of the disturbing dream, in the secret places of her mind. Over, finished, period: Today is the first day of my new life. What had the graffiti in the women's lounge at the network advised? Scrawled in bright red lipstick, like blood from an open vein: *Optimism is thinking the next one will be better.* A testament to disillusion and farewell from one of the older staff, some woman who had been around too long and was fed up with the second, third (fourth?) office romance.

Not that Karen believed herself fully recovered from Delos Burke, even now, with her new life with Peter to look forward to. But she recalled her Grandmother Wickersham and that wise, tart lady's antidote for disappointment. "Karen, we move on to new areas of life. The door that closes on one set of experiences prepares us to deal with the next set . . ."

She clung to these reassurances, to the faint rays of optimism.

Delos could no longer hurt her as he had others. She was safe now. Peter is my protection, she assured herself, Peter is my future . . .

She raised herself slightly in the bed, propping her arms in back of her head, hands clasped above the sturdy, shoulder-length braids that kept her fine blonde hair from tangling when she slept. She allowed her legs a luxurious stretch, feeling the pull of the muscles in her slim thighs, glanced at the brown of her skin, the result of a week in Palm Beach and Hobe Sound.

Her spacious bedroom was dappled with spring light, not yet as brilliant as a summer sun but soft, incandescent. She had loved coming back here from prep school and Bennington vacations, and returning to sleep here every night—well, *nearly* every night—during her disastrous season at the network.

This room was her retreat, her secret garden. She understood why children always searched out caves or secret places, totally inaccessible, where nobody from the prying outside world could reach them. Even her mother's miniature champagne poodle always dug himself a retreat, using his paws as tiny shovels, whenever they spent a weekend at the old family place in Rhinebeck. Not to dig out into the world but to hole in, as she had done after the shattering confrontation with Delos's wife.

My cave, Karen thought, looking around her. She had put on the silver-rimmed glasses she often wore in lieu of contact lenses.

The "cave" was furnished with English antiques, a graceful Duncan Phyfe writing desk, a rare tester bed, Queen Anne wing-chairs. Nothing as cluttered as the nursery on the top floor, which now served as an attic for her dolls, well-loved books and other assorted relics of the Cole family that would eventually be distributed to museums and thrift shops. There were pots of plants at the windows and her mother knew each by its Latin name. Karen wasn't even sure of some of the English names; she simply enjoyed them.

She averted her glance from the Pembroke table, still covered with piles of books that she'd been obliged to read and outline for Delos before the authors appeared on his special program on contemporary life. And a book on future shock of the 1980s, written by a young friend of her Grandmother Wickersham's and autographed for Karen: *To Sarah's grandchild, who will, I pray, inherit Sarah's grace, vision and courage.*

Grandmother had such high expectations for her. She was the last of the Wickershams; the distinguished old line had petered out in distant, careless relatives. I hope I won't disappoint her, Karen thought. Her parents expected much less of her—just adherence to their own traditional values, which were tempered by a tolerance for the contemporary lifestyle of the younger generation.

Karen's soft canvas bags lay open on two luggage racks, crammed with clothes she'd need in Belfort. Jeans, bleached and washed to a mottled robin's egg blue, sweaters in rainbow colors that set off her apricot tan, boys' shirts and the newly purchased feminine blouses and wraparound skirts from her mother's favorite Madison Avenue boutiques.

She pushed aside the sheet and swung her legs over the edge of the bed. Her trim lines were a result of good nutrition and active sports, with a lucky inheritance of long narrow bones. The emotional excesses that marked her brief but troubled affair with Delos had not affected her outward appearance. Only the inner self had been bruised, and that, she thought gratefully, left no visible scars.

In the large blue-tiled bathroom she splashed cold water on her face, brushed her teeth, skipping a shower because she didn't want to miss Peter's call. She needed the reassurance of his calm voice to give her courage to face her parents over breakfast. To announce—to explain—to defend her next move. It would, she suspected, take more courage than she could summon up without the reinforcement of Peter's voice.

Peter would telephone on his first break. He was scheduled for the emergency ward today.

She shared only a small part of Peter's life, Karen knew, but she did not mind. The time he spent away from her was given over to his medical obligations. Not to dazzling women to gratify his ego, like Delos. Delos . . . a case of ultimate ego.

You're lucky, Karen, she told her unblinking image in the mirror, that Dr. Peter Norris came into your life when he did. Few women were so lucky. She'd witnessed the anguish of her friends at the network, trying to recover from office affairs that had left them shattered while the man in question went on to fresh and presumably greener fields . . . Even in this day of women's liberation, it was still the female of the species who suffered most. She cried or grieved in-

wardly, in silence, or vented it to a psychiatrist who too often helped
transform the lingering love into anger and even hate. But she could
not hate Delos. She could only consider, in the aftermath, how badly
she'd been had. And that it was her own doing. . . .

Peter would ask, when he called, how her parents were taking the
news of their plans.

Perhaps he'd sound anxious; he had respect for the Coles.

Well, she'd tell him the truth. Playing games was part of Delos's
lifestyle, a tissue of small deceptions and little white lies. But with
Peter she had to be honest—she *wanted* to be honest. Her integrity
should be no less than his.

She rehearsed her answers to his questions. "I'm chicken," she
would admit. "But I mean to tell them at breakfast. We're eating together because father and mother are leaving for London on a business trip. So they'll know."

Peter would worry it. "You know what, Karen—we should have
told them right off—last month. As soon as we decided."

"I know you wanted to," she would say. "After all, it's not like
you're the villain seducing the heroine. You're so straight, Peter—and
I love you for it. But not to worry, darling. They'll listen."

A tap on the door and Verna, the heavyset middle-aged housekeeper who'd been part of Karen's childhood and privy to her misery over Delos, came in. Under the topknot of grey-brown hair her
plump, ruddy face was set in lines of distress.

"Karen, you will come down for breakfast?"

"In a minute, Verna."

The woman looked at the books ready for packing, the shelf of antique toys that Mr. Cole had collected for his daughter, the family
photographs in silver frames, the albums of rock records that Karen
had once brought back from London. She kept her eyes discreetly
away from Karen, who was stepping into a pair of jeans and a white
cotton turtleneck.

"I'll pick these up later." Karen tightened her lips, concealing the
slight overbite that orthodontia had not corrected. Verna read her
tension. Verna knew; Verna, in fact, knew more than her parents.
Not that it was anything to be ashamed of, not today. But Verna's
roots went back to the village near Prague where a girl who
transgressed the bounds of modesty was branded for life. Oh, Karen

knew the images in Verna's head. The only child of Eleanor and Phipps Cole should be dressed in Alençon lace and silk and seed-pearls from Priscilla of Boston; there should be an overflow of bridesmaids, ushers and houseguests, with Verna's husband, Otto, passing silver trays of champagne and an off-duty policeman stationed near the diningroom, where the display of wedding gifts would resemble the third floor of Tiffany's.

The whole *Bride's* magazine production.

How could she make Verna understand about Peter?

Verna's reaction mattered to Karen; she couldn't bear to jeopardize the older woman's affection. She took Verna's hand in hers, feeling the work-roughened skin. The staff was all remarkably loyal, a tribute to the Coles' generosity. Verna and Otto, for instance, had been part of the household ever since Karen could remember. She suspected that she was the surrogate child they had lost when the Russians marched into Prague.

New sorrows deepened the lines in Verna's flushed face. "This time, think carefully, Karen. Be sure."

"I *am* sure, Verna. He's just the kind of man I need . . ."

"Yet he hurts you with this first step."

It was, Karen knew, a testament to Verna's love that she spoke her mind. A devout Catholic, Verna had eased her rigid moral code for Karen when she broke up with Delos. When she was too devastated to face her family, her friends, her job, it was Verna who had sat up with her during the long nights. Not talking, just being there.

"When a man loves you, he will *marry* you." Verna's hoarse voice affirmed the ethics she knew and trusted.

"You don't understand, Verna—"

"Oh, but I do . . ."

"Well—I don't want to discuss it." Instantly Karen regretted saying it. She took a deep breath, averting her glance. "I'm sorry . . . I didn't mean it—forgive me . . ." She turned away hastily, before the tears spilled down her cheeks. The housekeeper left, closing the door after her.

Karen opened the door to the hall and went down the stairs. The rare hunting prints her father had brought from London seemed to reproach her from the rich red damask wall of the stairway.

Everywhere in the house, on priceless chests and carved or marble mantels, graceful English pottery served as receptacles for spring flowers brought back from the Rhinebeck greenhouses. Mrs. Cole's obsession with the greening of Manhattan had transformed the townhouse into an indoor botanical garden. The April sun kissed the blazing reds, yellows and violets of the tulips, daffodils and hyacinths, framed by sprays of pale gold forsythia.

At the foot of the staircase Karen paused, taking a deep breath as she prepared to face her parents. She reminded herself that they had always been considerate; during her college days she had always bragged that they were so tolerant she could tell them anything . . .

Suddenly she was far less confident. She remembered a friend who had moved abruptly to the west coast, three thousand miles from her mother's hurt glance and accusing voice. And Janice hadn't even been living with Scott.

Why didn't Peter call? Right now . . . God, how she needed him . . .

In the Cole townhouse the diningroom was on the ground floor, beyond the hall and opening on a walled brick garden that offered privacy and protection.

Karen's mother and father were facing each other at a small table set in a bay window banked in flowering shrubs, their buds tipped with scarlet and gold. An elderly gardener was snipping at ivy that stretched over the faded brick wall, its young leaves reaching for the sun.

The garden reflected Eleanor Cole's flawless horticultural taste. Phipps Cole ignored the sheaf of papers at his place and joined her in admiring the effect. The April dew had left a scattering of brilliance on the lush greenery.

Karen's father still marveled, after twenty-five devoted years with his wife, what a charming contradiction she was. She looked precious and ornamental, an aura that had at first fascinated him until he got to know her and discovered that her mind was quick, lucid, with a kind of no-nonsense approach that inspired awe and respect in tradesmen, art dealers, hairdressers and friends. She was always ready for every day, structured with meetings, conferences and an hour at the exercise salon. In spite of her long nose and narrow face, there was a suggestion of beauty and elegance about her, and she was invariably on the lists of outstanding women in fashion, art, civic affairs.

"Thank heaven Karen takes after her father in her looks," Eleanor often said, "that marvelous bone structure and fair coloring."

This morning Eleanor wore a becoming royal-blue tweed Chanel suit in preparation for their flight. Her collection of Chanels had started on their honeymoon in Paris when she wandered out of the Ritz bar to the Rue Cambon and was lured into Madame's establishment. Afterwards, she always wore several chains of pearls and gold all looped together around her thin neck. As she sipped her coffee now, her dark eyes shone with affection for her husband. Her hair so black the sunlight gave it a purple sheen, was styled in a pompadour that allowed her small ears to show the gold and pearl earrings that matched her chains. She looked cool, inbred, aloof, until her sudden intimate smile reminded Phipps of the very human woman who had shared his life and bed for the last quarter-century.

"Dad, mother—" Karen said and slipped into the chair between them, looking like a teenager with her thick braids and flushed face. Phipps Cole loved his only child deeply but they were no longer as close as they'd been during Karen's adolescence—which was natural, he supposed. He counted on Eleanor's wisdom and good sense to guide their daughter into womanhood.

As Karen and Eleanor talked about Peter, Phipps listened absently, his mind on the complex issues he would confront in London the next morning. But suddenly he grew alert; there was a note of panic in Eleanor's voice.

"You mustn't go through with it, Karen. It's too impulsive. Too sudden . . ."

"It's not really sudden, mother," Karen protested gently. "I've known Peter for nearly five months."

"Karen, are you pregnant?"

Phipps Cole looked at them, startled. His handsome middle-aged face blanched. He had schooled himself to present his business associates with a bland mask, a defense in the verbal war games that whirled around him during bitter jousts at the economic council sessions. But his composure dissolved in the face of domestic trouble. His eyes, deepset under his sharply defined forehead, narrowed. He set down the cup of coffee he had raised to his lips.

"Eleanor, what on earth . . . ?" Not a question, more an entreaty that she unsay what he had just heard.

His wife clamped her lips together as though sealing them against an impulsive remark.

Karen was unwilling to meet her father's fierce look. She was upset for him, more than for her mother. Although at fifty Phipps Cole was marvelously youthful—even turning in a creditable performance in the most recent marathon—as a father he was a strictly traditional *paterfamilias*. Karen longed to tell him to be realistic, to understand that she and her friends were no longer hampered by the straitjacket of conformity. Still, she was afraid to meet his glowering expression, so she answered her mother instead. "If I were pregnant, we'd probably get married, or I might choose to have an abortion—"

"*Karen!*" The surge of blood to his face emphasized the thatch of prematurely gray hair.

"I'm sorry, dad. I didn't mean to alarm you. I'm not pregnant. I'm simply going to share Peter's apartment and we'll see how we get along . . . if it works out . . ."

She left any discussion of the future vague, which was hardly dishonest because she had no idea whether she and Peter would ever marry. What she wanted now was to let her parents down gently. My God, here they were having a fit about Peter—solid, eligible Peter Norris, M.D.—how would they have reacted if they had found out about Delos?

She knew from past experience that it was useless to play one parent against the other. But she knew also that if her mother could be won over, her father would prove less of a problem.

Eleanor's face was stern, displaying the chilly authority familiar to her fellow members on civic boards, an expression announcing, in fact, that she had come to a decision.

"Karen, we've always been proud of you. You've given us a lot to be proud of and no more than the usual problems involved with growing up. What you want to do is indicative of the way you and your friends regard established morality. We want very much to be sympathetic and understanding—"

"Mother, I'm *in love* with Peter." Karen added privately: I think.

"I don't doubt it. He's a very attractive young man. But if he has managed to persuade you—"

"No, he hasn't. It's what I want too. We've been discussing it for weeks."

"And if it doesn't happen to work out . . . ?"

"We'll call it off." Karen shrugged. "At least this way we'll bypass the heartache of a divorce."

"And you think a breakup between . . . roommates . . . lovers, whatever, is less of a trauma than divorce?"

"How did we get started talking about a breakup? We won't break up. We have commitments to each other . . ."

"Enough of this nonsense." Her father stood up, a tall commanding man in the dark pin-striped suit; urbane, polished—and distressed. "I absolutely forbid this move, Karen."

"But you *like* Peter. You said he had character and vision."

"That was before I knew he was seducing my daughter."

"Oh," she tried to control the tremor in her voice, "you're so Victorian."

"Karen, I won't allow this. I put you on your honor, since your mother won't be here . . ."

"I believe I'll remain here, Phipps," her mother said quietly.

"No reason for you to stay here, Ellie." His authority was low-keyed but effective. "You'll come with me. And Karen will join us—"

Karen was furious. Couldn't they accept her right to control her own life? Fortunately, just then Otto entered with a rack of fresh toast and another pot of coffee.

Eleanor dismissed him. "We've finished, thank you, Otto."

After the door closed quietly, she said crisply, "Your father's made a sensible suggestion. You love London."

"That's beside the point. I'm going to Belfort this morning."

"You'll do nothing of the kind." The vein in his temple pulsed, deeper in color than his flushed face. "Eleanor, you'll take care of it."

Karen wondered if she would have been smarter to lie to them, to say casually that she was taking a small flat in Belfort, because she wanted a break from city life. She could have said she was planning to take courses at the University of Connecticut, which had a branch in nearby Stamford. Suddenly she was terrified, that this could mean a break in their warm family relationship.

"Dad, please don't make mother the patsy. I'm old enough to make my own choices."

Her father shook his head, but it was, she felt, a gesture of frustration. He looked at her mother, as though Eleanor had the key to the secret of his daughter's baffling behavior. Eleanor remained seated, her face impassive except for the faint double lines between her arched eyebrows.

"Karen, I thought I knew you . . ."

"Knew me, dad? You know the Karen of ten years ago, daddy's little girl. I guess it's partly my fault, but you really have no inkling of what I've gone through these past months when you were so pleased with my progress at the network, with the help I was getting from that brilliant anchorman, Delos Burke. You knew the baby, the adolescent, but not the woman. It's never occurred to you that I have . . . a sex life, that Peter Norris might be all that stands between me and the 'singles scene' . . ."

"Karen—"

"I'm sorry," she said stubbornly, "my mind's made up."

"Karen, you're of age. We're only trying to pass on to you the wisdom of maturity, but I suppose you'll have to learn from your own experience. I hope it works out. Your father and I will try to understand—we've no objection to Peter personally."

Why had her mother just done an about-face, Karen wondered. Deeply touched, she could only nod in gratitude, aware of the signal her parents had somehow just exchanged. They disapproved but they did not want to lose her.

"Just one thing, Karen," her mother said.

"Yes?"

"I wouldn't tell your plans to your grandmother. There's no reason for upsetting her."

"All right, mother."

She was the first to leave the diningroom. She rushed upstairs to her own room, shaken but adamant. She was closing the zippers on her travel bags when the telephone rang. Peter! she thought, and it was a shot of adrenalin to her heart.

But it was Delos's voice that greeted her. More adrenalin . . .

"Karen, what's this I hear about you . . . ?"

How she wished she could say, "I'm getting married." *That* would have been a victory. Although she would never admit it to her parents or Verna or anyone, the fact that Peter had never even spoken of marriage nagged at her. She wasn't sure she wanted to marry him, but somehow it was important to her that *he* want to marry her.

"My secretary told me of your plans." His voice was low, not the familiar confident one that went out over the airwaves every night, but one that had a note of dejection. A signal for her to cheer him up.

"I hope you're not being rash," he said.

"Rash?" He sounded like her father. "Not at all, we've been dating for some time." No need for Delos to know about the weeks she had spent brooding in her bedroom.

"Who is he?" Delos asked gruffly.

"A very nice man," she answered simply. "A doctor."

Inwardly, she was crowing. Although the sound of his voice had brought a momentary return of confusion and hurt, it didn't last long. She was in control now; the very fact that he had called renewed her self-confidence. Delos was not known for his post-affair courtesy. Which meant that he missed her; the trip with his wife had evidently done little to restore their marriage.

"I think we should talk, Karen."

"Everything's been said; there's no sense in rehashing the past . . ."

"Well, we could still have a drink together sometime. Why don't you call me . . . ?"

"I might," she said. "Sometime."

Before returning to her packing, she went to the carafe on her bedside table, poured a glass of water and rinsed the taste of Delos Burke out of her mouth.

CHAPTER III

Twenty-four hours earlier Peter Norris left the house on Buxton Avenue, silently closing the front door. Sundays Mrs. Thalberg, his landlady, slept late.

He headed two blocks south toward the hospital, which sprawled over the length of High Street. He was a tall young man with a long brisk stride and an air of perpetual enthusiasm. Four years of medical school, three of residency had not dampened his commitment to medicine, although he was by no means a naive beginner who thought the physician's black bag contained the cure to all the world's ills. Besides, his class would be the first to graduate in family practice residency, a new specialty, and he was proud of it.

Over his khaki pants and a white shirt and tie he wore his white hospital coat, the pockets bulging with stethoscope, electric pocket beeper, tongue depressors, scissors, pens, a rubber tourniquet. Despite the grind of medical school and residency, he looked as healthy and vigorous as when he had come east from the lakes region of Wisconsin. His clipped sandy hair was bleached by the sun, his ice blue eyes were alert and probing, his skin had a healthy glow, even when he was tired. He looked less like a doctor than like one of the All-American athletes from the Wisconsin farmlands who were on football or basketball scholarships at the eastern colleges.

Peter Norris was, in fact, a mean basketball player, but in college he had chosen pre-med; doctoring was in the family.

He walked along High Street, past the century-old Victorian mansions where a scattering of the affluent first families of Belfort still lived, defying mounting real-estate tax assessments and reminding the new arrivals in town—the new rich, the new powerful—that the former lions were still watching out for the old town and its Puritan heritage.

At six-thirty Sunday morning, Belfort looked more than passably good to Peter. The sparkle of dew touched the white dogwoods, the miniature golden bells of forsythia, the lavish pink-purple petals of the tulip trees that framed the old mansions. A lonely tan-and-cream springer spaniel followed him. Peter petted the animal absently, feeling the soft long fur, then sent him back to his nearby home.

You could clean out your lungs with this air, he thought. No fumes, no pollution. The only person he met was a newsboy delivering the thick Sunday papers, but at the hospital parking lot cars were arriving in a steady stream, jockeying for places in the shade. The cars of the hospital staff were set in neat rows like colorful beetles, but the doctors' parking lot was still half empty.

Peter looked forward to a quick breakfast in the cafeteria, with black coffee, steaming hot. He wasn't thoroughly awake and he had a brutal shift ahead of him. He envied doctors who managed on four or five hours of sleep a night. Even Peter's father needed seven hours, which he seldom got, although recently, his mother had written, "Dad comes home for lunch now whenever it's possible, and then takes a nap in his Barcalounger."

The seven o'clock shift was coming into work, nurses, technicians, some of the hospital maintenance and housekeeping staff.

Belfort Hospital was very much controlled by the board of directors, the old guard—tough, inflexible, conservative Yankees who also owned the newspaper, the radio station, the important banks, the sprawling old clockworks.

However, new corporations were coming into the area and beginning to take an interest in the community. Many top executives were now serving on the hospital board and had participated in the recent drives for a new wing and a CAT scanner. Dr. Macray, the chief of staff, hoped the hospital would add more nurses to the patient floors instead of spending over a half million dollars on the scanner.

"The nursing care in this hospital is outrageous," Dr. Macray complained. "Two nurses and an aide for twenty-eight patients."

As Peter approached the main building, which housed the older wing of the hospital, he recalled his first impression of the place, nearly three years ago. It was grim, forbidding, like an institution in a Dickens novel, with narrow windows, ivy growing up the brick walls and turrets crowning the third floor. It seemed no better than the outdated urban hospitals in the inner cities—just the kind of residency he had hoped to avoid. But his spirits had lifted at the sight of the new wing, built by old-guard concern and new-rich money, an arresting complex of white-painted brick, a curve of concrete, steel and glass. Flowing transverses connected the gleaming new wing to the decrepit-looking main structure.

The new wing was spacious, with ceiling-to-floor plate-glass windows facing east and looking out on the doctors' parking lot.

The inside of the lobby, which was used as a waiting room now that renovations were complete—not only by Emergency but by the rest of the hospital as well—was bright and cheerful, with blue carpeting and rows of orange and white chairs like the plastic shells in airports. The tables were piled high with magazines, and the receptionists behind the high polished curve of the front desk were friendly and helpful.

Porters were usually on hand mornings, washing, cleaning, vacuuming. Whatever complaints the Board had lodged against the old administrator, he couldn't be faulted on cleanliness. The hospital was known for its cleanliness, going beyond traditional housekeeping standards. The new one, Dr. Hilton, had better be good.

Located off the lobby and beyond the emergency room was Dr. Macray's office and beyond that the cardiology and pulmonary disease departments. On the second floor were the new pediatrics and adolescent units, the maternity ward, the nursery and the delivery rooms. In one there was an extraordinary new bed, brought over from France, to be used in the Lamaze method of childbirth.

What Peter especially liked about Belfort was that all patients were treated with equal concern, from the wealthy old Yankee families and well-to-do professionals, to middle-income groups like the second-generation Irish and European immigrants, to the less well-off blacks and Hispanics who had recently ventured beyond Harlem into Fairfield County. In many metropolitan hospitals these patients —especially if they were on welfare—were treated callously and often subjected to long waits. No matter what the illness—stomach ulcers, vaginal bleeding, breast masses—often these poor suffered doubly. Not so at Belfort, although Peter had recently discovered that some of the staff doctors would not take on patients with Medicaid coverage. This practice had recently been reinforced by the case of a woman who had taken the insurance money for her hysterectomy, gone to Florida, and never paid the surgeon.

But he was reasonably happy here, Peter reflected. Not because Dr. Watling, chief of the family practice residency program, was of any help. Watling believed that abusive language, harsh treatment and unrealistic demands resulted in a star performance. But at least the rest of the hospital staff—the attending senior physicians, the nursing supervisors and others—were competent professionals, civilized human beings, and many of them went out of their way to help the residents.

Several of the nurses were especially accommodating . . .

It hadn't been easy, but Peter had managed over the past three years to avoid anything more than casual affairs, enjoyable for himself and for the nurse, but with no commitments. He'd grown particularly wary of playing house. It was often more seductive than sex during this period of overwork and lack of sleep and need to learn.

Several residents in his group were already married. When Peter saw a young doctor and wife look at one another with shy devotion, he felt a pang of loneliness, of envy. Once during a coffee break, Dr. Bruce Bennett had noticed Peter staring wistfully at a couple and told him, "Don't get taken in. Women marry doctors for all the wrong reasons. The same applies to doctors. I married a nurse in the hospital where I was a resident. I made thirty thousand clear the first year—now I shell out twenty-five thousand a year alimony . . . until she marries again. Which isn't likely." He rubbed his chin. "Pretty good pay for a couple years maid's work, which is all she did."

Peter had thought about that a lot. The thirty-six-hour shifts were one hell of a test of a man's staying power. It was an endurance race that drained you until you could no longer make decisions. There was never enough rest or decent meals. The thirty-six-hour tour of duty every third day played havoc with his inner time clock, brought on a kind of jet lag. No wonder the doctors were easily seduced by women who were willing just to look after them a little. . . .

In the large lobby, the receptionist had just come on duty. A police car had pulled up to the emergency entrance, and the officer escorted a scarecrow of a man, in a torn army shirt and baggy pants, to the reception area where one of the staff doctors was making out the patient reports.

"James is back again," Peter said. He was a regular customer.

"Doctor, he's all yours," the officer said.

The two-inch cut over the man's forehead was oozing blood, and the bruise along his jawline was spreading in ugly purple splotches. His ankles were swollen and his abdomen jutted out like a football, straining the thin skin of his body. Miss Tracy, the small black-haired nurse who looked doll-fragile but was expert in judo, helped Peter maneuver James into a small treatment room. He made a futile struggle to keep his shirt and pants on, then gave up. Peter examined James as he squirmed on the table.

He was ageless—alcohol had embalmed him from his early manhood—yet his face had a certain patrician cast. Sometimes he stumbled in on foot, other times a police car brought him in, to be patched up, fortified by vitamins and intravenous feedings, and returned to the depths of West Street, where the inner city was now rubble, preparing for urban renewal, and where the dregs of Belfort met in a kind of wayward kinship. Peter was concerned whenever James showed up. In his more lucid moments he revealed a high intelligence, but he worked as a janitor. Several of the nursing staff hired him once in a while, when he was sober, and they reported that nobody polished a floor as well as James did.

The April rains, the worst for Connecticut in a decade, had marked James with a kind of permanent decay. Peter wondered if there were some way to get him into Lazarus House, a halfway house for chronic alcoholics. He reminded himself to ask Sheila Ryan, the head of social services, to see what she could do. He often referred these hapless creatures to Sheila, who did her best for them. But she was more resigned than Peter; in the five years she had been a social worker her relentless battle with the Medicare and Medicaid people had escalated tenfold.

He brought a mug of coffee and a Danish from the refreshment station near the utility room and found an empty armchair in the nurses' room. The coffee was strong and hot, as good as it was in the cafeteria, where the food too was excellent—wholesome and tasty. The kitchen was a carry-over from the days when the hospital had been a small-scale operation, long before the advent of department chiefs, each seeking to enlarge his own enclave by waging an insidious battle for power.

The power game at the hospital was an exercise of brains and influence—all at the cost of patient care. Peter was aware of it early in his residency, perhaps because the behind-the-scenes rivalries were so unlike the manner in which his father—and now his brothers— managed their Wisconsin clinic.

But there were two men at Belfort Hospital whom he genuinely admired, almost idolized: Dr. John Paul Macray and Dr. Malcolm Stone. They seemed content with their positions in the medical constellation and had earned them. It was Dr. Macray who gave Belfort Hospital its extraordinary reputation. He was a titan among surgeons even in these uncertain times; with inflation going out of bounds and hospital costs increasing wildly, he was a sound chief of staff. And Dr. Stone, at forty-two, was head of Belfort Hospital's cardiology department and, rumor had it, Big John's heir apparent.

Emergency was quiet. For the first time all morning Peter thought about Karen. Her name was soft on his lips, the vision of her vivid in his mind. He had hoped to meet her in New York the next morning and drive her back to his place at Mrs. Thalberg's. But he was on duty for the damned thirty-six-hour shift, which meant all of today, all of tonight, all of tomorrow until seven in the evening. He had tried to switch with his friend Fred Farley, but though Fred was agreeable, Dr. Watling would have none of it. The inflexible bastard would tolerate no deviation from the schedule he set up. You were on duty for a three-day cycle of two twelve-hour shifts and one thirty-six-hour shift. You were a slave to the hospital. What was curious, Fred Farley said, was that the older physicians had no sympathy for the grueling hours. "They have it so good now," Fred added.

Peter's feelings about his profession and his future were currently in limbo. He was still tired from his last twelve-hour shift and totally unprepared for the day ahead. Sunday in Emergency was apt to be an ordeal. Not only because of accidents, big and small, but because people who had been dragging around for weeks, sick and upset, would finally decide to make it to the hospital that day.

He drained his coffee, left his Danish half-finished, got up. The parking lots were filling up as physicians arrived to make their rounds. They would all gather in the coffee shop soon, to exchange information about patients, perhaps to speculate about Dr. Hilton, the new administrator. The sound of food caddies drifted through the corridor; patients were being served breakfast and the technicians were setting out on their rounds.

You could tell it was spring by the type of accidents, an elderly man with emphysema aggravated by the budding trees and spring grasses, a fisherman with a fishhook lodged in his hand, a boy who'd braked his new ten-speed bike too quickly and had sailed over the handlebars.

After he'd patched up the first batch of accidents and looked in again on James, who lay in a dead-to-the-world sleep, Peter went out to the public telephones to call Karen.

In the booth he dialed and waited. But it was Otto, the butler, who answered. The Coles were not home. Peter left his name and said he'd call again.

He wanted to tell Karen that he couldn't see her tomorrow morning but would have Tuesday afternoon off. Mostly, though, he wanted to hear her voice, to reassure himself that she was actually coming here to live with him.

It was much later that day when Peter tried to call Karen again. And by then he was too heartsick to even talk.

CHAPTER IV

The girl was in her early teens, a slim, delicate child with beautifully chiseled features, chestnut hair that rippled over her shoulders, a mild face, with a vacant far-off gaze. Unlike the retarded, for whom the center was a therapeutic retreat, Jenny Emerson was not a victim of Downes syndrome. As a young child, loved and nurtured by adoring parents, she had been stricken with encephalitis, which had left her forever with the intelligence of a four-year-old.

There were no nearby schools for girls like Jenny, and her mother was determined to keep her at home, teaching her the simple routines of living that were within her grasp. Then, ten years ago, some Connecticut parents had met and decided to open a center and school for retarded children in nearby Stamford.

Jenny's mother, fired with enthusiasm by this example, generated enough interest in Belfort to take a similar course of action. She found a small abandoned plant in Belfort's inner city, and with her dedication and enthusiasm the new headquarters came into existence.

It turned out to be an ideal situation for Jenny. She liked the other retarded children; like her they were docile, generous, with none of the anger or jealousy to be found in normal groups of people. Sometimes Jenny said angrily, "I'm not like them!" But most of the time, she was amiable and in a touching, clumsy way, nurturing.

Her mother brought Jenny to the center before going to work. Mrs. Emerson worked in the Belfort school system, in the principal's office. Jenny's father, unable to accept the tragedy that had left his daughter a permanent infant, had cut himself off from his wife and child and moved out.

What will happen to her when I die? Mrs. Emerson often fretted in the dark of night. Who will look after her, how will she manage?

There was no place for Jenny except in a state-run agency, which made her mother shudder. Reading was difficult for her, but her fingers were quick and unerring when it came to doing certain chores. A number of manufacturers gave the retarded children jobs making small electric gadgets, which they turned out satisfactorily. The work not only added to the center's income, but added to the children's self-confidence.

One April weekend Jenny's mother was obliged to go out of town, to attend a conference pertaining to her job. She made arrangements for one of the local teenage girls to take Jenny home from the center Saturday night and stay over with her all of Sunday.

But the babysitter couldn't make it; her boyfriend was taking her to Bridgeport Saturday night and she wasn't going to miss *that*. So she arranged with a friend to pinch-hit for her.

Jenny waited at the center until nearly everybody was gone, then the superintendent, an elderly arthritic man, decided to take her home.

"You gonna be okay now," he said. "You lock your door and don't let anybody in—until the sitter comes over to stay with you."

It was all confusion, the absent babysitter later claimed: she was sure her friend would pick up Jenny and take her home—her friend owed her more than one favor. How was she to know her friend didn't know her way around and had gotten lost.

So there was Jenny alone in the apartment. Being alone was a strange, unnerving experience. She wandered through the bedroom into the kitchen, looking for her mother. She was hungry, it was past her suppertime. In the refrigerator she found a carton of milk. Holding it in both hands, she opened the spout, lifted it and poured the milk into a glass, scarcely spilling any. She wished her mother were here to see her do it. She found some Ritz crackers in a drawer and nibbled on them. Then she went to the front window and looked out on the darkening street.

She shivered. Where was her mother?

Jenny and her mother lived in a four-family brick house with a flat roof that looked like part of a shopping center. Nearby was Dairy Queen; she was allowed a butterscotch Dairy Queen almost every day, and she loved the taste of it on her tongue. Maybe she could walk to the Dairy Queen . . .

Her mother had warned her never to go out alone at night, but Jenny's mind did not retain such warnings. She began walking along the edge of the road, with traffic. She was wearing blue shorts that hugged her rounded buttocks and a T-shirt that, after numerous washings, clung to her well-developed breasts.

There were cars filled with teenagers at the Dairy Queen; two cars with lots of noisy kids, who had their portable radios blaring. They whistled at Jenny, who thought she knew one of them, but they dashed off in their cars before she got her ice cream. Before the fellow handed it to her, he said, "Forty cents, please." A small frown appeared between her eyebrows; she didn't understand.

"Come on, pay up." He was impatient.

Jenny was bewildered. The man behind the counter moved to grab the ice cream cone from her. But a black boy who was next in line said, "Let her have it, man," and tossed down a quarter, a dime and a nickel. The server told her to get lost and never come back.

She no longer wanted the ice cream; the anger of the fellow who had waited on her was shattering. She walked hurriedly down the road, not realizing that she was going farther away from home. Confused, hurt, she pressed her trembling lips against the cool custard. Where was mother? She was walking deeper into the lonely road and the budding bushes were mysterious and alive, darting out to frighten her. A couple of cars were coming toward her; their front lights picked her out. The first was a station wagon with three young men in the front seat, grinning like Halloween pumpkins. The wagon braked, the driver leaned out and offered her a lift. The side door opened and a big fellow in a sweatshirt and running shorts jumped out, bowed low, took her by the arm and half-helped, half-shoved her into the second seat, where another young man grabbed her and said, "Hiya kid, welcome . . ." She was bounced into the car, one of them lifted her up and held her captive, face down on his lap. They were smoking; the smell was funny. Then the second car, a jeep, whose occupants were friends of the youths in the first car, slowed down. With whooping and laughter the cars swung around on the empty road and made a dash back to the cove. The cove was closed to cars at nine in the evening because of the problems police had had with teenagers who got into fights at night with derelicts from the inner city who camped out there in the balmy months.

The girl wasn't frightened. At first. Nobody had ever been cruel to her. But she was uncomfortable on the big fellow's lap because something was happening she couldn't understand. It began to frighten her. As she squirmed, he stretched her out on his lap, face down, so her head was on the lap of the fellow by the door and her legs stretched across the width of the car, her feet dangling out of the half-open window. In squirming she lost her slippers.

"You don't need shoes, baby. I'm gonna carry you piggyback," the big fellow assured her. She was badly frightened now, knew she must try to run. But by the time she began to struggle, they were on the beach, with the car headlights off and the shore bleak and menacing. She cried out, and one of them put his hand over her mouth. She bit him, he slapped her. Hard. Across the mouth. Then the bunch of them carried her toward one of the deserted bathhouses, making a bean bag of her. Whenever she struggled, they tightened their grip and muttered obscenities. The big fellow spit in her face. She was now like a small wild animal, crazed with terror, but her terror seemed to excite them further. Two held her down while the others lined up, watching and laughing as each one took his turn. Then they flipped her over and tried tricks they'd heard about. Mercifully, Jenny lost consciousness. Her captors, still laughing, still kidding, all more than a little stoned, left the inert body on the beach, climbed into their cars and drove off.

When the police car patrolled the cove in the morning they saw something odd staggering toward them. It looked like a girl; it looked as though somebody had doused her with red paint.

When they ran out to check, they saw that it wasn't paint.

The police radioed for an ambulance. As they approached the blood-streaked girl, who was naked and shivering, she shrank from them in terror, tried to run. She stumbled in the sand, fell; fortunately the cops had a blanket in their car.

Luckily there were no other critical patients in Emergency when Jenny was brought in.

She was brought by an ambulance, its red lights flashing, the police car clearing the way through shore traffic. In the ambulance a young attendant was monitoring the girl's vital signs and talking to the emergency room via direct radio connection. She was unconscious now and the attendants were concerned, anxious to reach the hospital quickly. She was covered by sheets, with mottled bloodstains coming through, and they were doubly concerned by the loss of blood.

At Emergency two nurses were waiting at the door. They walked alongside as the moving stretcher was pushed into the trauma room, where the girl was transferred to a hospital stretcher. Peter prepared to hook her up to an intravenous line. When they unwrapped the sheets, she moaned faintly. The body was battered, there were bruises on the pear-shaped breasts; a knife cut below the navel; she was bleeding from the vagina and the rectum.

"Which doctors are in the building?" Peter asked the nurses.

"Dr. Monroe was delivering earlier this morning. He may still be here."

Dr. Monroe, an outstanding ob/gyn man, was in the maternity wing, talking with a woman who had an hour before delivered premature twins, now being warmed to life in isolettes. He came down to Emergency, still in his white scrub suit, tall, lanky, with a boyish face that aroused instant trust.

When he reached the trauma room Dr. Monroe saw the head nurse, Miss Tracy, standing by the stretcher holding Jenny's hand, speaking softly, soothingly. Dr. Monroe was not unfamiliar with rape victims, but he still felt the initial shock whenever a new one was brought in. As he looked up and met Peter's glance, he realized it was even tougher on the inexperienced young doctor.

They would make preparations to take Jenny to surgery to repair the lacerations. She was awakening now; her eyes opened in bewilderment. She was moaning again.

"Who is she? Has her family been notified?" Dr. Monroe asked.

"We don't know, sir," replied the police officer who was standing in the doorway. "Wasn't any clothes or bag or anything we could use for identification. No girl reported missing, so far as we know."

Miss Tracy was still holding Jenny's hand when Miss Sandowsky, the representative of the rape crisis center, hurried in. She wasn't allowed to see the girl yet, so she waited nervously at the nurses' station for Miss Tracy.

Miss Sandowsky was there to help, to counsel; it was important that the rape victim receive the benefit of counseling before she left the hospital.

"The law doesn't require that she lodge a complaint," Miss Sandowsky said, her full face mottled with suppressed anger, "or even that she report the assault to the police. But I hope she does." She turned to Peter. "Have they found out who she is?"

"Not yet. They're checking. Poor kid, she's going to have a rough time. I hope they find her parents . . ."

Peter drained his coffee and went out to the nurses' station. The most recent local case of rape had ended in death; a schoolgirl was found, battered, choked to death and unspeakably mutilated in a grove off the Merritt Parkway. He had not been present at the autopsy, but the young pathologist had told him it was a grisly experience. But this was by far the most emotionally wrenching case he had encountered yet. He'd seen some pretty bad injuries before: accident victims with their abdomens ripped open and the vital organs spilling out; severely burned patients, assault victims and battered wives. But to think that human beings could willfully, wantonly reduce a young girl to the bloodied body on the operating table—was hard to accept. And then there were the psychological wounds . . . Perhaps the Merritt Parkway victim was better off dead.

This one would be given shots to prevent a possible pregnancy. There would be counseling, follow-up care. But it would not repair the damage permanently.

He lost track of time as the emergency room began to fill up, and he worked unflaggingly through the next hours with patients, mostly older ones, taking histories, asking questions. What happened, when did it happen, how? Do you hurt anywhere else? Was there dirt or rust? Did you get any splinters? How far did you fall? Did you faint? When was your last tetanus shot? Are you allergic to any medications? What medications are you taking?

The ER secretary had already typed up the treatment sheet: name, age, social security number, employer, medical insurance coverage. And had got the important signature permitting treatment.

Peter continued to collect data, cared for a number of injuries—an elderly woman with osteosporosis who had stepped down from a curb, stumbled and broken her hip; a young boy who fell off his skateboard, skinned both knees; an old man who insisted his pain came from indigestion—it was the damned spareribs—not a heart attack. Denial, denial, Peter thought as he attached electrodes to the bony chest, watched the revealing answers on the EKG tracings.

The hospital lights glowed in the gathering twilight, the waiting room was still full. The housekeeping staff were kept busy scrubbing the rooms. In a brief respite between rounds Peter realized that he was hungry. He'd skipped lunch, substituting coffee and a couple of chocolate cookies that a grateful patient had brought to the nurses. He looked at the clock; the cafeteria had closed at 6:30. Well, he could get a sandwich in the coffee shop, which was like the old-style automat. You inserted your coins, a slot opened, you took out an uninviting sandwich: bread soggy, ham dry, cheese stale. More than food, he craved rest, a ten-minute breather away from the antiseptic smell of the rooms being prepared for the next patient. Before he could summon the energy to walk down the corridor, a police car and fire-company ambulance arrived, lights flashing.

Corpsmen opened the ambulance door; the stretcher held a young black man. The nurses greeted the newcomers, directing them to the trauma room. Miss Tracy followed.

"He'll probably need immediate surgery," she said. Knife wounds had opened the flesh on the upper arm, a bullet had entered the abdomen just above the navel. The smell of brilliantine, blood and sweat followed them into the room.

"Get Dr. Macray," Miss Tracy said. "He's in the building."

The summons went out on the loudspeaker and within five minutes Dr. John Paul Macray entered the room. He was a big man, with a sinewy body, a long, hawk-boned face topped with thick white hair and a deeply tanned face. His eyes were blue and keen, his habitual expression affable. Most of the attending physicians, especially the men at the top of the hierarchy, were apt to be aloof, even pompous, letting the staff understand by their objective manner that they were the élite; but Dr. Macray was a paragon of human decency and warmth. Behind his back the staff affectionately called him Big John; he was big in more than physical stature. He was known throughout the medical field as a great surgeon; patients came to him from New England, the Middle Atlantic states and even the West Coast. For thirty years he'd been the symbol of Belfort General Hospital. He could be brusque and impatient in the operating room if his pursuit of excellence was offended by negligence or stupidity. Otherwise he was courteous, very much a gentleman of the old school, considerate to everyone from the housekeeping crew to the administrator. He was constantly behind schedule, yet he had time for anyone who needed him. Peter had his own father as a role model, but he worshiped Dr. John Paul.

While Peter was working on the intravenous needle to be inserted in the youth's arm, Dr. Macray examined the victim.

"How'd it happen, son?" he asked.

The youth's face went blank; it was evident that he was afraid to tell.

"Any of his family here?" Dr. John Paul asked the nurse. She said the boy's mother was in the lobby, to sign the consent for his surgery. Dr. John Paul watched the nurse wheel the moving stretcher to X-ray.

When they were alone for a moment, Peter asked the older man if he knew about the rape victim.

"They tracked her mother down and she gave verbal permission to operate. The girl is in surgery now, I guess it's a mess."

"Will she make it?" Peter asked.

"I didn't examine her. But she's got every chance, with Monroe working on her."

The next two hours were busy, as Peter worked steadily. By seven o'clock in the evening he had taken histories; checked sprains, bruises, open wounds; restored the breathing of an overweight woman. Just as he was congratulating himself on getting through the first twelve hours, an ambulance brought in a victim of an auto accident. The elderly man who had been driving the car was ashen and near collapse. He kept repeating, "I didn't see her." She had run out behind two parked cars; he braked but the car skidded—and there she was, crumpled under the front right wheel.

They wheeled the little girl into the trauma room. Like that morning's rape victim, this one looked ghastly: the drops of blood left a trail from the entrance to the trauma room and one of the police officers mopped at the stains with a towel.

Nurses, residents, pediatricians, a neurosurgeon who happened to be in the building—all worked blindly, automatically, frantically, balancing their skill and will to save the child from the irreversible approach of death.

The driver of the car stood at the nurses' station, his head buried in his hands, sobbing hysterically, a police officer nearby trying to write up his notes. The girl's mother walked back and forth, too numb for tears, trying to look down the corridor into the trauma room. Finally they allowed her in—after the room was cleaned of instruments and blood, after the sheets had been drawn over the crushed body.

The mother's cry was wild, primal. It was unnerving, confronting them with the painful truth: they had worked no miracles.

"Oh, dear Jesus," she was whimpering. "My baby."

"Where's the woman's family?" Miss Tracy asked. "She can't go home alone." The child's mother had been given a sedative, had her arms folded to her and was rocking back and forth in her seat, mourning. The police officer who had escorted the ambulance drove the woman home—he had a daughter the same age. Meanwhile, the driver of the fatal car sat alone, tears staining his swollen cheeks.

It was eight in the evening and Peter had been on duty for more than twelve hours. Adrenalin was surging through his body. He knew he should be tired but he wasn't.

He checked with the switchboard to find out if he had missed a call. None had come in. It was briefly quiet; he stumbled out to the public telephone and dialed Karen's number. There was no answer; perhaps she'd gone to Rhinebeck with her parents today and the staff might have the day off. There was no way to reach her until tomorrow. Tomorrow night he would see her; they would be together, he thought with a surge of elation. But abruptly his mind darkened. Maybe. If she had not changed her mind. She was often upset if he didn't call her when he'd promised. He explained that it was not always possible. She listened politely, but he had a feeling she did not quite trust him. The affair with that damned newscaster had made her wary. Yet trust had to be the foundation of their relationship. Especially with a doctor's schedule, uncertain hours, last-minute emergencies, meetings, rounds. Karen had led such a sheltered, privileged life, someone always there to meet her every need. Would she understand, when he couldn't be there for her, that he had to make his patients his first priority?

It was almost midnight. Emergency cases had tapered off. The nurses were having coffee, most of them feeling fresh since they had come on only an hour before, and were full of their day's activities. Several were sunburned from a day at the beach. They all had heard about Jenny Emerson and plied Peter with questions. Did the police have any idea who the boys were?

"Belfort is changing," one of the senior nurses said. "It used to be that you could walk downtown at night without fear." Not anymore. Muggings, mostly, or rape that wasn't reported. It made them jittery.

The emergency doors opened. It was a youngish woman, attractive and very distraught.

"I'm Mrs. Emerson . . . my daughter was brought here this morning . . . I just got home a little while ago . . . Can you tell me how she is, where she is . . . ?"

The nurse at the desk called the intensive care unit. Yes, Jenny was there. Mrs. Emerson would be right up.

Peter offered to take her up. As they walked along the corridor, she asked a hundred questions. Peter led her through the long hushed corridors to the bank of elevators. They waited in silence until the doors opened. Peter pushed the fourth floor button. She was, he saw on closer inspection, perhaps in her mid-thirties. She was wearing a tan raincoat, with a shoulder bag that left her hands free. She dug her hands in her pockets, as though seeking control.

"Tell me . . ." she began again, but the elevator stopped and

Peter led her down the corridor. With the recovery room closed on weekends, Jenny had been taken to the intensive care unit, where she was watched closely until she came out of anesthesia. They would keep her overnight. Mrs. Emerson made a move to enter, then froze as he held her back. He opened the automatic door cautiously and they slipped into the room. The shaded lights revealed Jenny lying on her back, her arm connected to an I.V. Her face was bruised, her mouth lacerated. The mother leaned against the siderails put up for Jenny's protection.

"Jenny—" she whispered. "Jenny, darling—I'm here—" The girl's slumber was deep, drug induced. God knew she needed the sleep— and the oblivion it brought. Her mother strained, listening to her breathing.

Peter gently touched her arm and led her out.

"Would it be okay if I stayed nearby?" Her face was taut, eyes wide with anguish and guilt.

He led her to the small family room outside the unit, returned to the nurses' room, filled a cup with coffee and brought it back to her. She was grateful, held the mug with both hands, trying to still the trembling.

"I hope they find him—I'll kill him. I swear to God, I'll kill him."

Emergency remained quiet. Peter had been on his feet for seventeen hours, his shift not yet half-completed. But even when the accidents, sicknesses, came in groups, he found the first half of his duty bearable.

He looked in at the quiet rooms where the emotionally disturbed patients were secluded. Three of them had been brought in and were to leave at ten the next morning for the state institution. The nightlight was on, and two patients, both middle-aged men, were sleeping in a fetal position, each with a hand buried in his genitals for comfort, their mouths making sucking sounds. In the next room was a large blowsy woman, formerly a brilliant scientist, who had succumbed to the bottle. It would take her a couple of weeks to dry out; after she came back from the sanitarium, Peter hoped she might be sufficiently motivated to move into Lazarus House.

He returned to Emergency. The two nurses were leafing through professional journals and dipping into a box of Russell Stover candies, which they offered to him. He couldn't remember now whether he'd stopped for supper or not; the chocolates and a cup of fresh coffee sent his blood sugar soaring. Before going back to his charts, he drank some orange juice. He had lost count of the day's cases, except for the rape victim and the little girl who had died.

CHAPTER V

Carmen was on duty at the intensive care unit. Her face was freshly made up, under the short copper-colored curls. She was in her late twenties but she fought the years with the skill of a model. She had, in fact, gone to a modeling school before she tackled nursing, but the rich indulgent husband she fantasized about proved to be as difficult to get as a Hollywood contract. So she settled on nursing because, as her mother always said, a man was at his most vulnerable and most appreciative when he was sick and helpless. The male patients in intensive care had private nurses, who kept zealous guard over them. The next best hope, Carmen decided, was one of the young residents. Her plan was simple: these fellows were so overworked, so exhausted, that they had no chance to live like human beings. What they needed was a good meal, a good lay, a decent night's rest. It could be the beginning of a beautiful relationship. She knew of other nurses who'd parlayed nurturing into a medical marriage.

She'd given up on Peter Norris, which left her two possibilities.

Choice number one was a young plastic surgeon who was chafing under his arranged marriage and his doting in-laws. Jewish in-laws were the best kind: they set up their daughters' husbands—the young doctors—in elegantly furnished offices, catered lavishly to them and smothered them with devotion and dollars. The young surgeon Carmen had her eye on was already bored with his compliant wife, his two children, his house in North Belfort. Carmen figured he was ripe for seduction. By now he could appreciate the kind of loving Carmen offered.

The other choice was Fred Farley. Macho man. She sensed that he had a great future and he wasn't bad to look at.

With smart clothes, exercise and a decent haircut, Fred would be just right. What she liked most about him was that he was street smart and hungry for money. He had a positive genius for attracting the good will of people who mattered in the medical community, Dr. Watling, for one. Dr. John Paul Macray for another. Fred was in the family practice residency program, yet Carmen had the feeling he would land wherever the pickings were best. God, the money these young doctors raked in after a year or two in practice!

In all likelihood the entire group would get offers for junior partnerships with the well-established Belfort physicians. Or else they would tie up with hospitals in other parts of the country. Fred Farley thought he might remain in Belfort. Which was a good idea; he was Dr. Watling's fair-haired boy, which promised him a good future. In no time, he'd collect the good things that came with a medical practice: a modern house in North Belfort, a condominium in Florida, a Cadillac, a little Volks for running around, a BMW for his wife.

She wondered if Fred Farley would remain in Belfort, as he'd said he would, either to join a group of doctors or set up his own office. Of course, opening his own place took money. So he might end up with a rich wife, to launch his establishment. Carmen had no money but she hated giving up on him.

Carmen watched Peter replace some charts and stride out. He was patterning himself after Dr. John Paul—tough to please. No mistakes, everything had to be right. Well, screw him!

As a matter of fact, she thought with a reminiscent smile, she had screwed him—once. Last year. It had happened on a week night, when he was on a twelve-hour tour of duty and lost a patient, an elderly man with a strangulated hernia. The primary physician had mis-diagnosed the problem. By the time Dr. John Paul was summoned, Peter had assisted another doctor who performed the surgery. He'd done all the right things; Big John's praise was unstinted. But septicemia was stronger than the patient's waning resistance.

Carmen happened to be on duty in intensive care when the patient died. The old man had no relatives and Peter had spent some of his free time at the bedside. She had the feeling, Carmen remembered thinking, that Peter was having a battle with death; that he refused to give up. When the body was finally wrapped in a shroud and wheeled out by stretcher to the elevator and the morgue, Peter went into the nurses' lounge, fell into an easy chair, buried his face in his hands.

She waited a few minutes, since she was going off at 11:00. After a while she went over to him, put her hands on his neck and massaged it. She could feel the muscles bunched up in knots and kneaded them rhythmically with her long, cool fingers.

"You're no good to anybody here," she said. "When do you get off?"

He looked up, empty, too drained to feel ashamed. "At midnight."

"Why don't you sneak out now. It's quiet and one of the guys'll cover for you. Isn't Fred on tonight?"

He didn't quite understand what she meant. "It's almost eleven, and I'll be leaving in a little while. Come on," she urged.

He followed her numbly; she was careful to make sure no one saw them. Her apartment was in the complex facing the hospital and she entered the lobby first, then waited for him to come in. He was staggering with fatigue. She opened the door to her studio apartment, switched on a dim lamp and said, "Make yourself comfortable, doctor. What will you have? Scotch, bourbon, rye?"

"Anything." Peter sprawled on the sofa, which was deep and comfortable, with cushions that supported his back. She made him a stiff drink, scotch on the rocks, and pressed his fingers around the glass. His smile was wan but grateful.

"Drink up," she said. "When did you last eat?"

"At lunch, I think."

"Well, let me see—" she had opened the door to the kitchen cabinet and brought out a can of chicken soup. She heated it, she fed him, and when he revived she seduced him. She undressed casually before him, tossing her uniform on a chair, stepping out of her white panty hose, which did nothing for her beautiful legs, she thought as she unfastened her bra. Standing before him, she gloried in her nakedness. She approached him, smiled, sat on his lap, putting her arms around him. "I'm just what you need," she whispered, "so relax."

She knew from experience what a death could do to a young doctor; the despair at having lost a patient, a battle. And in the aftermath, the overwhelming need to reaffirm life, reaffirm the vitality of the human body. Well, what better way than to have sex with an obliging partner, who'd learned from the best of the M.D.s the fine art of making a man feel good.

As she had anticipated, he was a good lover. That lean, muscular body, the skillful, gentle thrusting—thank God he's not a banger, she thought, remembering the last resident she'd slept with. She didn't ordinarily come the first time. But Peter plunged her into a series of wild orgasms, each intense wave of pleasure surpassing the last—like the kind she had read about in *Cosmopolitan*. Life! Hey, Dr. Norris— Peter—we're alive and to hell with all the sick and dying and dead across the street!

She hoped he'd stay the night, but like a fireman he was in the shower, drying himself and ready to leave.

"They sure have you on a tight schedule," she said snuggling down into her bed, lazy, sensuous, anticipating a marvelous sleep.

"One half-day off each week and every third Sunday," he said. "The rest of my life belongs to the hospital." He leaned down and kissed her cheek. "Thanks," he said and sounded as though he meant it.

"See you around some time," she said brightly, figuring it would happen again and maybe develop into a habit he couldn't break.

He nodded, and let himself out the door. A few minutes later she went to the window, watching for him as he passed the small fountain. He had a long easy stride, even when tired. There was something about him that attracted her and made her feel good.

Maybe he'd need her again, even when he wasn't feeling so vulnerable. But then she recalled that he lived in the same house with Sheila Ryan, the social worker, and Sheila wouldn't let a plum like that dangle. Not Sheila . . .

He never asked her for an encore. He was always courteous and considerate, not like some of the other snooty residents: but there was never another occasion. And now, like the others, he was showing his displeasure. I'll bide my time, Dr. Norris, she thought. You'll trip up somewhere . . .

It was now five o'clock in the morning and Peter was still on his feet, although he was exhausted. How the hell was he expected to remain alert, to make sound judgments when his brain was fogged, his reflexes dulled with sheer physical exhaustion?

The hospital was at rest, quiet, but with a grim, foreboding silence that marked the lowest point of the dark night, when the dying seemed to drift quietly out of the painful, indifferent world.

Peter found an empty call room with a bed intact. He took off his shoes and white coat and stretched out. Almost instantly, he fell into a deep sleep, from which he was rudely awakened by his beeper, summoning him to the next twelve hours of duty.

He was awake but not yet alert; his body, demanding more rest, refused to function for him. He got up slowly, like a man with a hangover, pushed his feet into the soft shoes, tied the laces, groaning as he righted himself. He washed his face—a shave would have to wait till later—scrubbed his hands vigorously, rinsed his mouth and went down to Emergency. One of the technicians was having trouble getting blood from an elderly woman. Her veins were small and deep and even though she made a fist and the technician had wrapped a rubber tourniquet around her upper arm, he had no success. Both technician and patient looked to Peter for help.

He sat down beside the woman, who was on the table in the small examining room. He told her to put her hand down: he began prodding the inner crook of her arm for a vein. She had screwed her eyes shut to avoid watching him, but her breath came in small moans and she was ready to scream at the first thrust of the needle. He managed it so skillfully that he had a vial half full of blood before she was aware of it. She stared at him now with a glazed look, like a hypnotized creature.

"There we are," he said, drawing out the needle and giving the vial of blood to the waiting technician. He covered the puncture with a bit of cotton, had the patient hold her arm up to staunch a drop of blood. Then, patting her on the shoulder, he left her in the care of the nurse.

All was quiet this Monday morning. The day's ritual was repeating itself; the parking lots filling up, the physicians checking in for rounds, the staff coming on duty to relieve the night shift. Peter caught the elevator as it was descending to the ground floor. It was filled with young nurses in freshly starched whites, their faces cheerful in the morning light. They laughed and shared their experiences of the previous day as they lined up at the cafeteria rail for Danish and coffee.

Peter was famished, having eaten nothing since his meager supper the night before. He ordered scrambled eggs, a toasted muffin and orange juice, pushed the tray down to the coffee urn, then to the cashier. She was a cantankerous woman, who seemed always to double-check the young doctors as though she suspected them of cheating her.

"You look beat," she said, more as a statement of fact than an expression of sympathy. "Bad night?"

He shrugged, gave her a meal ticket and carried his tray to the table near the windows that was reserved for the residents. Coffee spilled. He was jittery.

Dr. Watling was eating his second breakfast at a small table for two, opposite Dr. Macray. They were in earnest conversation and Peter wondered if it had anything to do with the graduating residents. He treated most of the residents with a lofty disdain, except for the three young women residents in the group, whom he verbally abused. He could barely tolerate the nurses; to him women had no place in the hospital, except to give enemas and carry bedpans. It was a mystery to the residents why the board of directors didn't fire Watling. Granted the man looked good on paper, with his impressive academic credentials and long list of publications. But what was the prestige of a name worth when it belonged to a failure as a human being? Politics, Peter thought ruefully.

He ate quickly. The food restored him; he began to feel human again.

He had enough time to call Karen but the phone booth in the corridor was occupied by one of the medical company salesmen who made the hospital rounds. Peter was growing more concerned about the day; he wanted everything to be right for Karen. She was, after all, coming to a strange place, and for all of her poise, it might, under the circumstances, be a strain for her.

The best thing, he decided, was to call his landlady, Mrs. Thalberg. She knew Karen was expected today and she could be counted on to make her feel at home. He hoped Karen would like her, that they would become friends. Because with his long hours, Karen would be on her own much of the time . . .

The hospital was coming to life, good smells of food wafted out from the main kitchens, food caddies were wheeled into the new private rooms above Emergency. He felt relieved by Mrs. Thalberg's response to his call: he was not to worry, she would greet Karen, whom she'd already met; they would have lunch together on the glassed-in side porch.

A young porter was swabbing the floors, a DANGER: WET FLOOR sign nearby. Peter smiled at him, pretended to slip, then continued on his way down the corridor. He was due to make rounds with Dr. Macray at eight o'clock.

Peter reached Dr. John Paul Macray's office just as the surgeon entered. His hours in the sun yesterday on Long Island Sound had deepened the color of his leathery skin and his shaggy white hair made a startling contrast to the burn. He nodded to Peter, asked him in, then hunted in his closet for a fresh lab coat.

There was an ugly bruise above his right temple. As Peter looked at it, Dr. Macray said, "I slipped on the deck yesterday." He rolled up the sleeves of his shirt revealing the powerful muscles in his arms. "How's it going, son?"

"Pretty well, sir."

"When are you off?"

"At seven tonight."

"The endurance test, eh?"

"Well, I guess it builds stamina." Peter sounded dubious.

"It's a crash course in doctoring. The idea is that even though you're strung out and exhausted, you absorb a hell of a lot in a brief time."

All of them had gone through it. It was considered a test of a young man's endurance and devotion to medicine, and a rehearsal for those times in private practice when the routine and the emergency piled up to marathon proportions.

Peter nodded. He didn't protest or suggest that after a while he felt like an automaton, wasn't sure of his judgment, stoked up on caffeine.

Early in Peter's final year, after he was chosen chief resident, he often made rounds with Dr. Macray. If the surgeon wasn't too busy, he'd ask Peter to have a cup of coffee in the cafeteria afterwards. Those were privileged moments for Peter; Dr. Macray would be talking to him and none of the other doctors would think of interrupting.

Peter was always inspired by making rounds with the chief of staff. He was a warm man, optimistic, caring. He answered the patients' questions honestly. He explained the surgery, the post-operative care.

They were joined now by four other residents, alert, interested, even obsequious. Dr. Macray stood at each patient's bedside, with the residents around him. He had Peter present each case, then he quizzed them all. At Belfort Hospital medicine was still taught by the apprentice system. The senior physicians taught the residents, who taught the interns and medical students.

Peter forgot his fatigue as he watched Dr. Macray with his patients. They stopped in to see a striking middle-aged woman whose lump in the breast had turned out to be malignant.

"Blanche, how are you feeling?"

She looked at him so abjectly that even the residents were shaken. It was the look of a woman who no longer felt herself a woman, whose loss of a small swelling of flesh had been accompanied by a far more dangerous loss of self-esteem.

Her pale lips quivered but she didn't answer. Dr. John Paul sat down on the bedside chair and took the thin cold fingers in his warm and gentle hands.

"It will be all right, Blanche. You came through surgery in good shape. In a few days a woman is coming to visit you. She has gone through what you have—but you'd never know it. She's back in the swing of life. As you will be. Matter of fact, it's all we can do to keep your husband from taking you home right now."

He spoke with such conviction that a faint reluctant smile touched her lips. This vital, handsome surgeon's interest made her feel intensely feminine.

"Have faith, Blanche. I'll see you again tomorrow." He pressed her fingers, touched her cheek.

It was like the laying on of hands, Peter thought, moved. What Dr. Macray gave his patients went far beyond his skill with the scalpel.

They left Blanche, her face still lit up by the smile, to continue with Dr. Macray on his rounds.

"It's important to restore the woman's sense of femininity, reassure her that she hasn't lost her sex appeal," Dr. Macray said to the residents after they had left Blanche's room.

When the others left Dr. Macray turned to Peter. "I'm sorry you aren't going into surgery."

"Thank you, sir. But I feel that family practice is for me."

"Well, maybe it is. But if you change your mind, let me know."

Peter returned to the emergency room buoyant despite his physical exhaustion. Dr. Macray had that effect on all of them—his peers, the other doctors and the nurses.

CHAPTER VI

Peter made it into the late afternoon, but by then he was punch drunk, not at all sure that he was making the right decisions. He stepped into the doctors' private lounge off the emergency room. It was a small room, with bright papered walls, deep leather chairs and a flowered carpet that one of the doctors said belonged in a Turkish brothel.

He was asleep before he leaned back in the easy chair, but after a good half hour's rest he was awakened by Fred Farley.

"Hey, how you doing?"

Peter shook his head to clear it. "What time is it?"

"Five P.M. and all's well at Thalberg's. Your chick arrived."

Peter jerked his face up, awake now, his blue eyes gleaming. "Karen? You saw her?"

"And how. She drove up in a station wagon filled with fancy luggage. She looks rich, Peter, stinkin' rich."

He made a calculated leer. "No wonder you kept her to yourself.

Hey, does she have a sister? I could go for a chick with money, especially if she was as cute as yours."

"Knock it off, Fred." Peter looked at the clock. A couple of hours more and he would be free.

He was charged with fresh energy. She had come; his fears were groundless. Already, he could practically smell the faint strawberry scent of her hair . . .

"Just showing my appreciation of your taste, Pete," Fred said, with a lopsided grin. "Isn't that what friends are for?"

Close friendships among the residents were rare in general—they seldom had time to exchange more than a few minutes talk over coffee in the cafeteria, or after they made grand rounds with an attending physician. Still, occasional intimacies did spring up—but not between two such opposite characters as Peter Norris and Fred Farley.

Perhaps the fact that the two young men both, in their different ways, stood out from the rest of their class had something to do with it. Looking back at their first meeting nearly thirty-six months ago, Peter recalled that Fred had immediately struck him as someone to take note of. Not for any special reason, it was just the impression he made of being stronger and bolder than the others. It was the way he held his head, the thick dark hair falling over his forehead and ears, his brown eyes an enigma behind the heavy shell-rimmed glasses, the pupils pinpoint sharp with hostility and suspicion.

Peter had sensed Fred's loneliness and was sorry for him, even though he knew little of his background until they were about to embark on their third year. The residents' opinions seemed to coincide with the judgment of the general staff. Farley was brilliant; the questions he asked the attending physicians often impressed them. He seemed to absorb more at the rounds than any of the others except Peter.

Yet from the very first year the residents had a name for him: Freddie the Freeloader.

"You can smell the poverty on him. He's obsessed with money," Miss Tracy reported to some of the nurses in the cafeteria. "He'll end up exploiting poor patients and getting rich off Medicaid mills."

Fred Farley was twenty-eight years old. At least that's what it said on his birth certificate. He was a graduate of the school of medicine of the Autonomous University of Guadalajara, the largest private university in Mexico.

In his third year Belfort Hospital paid him thirteen thousand dollars a year; he knew Peter, as chief resident, received five hundred more but then, even with Dr. Watling's influence, he couldn't aspire to that position. But Fred was alert for anyone who could help him. He had an uncanny talent for molding himself to please a possible benefactor. And so he made himself Watling's admiring protege.

Hero-worship from a brilliant young doctor with an IQ of 160 was a restorative for Watling's ego. Some of the residents griped that he didn't teach them anything, but young Farley was always telling him what a great teacher he was.

When he had first arrived in Belfort, Fred was horrified at the rents for single rooms. His few possessions were stashed away in an unused locker in the hospital basement. He slept in vacant call rooms, those rooms reserved for the staff on a long tour of duty. Sometimes he scrounged meals from the nurses who brown-bagged their lunches. He was friendly with the assistant to the chef, and often he was able to feast on leftovers from the fund-raising dinners that Roscoe Osgood, the development head, gave.

Dr. Watling would have offered Fred a room in his own house, but his wife, Clementine, was being damned difficult these days. She was reacting badly to menopause, was touchy, prone to hysterics, a great nuisance to him.

In their younger days Watling had been strict with Clemmie. He expected an immaculate house, six-course dinners, starched shirts. He demanded that she stay slender—the fact that she was now putting on pounds annoyed him.

She wasn't even a wife in the bedroom anymore. Not that she'd ever been much for sex; even as a bride she had always been making excuses, acting like a martyr when he finally demanded his rightful due.

Women! As if he didn't have enough problems with the female residents who were about to graduate from Family Practice. The Germans had the right idea. Keep them pregnant and in the kitchen . . .

He spoke to Clemmie about Fred Farley. The poor kid was trying

58

to pay off loans for his education. He slept wherever he could, which wasn't right; a call bed in the hospital wasn't always free.

"No," Clemmie said. He had never seen her little mouth set in such a firm line. He considered insisting but decided against it. She was so unpredictable these days, God knew what she'd do. More than one of the unmarried nurses would have been delighted to share her bed and board with Fred Farley and had there been an heiress among them he would readily have agreed. But there were no heiresses . . .

It was Peter Norris who finally got Fred a place to live. Peter had an excellent relationship with his landlady, Mrs. Thalberg, a doctor's widow who saw in Peter an image of her dear Harry, who'd been so dedicated to his patients. She had some vague notion of playing matchmaker to Peter and Sheila Ryan, the pert head of the hospital's social services department, who had become Mrs. Thalberg's second tenant. A romance with Peter would, Mrs. Thalberg suspected, please Sheila. But Peter seemed to consider her only a good friend.

Peter had brought Fred Farley into their domestic circle, persuading Mrs. Thalberg to let Fred share his room. He explained that Fred couldn't contribute a fair share of the rent since he was obliged to pay off some college debts.

Their living situation cemented Peter's and Fred's growing friendship, but it was some time before Peter learned anything of his roommate's background.

Then, late one evening in their third year, Fred and Peter had gone to a bar for a few beers after having come from the hospital auditorium where Dr. Virginia Carruthers had given a talk about the emotional problems of very young children.

The brass expected them to attend, so they had sat through the hour's lecture. Dr. Carruthers, who was head of pediatrics, had looked like a model in her jumper with a white blouse edged with ruffles. She was using a pair of half glasses, which kept sliding off her small nose. Fred muttered in an aside to Peter that she was one cute little piece of ass.

But once she began to speak, he grew silent. Peter glanced at him, realized Fred was listening with puzzled, sullen intensity.

Dr. Carruthers was talking about adopted children.

"If a child is deprived of a mother's love, he becomes an adult in body, but not emotionally. Emotionally he doesn't grow up. His anger, his fury, his frustrations can be traced back to his deprived infancy. Yet once in a while, a youngster who has all the strikes against him turns out well adjusted, makes a stable, successful life for himself. Adversity seems a challenge which he can overcome."

"That's a lot of crap," Fred muttered when the lecture was over. They filed out of the crowd of nurses and hospital attendants. Peter wondered at his vehemence but said nothing.

When they emerged from the hospital reception room, Fred suggested that they go to the nearby bar. As they headed down Main Street toward the station, bucking the wind coming in from the Sound, he was silent. To Peter, he seemed more moody than depressed, as though he had something on his mind.

That night as they sat in the shadowy tavern, glasses of beer on the table, a scattering of workmen grouped around the bar, Fred spoke to Peter about his early life for the first time. Not in sequence, but in bits and pieces, fragments that Peter put together to form a coherent story.

Fred Farley had no memory of his parents. He had been found huddled on the steps of an abandoned house in one of those dreary streets of Los Angeles by the cop on the beat. He remembered how cold the night air had been, how hungry, tired, frightened he had felt when the policeman discovered him. He was brought to the police station and fed a hot dog and a glass of milk while the officers checked around. There was no report of a lost child. Abandoned kids were checked in at a children's center, kept there until they were claimed or sent to foster homes. The police thought he was about three years old, but small and skinny, with enormous dark eyes, curly hair spilling over his forehead. He had a puppy's eagerness to please.

For a three-year-old he had a meager vocabulary. They kept asking him what his name was, and when he shaped the word it came out like "Fweddy." They got no more from him. His tiny body was covered with bruises and scars.

The girls in the children's center liked the boy; he was shy but lovable. Before he was placed in a foster home they tried to guess his nationality. His coloring was dark, but he had Caucasian features and didn't seem to understand Spanish so he couldn't be Mexican. Nor was he Jewish, since he wasn't circumcised. Portuguese maybe, or Greek, they decided. The scars on his back were cigarette burns. Purplish bruises stained his small ribcage and his arms. An x-ray of his wrist showed a break.

A battered child, born perhaps to a young girl who'd come to Los Angeles, movie struck, fantasizing that she would become another Marilyn Monroe. The social agencies saw many such victims of the glamorous movie syndrome, girls who'd tried to take the bedroom route to stardom, or had taken to the streets when the glitter had worn off their daydreams.

As Fred unreeled these facts, his face was noncommittal, his voice factual. As though he was reciting the story of a stranger.

By the time he was a tormented confused teenager, his life was a series of denials. Yet his refusal to face his early years seemed to create in him a drive and perception that were extraordinary. His battery of psychological tests fascinated the psychiatrists.

Fred learned to survive in a series of foster homes where he was tolerated only because of the money paid for his keep. Out of necessity he learned to lie, became street smart, developed as a dangerous, wily fighter. He ran away and was discovered by the authorities. He ran away again, was branded a juvenile delinquent. He was scheduled to leave for a boys' town for emotionally disturbed children when he was rescued by a new psychiatrist.

The boy was bright, deserved an opportunity, the psychiatrist concluded. He was a sympathetic man with a genuine interest in reclaiming wayward kids. One of his friends was an elderly and well-to-do widow from a solid Los Angeles first family. He interested her in Fred and she agreed to sponsor the boy through his last two years of high school. If he made good grades and kept out of trouble, she would underwrite his college education. She was isolated from her own family, living as a recluse, relying on her lawyers and the psychiatrist who was her friend and confidant.

Fred never heard from his benefactress directly. Her lawyers kept in touch with him and her grant was generous enough so he was not short of funds. But the craving for money was strong in him by that time, as was the craving for education as a means of making money.

He sent her an invitation to the graduation exercises at UCLA. She arrived in a long black limousine that looked like a hearse. Her maid and her chauffeur helped her out of the car, frail, her face very brown and as wrinkled as a mummy's. Fred greeted her before the ceremonies and met her afterwards.

He felt enormously shy with her, very constrained. His feelings were tumultuous; he could scarcely control them.

"I understand you want to go into medicine." Her voice was high, tremulous with age.

He nodded, said smoothly, "A doctor can do a lot of good in the world." He sounded sincere, although he was partly lying. He really didn't know *what* he wanted to do. In the recession of the early 1970s, the job market was terrible even for college graduates, and M.A.s and Ph.D.s were teaching in high schools. Even law school graduates were having a tough time finding lucrative positions; medicine was the only sure bet.

"So it's medicine you want?"

"I think I can get into medical school . . . my marks are high. If I can get a government loan or a grant—"

Her rheumy eyes glittered. "Let those who need help apply for it. You'll be taken care of."

Chance, Fred thought forever after. If the second psychiatrist hadn't given him a second battery of tests. If the doctor hadn't happened to have an elderly woman friend who needed some reason for living . . .

He never saw her again. Her lawyers arranged for his tuition and expenses at Guadalajara. He wrote to her in care of them and an answer came back from the firm's senior partner. His good Samaritan was in a sanitarium. No mail could be forwarded to her. The lawyers wished him well.

"Her psychiatrist friend was trying to help her," Fred said as he finished telling the story to Peter. "He thought if she took an interest in a kid, in me, it might restore her. But she went haywire. I guess she's still in the nuthouse. I feel funny about it." He paused and looked down at the empty glass. "I kind of wish I could see her again. She was the nearest thing to a family I ever had." He looked away.

In the dim light Peter thought he could make out the glint of tears behind Fred's glasses. He picked up the check, threw some bills on the table and got up. Fred continued to sit in the booth, staring across the table. Peter nudged him gently, linked his arm through Fred's and lifted him to a standing position. Then the two young doctors went out into the midnight darkness, to hail a cab back to Mrs. Thalberg's.

CHAPTER VII

Karen left the Manhattan townhouse at eleven o'clock Monday morning.

Otto had stacked her bags in the station wagon, which she would use while her parents were in London. In a way, she thought, pulling out of the parking space outside of the house and aiming for the East River Drive, it was like going off to college.

She wondered what it would be like to share a room—a life—with Peter. She knew him, or so she thought, but she wondered soberly if you knew any man until you'd actually lived with him. The strange thing was that never during her anguished, ecstatic affair with Delos had she been able to visualize living with him on a permanent basis. She had lived from hour to hour, the uncertainty of their relationship heightening her passion.

She shook her head to banish the memories; it was too late to turn back. And she didn't want to, did she? She had chosen to go to Belfort, to live with Peter Norris and be his love . . .

She swung onto the expressway that would lead her into the Hutchinson River Parkway, keeping the wagon at a steady 55-mile speed. A visit to Grandmother Wickersham was in order; she'd like to include Peter in that visit, but she had promised her parents that she wouldn't tell her grandmother about the arrangement. Dammit, the whole thing was beginning to seem like a repeat performance of Delos. The deception, the furtiveness . . .

I lied to mother and dad, thought Karen, I've been lying to myself. This is Peter's arrangement, I've only gone along with it to please him. Did that mean she was passive with Peter, as she had been with Delos? What did Peter want from her, anyway? At first he'd seemed to imply it would be a kind of trial marriage, but once she'd agreed to live with him, there'd been a subtle shift, he'd started using that word arrangement. What did he really mean by it . . . ?

She hadn't quite figured Peter out; she was following her instincts, trusting him. Surely he was acting in good faith, not taking her for granted as some kind of permanent concubine. No, that was more Delos's style. She had to stop confusing them.

She cautioned herself to slow down as she automatically obeyed the signs for the toll booths leading into Connecticut. It would be disastrous to reveal any of her anxieties to Peter. He had enough worries of his own, the brutal schedule at the hospital for one. She was supposed to provide an oasis from all that. And he would be her oasis. So why was she frightened?

She guided the car off the Merritt Parkway exit and south along a main artery; she'd visited the Thalberg house once with Peter and her sense of direction was unerring. The town's older area, with its costly Tudor homes, was shut off by imposing gates. Just beyond it was Buxton, an avenue of older houses set in a splendor of gardens welcoming spring with a promise of peonies, irises, and pink and ivory dogwood.

Most of the houses were of early Italianate architecture so popular at the end of the nineteenth century. The Thalberg house seemed out of context with the others—it was asymmetrical, the front door to one side instead of fixed in the center; beyond it, to the right, was a deep bay window, outlined in tiny squares of colored glass: red, orange, and a deep blue-purple. The first floor was white clapboard, the second was covered with shingles, and the attic was an intricate blend of materials, topped by an open tower with a fretwork of stick-style embellishments.

Karen turned into the driveway, shut off the engine and got out of the car. Before she could mount the front steps, the door opened and Mrs. Thalberg emerged with a welcoming smile. She wore a becoming gray knit pants suit with a white turtleneck.

"Karen, hello. I'm so glad you made it for lunch." She took Karen's hands in hers with genuine delight. "Come in. We'll fetch your bags later."

She led Karen into the long hall, which ended in a bright kitchen that was more like a family room, the woods dark, with white plaster above the wainscoting; open shelves setting off the colorful china; built-in cabinets and a sunny breakfast alcove, which was set for their meal.

"You'll want to wash up," she said. "Why don't you use this bathroom?"

Her warmth allayed Karen's nagging sense of insecurity. Mrs. Thalberg did not seem to disapprove of her. She treated Karen as cordially as if she were Peter's bride.

After she washed in the old-fashioned immaculate bathroom, Karen returned to the kitchen, where Mrs. Thalberg was preparing for lunch. From the refrigerator she took two pottery plates of chicken salad and mixed fresh fruit bathed in a delicate curry dressing. She placed the plates on red mats on the circular breakfast-nook table and went to the range, where she had blueberry muffins heating.

"Iced coffee?" she asked.

"I'd rather have it hot," Karen said, sliding into the circular seat.

"I like it hot, too, even when the weather is warm. It kind of restores you," Mrs. Thalberg said. She added a butter dish and sat down beside Karen. "It's such a shame Peter couldn't be here to meet you."

"When will he be home?"

"Probably about seven, or a bit earlier. This is his long day. He will have been on duty for thirty-six hours straight."

"Without a break?" Karen was startled. Peter had told her about his demanding schedule, but she hadn't understood what it entailed.

"It's very rough on the boys. I remember when my husband was an intern, he was always exhausted and I used to ache for him. It hasn't changed much since those days. I've seen Peter come home absolutely drained."

Karen realized she didn't know what Peter did at all. He seldom talked about his work, except when he was concerned about a particular patient. Usually they socialized with Karen's friends; sometimes, if more than one of his fellow residents was included, he and Peter talked shop.

Mrs. Thalberg enjoyed serving her guest and replenished the coffee. "I'd love to have you both to dinner tonight . . ."

Karen said quickly, "Shall we leave it up to Peter?"

"Of course, you're right. He'll be tired and you'll want to be alone this evening. That wasn't very thoughtful of me."

"Not at all. You're very, very kind." Karen hoped Mrs. Thalberg would sense that she was referring to more than just the offer of dinner.

"Well, I didn't mean to sound so—so smothering." Mrs. Thalberg looked conscience-stricken. "But I'm so pleased to have you both living here. It takes me back to my own early marriage—but that sounds hopelessly sentimental, doesn't it?" She slid out of the circular seat. "Would you like to see the rest of the house before you go upstairs?"

"Yes, I'd love to see my new home."

Mrs. Thalberg brightened at the words. "This is an odd-shaped house, the living quarters all take off in one direction from the hall."

In the front parlor a deep old-fashioned sofa, easy chairs and a Steinway baby grand were set precisely in place on plush gray carpeting. Watercolors of harbor and garden scenes framed in gilt lined the walls, and early plants in glowing brass containers graced the windowsill. It looked comfortable, but not lived in. This was true of the diningroom too; the oval table surrounded by heavy Chippendale chairs, the buffet with its silver tea set protected from tarnish with a plastic cover.

What Karen liked best was the backyard: a grape arbor, with greenish buds that promised a rich harvest, a small rectangular rose garden and a badminton court.

"It's charming—just like my grandmother's house," she said, clapping her hands with delight.

"Peter and Fred—he's the other resident—play a wicked game of badminton when they're both off."

There was also a wooden glider, the kind seldom seen any more. Mrs. Thalberg said it had come with the house, when they bought it in 1965. Bird feeders hung from the lower branches of a maple, and a fat old calico cat was hidden partly under the forsythia bushes that edged the property line, watching the wary progress of a robin. The atmosphere was so comfortable, so friendly that Karen felt much more cheerful than she expected to.

"Shall we sit in the swing awhile?" The older woman evidently hated to let her go; she was eager to share her time, which Karen realized, with sudden insight, must hang heavy when she was alone. Several of her mother's friends were widows but Karen had never given them any special thought. Of course her own Grandmother Wickersham had been widowed now for five years, but she had never thought of that energetic lady as being alone or lonely. Her life was so active, so purposeful and busy.

It was pleasant sharing the swing, which rocked gently under Mrs. Thalberg's prodding. Karen was sleepy from the drive and the substantial lunch. She considered taking a nap before Peter's arrival. She wanted to be fresh for him.

"Have you and Peter made plans for after his graduation?" Mrs. Thalberg asked.

"Not really."

"Well, do stay here as long as you'd like. Make my home yours. Feel free to use the kitchen, too, whenever you feel like cooking. Sheila often does—"

"Sheila? That's the social worker, isn't it?"

"Yes, she's head of social services at the hospital. She says that cooking is a form of therapy for her—it keep the frustrations of her job from driving her crazy."

"What kinds of frustrations?" Karen asked.

"Mainly the nursing home shortage. There are so many helpless old people, who aren't really sick but still need supervision. Or who are sick but not sick enough for care in a hospital. Which is where they sometimes end up all the same, because the nursing homes in this area don't have enough beds for them."

This was a revelation to Karen. She knew next to nothing about the indigent elderly and their problems. Verna and Otto, the couple who attended the Coles' Manhattan apartment, would probably be with the family until they were pensioned off, like Karen's old nanny.

After a while, Mrs. Thalberg said, "Let me show you the rest of the house." Linking her arm with Karen's, she led the way indoors.

"We bought this place in nineteen sixty-five. That was the year Harry finally had a good income and we could afford to move. Up to then we had lived in a two-family house in the south end. I only wish Harry were still alive to enjoy it. He loved the space and the garden . . .

"He'd always dreamed about medical school, but there was no way he could afford it. The GI Bill gave him the chance to complete high school, then go on to City College in New York . . ." Mrs. Thalberg paused at the piano and showed Karen a photograph of herself and her husband when they were young. He was a slender man, rather gaunt, with light hair and a contagious smile on his face.

"He looks happy," Karen said.

"He was. He loved life and his family and later on, his patients. I was always the melancholy one."

But her photograph showed a smiling, slim girl in one of the post-war full Dior skirts, dark hair pulled off her face in a chignon, brilliant eyes under heavy, sensuous lids and stunning high cheekbones.

Karen said, "Did you model?"

"Nothing so glamorous. I worked as a teacher in the public school system. We were very eager to get married, so I saved every penny and Harry took any job he could find during the weekends and vacations. We just about made it—until I became pregnant. I wanted to have a baby, but it was a problem with money. Then, when my second child came a year later, we really were strapped. I worked nights, when Harry was home with the babies.

"After he finished medical school, he was offered an internship at Belfort Hospital. We were eager to leave New York and his salary of one hundred dollars a month seemed like a good deal. Only a short time before the war interns were getting thirty dollars a month in metropolitan hospitals.

"One night Harry came home very excited. The head of the hospital had just bought his own home and offered to rent us his old one, which was very nice, far superior to what we were accustomed to.

What he didn't tell us clearly until after we moved in was that the rent was eighty dollars a month."

"You mean eighty out of the hundred dollars?"

"Exactly. That left us with twenty dollars a month. Enough to buy milk for the babies."

"Good Lord, how did you manage?"

"We starved a little and borrowed a little, not from our families, who had nothing themselves, but from friends. I wanted to go back to teaching but there was no one to look after the babies during the day."

"How awful!" Karen thought of her own privileged life, how much she had always taken for granted.

Inspired by a sympathetic listener, Mrs. Thalberg went on, telling Karen about her husband's first office. "There were few patients at first, so he took night calls for other physicians who were either too old or too affluent to do night work. When a patient asked him, 'What do I owe you, doctor,' Harry was at a loss. He'd say that the regular doctor would send the bill. Harry never collected half of his fees." She made a wry smile. "His first month in private practice he made forty-six dollars."

"Peter said the residents today have it much easier."

"He's right, they do. The residents at our hospital earn thirteen thousand dollars a year. That's more than my Harry made until his fifth year in private practice."

Karen was silent. She had no idea what her father's income was.

"In the sixties he began to do well, though. His talent as a diagnostician brought him a lot of consults. Then he made a wise suggestion—as though he knew his future was limited. 'Let's see the world,' he said. So he took time off and we traveled. It was Harry as I'd never known him, boyish, fun-loving. He loved his work and his patients and he always had time for the ones who needed him . . .

"Until his heart attack. He died five years ago, but the older physicians still talk about him. If it's a difficult case they say, 'If only Harry were here.' They're honoring his memory by a series of lectures in his name this fall."

"That must make you very proud."

"Yes." Mrs. Thalberg's dark eyes were glowing. "And that's why I like having young people from the hospital living here. My own son and daughter are in California. I work in the auxiliary too. The medical wives stick together—until one is widowed." She bit her lip, rose rapidly from her chair. "But I do run on, you must want to go to your room. Come on, I'll show you the way."

Freshly showered and into spotless powder-blue slacks and a matching silk shirt, her long narrow feet in Gucci loafers, Karen wandered around the front lawn, stopping to inspect the flowering bushes, petting the cat who was sunning herself on a stone bench near the birdbath in the middle of the front lawn. A bird skimmed through the clean spring air. As far as Karen could see, the tree-shaded street was deserted in the late afternoon. It was not yet time for the homeward rush of commuters.

The heavy fall of fair hair cascading over her shoulders was uncomfortably warm on the back of her neck. But she didn't want to pin it up, Peter liked the Alice-in-Wonderland look.

A newsboy on a bicycle tossed a rolled-up copy of the *Chronicle* at the front steps and missed. It fell on the lawn and instantly the front door opened, as though Mrs. Thalberg were waiting for it.

Karen retrieved the paper and handed it to her.

"You look lovely, so cool and composed," Mrs. Thalberg said. She unfurled the paper, scanning the headlines. "The hospital is going out for a capital fund drive. They've got this new director of development, he was originally from some small-time children's fund. I don't believe he can hold his own with the top corporate executives. He doesn't have their sophistication." It was clear to Karen that Mrs. Thalberg still had an interest, and perhaps an influence, in the medical community.

"Well," Mrs. Thalberg settled herself beside the cat, "Peter will be awfully busy for the next two months—until he graduates. You should try to keep busy too." She reached out and touched Karen's arm. "My dear, I don't mean to be a busybody. But I can't seem to keep my mouth shut when it comes to the young doctors and their wives. I always hope they will benefit from what my generation went through."

"I'm very grateful to you," Karen said.

"It's just that I believe you'll find adjustment much easier if you have some work of your own, Karen."

"I realize that, I couldn't be idle. I worked in broadcasting in New York, so I wrote to the local radio station here and they sent me an application to fill out. I don't know anything positive yet, but I'm to call for an appointment."

"That's very wise. Most of the wives of my generation stayed home, kept house, raised the kids—and walked in the shadow of their husbands. Many of us ended up with nothing, suffering not so much from the empty nest syndrome as from the empty life syndrome." Mrs. Thalberg plucked a withered bloom from a pot of tulips she'd set out too early. "But even if you find a good job, Karen, I hope you'll still join our auxiliary."

Karen brightened at the thought.

"It's the women's group of the hospital. We manage the thrift shop, the coffee shop and the gift shop, we run all of the annual events, such as the May fashion show, the annual ball, the dessert-bridge—all to raise money for the hospital. Last year we gave Obstetrics that marvelous new bed from France that's used for natural childbirth. I'll ring Mrs. Macray—she's president of the auxiliary board—and tell her that Karen Norris is in town and should be in the auxiliary—"

Karen's heart sank. Mrs. Thalberg's warm reception of her had been based on a mistake. She hadn't known after all, hadn't been trying to show Karen it was all right. She took a deep breath.

"Mrs. Thalberg, my name is Karen Cole. Not Karen Norris."

"You're keeping your maiden name? Why don't you hyphenate it—Karen Cole-Norris."

"We're not married, Mrs. Thalberg."

"Oh. You and Peter, er . . ." the older woman floundered.

"We have an arrangement." She was beginning to hate the sound of it.

Mrs. Thalberg seemed to understand Karen's embarrassment. She reached out and pressed her hand reassuringly. "You're like my daughter. She went to San Francisco to lead her own life. But may I suggest something—for your own good?"

Karen waited, tense. Mrs. Thalberg's manner was still cordial, but there was something like pity in her eyes.

"Don't bandy it about. Most of our medical wives are *very* proper. Oh, they probably slept with their men before they married but they've conveniently forgotten. And they're the first to pass judgment. Sinners—" there was a humorous gleam in her eyes, "become the most saintly reformers."

Leaving Karen to digest the well-intended advice, Mrs. Thalberg scooped the cat under her arm and marched it back into the house. Karen remained on the stone bench, stunned.

She was so angry with Peter that she wanted to cry. How could he have put her in such a humiliating position? Was he simply thoughtless or had his concern been a projection of her need? Surely he should have found some way to tell his landlady of their situation. Suppose Mrs. Thalberg hadn't been so understanding, suppose she had demanded that Karen leave her house at once? Or was it Peter's idea to pretend they were married—well, he might have at least informed her of it.

She suddenly realized how little they had thought through this move together. Oh, they had talked, but it had been romantic talk, with no discussion of the practical aspects of the matter. And hadn't Mrs. Thalberg warned her just now that she was being thrown to the wolves? "Our medical wives are *very* proper . . ."

Thank you for warning me, Dr. Peter Norris, Karen thought with a fresh wave of resentment. Oh, God, to be faced with a whole town of catty women, when she had only recently crumbled under the strain of the confrontation with Delos's wife. Well, she wouldn't go through with it, she couldn't. She stood up; she was going home.

But something prevented her. She sat down again. Was she being fair to Peter? It was unlikely that he had deliberately misled Mrs. Thalberg. Maybe she had just inferred that they were married because Peter had been so excited about Karen's arrival. He was so absorbed in his work—even more than Karen had realized before her conversation with the landlady—he had probably never given a thought to the Belfort doctors' wives, had no idea what they were like.

No, Karen thought, they'd both been so full of each other, so enchanted at the prospect of sharing the same bed every night, neither one of them had seen past their private paradise to the greater community in which they were to live. She was glad that she had already anticipated Mrs. Thalberg's suggestion about scouting for a job in Belfort. And Peter, no doubt, had thought the only problem would be the demands of *his* work, the large amounts of time they would have to spend apart. Oh, the wisdom of hindsight . . .

Well, it wasn't too late, Karen realized. Luckily, Mrs. Thalberg had alerted her to the dangers, and now she and Peter must sit down and talk together. There were other details that had been left vague, the financial aspects of their relationship, for example. She hadn't realized Peter's salary was so low until Mrs. Thalberg had told her what the residents made. She had let him know that she was willing to do her share, but she needed his support too, in paving the way for her in the medical community. They were in this together . . .

She heard the sound of the front screen door. A young man in hospital whites emerged from the house and stood at the top step a moment, peering behind his dark glasses as he looked around. Then he walked deliberately down the steps and padded on his white rubber-soled shoes across the lawn to her.

"Hi." He raised his hand in a careless salute. "You're Karen, I take it."

"Yes."

"Peter told me you were due today."

She smiled politely, aware that he was giving her the once-over. "Are you one of the residents?"

"Right. And Peter's former roommate. But I'm sure he'll be happier with his new one."

She was puzzled. His manner was offhand, with a touch of insolence, a kind of *I dare you to impress me*. She recalled now that Peter had spoken of his former roommate, Fred, or was it Ted? She hadn't pictured him like this. He looked disheveled. His dark hair was parted on the right side, falling over his forehead into thick beetling eyebrows that his sunglasses couldn't hide. He had a prominent nose and Adam's apple, a heavy sensual mouth and a faint growth of beard on his olive skin. His white coat was open, his pants too snug. She couldn't decide whether he was an egotist or whether his abrasive manner hid some insecurity. He certainly wasn't her type, but she recognized a naked sexuality about him that might attract some women.

"I'm heading for the hospital. Got a message for Pete?"

"No. I'm just waiting until he's free."

"He's never free of that place. He's so accommodating that Watling exploits him."

"Watling?"

"Captain Queeg of the medical staff. By the way, my name's Farley. Fred."

"Oh, yes. Peter's spoken of you."

Fred grinned. "See you later." Karen didn't like the glint in his eye.

She watched him amble up the street toward the hospital. A rover. Who would want to put their life in Fred Farley's hands, Karen wondered. But Peter had said he was a brilliant doctor.

The sun was as potent as a sleeping pill. She felt languid, drowsy, and was about to doze off when she saw Peter at last coming up the walk. She jumped up and walked toward him. He looked bedraggled, with lines around his mouth. Then he saw her, his face lit up and he held out his arms.

"Karen, God, I can't believe you're really here." He buried his face in her hair as if to confirm it.

"I said I was coming today—didn't you believe me?" she teased, raising her face to be kissed.

"Sure." He ran his tongue over her lips, parting them gently. They kissed, not once but several times. "I knew you were due, but I called and didn't get you . . . it was such a crazy tour—"

"Thirty-six hours."

"Yeah."

"Without any sleep."

He smiled, touched by her concern. "I took a few naps. There's always a bed to park on." His embrace tightened. "God, you're lovely." He carried the smells of his work and himself, the clean acrid smell of a healthy male, and she loved it.

His arm around her, he led her into the house. "If you give me time for a quick shower and change—"

The front hall was cool and shadowy, pervaded by the aroma of home cooking. Peter looked through the letters on the small table. "Mail from my folks," he said, pleased, as he put the letters in his pocket.

"Don't you want to read them?"

"They'll keep. For the moment I just want to look at you—hold you . . ."

They mounted the stairs together and Peter tried to lead her directly ahead to his room.

"We have a change of rooms," she said, guiding him to the right.

The door to the master bedroom was ajar. Peter had been here once, when Mrs. Thalberg had caught a viral infection, and he had treated her here, admiring the space, the delicate English floral wallpaper matching the coverlet on the handsome brass double bed. He'd particularly liked the old-fashioned rolltop desk, with pigeonhole slots, small drawers, the oak and brass gleaming. It was here that Dr. Thalberg used to write. There were two chairs tufted in royal blue and a low glass table by the windows overlooking the backyard. The bathroom was spacious, in blue and white tiles, with a glassed-in tub and a strong shower head. Plenty of towels on the racks.

"But this is her room," he said.

"Yes, but she says it's meant for two and we're to have it. Isn't she a dear?"

"I guess she expects us to stay here after I graduate."

"Wasn't that your intention?" Karen fought the return of her earlier mistrust. We'll talk it out later, she told herself.

"Well, no. I thought we'd hunt for a small apartment—but this is too good to be true."

"A good start for our life," she agreed.

He had stripped off his soiled hospital coat and shirt. "Five minutes," he said, kissing the palm of her hand. "Give me five minutes—"

When he emerged from the bathroom, a towel wrapped around his waist, his face with its usual high color restored, he found her sitting in a yoga position on the bed, legs crossed and calves draped under the thighs, hands folded, palms together. He came to the bed, looked down at her. She saw the rugged spare frame, the well-muscled shoulders, wanted him. He let the towel fall to the floor. Just then Mrs. Thalberg called them from downstairs.

"I don't mean to rush you, but dinner will be in ten minutes."

They stared at each other, in surprise and regret, and then a burst of laughter. He kissed her with infinite tenderness. Karen said, "I told her we would want to be alone."

"Oh well," he said. "The night is young . . ."

After champagne toasts, a magnificent roast capon, endive salad, fresh strawberries and cream; after grateful goodnights to Mrs. Thalberg, who refused their help in the kitchen; after they came into their new quarters; after they undressed each other and got into bed, Peter felt more like himself. The horror of the weekend's tour of duty was obliterated by the champagne, by Karen's delicious presence.

The first time he climaxed too quickly, cursed himself, apologized to her.

"The night is young," she reminded him with a smile and caressed his thigh lightly as they lay side by side in the soft darkness of their bed. When they made love again, it was less hurried, he was patient, considerate, restrained, bringing her to orgasm just as he felt he could hold back no longer.

"I want to hold you." He touched her hair, her temples, the corners of her trembling lips. "Karen, I love you. I love you."

Karen basked in the sound of it. He didn't shower her with pet names like Delos did, but she loved the way he made her own name into an endearment more meaningful than Delos's "sweetheart" or "baby." Delos, she realized suddenly, had never called her Karen in bed, and though he'd waxed eloquent on how much she meant to him, the word love seemed to be missing from his vocabulary.

The third time was even better than the second; he was no longer greedy, his slow rhythmic loving brought her to a sharp peak of delight.

At last, toward dawn, they slept, deliciously spent, their bodies curled around each other.

When she finally awakened, every pore of her skin permeated with his scent and touch, she knew it was far better than her dream of the previous night. Eyes still closed, she reached out, her hand groping at the other pillow. It was empty. She sat up on her elbow; the pillow bore the imprint of Peter's head. Then she saw that the bathroom door was ajar and heard him singing to himself as he shaved.

"Peter!"

He came out wearing only boxer shorts, his rugged body still damp from the shower. He smiled at her, and there was so much affection and gratitude in his smile that she felt a catch in her throat. Let it always be like this, she thought, no anger, no scenes, no pain.

"Karen—" he sat down on the bed beside her, "you don't look happy. Aren't you happy, love?"

Love—he'd never called her that before. "I'm *too* happy," she told him. "I'm afraid something will happen to spoil it."

He cradled her in his arms and she was content. If they could only stay like this forever. He was nuzzling her ears, the soft folds of her neck, and then, abruptly, he moved away. "Let's not start something we can't finish," he said, "or I won't be able to walk out of here."

"And you have another long session at the hospital."

"Ten hours . . . I'll be back in time for dinner." He moved his fingers over her lips. "Don't look so down, love."

"I am—not for myself, but for you. I mean, all those hours, dealing with pain and misery and waste—"

"It's not all that terrible."

He stepped into his white pants and shirt. "What's your agenda for today?"

"Nothing spectacular. Mrs. Thalberg is giving me a Cook's Tour through Belfort."

He kissed the top of her head. "It'll be a long day, but easier knowing you'll be here." He kissed her, and then he was gone. They had not yet had that talk together about their future, she remembered —but somehow it no longer seemed so urgent.

CHAPTER VIII

Dr. Malcolm Stone made an appointment with his accountant at three P.M. Thursday afternoon. Since he had no office hours today, it gave him time to perform two stress tests at the hospital as well as a cardiac catheterization of a writer from Westport. He also allowed extra time to look in at his patients in the coronary care unit.

He put on a dark blue knit suit, a blue-and-white striped shirt and a figured red tie, all purchased for him by Silvie during a sale at Paul Stuart in New York. He allowed Silvie to shop for him because she had an eye for values—and a mouth for a bargain. In that way she was like his mother, with an instinct for good buys. In his bachelor days, he used to drive his mother up to Vermont so she could look at a piece of white ironstone or a pine baby's cradle and offer the seller just enough below his established price that he could still make a profit on the sale, if not the hundred percent markup he'd counted on. She nearly always won, and took such pleasure in bargaining that it offended nobody.

Malcolm must have absorbed some of her psychology of buying, because when it came time for the new car he allowed himself every two years, he made the rounds of the automobile showrooms as soon as the latest cars were being shown. He'd choose last year's model, add a radio, air conditioner and other extras, and then make the salesman an offer of, say, two hundred dollars above the cost he had computed with the aid of *Consumer Reports*. It nearly always worked, and he saved plenty by using the methods that his mother had taught him.

It was a damned shame his talent for bargaining hadn't shown a profit in his major investments. He tried to be philosophical about his latest loss, so he could face his accountant, Jack Palfrey.

Facing Silvie would be another problem. But he still had the whole day ahead of him to figure out what to tell *her*.

Silvie no longer got up to share orange juice and coffee with him. "What for?" she said. "So I can sit and watch you worry about your patients?"

She was still sleeping when Malcolm left the house at seven A.M. Silvie was a night person and so were their children. Barbara had come in at God knows what hour; at seventeen, she ignored Silvie's midnight curfew. So did fifteen-year-old Norman, but at least they always knew Norman was with his classmates at Regent's School. With Barbara, even Silvie was unsuccessful. Sometimes when Malcolm returned home late from a medical meeting or an emergency call, he found Silvie and Barbie in the kitchen, going at it hammer and tongs. They hadn't got along well since Barbara had got her period five years ago. It wasn't that Barbara talked back to her mother. She simply tuned out, grew sullen, remote. Malcolm knew his daughter wasn't a beauty, but her youth and freshness caught his heart. He wanted to put his arms around her—which he hadn't done since she was a little girl—and speak soothingly to her . . . Barbie, it's a woman-sized job to grow up. It's tough and bewildering—all those hormonal changes in your body and making confusing demands on you. Be patient with your mother; she means well. Be patient with me too. I love you, Barbie, even if I don't always show it . . .

Sometimes Malcolm wondered if doctors should have families. Doctors needed wives, yes, to do the work that made their lives comfortable, so they could concentrate on their careers and their patients. But children, who needed supervision, craved attention . . . Maybe not.

There was a memo written in Silvie's precise hand attached to the refrigerator. It reminded him of the date of graduation exercises at Locust Ryse. He'd have to check his calendar and make sure his secretary kept the hours free. After graduation, he remembered, Silvie was inviting a group of friends, mostly from the medical community, for lunch.

He knew Silvie was concerned about Barbara. The girl was smart as a whip and obstinate as a mule. You couldn't force her to do anything. "What about college?" he had asked Silvie. He knew that the headmistress of Locust Ryse had suggested they apply to two-year colleges, because she didn't think Barbara stood a chance at the seven sister schools, even though they needed applications this year.

"She doesn't want a college in a rural setting. She wants to be in a big city," Silvie had told him. "You know where I think she should go?"

Malcolm's hopes rose; Silvie was always ahead of him when it came to handling the children.

"Katharine Gibbs, that's her speed. If she would learn to be a good secretary, she'll never be out of a job. She may even—" Silvie wrinkled her exquisite nose, "marry one of her bosses." She added drily, "You'd better face the truth, Mal. She's bright, but not motivated."

Malcolm was concerned. If only Barbara would confide in him, if only he had the time . . .

He went out the kitchen door and into the two-car garage where his Stingray and Silvie's Cadillac sat side by side. The Cadillac was ten years old but they'd had it only four years; Silvie had bought it from a doctor's wife who was divorcing her mate and needed the cash. It was a beautiful machine and Silvie kept it in top shape, persuading Norman to help her wax the body and scrub the whitewall tires. With the increasing price of gas, Silvie didn't use the car often, except when she wanted to make an impression.

He got into the Stingray and backed out on the blacktopped turnaround.

"Mal! Oh, Malcolm—"

He opened the left door of his car; Silvie was coming out to speak to him. The morning was crystal clear but on the coolish side, which didn't bother her. She wore a baby-doll nylon nightie sprigged with violets, and her wild auburn hair stood up in curls all over her head. She was always at her sexiest when she had just awakened from a deep sleep. He felt a stirring of desire. Funny, her body was like a reed—she had a need to look thin, no flesh, just skin and bone and small pancake tits—yet there was something about her that always got to him. Maybe because she'd been his first real success in bed, and he was both grateful for the memory and excited by it.

He waited, car door open, as she approached.

"You know about tonight," she reminded him.

"Yes. What time?"

"Maureen said about seven."

"I'll be back before that."

"Don't be late, for God's sake." She stooped to pick up the skate-board that Norman had left in the path of the Cadillac. "I'm taking Norman down to have his eyes checked. He lost his second pair of glasses. And it's been two years since his last check-up . . ."

Malcolm nodded approval and shut the car door. Silvie was meticulous about the health of the kids. Norman was at a difficult age; fifteen was tough for a boy, especially when he had to wear Coke-bottle lenses. Malcolm thought that the boy ought to go to a camp this summer, one that stressed outdoor sports, field and canoe trips. But Silvie wanted him home. Why should they spend a thousand dollars, she said, when they had a fine pool, tennis courts nearby and his school friends at the swim club?

Malcolm guided the car down the winding drive to the main road, which was somewhat wider and flanked on both sides by fine old country houses, some of them Belfort's earliest and most elegant. They were interspersed now with newer ones that blended well into the stony Connecticut hills and marshy valleys. He turned on the tape deck, listening to Mozart's *Jupiter* symphony. He'd learned to appreciate classical music as a kid; when his father was still alive, his parents had taken him to concerts. Whenever a musical group, a quartet or a philharmonic group from Pittsburgh had played in the school auditorium of their small town, they had always attended.

He and Silvie now had season tickets for the Greenwich Philharmonic, but invariably, he was summoned on an emergency the night

82

of a concert or Silvie begged out. Her once and forever idol was
Sinatra. How could she scold the kids for their rock music, or whatever it was, when she played Sinatra records all day?

The music was soothing; it prepared him for his day. The sky was
swept clean after last night's showers; it was a serene morning, the
birds were testing their voices, a red setter ran along the edge of the
road, followed by his master in a jogging suit and a sweatband across
his forehead. Malcolm wondered if he were a recovered cardiac victim doing his prescribed exercise.

Malcolm saw people not as people, Silvie said, whenever she was
irritated with him, but as appendages to the heart. It was true. In his
mind he always visualized parts of the human heart, especially that
left anterior descending coronary artery. His enemy, the widowmaker.

If a dam of waxy yellow matter clogged the artery, a life was lost.
A family was robbed of a parent, broken up or scattered. He
detested the widowmaker more than any other part of the heart. It
was the chamber of death.

His father had died suddenly at thirty-eight of a massive heart attack. Malcolm had always had a secret fear that he would die at the
same age. But here he was, forty-two already, and maybe if he was
careful with his lifestyle, the way he tried to teach his patients to be,
he could beat the odds.

He slowed to a stop sign. He reminded himself to call his mother
tonight; it was the anniversary of his father's death, the *yahrzeit,* and
she always fasted and lit a candle in his memory. Malcolm, who had
worshiped his father, often wondered what his life would have been
like if he had known him longer. A different life. Possibly no Silvie.

Would his father have tolerated Silvie, a *shiksa,* their intermar-
riage? His mother made the best of it, but he knew that deep in her
heart she was unreconciled, unforgiving, the orthodox *mameh* who
draped her mirrors in black when her son married a Gentile girl,
whose love for her grandchildren was not given a chance to grow
strong enough for her to overlook their mother.

He recalled the comment of a friend of his, Herb Langston, a
young psychiatrist who was affiliated with an East Village clinic.

"The orthodox Jewish mother is utterly destructive to her sons,"
Herb had said. It had never occurred to Malcolm that his friend was

talking about him—until the year when his mother at last agreed to visit them in their new Belfort house for the summer and Silvie had shortened her visit to two weeks.

"You already have a wife," Silvie said, her voice quiet but menacing, "your mother is *not* your wife . . ."

Silvie did not understand, of course, how close he and his mother had become after his father's death. You're the man in the family now, she had said. And he did his best, he was an only child, a son, living in a house of women—his mother and her two sisters. They all looked to him, took pride in him, the two aunts contributed from their scant earnings as salesladies to fund his medical education.

He'd paid them back, and generously; his secretary wrote out their monthly checks; she was never to allow Silvie to see his private checkbook. No sense in starting a ruckus, particularly since there was enough money for everybody and everything.

He was lavish with money for his mother and the aunts. What upset them was that he was so niggardly with his time. Well, he couldn't spread himself any thinner. There was not enough time for Silvie, not enough time for the kids, not enough time to prepare the seminar in cardiology that he'd be presenting in September, not enough time for his patients, who needed him the most . . .

He drove into the doctors' parking lot at the hospital. He noticed John Paul Macray's old black Chrysler and parked his Stingray in the space beside it. The chief of staff was one of Malcolm's favorite people at the hospital—he was a top-notch surgeon and a first-rate human being. But John Paul was getting on in years, should be retiring soon. Malcolm wondered who would take his place.

"Nobody's more suited than you," Silvie often reminded him. In some ways she was right. But this was not a hospital that might consider a Jew as its head. There were too many Yankees on the board of directors.

He walked into the coffee shop, the volunteers looked cheerful in their bright pink smocks, pleasantly flirtatious with the physicians who were straggling in. He asked for a toasted English muffin and black coffee, then took a seat at the doctors' table between Dr. Macray, looking like a sunbrowned Maine guide, and Dr. Virginia Carruthers, who reminded him of a tousled-hair doll, swimming in her size-five doctor's coat. She was tiny, with the small bones of a bird, a mass of dark curling hair and enormous eyes. There was a shyness about her that Malcolm always found appealing. He couldn't quite believe how large her practice was. The doctors treated her with a respect they seldom gave to women in their field.

John Paul was quiet; he sipped his coffee slowly, lost in thought. Malcolm spoke to Virginia; she'd recently treated a blue baby, who was sent to Yale-New Haven Hospital for surgery. The little girl was Dr. Carruthers's patient but she had called Dr. Stone for a consult when the heart defect was discovered, in the infant's first month of life. Both doctors were cautiously optimistic about the child's progress. She would be needing surgery again. They talked more, then Dr. Carruthers gave Dr. Stone a bright, appreciative smile and left for Pediatrics. It was the kind of smile, Malcolm thought, he'd not received from Silvie in years.

Dr. Macray looked up. "We're expecting you and Silvie tonight."

Malcolm was pleased to be reminded. Then his observant eyes caught the fading bruise nearly hidden by the shock of white hair on the older man's temple. And the vein, which was corded and pulsating. Dr. Macray saw him looking at it.

"Mal, will you have some time in the next couple of days?"

"Certainly. Is there a patient you want checked out?"

Dr. John Paul was unsmiling. He looked tired and dispirited. "You might say so. It's time for a stress test, I think."

Just the two of them were at the doctors' table now.

"For you, John Paul?"

"Yes, for me, Mal."

"Have you ever taken a stress test?"

"I've never felt the need of one."

"Have there been any changes in your blood pressure?"

"It's a bit high." John Paul rubbed his temple with his fingers. "I slipped and banged my head on the boat Sunday. At least that's what I told Maureen. The truth is, I passed out."

John Paul knew the significance of the pain that had gripped him lately. It was not bursitis or arthritis. The tight bands around his chest . . . the nagging awareness . . . the ache in the jaw that wasn't a toothache. The dizzy spells he had been having.

Denial was characteristic of a man with a suddenly failing heart. There is nothing wrong with me, oh, a bit of indigestion, maybe, but those spareribs were too fat. He was out of shape, that's what bothered him. It was foolish to play three sets of singles tennis with the new tennis pro at the club. John Paul knew he could no longer deny what was happening to his body.

"What about tomorrow morning?" Malcolm looked worried now. "We'll work you in early."

"I'm not in that much of a rush. I just thought it was something that needed checking."

"You'll let me know—?"

"I will, Mal. When you see Maureen tonight, don't mention it to her."

Malcolm nodded. He respected John Paul's right to privacy. Besides, he was flattered that the chief of staff had turned to him.

Carmen was coming down the corridor, swinging her hips. A halo of red-gold curls came over her forehead, nearly covering her bright, vivacious face. She greeted Malcolm with a seductive smile, as though her generosity to the medical professional could easily include him. Malcolm's interest was piqued but he passed her with a mere nod. He couldn't understand his attraction for redheaded women. Carmen, he decided briefly, was someone to keep at a distance.

Peter Norris was waiting for him in the secretary's office of his suite. He greeted Peter cordially and unlocked the door to his private office.

"Come in," he said.

On his desk were manufacturers' photographs of the latest technology in echocardiography and vectorcardiography . . . instruments to guide the cardiologist in making a diagnosis of various kinds of heart disease.

He motioned Peter to take a seat while he went through his telephone messages and mail from the previous day. "What do you think of our new administrator?"

"Dr. Hilton? Oh, he has an impressive background," Peter said warily.

"I think he's just what this hospital needs. A man who understands the medical needs, but is aware of the cost end too." Malcolm changed into a white coat; he had to check a couple of patients in intensive care and he wanted Peter to accompany him. He liked Peter.

He even envied him his youth, his lean broad-shouldered body, his open friendly face, not movie star handsome but attractive, inviting respect and confidence. Malcolm had watched the young residents playing handball at the YMCA one evening and Peter's speed and grace had aroused his admiration. Peter reminded him of all he had missed out on as a child, the stifling environment he had grown up in.

"I suppose you'll return to Wisconsin after you're finished here."

"No. I'm planning to settle in Belfort."

"In family practice?"

"Yes. I feel comfortable in it. Both my grandfather and my father are in it—they're country doctors."

"I think your father had an article in *Medicine Today* about the effect of the thyroid on heart disease?"

Peter flushed with pleasure. In the Midwest his father was greatly respected by his peers; he was an authority on problems of the thyroid gland and often other physicians sent their patients to him for evaluation. While he practiced—almost thirty years now—he experimented and researched. The results were often illuminating; his insights into the behavior of the master gland and how to treat it had saved many patients from surgery.

Peter looked at Malcolm as they walked out into the corridor. "We all wanted to take after dad. My two older brothers practice with him now. And my kid brother wanted to heal animals, so he's in veterinary school."

Malcolm didn't volunteer his own reason for going into medicine, although he suspected Peter would have liked to hear it. How could he confess to this young idealist the truth: that he had gone into medicine because his Jewish mother wanted him to. Few cultures, he thought with dry humor, revered doctors the way orthodox Jewish families did. The awe and respect for the man of medicine was something akin to the awe and respect for Yahweh himself.

As he and Peter walked down the blue-carpeted corridor to the intensive care unit, an urgent voice came onto the loudspeaker.

"Code 99, ICU . . . Code 99, ICU . . . Code 99, ICU."

They quickened their pace to a run. Code 99 meant a patient's heart had stopped beating.

"God, I hope it isn't Tom Gordon," Malcolm said, sprinting now. Gordon, a former college fullback, now an engineer involved in the construction of the new shopping center just off the turnpike, had collapsed twenty-four hours ago with what appeared to be a full-blown myocardial infarction. He was scheduled for a cardiac catheterization after his recovery from the attack. But Malcolm knew there was little healthy muscle left in his heart.

As they entered the unit, one of the nurses was wheeling the crash cart to the bedside. From the stairs outside the unit, physicians, nurses and technicians emerged and headed inside. A nurse was laying out the medications, drawing up the liquid in syringes and arranging them.

Malcolm hurried to the bed; it was Tom. His face was turning gray and giving way to a bluish cyanotic tinge. He wasn't conscious but his hands reached out, begging for help.

Malcolm heard one of the nurses outline what had happened, what medications had been given. He placed his stethoscope on Tom's chest and listened. He watched the tracing on the bedside monitor. It was flattening out. He asked for the defibrillator paddles and motioned everyone to stand away from the bed. He pressed the button on the handles. Tom's body arched and fell back as the jolt of electricity went through him. Malcolm tried a second shock treatment, then injections.

With each shock, each injection, the heart had more difficulty responding. There was no strength left in the muscle. Tom couldn't survive this. They took their hands from his chest. Malcolm and Peter each held one of Tom's hands, watching the monitor as the beats got smaller and further apart and more irregular. Until the tracing of his heart went flat . . . a straight line . . .

The nurses took over.

Malcolm and Peter parted at the nurses' station. Malcolm was pale under his olive skin. He sat down and reviewed Tom's case, wondering if somehow he could have prevented the heart failure.

Dr. Brickton had been Tom's primary physician. Malcolm rang his office and the secretary put him through. Malcolm reported what had happened. "Do you want a post-mortem?" he asked.

"No need for it," the physician said brusquely.

"Brickton—"

"What difference does it make?" Brickton added as an afterthought, "I'm glad you handled the arrest. I've never managed a cardiac arrest. I wouldn't know where to start."

"Okay."

"But thanks, Stone."

No doubt, Malcolm thought bitterly, the fee for Brickton's services will go out in the mail tonight. He returned to his office and changed into a clean shirt, tie and jacket and went out to the doctors' parking lot. He still had that appointment with his accountant.

He felt an ache somewhere in the pit of his stomach. Brickton's reaction had filled him with contempt. Most of his own fees were arranged through private insurance from the big corporations who sent him their executives, or through Medicare. He no longer thought much about his fees, except in the case of elderly patients living on social security. He was always careful to find out whether the patient could pay anything. He believed, a residue from childhood maybe, that the rich should pay for the poor. But still the money poured in. There wasn't one doctor in Belfort who netted less than $60,000 a year.

He got into his car and switched on the ignition. He decided he'd make better time into Manhattan by taking the Merritt Parkway. He handled the wheel easily. His hands, the fingers long and flexible, weren't on a par with John Paul Macray's, but nobody did a catheterization better. Even though he had lost Tom Gordon, he was good and the profession knew it. And Dr. Macray thought highly of him. If other physicians knew that the chief of staff was his patient, he could count on other doctors' families switching to him. At last, he thought, he was gaining stature in the medical community.

Recently he'd been invited to speak about coronary heart disease to the Exchange Club, the Rotary, the Lions and other service clubs. He was careful to make his talks simple, in nonmedical language, with charts and diet suggestions. Since most of the members were local businessmen, anywhere from thirty to sixty years old, he could expect, in time, a number of new patients.

He had also addressed the auxiliary of the hospital, on his favorite topic: How Not To Be a Widow. He had some charts made up by one of the nurses, pictures the layman could understand. He described the action of the heart. He explained the beauty and the miracle of the pump when its owner treated it with respect, the importance of low-fat diets, not smoking and the need for exercise. He inspired the women to save their middle-aged husbands from sudden death, tracing the arteries and showing them where blockage caused the most fatal damage.

Even Silvie at her most critical agreed he had a talent for teaching. He made everything concerning the problems of heart disease easy to understand. Of course, he would enjoy teaching at a medical school but his income precluded any chance of his going off in that direction. Compare a quarter of a million a year—and more—with a professor's salary.

It was unthinkable . . .

CHAPTER IX

"Cows!" Jack Palfrey cried, slapping the palm of his hand to his grooved forehead. "Cows—for a tax shelter?"

"Bulls," Malcolm corrected him.

"Cows—bulls—whatever. Why did you do it? For God's sake, Mal, why didn't you call me before you went off the deep end? I'm your financial advisor—I like to think—as well as your accountant." He was a slender man, under fifty, with dark, thinning hair, shrewd eyes behind heavy shell-rimmed glasses. He was conservative in business, a trait that was in conflict with his emotional personality. Over the years he'd saved Malcolm a lot of money.

He swiveled his chair away from the desk strewn with the records of Malcolm's financial state.

"I didn't have time . . ." Malcolm said lamely.

"Will you take the time—before you become a pauper?"

"It looked good, the price of beef was shooting up." Malcolm figured it was a sound investment. A couple of other doctors were in it too. He was supposed to see some earnings at the beginning of the third year but had received nothing.

"Beef on the hoof and beef on the butcher block are two different things." Jack shrugged. "Well, we'll take a loss on it this year. What does Silvie say?"

"She doesn't know. And I'd be obliged if you don't tell her." Why was he always on the defensive with Jack?

"She'll have to know come tax time next year."

Malcolm had incorporated himself which saved him from paying more taxes; but his expenses, particularly malpractice insurance premiums, were out of sight.

"Malcolm, instead of taking fliers on tax shelters, why don't you turn some money over to Silvie? She's got a damn good head for business."

"You may be right." Malcolm was relieved to be off the hook. "She's been bugging me to invest in real estate."

"How's the office space coming along?"

"So far, so good."

"You should have no trouble renting the other suites."

"I've already had inquiries. I'd like to make it a medical complex: an internist, a family practitioner, a gynecologist, an orthodontist."

Jack Palfrey stubbed out his cigarette, gathered Malcolm's papers and slipped them into a portfolio.

"Some day," he said, "I'm going to give a seminar on what doctors should know about money. To show how their innocence—shall I say naïveté—is contributing to the appalling medical costs we have today. Not to mention the practice of defensive medicine, running thousands of dollars in extra tests to cover themselves against malpractice suits."

"But I have a responsibility to do everything in my power to find out the cause of the disease and plan a treatment."

"I'm not criticizing you," Jack said, reminding Malcolm that he had other medical clients, including several Park Avenue physicians, who were just as helpless as he was when it came to handling their own money. There wasn't much difference between the waitress who became an overnight movie star and the young medical resident who was accustomed to deprivation and several years later was earning a hundred thousand a year. It was enough to ruin him and his family for life.

Then, because he was genuinely attached to the Stones, he asked, "Malcolm, what do you want from life? You've got all the luxuries, plus a great reputation in your field. Are you happy?"

Malcolm stood up, easing the tightness in his shoulder blades. He always felt uncomfortable when the conversation got personal.

"Oh, I guess rehabilitation is what fascinates me. I'd like to create a rehab center for patients with heart problems."

"That would be a good place to stockpile your money." Jack was approving as he walked Malcolm to the door. "When you really get serious about a project like that, let me know. I can rustle up some silent partners for you—and I can guarantee them real tax shelters, maybe even real profits, heaven forbid."

As Malcolm waited for the elevator, the thought of a cardiac rehab center remained in his mind. He'd thought of it often enough, but it was, he figured, pure fantasy. He had a wife, kids to put through school and college, an elderly mother and his two infirm aunts. The rehab center was a dream to be explored when he retired from active practice . . . But he wondered if he'd make it to retirement. There were a dozen physicians in the medical building off High Street and out of those twelve, eight had had bypass surgery within the past five years. It never occurred to patients, he thought, that the practice of medicine is hazardous to a doctor's health.

He left Jack's office building at Madison and Forty-ninth Street feeling depressed. He wasn't looking forward to the Macray party in spite of his respect for John Paul and Maureen. It was important to Silvie, though. To be accepted by the Macrays was the mark of upward mobility, and Silvie had certainly worked hard at gaining acceptance. It had taken her years and many rebuffs, but Silvie, he thought, had a single-minded determination.

He'd better tell her about the failure of his cattle investment tonight, when she was in a good mood.

Other physicians among his friends were able to keep their business and personal lives separate—unless their wives happened to be their office nurses. But Silvie, he thought with a mixture of admiration and annoyance, had the instincts of a bloodhound, or a clairvoyant, maybe. She could divine what was in a letter without steaming open the flap of the envelope; she could surmise what went on in a telephone call without really listening in.

Privately, he credited her insights to the experiences she'd had before they met. And to the other training, which she had good reason to keep hidden. Now she seemed to have a pipeline to all the undercurrents in the medical community. She was bosom buddies with Eve Rothschild, the wife of the internist Barnet Rothschild, and they were forever on the telephone . . .

Malcolm swung his way through the crowds on Madison Avenue with the agility of a tennis player. He blended with the executives headed toward Grand Central Station and the 5:10 express to Stamford and New Canaan. He caught a glimpse of his image in a store window and decided that for autumn he should get a conservative gray flannel suit; it would be more in keeping with the image he wanted to project in his lectures at New York Medical College, where he was an associate professor of cardiology.

At the garage he stood in line, offered his ticket, waiting impatiently for the arrival of his blue Stingray. Malcolm tipped the driver, slid into the leather bucket seat, adjusted the mirror and caught a glimpse of his olive skin, with the shadow of tomorrow's beard on his chin, his eyes hidden behind the aviator sunglasses.

He wondered if he ought to listen to Jack, let him and Silvie take care of his income, expenses, investments, and allot him two hundred dollars a week for spending money. Which was what Eve Rothschild did for her husband, but then Barnet Rothschild was a compulsive gambler, so it made sense. Malcolm didn't feel comfortable with Silvie knowing how much money he had been depositing in his mother's bank accounts. It was his mother's idea for him to squirrel away some of his income without Silvie's knowledge; she still believed their marriage would break up and Silvie would get everything in a settlement.

But Malcolm knew differently. He'd never leave Silvie; he would accept her temper and her temperament, even her infidelities, because she gave him something that he found missing in other women. And it sure as hell was nothing he could discuss with his mother.

Or even with a psychiatrist . . .

Idling the motor as he waited for a traffic signal, Malcolm thought, three hundred thousand . . . he, Malcolm Stone, had earned three hundred thousand dollars last year. When he had proposed to Silvie, captivated as he was, he'd vowed he would take care of her. Soon, he had forecasted then, he should be making ten thousand a year—a promise that seemed reckless eighteen years ago.

Three hundred thousand a year. He still could not believe it. It was like winning the Irish sweepstakes, except that it went on year after year, as long as he remained in practice.

The monthly statements went out; the return envelopes flooded his office during the early part of the month, checks fluttering in like leaves falling from a tree. His bookkeeper made several weekly trips to deposit the money at his bank. God, he could buy anything he wanted. He could travel first class, stay at the best places. He could toss greenbacks out of the window and watch crowds scramble for them.

Then why the devil was he so jittery?

Bruckner Boulevard always depressed him with its monotony. He felt better as he swung into the expressway going toward Connecticut. The Stingray made contact with the new lanes; motor and tires were singing in his ears. If there were no delays in traffic, he would make it home by seven. He was headed for the thruway, which passed the point where the Macray house sat on a grassy plateau overlooking Long Island Sound.

The car responded to his touch like an eager woman. He wove between the heavier cars, unconsciously making a game of it, feeling a sudden recklessness that surprised him because he was, most of the time, so cautious, so . . . uptight.

Fragments of the landscape made jagged impressions on him. This was the part of Fairfield County that real estate brokers seldom mentioned. Car dealerships, fast food drive-ins, gas stations, here and there a shopping center. He was approaching a Howard Johnson's, used mostly by traveling salesmen. And beyond it was the half-moon of red-brick, soot-stained buildings, a tenement known as the Million Dollar Slum, home for the ethnic gangs whose activities in Belfort's south end added to the reports of muggings, robberies, rape and break-ins that the chief of police kept on his desk—along with the high blood pressure medication Malcolm had prescribed for him.

Abruptly, the Stingray reached the crest of the macadam lanes, and ahead lay the new part of Belfort. In the cup of the valley and pouring out to the Sound, the new city was a modern miracle, its shafts of steel, mortar and glass towering in the late afternoon sun.

Here was the final piece of Belfort's urban renewal, at last a reality after fifteen years of modifications and enlargements, all firmed up at a laggard's pace by those advocates in Washington who were repaying their local constituents for their loyalty.

There were still promises to keep; those of the great mercantile corporations who had agreed to open major shops in the multi-million dollar parkade; who were waiting for the new exits off the turnpike to be enlarged and plans for the five-story public parking garage to be unfurled.

Much of the land by the old railroad station looked as though a cyclone had destroyed it and decapitated century-old trees. Soon this section would be filled with shops, arcades, entertainment centers.

Progress. Malcolm was all for it. It was good for business.

CHAPTER X

At four P.M., while Malcolm was in New York City conferring with Jack Palfrey, Silvie Stone stepped out of her rose-colored Aurora marble bathtub and slipped into a white velour robe. At the door of the custom-designed Sherle Wagner bathroom, Silvie paused to admire the luxury of it: the imperial swan basin, tub/shower and towel rings, all in 24-karat gold plate; the recessed malachite soap dish and matching paper-holder; the antique white-and-gold *chaise percée* commode; and the pièce de résistance, a hand-carved rose Aurora marble bidet, with gold knobs and malachite handles, mounted on a platform of solid malachite.

"What the hell do we need with a bidet?" had been Malcolm's response, "let alone one that costs over fifteen thousand dollars?" He couldn't understand how Silvie, with her usually shrewd eye for a bargain, could have splurged on decorating a bathroom.

What Malcolm didn't understand, thought Silvie as she glided into the chartreuse and white master bedroom and sat down at her dressing table, was that it wasn't a bathroom but a kind of shrine, the temple where she anointed her sleek, well-kept body for what had once been a nightly ritual, the sexual performances that she now gave to Malcolm on a limited basis.

She sat down at the dressing table and turned on the hair dryer. As the heat attacked her hair, she ran the fingers of her free hand along her scalp, so the short coppery curls bounced over her well-shaped head. Moisture from the shower gave her pale skin a porcelain luster. She intended to use false eyelashes tonight, even though none of the other doctors' wives wore them. They gave her light green eyes depth and irresistible allure.

The vodka martini on the dressing table was half full and she finished it. Too jittery to stretch out on the chaise, she walked barefoot on the creamy shag rug and looked out at the curving swimming pool, which reflected the clear blue of the sky. It was still too cool to use an unheated pool, but by Memorial Day she would arrange the summer furniture and open the small poolhouse for the season. To her thinking, their one-story sprawling white house wasn't that attractive, but it was the only one within their price range when they'd first moved to Belfort eight years ago. They could now well afford a house triple the value of this one, but she and Malcolm couldn't agree on the choice of a property. She wanted a place in Greenwich, while he felt they should remain in Belfort, since most of his practice was there. She'd gladly settle for a house on the Point, like Dr. Macray's, for instance, but Malcolm balked at that, too. He could be so damn stubborn at times. Well, at least she had gotten her bathroom.

Before she could rinse the glass at the bathroom basin, the telephone rang.

"How did it go?" Half relief, half suspense.

"It didn't. I lectured him. A medicine man and his money are soon parted. But he wasn't buying it."

"What's he into now . . . that he's keeping from me?"

"Shares in the ski resort at Aspen."

"I know about that. It's just apt to make a profit."

"There isn't one sound investment in his portfolio." Jack Palfrey was impatient. "I swear to God, these doctors shouldn't be allowed out on their own. They're conned into bad investments—and instead of cutting their losses, they hang on."

Silvie inspected herself in the standing mirror. "Did he listen?"

"Are you kidding? He tuned out. The only news that upset him was the notice that his malpractice insurance is going up again. It's almost out of sight now. In that case . . ."

"Yes, Jack?"

"The smart doctor will turn over all his assets in his wife's name."

"You'll keep after him, Jack?"

"I'll do my best."

"I'll be driving into the city next week."

"Good. I'll take you to lunch."

She hung up, more disturbed than she had let on.

At five P.M. the school bus from Regent School for Boys and Locust Ryse School for Girls stopped at the front of the Stone driveway and Norman and Barbara stepped off.

Silvie, pausing to watch them from the kitchen window, mused that nobody in the world would ever take these two for brother and sister.

Norman took after Silvie: the long, sleek frame, burnished red hair with a life of its own, chiseled head and small, regular features, skin that freckled but never tanned. People thought he looked Scottish, as she did. But her genes were German and Irish. How well he looks in his gray flannel slacks, striped tie and navy blue blazer, she thought proudly. She was partial to her son. What a pity his eyes were so nearsighted; he'd worn glasses since he was five years old and they were always slipping down his nose.

Then there was Barbara . . . Barbara took after Malcolm and seemed to have inherited his worst features—the dark, prominent, restless eyes, the nose too large for her face, which was a plump testament to the sweets she craved and ate in spite of Silvie's disapproval. At least her teeth were in shape now, with a fine arch, white and even. She only had to wear a retainer at night, but last night she had said she'd lost it again. All that money paid out to the orthodontist—even though he gave Malcolm a break on it—was still a big sum. And for what?

It wasn't the teeth men cared about, Silvie reflected. A woman's passport was her figure—and Barbara's was hopeless. Her summer uniform, a brown-and-white striped cotton seersucker shirtwaist, was bunched up around her middle, and her brown senior blazer was too snug. Silvie found the sight of her depressing.

"If God meant us to be mothers of adolescent daughters," she had said to some of the auxiliary board members over lunch in the hospital coffee shop, "why didn't he equip us to deal with them?"

Other mothers agreed with her, though they kept their criticism on the light side. But she knew they all had problems.

It was a pity the women couldn't enjoy their station and affluence. In her secret mind Silvie considered the medical community a clique —a group of deified witch doctors with wives who bathed in their reflections. She hadn't liked Belfort at first—and still didn't. The community reminded her too much of her adolescence, when she was always on the outside, trying to get in with the right crowd and facing rebuffs.

But she had a tough hide and made herself immune to taunts and snubs. Her mind worked like a calculator, storing away the hurts of indifference and snobbery. She would be ready at the right time to spit out the total and show the world that she was smarter, richer, more desirable than anyone.

It had taken a while before the local primary physicians started sending patients to Malcolm for consults, but now he was regarded as *the* cardiologist in Belfort. At Malcolm's request, Silvie recompensed his colleagues for their referrals: a case of J&B at Christmas, imported wines; gifts from Tiffany.

The women, however, were ignoring her, forming a circle to keep her out. When she raged, Malcolm suggested that they were jealous of her. Few of them were as sexy, especially as they matured; they were so careless, playing tennis and golf and swimming when the sun was at its peak. They stayed thin but got wrinkled. No wonder the plastic surgeons had a waiting list as long as the country club's.

She suspected Malcolm was at the root of the women's cool behavior. She'd have loved to join the Yacht Club, even though it was expensive, but Jews weren't encouraged to become members. They had been invited more than once to join the quite beautiful Jewish country club near the borderline of Pound Ridge, but how could the children belong there when they went to Episcopalian services and

Sunday School? Most people considered them Jewish, because Malcolm attended Rosh Hashanah and Yom Kippur services at the Reform Temple. No doubt Malcolm was the reason they'd had a tough time getting Barbie accepted at Locust Ryse, a preparatory school Silvie suspected of having a minority quota. It was only after Malcolm had spoken to Dr. Macray and Dr. Macray had spoken to his wife, that Barbara was finally accepted. Of course, the generous check Malcolm sent to the building fund for the new middle school had greatly expedited things. So had Silvie's generosity to the Parent Teacher Association, her willingness to work on committees, her participation in everything that would solidify the family standing in Belfort.

She had her own standards and goals, but she also knew what the community expected of her. She hid her boredom, stifled her impatience, planned carefully and was unstinting in her efforts to impress the right people.

At last she was getting recognition from Maureen Macray. Silvie was now treasurer of the auxiliary, which meant that next year she would automatically become vice president. There was a clique at the head of the auxiliary; the richest of the Belfort newcomers, Pamela Shaw, was heading the committee for the auxiliary ball and Silvie had knocked herself out to ingratiate herself, selling space in the souvenir booklet as well as tickets for the event. She was hoping that Pam would invite her to lunch aboard their yacht, which had just come up from Florida and was anchored at the marina.

The trouble with Malcolm, she decided, was not just that his money was too new. They weren't *spending* their new riches properly. So she was doing as the women from old families did, learning to play golf though she was obliged to use the public golf links, which annoyed the hell out of her. And before the summer was over, she was determined to rent a boat and find out how to sail. They'd do it as a family, and when Pam Shaw, her husband and kids sailed to Bermuda—they had a captain and a crew, naturally—Silvie could use the nautical terms she'd learned.

Last winter they'd gone to Vermont during the Christmas vacation, which lasted three weeks. Equipped with brand new ski outfits, skis, après-ski outfits, they drove off gloriously, full of excitement. The kids did well; they graduated from the beginners' slopes in the first week. But Malcolm hurt his back and was on crutches for a month and she got some bruises herself. Why was it, she wondered, that Malcolm's generation of orthodox Jewish boys was not athletic—except for tennis? And they didn't like dogs. "We had cats," Malcolm explained. Whenever she suggested a German shepherd or a Doberman pinscher for security reasons—there were so many break-ins in this part of North Belfort—Malcolm refused to consider it. If they owned an animal with a good pedigree, it might open the doors of Ox Ridge; even, she thought grandly, the Westminster show. Horses, dogs, art, charity affairs, and auctions, the right schools, volunteer work at the hospital—these were the rungs to acceptance. A damned nuisance, working your ass off to impress those bitches, but in time, you were accepted. And though she didn't really like the women of Belfort—didn't like women generally—Silvie wanted them to accept her.

Norman and Barbara came into the hall, dropped their briefcases and bookbags on the Shaker pine bench and clattered into the kitchen, where Silvie had shut her mind to the medical wives and was setting the table. They could wash up and have an early dinner—no television until homework was completed. They knew without prompting that they were to change into T-shirts and jeans. By the time she had sliced the meat loaf, arranged the salad, poured their milk and set out two cookies apiece, they had returned to the kitchen.

"Where are you going, mom?" Norman asked.

His gentle face, his solemn unblinking eyes with thick lashes, his finely etched features tugged at Silvie's heart. She loved him to the point of anguish, she cherished him, had grandiose dreams for him. Norman would go places, she had decided when he was still an infant. The right school, the right church, the right friends—who would be his friends for the rest of his life—Harvard or Yale . . .

"A party at the Macrays," she said. "We'll probably be home late."

Barbara didn't respond; she was concentrating on her food, washing it down with gulps of milk.

No use nagging at her about manners, Silvie thought. A scene with her daughter was the last thing she needed tonight. She was determined to maintain her composure; she wanted the evening to be successful, both for herself and Malcolm. Smiles on a spring night, she reminded herself.

By the time Malcolm drove into the garage, the kids were finished with supper and had gone to their rooms. Silvie was dressed, in a black crepe pants suit and a sequined tank top that she'd bought at Loehmann's. Her make-up was striking, pale bisque foundation blending with her auburn hair, velvety false lashes that gave her eyes mystery and allure, and a Clara Bow pout, deftly drawn with a rose-purple Mary Quant lipstick over her thin, disciplined lips.

Malcolm walked through the kitchen, into the living room and directly into their bedroom. He was stripping off his jacket, loosening his tie as he came in.

"Sorry to be late," he said. "Give me ten minutes to wash and change my shirt."

She nodded, taking another look at herself in the full-length mirror. She liked the way the sheer material of the pants clung to her skin, showing off her tight ass and slim hips. Malcolm went to the built-in chest that held his shirts and picked out a fresh white one. He was drying his face when he returned to the bedroom.

"Is that new?" he asked.

"You like it?" she asked, preening.

"It's stunning. But, uh, isn't it a bit much tonight? This is just an informal party for the residents."

"All the wives will be there." Silvie fussed with a curl behind her ear. "I mean to give them an eyeful."

"That you will do," he said, planting a kiss on her forehead. He considered her the best-looking woman in the group.

CHAPTER XI

Not all of the new medical wives had met Maureen Macray, but they were all aware of her. Even unseen, she was a V.I.P.

She was president of the auxiliary and was on a first-name basis with all the local political bigwigs. A devout Catholic, she was also the perfect wife to the perfect doctor.

Her party tonight was in honor of the twelve residents who were graduating from the family practice residency program. They were coming with their wives or girlfriends and a number of the older physicians and their wives would be there too.

Early in the afternoon Eve Rothschild had telephoned to convey some news. "Maureen, did you hear—Jim and Judy Denker have split."

Maureen, her mind on the evening ahead, expressed surprise. Jim Denker was a psychiatrist who gave time to the community mental health clinics and his wife, Judy, was one of his former patients. Maureen wasn't exactly surprised by the news; the marriage had been foundering almost from its inception. Judy had proclaimed to anyone who would listen that they'd had much better sex before they were married.

"I don't know why some of these doctors get married," Eve had said. She was a former president of the auxiliary and an insatiable gossip, and according to her evaluation of herself, gifted with uncommon artistic talent. She was the self-appointed photographer of the auxiliary and she could turn out dreadful snapshots with a Polaroid camera. Her husband, Barnet, was an internist, one of the few doctors, Maureen remembered, who refused to take Medicaid and Medicare patients. The Rothschilds were active in the medical community but their real friends were in financial and social circles.

"There are plenty of easy lays among the nurses," Eve continued. "I mean, really, most of them are fooling around, anyway—why bother getting married in the first place?"

After she hung up, Maureen slipped into a silk caftan and went downstairs to check on the maids, who were setting the tables on the terrace. She mulled over Eve's remarks—maybe, for once, she was right about something.

So many of their friends, mostly doctors younger than John Paul, set themselves up as targets for trouble. Bored with their wives, they were not only willing but eager to stray. And female patients, in all age ranges, seemed to find their doctors irresistible.

Sometimes Maureen wondered if any doctor remained faithful to his wife. Even John Paul—but that was absurd . . .

She had never had any doubts, even when the boys were growing up, when she had little time to devote to her husband—as little as he had to devote to her. Yet the ties between them had been strong and durable despite the stress and strain. They had not had caviar, champagne and moonlit nights, but good home-baked bread and home-made apple butter. They were friends and companions, as well as lovers.

Yet it was the doctoring that had caused the gap—if it was a gap—between them. Success came less easily to John Paul than to the later group of surgeons, but he was fiercely dedicated to his field. The demands of his patients, his classes at the medical school, his devotion to the clinics where the poor gathered to wait until the clinic doctors could see them—these were her rivals for his time and attention. He was increasingly depressed by the everlasting struggle to care for the people from the slums, increasingly exhausted in body and spirit. During their courtship, when she'd been a student nurse at Grace-New Haven and he an intern, they'd talked shop constantly. And afterwards, in the early years of their marriage, when she'd been his office nurse. Then, suddenly, he'd ceased talking about the hospital, the sick and the dying. It was as if he wanted to shut them out of his mind when he came home at night. Until then Maureen had known both parts of him, all parts of him; she thought they had few reservations from each other, few anxieties left unshared. But as his workload increased, John Paul seemed to detach himself from the family they had built together and began to revolve around it like a satellite, influencing it, but not participating in it.

Perhaps the break had started earlier than she'd realized; while their four sons were growing up, John Paul had had less and less time for them. Maureen made the boys aware quite early that when their father was absent he was not playing golf or cards. He was traveling to medical meetings or treating his patients either in his office or at the hospital. Many people counted on his skill and humanity. Sick people came from all over the country, and sometimes even from Europe, hoping he could cure them. A lot of people depended on their father and he knew they would understand and help him by not being upset because he wasn't around, like fathers with nine-to-five jobs.

They listened to her and understood with their minds, if not with their hearts. They were handsome boys, with John Paul's good looks and generous heart and she'd done everything she could to compensate for their father's absenteeism. Some of the younger doctors who had time for their sons would include the Macray boys in trips, camp outings. And Maureen drove them to Little League practice and Boy Scout meetings. One year she was voted by the boys and their friends the best den mother ever.

One morning, she recalled, when she was driving Pauley past the hospital on the way to nursery school, he'd asked, "Mommy, is that daddy's other home?"

It made an amusing story to share with other wives who had similar problems. She used it to vent her own frustrations and warn the youngest medical wives that though the perks of being a doctor's wife might include expensive cars, real jewels, designer clothes, travel, membership in the best country clubs, there were also "negative perks"—loneliness, the grass widow syndrome, the constant fear that the good husband was enjoying his female patients. Of course she'd had no such fears about John Paul then. But she was beginning to understand that in her preoccupation with being both mother and father to four growing, demanding sons—not to mention her devotion to the auxiliary and her community work—she had ignored the imperceptible separation between herself and her husband that now, with the children grown and gone, seemed to stretch between them at times like an abyss. And yet they were considered by all of Belfort to have a perfect marriage. Well, maybe her standards of intimacy were too high; no one could be everything to one person. But if, after all they'd been through, John Paul were seeing another woman . . .

She passed through the large airy rooms of her house, aware of the furniture she had chosen with such loving care, from the first chair she and John Paul had so frugally saved for to the beautiful old Hepplewhite chairs in the diningroom that they had brought home, many years later, from a London antique shop. All the furniture and paintings had been chosen together, usually when John Paul got a brief vacation or attended a convention where Maureen could accompany him. Those snatched moments had an almost illicit flavor—away from his office, his patients, his students, they had enjoyed a kind of abandon, a return to youth and to each other. Those second honeymoons had been the fuel that kept her supercharged during the hectic days with her sons, their friends, her community activities, her work as a volunteer at the hospital, her membership in the auxiliary.

In the early married years, there were few divorces among the doctors and wives. They were still building toward the future. The trouble came when the couples reached thirty-five or forty. Any number of local physicians had an understanding with their wives. Each man went his own way, without jeopardizing his standing in the community by separating from his wife (which still shocked many Catholic patients, particularly if the doctor involved were Catholic). It evidently agreed with the wives, who retained their social standing and income.

Not all of the wives had even that to hold on to. It was especially tough on older women, women who had been married thirty years and were suddenly divorced, the structure of their lives gone. Younger wives, newly divorced, might receive money for a few years so they could learn new skills and become self-supporting. But it wasn't so easy for the older ones to start over—schools rejected their applications, employers refused to hire them.

When wives of John Paul's colleagues called on Maureen for emotional support and sometimes more, she used all her resources to help them. Fortunately Maureen was friendly with many of Belfort's civic leaders. She found places for the dispossessed wives in a number of social agencies, which were being expanded during the years of Lyndon Johnson's Great Society.

Maureen sat in on the formation of the Belfort Commission on Aging, organized a child guidance clinic and was also a strong supporter of the Citizens' Committee for Housing.

With each year, more projects developed. She was particularly interested in the Friends of Youth, a group of adult volunteers who worked toward activity-based relationships with youngsters and encouraged the kids' interests and talents by helping them achieve positive goals.

Into the midst of these burgeoning projects, Maureen brought the wives and the organizations together. She became one of Belfort's richest human resources, since she had a talent for bringing the right volunteers to the right projects.

The root of Maureen's dedication, beyond her generous, warm nature, was a kind of gratitude because she had it so good. She was one of those rare women who had married the man she loved, borne his children, helped him in his early practice when he couldn't afford a nurse-secretary. Later, when his reputation grew, she was not only understanding, proud, warmly supportive of his new activities, but she also created a lifestyle that kept his career free of nuisances and extraneous demands. Despite her moments of insecurity and doubt, it seemed to her they were as close as a husband and wife could be. If thirty-three years of being together had taken away the mystery and some of the romance of their marriage, it had also strengthened the bond of shared experiences, the beautiful house, the four fine sons, her husband's career and her unstinting work in the community, for which five years before she had been honored Belfort's Woman of the Year.

Maureen sighed. There was more work to be done before the party could begin. Then she heard John Paul coming up the stairs, his step tentative, and she hurried out to the landing to greet him.

John Paul, she thought, my husband. Mother of God, please let my fears prove unfounded . . .

CHAPTER XII

Dr. Harlow Hilton, the new president and administrator of Belfort Hospital, had promised Maureen that he would come to her party.

He made it a point to accept every invitation he received from the medical community. There were some fine men on the staff, men of stature in their medical specialties. Besides, he was feeling lonely. Harlow's family was staying in California until the children finished the school year. He missed Esther, his supportive wife, too . . .

His office was in the main section of the old building. The corridor was lined with large studio portraits of physicians now deceased. He knew the names of some of them, the reputations they had carved from the time the hospital opened, when the late Dr. Harry Thalberg had made his reputation as the last of the great general practitioners in Belfort.

I wish I'd known him, Harlow Hilton thought. He knew this town well. He could have given me practical insight into the medical politics, the rivalries between the doctors, the power plays. Why some of them—such as Wilbur Watling—had been allowed to remain here, he didn't know, but he would find out.

Harlow Hilton, with a master's degree in Hospital Administration and a Ph.D. in Public Health, was on deck. On the west coast he had been responsible for the rehabilitation of a half-dozen small-town hospitals that were on the verge of extinction even before skyrocketing inflation had come along. He had used his considerable tact and skill to put each of these institutions in the black.

As his reputation grew, the state hospital organization asked him to join them as a consultant. But soon afterward one of the largest health groups in California invited him to take on the job of administrator. He was happy in his work and he adapted well to the unique lifestyle of southern California. His wife, however, simply could not adjust. She was a Mount Holyoke graduate from Massachusetts; she loved the change of seasons; was comfortable with the New England character. She didn't say much about it, but he knew her feelings, and when the position in Belfort was offered to him, he accepted it.

But before Esther and the kids arrived, Harlow Hilton had plenty of problems to solve.

This afternoon, with half a dozen folders spread across his desk, he chose what he hoped was the least aggravating group. He took off his dark pinstriped jacket, hung it in the closet, loosened his tie, rolled up his sleeves. He poured a glass of ice water from the carafe on his desk and went to work leafing through a pack of recently returned patient questionnaires, the patients' unsigned comments on the hospital's services.

Dear Patient: Our most treasured asset is the good will of our patients. We can earn your good will only by giving you a complete and gracious service. You can help us do this by kindly taking a few minutes to complete this confidential questionnaire.

His dark glossy eyebrows drew closer to the bridge of his classic nose as he read the responses:

Room could have been cleaner . . . sanitary conditions in bathrooms poor . . . Very disappointing nursing care . . . My father's buzzer was out of order and was discovered only the day before he was discharged. He was not helped to wash despite the fact that he had a broken arm. Icepacks placed on his arm melted and wet his pajamas, had I not brought this to the attention of the nurse, he would have stayed like that all night . . . Nurses left many tasks for patients to do for themselves, which they were unable to do because of lack of strength or because I.V.s in the arm prevented using that hand . . . Very bad care and service . . . Please tell Dietary to make better coffee, I don't think they'd drink it themselves . . .

Harlow Hilton leaned back in his black leather revolving chair, closed his eyes briefly. There were hundreds of complaints. Granted sickness brought out the anger and frustration in patients, who sometimes overreacted, but there was still no excuse for this many negative comments. Yes, there were some questionnaires with "thanks for the good care" written on them, but his job was to see to the others.

It's time to quit protecting not only the doctors but the nurses, the entire structure of the staff, he thought. The problem of personalities was impossible to solve completely. Few of the younger office workers stayed more than six months or a year before moving on to other jobs. Sometimes he thought it had been that way ever since the sixties . . . the minute young ones accumulated a little money, the minute the job and their co-workers irritated or bored them, the minute they didn't get the vacation schedule they wanted, they split.

Many of the more mature nurses were leaving too. Some had come back to nursing in order to help put their children through college, but once the children were on their own the women looked to their own futures. They went to the local branches of the University of Connecticut to expand their skills and found jobs in real estate, education and the corporations that were changing Belfort's skyline.

Hilton pushed back his chair, walked over to the small side table that held a pot of coffee and mugs. He poured a cup and stood at the end window, looking out on the parking lots. There were too many cars and not enough spaces. The question of additional parking was uppermost in his mind. And office space for physicians. And housing for staff and residents . . .

Behind the old buildings and fronting a private dead end street, the hospital owned two acres of inestimable value. The board of directors had considered selling the property to meet interest payments on the loan that built the new wing. But Harlow was more interested in generating revenue, and had suggested going in another direction.

"We need a building," he had explained to the Executive Committee at the most recent monthly meeting. "The first floors for parking;

the next couple for office space for the physicians, and above that efficiency apartments for some of the hospital staff who have trouble finding affordable housing in the area, and for our medical students and residents who rotate through here."

The executive committee had liked the idea and wanted it presented to the full board at their next quarterly meeting. The board was composed of sound, practical businessmen. Harlow was currently discussing the project with Valentine Secca, whose construction company was involved in much of Belfort's redevelopment.

Hilton rubbed his cheek thoughtfully. He was a tall man, whose presence suggested courtesy and conviction. Everyone was impressed with him so far, and he wondered when the honeymoon would be over, when they'd start carping and criticizing. Did they expect miracles? The hospital was sagging badly; it would take skill, money and prayer to save it.

Hilton replenished his coffee and went back to his desk. He missed his family. What were they doing now, he wondered. At the pool, perhaps, with other friends from the neighborhood in Westwood. They were such healthy specimens, his son and daughter. They loved the life in California, the freedom from fierce winds and bitter snows, the relaxed pattern of their days: school was not too demanding; and after school and weekends they had the delicious long hours at the beach.

But Esther worried about their intellectual growth. They were bright kids, Roddy and Jean, and Esther thought they hadn't reached their potential—and never would as long as beach parties took precedence over books.

His phone rang. He hoped it was her calling; they spoke to each other nearly every day. If she had problems, he was not aware of them. She was, he thought, the ideal mate. She never bothered him with family problems; the children had always been good humored and never complained when he was home. She had a list of first-rate, accommodating workmen—electricians, plumbers, gardeners, pool mechanics. The household always ran smoothly.

And she was a warm, responsive woman, creative and demonstrative in bed. He missed her terribly and meant to tell her so.

But he heard Dr. Watling's unctuous voice.

"Harlow, have you got a few minutes?"

"Certainly. Come on by."

Watling must have been calling from a house telephone in a nearby corridor; he sailed in, the white hospital coat open to show his expensive shirt and tie. He was a big man, whose abrasive personality cowed the medical students, interns and residents. He sat down without being invited, pushed his glasses up his nose and peered at Harlow while moistening his narrow lips with the tip of his tongue.

"Pictures of the incoming group." He spread their folders and the glossy prints fanlike on the desk. Harlow looked them over.

"They're a smart group," said Dr. Watling. "I expect good things of them."

"How many from American medical schools?"

Dr. Watling bristled. It was a sore point with him. "I hope you're not prejudiced . . ."

"Not at all, but Watling, you know as well as I do about some of these foreign diploma mills." He wanted to cut it short. "I presume they all speak good English?"

"Adequate."

"That's encouraging. I remember one foreign intern who was supposed to speak English. His vocabulary consisted of three words: yes, no, thank you. And he was supposed to take histories on the patients."

Dr. Watling gave him a perfunctory smile. Behind his glasses, his eyes were shrewd and appraising. Harlow suspected that the man was trying to decide how far to go, to show his superiority to the administrator, to jab him a bit but without going too far.

Harlow pulled out a newspaper clipping from under the blotter on his desk. "Wilbur, it seems you made some waves at the Miami convention last week."

Dr. Watling chuckled, pleased. "I believe that some of the Ten Commandments are obsolete in our modern world. Fidelity to a single love object over the years can be debilitating."

"You forget that there is a powerful right-to-life movement in this town, which fights us constantly about doing abortions in the hospital. And we have practicing Catholics on our own staff. Our chief, Dr. Macray, for one."

"You mean John Paul hasn't lusted?"

"Come on, even President Carter admits that. But your personal advocacy of abortion and open marriage in that interview was perhaps a bit unfortunate. Well, we'll forget it. There's another problem, which concerns me more."

"What's that?"

"Drugs are disappearing from the drug room, the medication stations, and the medication carts. We haven't pinned it down to anyone, but it's beginning to be a problem. I wondered if you had any ideas."

"None of my boys is responsible."

It was the first time Harlow had heard Dr. Watling defend his residents and students. Usually he was critical and caustic, neglecting to commend their progress. He seemed to take an admiring interest in himself in relation to the residents. He expected them to accept and admire his decisions, to be agreeable to his concepts. And whenever they failed to give in to his wishes, he showed the ugly side of his complex personality, all too familiar to his wife, his girlfriends and his secretary.

"Wilbur, I'm not suggesting that they are. In fact, I wanted to tell you that with the new group coming in perhaps you can be more flexible. At least until they become acclimated. It would be unfortunate if any suffered nervous breakdowns—like those two fellows did last year—"

"You mean the two that sent you letters about me? They were psychotics—we're well rid of them."

Harlow stifled his anger. He had heard of Watling's paranoia, his tantrums and excuses. He wondered if Watling was having any medical problems himself. Several of the residents had gone to John Paul and suggested that Dr. Watling was suffering from TIA—transient ischemic attacks. He *was* increasingly forgetful.

Harlow stood up and walked Watling to the door, his hand on the doctor's shoulder.

"I guess I'll see you later at the Macrays'," he said.

Watling stopped, turned to him, his face grim, all the deep lines around his mouth prominent. Behind his glasses, the deep eyes were shrewd and suspicious.

"That's another thing—a party for my boys, and the Macrays didn't invite me."

"Check with your secretary, I'm sure you received an invitation. Maybe it went to your house. I remember your wife saying she'd see me there."

Harlow returned to his desk. He tried to put Watling out of his mind, but the man's belligerent manner annoyed him. He was so rich in book knowledge and so poor in human relationships. His academic credits were impressive; he had written several texts that were required reading in the medical schools. But on the human level, he was an utter failure. Even his wife, Clemmie, admitted it in confidence to Harlow. Watling did not like women doctors; he made their lives miserable. He was rude and dictatorial to the nurses. And Harlow had hardly been surprised when, the other morning, he'd stepped into Watling's office to find his secretary updating his scrapbooks.

Yes, there was something out of whack in the character of a man in his fifties, with his academic record, who left a large teaching hospital to take a post in a small three-hundred-bed community hospital. For all his knowledge, he was a poor teacher. Harlow had heard it was his habit to pounce on an error a resident made and announce, in his raspy voice, that the young man was a disgrace to his teachers, that there was no hope for him.

Harlow wondered if it would do any good to speak to one of the psychiatrists about Watling. Perhaps analysis would help him. He was obviously fighting old nightmares and, unless he could get control of himself, might do something dangerous.

But where do you get another knowledgeable man for the family practice residency program? There were none anywhere.

Harlow paced back and forth in his spacious office, mulling over the other problems. He filled his pipe with specially mixed tobacco, lit it and took a deep pull.

Okay, Hilton, he said to himself, as president and administrator of the hospital, you are responsible for everything that comes in here. Two thousand items, from plastic garbage bags to surgical instruments, must be ordered, received, stored and rotated. There was a steady stream of trucks to the loading dock.

And this morning's newspaper spoke of increases in the price of oil. It wasn't just fuel, electricity and oil for the furnaces and the hospital's lights and x-ray equipment and sterilizers and food lockers and computers. It was all the other products of the petrochemical industry—the disposable tubing used for oxygen therapy and respiratory therapy treatments, the plastic bedpans and basins, the I.V. solutions encased in plastic rather than in glass bottles.

And the paper goods—bed liners to protect the sheets, paper for the copying machines, drinking cups.

And the ballpoint pens and the lightbulbs . . .

What are you doing about the budgets for the state's cost commission, Hilton? They have to be ready for submission on July first. He'd heard that the budget submission for one Connecticut hospital was a stack of paper six feet high; they had taken a picture of it.

Every department was clamoring for new pieces of equipment or for replacements for old ones. The laboratory, cardiology, pulmonary, surgery . . . And he had to appease them all.

Have you thought through the proposal for one-day surgery?

What are you going to do about the proposal for a hospital-based home care program?

The hospital had been cited by one of the many regulatory agencies for keeping patients longer than was allowed. But elderly patients didn't heal as quickly, were apt to develop complications. Sheila Ryan was frantic. Social Service and Discharge Planning was overworked, understaffed, helpless in trying to find enough resources for these old people.

"I'm a basket case at the end of the day," Sheila told everybody within hearing distance. Harlow Hilton, for one, understood. Trying to deal with a hundred fifty-six regulatory agencies was enough to drive anyone up the wall. Talk about Catch Twenty-two . . .

The Joint Commission on Accreditation of Hospitals recommended one thing.

The federal government said another.

The state contradicted the feds.

And then there was the daily everlasting albatross: the cash-flow problem.

Ah yes, and a few niggling matters. What about the lawsuit instigated by that smart young whip, Jedd Cramer?

True, it was hardly monumental, a mishap in surgery, a sponge left in a patient's body due to the carelessness of a nurse. The insurance company had offered the patient a generous settlement, but by that time Jedd Cramer had taken over the case and blown it way out of proportion.

And juries were unusually generous in malpractice suits these days.

That was another thing—the hospital's malpractice insurance carrier had sent them a detailed letter that their premium was going up again this year. *That* would have to be plugged into the budget being prepared, along with the skyrocketing costs of everything else. He'd heard one story about a hospital whose malpractice premium was raised and the cost commission hadn't allowed enough in the hospital's budget to cover it, requiring detailed documentation for additional submission before the expenditure was finally approved—

Oh, the hell with it. Dr. Hilton looked at his watch; it was nearly six. He had time to go home and shower and change and then go to the residents' party.

God, he needed something pleasant to ease his mood.

Where was Esther when he needed her?

CHAPTER XIII

Seven o'clock.

Guests would be arriving within the next half hour. The big Mediterranean house jutting out on the Point was brilliant in the golden wash of sunset. The lawn dividing the patio from the rocky shore held candles protected by tall glasses to discourage insects. Candles made flickering golden patterns on the deck, and the long table in the glassed-in veranda was also illuminated by groups of candles in gleaming glass hurricane lamps. Two middle-aged women in black uniforms with frilly white aprons, part of the catering staff, were busy around the table. A bartender in a white jacket was setting out glasses, checking his ice buckets and making sure there was enough Perrier water for the physicians who might be on call. At the wall near the double doors the iron French baker's stand was filled with vivid Italian dessert plates in assorted flower patterns, handsome coffee mugs, and flaring amethyst handblown glasses for iced drinks. Two electric coffeemakers were already perking with fresh ground coffee and hot water for Earl Grey tea. The three-section silver chafing dishes on the long buffet held spicy little Swedish meatballs, slivers of ham in raisin sauce, bite-sized Vienna sausage. Silver bread baskets were heaped with hot biscuits and long loaves of Italian bread, sliced, spread with garlic butter and kept warm on a hot tray.

"Tonight," Maureen had said to John Paul earlier, "we'll forget about cholesterol and triglycerides. Those young fellows are entitled to a decent meal after three years of eating on the run . . ."

In their gold and white bedroom, part of the master suite overlooking the Sound, Maureen was changing her caftan for a pair of white silk evening pajamas, the loose jacket painted with purple and pink hyacinths. She slipped into a pair of white kid sandals with low heels—she'd be doing a lot of moving around this evening—brushed back her soft blonde hair and caught a lock off her forehead with a gold barrette. The style was similar, she thought, to what she'd worn as a girl, except for the color, which had been mousy brown in those days. She'd been blonde for over a decade now, and whenever she was tempted to let her hair grow out—it would be streaked with gray now, she suspected—John Paul, her sons and her friends objected. The simply cut ash-blonde locks sat on her head like a stylish cap, leaving her forehead bare, her small ears visible. She had spent time with her make-up tonight, more than usual, and the soft peach called attention to her cornflower-blue eyes. A bit of lip salve, small diamond posts in her earlobes, a sunburst of beaten gold and diamonds on her shoulder. She walked a few steps backward, to get a full view of herself.

John Paul came out of the bathroom, a white towel around his waist, his feet in Italian slippers. His wet hair was clinging to his forehead, his dark lashes were spikes against his eyes.

"You look like one of the Caesars," she said, smiling. "A man just out of a shower, a bath towel around his middle, is the male equivalent of a lady in one of Frederick's of Hollywood sexy black nighties."

He came to her and put his powerful hands on her shoulders, leaving damp fingerprints on her loose blouse.

"You have any ideas in mind?" he asked.

She felt herself respond to his touch, but resisted: it was getting late. "Lots of ideas, but no time," she said, then asked his reaction to her new perfume.

"Now, *that's* sexy," he said. "What is it?" So he would remember to send her some when he was on a trip.

"It's called Opium. Isn't that outrageous?"

He was drying himself; his body, brown and sinewy, could pass for a young man's, except for the telltale slack around his middle.

"That reminds me," he said, letting the towel fall to the floor, "we seem to be having a drug problem at the hospital."

"Oh?"

"Yeah. I think the nurses may have been careless. Hilton's upset."

"Do you think any of the residents are involved?"

"Perhaps, though I doubt it. Oh, they probably mess around with marijuana and Quaaludes, but not hard drugs."

"Well, try not to worry about it." She stood on tiptoe and put her cheek against his. "If you're tired, why don't you lie down for a while?"

"What makes you think I'm tired?"

She didn't answer, but she was surprised at his irritation. His staying power was the talk of the staff. There were days when he went into surgery at seven in the morning and took one case after another through a long round-the-clock day. Not easy cases, either. At the end of a day like that, when his team was ready to crumple, he would look up with that boyish smile and ask, "Next? Who's next?"

Pausing at the top of the curving staircase, Maureen looked down at the hall, where tubs of plants and vases of flowers were spaced with greenhouse splendor. The scent of flowers, combined with the streaked sunset, vivid with magenta, orange-gold and aquamarine, the rich balmy air, the gentle lapping of the waves, suggested a summertime aphrodisiac.

She saw a battered station wagon turn into the crushed stone drive. A half dozen young men and their girlfriends got out. They were all destined to become primary care doctors—the medical man, or woman, whom a patient initially saw when he needed attention.

Most of the residents and their wives were already here. They stood around on the deck, ill at ease and too conscious of the abundance of hors d'oeuvres and drinks. As she came down the stairs Maureen noted with approval that the waiters were taking orders for drinks. The residents had drifted away from their women and were huddled in a circle around Dr. Malcolm Stone. She greeted them warmly, remembering their names, putting them at ease. They were from India, Pakistan, the Philippines, Taiwan, Mexico, and, of course, the States.

She left them and approached the small group of their wives and girlfriends. They were pretty, all slim, most of them with long flowing hair and a small-girl fascination with the spacious and tastefully furnished house. Later, Maureen decided, she would give them a tour.

She excused herself and went to greet the Stones. Silvie looked striking—the flaming hair, the artificial lashes, the bright bold mouth outlined above its natural thinness, the gleaming sequins on her jacket. Toulouse-Lautrec should have made a poster of this, Maureen thought, she's sensational.

Silvie pressed her cheek against Maureen's, a suggestion of a kiss but really touching the air. Malcolm kissed Maureen warmly. Dear Mal, she thought.

"I made Mal hurry," Silvie said, "I thought with this mob, you might need me."

"I'm delighted you're here. I think our young residents need some stroking."

Others were arriving, alone and in couples; more of the older physicians and their wives; the department heads and Wilbur and Clemmie Watling. She'd looked for Watling's secretary, who, she understood, ran the entire family practice program with scant help from her boss, but he had evidently forbidden her to come. Maureen suspected Wilbur Watling was one of Dr. Hilton's problems. What good is a man's brilliance, John Paul often said, if he has no humanity?

The Watlings were talking to Silvie now; they were sipping champagne and looking animated. Clemmie Watling was small and plump, while her husband was tall and hulking. In a flash of mischief Maureen wondered what they were like in bed. A man who raged at his female residents, who accused them of wanting to ruin him, must be sexually frustrated. Was it his unattractive body, she wondered, or his dark, peering eyes, darting from the corners, never looking at you straight on, or the way he hunched his shoulders? He reminded her of a former president.

A group of physicians were coming in together, greeting the residents, joking with them. In the convivial atmosphere the physicians were shedding their formality and the residents were cautiously responding.

Maureen knew there was less mingling between the highly successful physicians and the lesser members of the medical community. The important men, the richest and most successful, had a tendency to stay within their own select circle. Their wives played the same game. The only time you saw all the women together was at auxiliary functions.

John Paul, in light pants and navy-blue jacket with the yacht club insignia, welcomed the men, then moved toward the women who were congregated around Maureen's collection of gardenias and orchids, arranged in small tubs in a protected corner of the livingroom. Silvie approached him, held out her hands and smiled. John Paul listened to her, putting his arm around her shoulders. John Paul, Maureen reflected, was a man who communicated physically; he always had a reassuring pat, a friendly squeeze of the hand for his women patients and women friends.

Silvie responded with a brilliant smile. Then she raised her head and whispered something to him. She laughed with her body. Other women were watching her. Silvie was a bit of an enigma to them, sometimes warm and friendly, other times remote. Often when she was alone with the auxiliary board members, she was apt to talk with surprising candor of her relationship with her husband and children.

Peter Norris and his bride were coming through the doorway. Maureen caught her breath. How beautiful they were, two young golden creatures; Peter in summer flannels, and Karen in white silk, slit to the thigh, offering a tantalizing glimpse of her apricot tan, her shoulders bare except for the spaghetti straps, her slim feet in sandals that were more decorative than practical. Her waistline was accented by a wide sash, her well-scrubbed face bare of make-up, except for the smoke shadow on her eyes and a lip gloss on her full mouth. Her hair was combed in a high knot on top of her head, with wispy curls above the ears. She was a vision of radiant good health, like a model in an orange juice commercial.

Today's golden youth, Maureen thought, unable to stifle the pang of envy. There has never before been a generation like them. She had first seen the new breed in California, the joggers, the swimmers, the surfers. Her sons had studied at UCLA, adopting the west coast as their habitat—except for Pauley, her youngest, now in his last year at the University of Vermont and still uncertain of his goals. But then, he had so much to measure up to—his father and his older brothers.

"Mrs. Macray, this is Karen Cole," Peter said.

Maureen clasped the girl's hand between her palms. She wondered if her own white silk was half as becoming as Karen's. "I'm so glad we're meeting at last, Irene Thalberg has mentioned you often. I hope you'll consider joining the hospital auxiliary."

"I'd love to," Karen said, "and if I can be of any help . . ."

"Karen is working for the local radio station," Peter said.

"Really? What field . . . ?"

"Mostly interviews and run-of-the-mill news, an occasional health interview." Karen liked Mrs. Macray already.

"Marvelous. Maybe with you at the station, they'll give the auxiliary a little more publicity. Our annual ball is coming up."

Maureen saw Silvie approaching, her arm linked with that of a resident . . . Fred Farley, she recalled. Was he the one John Paul said was too smart for his own good? Brilliant but unstable. Well, he'd probably straighten out. There didn't appear to be any potential suicides in this group.

They all seemed outgoing, animated, amiable. They were gathered around Dr. Stimson, the orthopedic surgeon, who was in an unusually affable mood. He was a stocky, peppery, balding man with aviator glasses on his blunt nose, nearly fifty and putting on weight, but with a heavy man's agility. He was always chewing an unlighted cigar, even between courses at meals; he had no interest in small talk.

Like Dr. John Paul, Dr. Stimson had an international reputation. Athletes and film favorites came to him from the west coast and Europe; his skills restored them to mobility. He nodded brusquely to the gathering and went out to the gardens to inspect Maureen's horticultural skills. His own flower gardens had been photographed for *House Beautiful* and won prizes at the annual flower shows.

Maureen watched as Peter Norris followed the orthopedist into the garden and introduced Karen to him. Dr. Stimson favored her with a surprisingly warm smile. He listened to what she was saying.

124

Maureen could hear none of it, but her heart warmed to the young woman and she thought, pleased, this lovely child will be a great help to Peter. She has the gift of simplicity, of reaching out warmly but not effusively. Maureen hoped that she and Karen would become friends. She loved her sons, but often wished she had had a daughter.

She returned to the livingroom to greet Dr. Spyros Kolis, the Greek internist, and his wife. They had arrived in Belfort shortly after World War II, as refugees. Their son was at Choate and their daughters at Radcliffe and Bryn Mawr. Maureen spoke to them, asking about their children, telling them about her sons. How fortunate that all of us have children, she thought, so we're never at a loss for something to talk about.

After she directed the Kolises to the buffet and saw that they were being taken care of, Maureen drifted back to join another newcomer, Joyce Tisdale, who had arrived alone.

"Ted will be along shortly," Joyce said. "He was detained at the hospital."

Joyce Tisdale was one of Maureen's favorites; a tall Boston beauty in her mid-thirties, with humor and wit, a bright, offbeat personality. Joyce was married to Ted Tisdale, a pathologist, who'd been on the staff at Peter Bent Brigham in Boston for a decade before opting for Belfort.

"How is he liking it here?" Maureen asked.

"He's very happy running his own show."

Ted Tisdale was the new man in the hospital; his background was impeccable and under his direction the department was well-organized and efficiently run.

"Have you met many of our medical wives?" Maureen signaled one of the waiters who came to take Joyce's order for a drink.

"A few. On a one-to-one basis. But there seems to be no real socializing."

"The generations don't often mingle, except for evenings like this. Or events for the auxiliary and the medical society's yearly dinner dance."

Joyce Tisdale brushed a lock of brown hair behind her ear. "It's almost like a caste system. I don't know where I am on the ladder—probably the first rung."

Maureen laughed; Joyce's candor was disarming. "The young

wives are busy raising their families, so the only friends they cultivate are women with similar problems—car pools, sharing sitters, that sort of thing. Most of the older wives are either going back to college or getting jobs—so I guess everyone is in her own compartment."

"It wasn't like that at home—" Joyce explained that she was from Gloucester, Massachusetts. "We all lived near the shore. The big houses were right off the beach. That's where the chief of staff and the senior attending physicians had their houses. But they were all very human and they made the younger doctors and their wives, who lived a few blocks in from the shore, feel equal and at home.

"Once a year, the streets to the beach were closed to traffic, and we had a block party—with ethnic foods, square dancing—it was like a big family . . ."

There was a touch of nostalgia in her voice. "We were all raising our kids, so we were busy at home. Nobody thought of doing any more . . . we expected to follow the pattern of our parents' lives . . ."

"We had the same here, but to a lesser degree. One thing we all have in common," Maureen's smile was mischievous, "we've learned not to consult our husbands if one of the kids is sick. I trained my sons to be stoics in daddy's presence, like the boy with the fox in his vitals. When daddy copes with illness all day, he wants healthy people around at night."

"Yes," Joyce laughed, "I learned early—when in doubt, call a doctor—but not the one you're married to."

John Paul was coming their way and Maureen motioned him to join them. His color had improved; the waxy highlights around his cheekbones had disappeared. He was holding a glass in his hand, but she knew it was only Perrier water, since he would be operating at seven the next morning.

"May I show you the deck," he said to Joyce. "I believe there is music and a moon."

He nodded to Maureen. "Is it okay, mama?"

"Definitely."

"Aren't you afraid of letting him loose among all these ladies?" Joyce asked.

"Oh, his life is so strenuous between his office, his surgery and his sailing, I figure he's entitled to the company of some pretty ladies."

She watched them move toward the deck, John Paul's strong tanned hand on Joyce's bare shoulder. You could tell the physicians who had a healthy attitude toward women, thought Maureen. John Paul was one and Dr. Monroe, the ob-gyn man was another. She felt sorry for the young women who wanted to go beyond nursing into medicine; it was still rough for them. If Virginia Carruthers hadn't elected pediatrics, she'd have met with obstacles too. The men were more tolerant of women in pediatrics, as though woman and child still belonged together and were no threat to them.

The party was in full swing now. Maureen walked from the spacious livingroom to the library and then out to the deck, where a three-piece orchestra was playing dance tunes by Rodgers and Hammerstein, Cole Porter and Jerome Kern. The one they were playing now was an erotic little number that had been the theme song of a movie of the late forties. It had made a star of Teresita, a dancer who traveled with the Bob Hope troupes entertaining the soldiers. Like Betty Grable and Marilyn Monroe, Teresita had become a favorite G.I. pinup. And the song, "The Dawn Comes Too Soon," was synonymous with her rise to popularity.

"I hear Teresita's cracked up again," said Eve Rothschild. "She's been readmitted to Sunset Hill."

There was nothing in the papers about Teresita's most recent sojourn at the glamorous rehabilitation retreat, but leave it to Eve Rothschild to have private access to such gossip.

"I understand Peter Norris is shacked up with that girl." Eve lit a cigarette, inhaled deeply and blew the smoke through her nostrils. "And who invited her to join the auxiliary board?"

"I did, Eve." Maureen fanned the smoke away with her hand. So they weren't married—Irene Thalberg hadn't told her that. It made no difference to Maureen, except that she now felt a certain protectiveness toward Karen. "I don't think their private life has anything to do with us."

"You don't think so? Even though you're Catholic?"

"Since Karen and Peter aren't Catholic, I don't see the relevance."

"All the same, I think the auxiliary should be restricted to medical *wives*."

Fortunately Maureen spied one of the residents whom she hadn't greeted. He was Fred Farley, looking as though he'd slept in his shirt and pants as usual. But for once a touch of sunburn gave his face some healthy color.

"Mrs. Macray, ma'am." He greeted her with more animation than he usually displayed, taking her hand and kissing her cheek. The scent of shaving lotion surprised her. Fred usually had an unwashed look about him and a perpetual five o'clock shadow.

Yet he seemed in good spirits tonight, and the girl beside him might be the reason. She was of medium height, dressed in a snug white furblend sweater and long flowered-cotton skirt, but her curly brown natural hairstyle added to her height. She had a bright, alert face, with a droll glint in her dark, button-round eyes.

"I'm Shulamit," she said, putting out her hand.

"Hello, Shulamit, and welcome. Are you a native too?"

"Definitely. I used to swim from your beach—even though it was marked private. I figured you wouldn't mind. I live on the other side of it."

"There's just the one house on the spit—doesn't it belong to the Soloves?"

"It does."

"You're a Solove?"

"I am, although sometimes my cousins are hard put to admit it. They're Harvard business school graduates—and they have no use for a Radcliffe activist."

"Forget about your activism for tonight and join the dancers. What are they doing now . . . a Jewish Hora or a Greek dance—I hope they don't smash my china."

The rooms were crowded now, all windows open to the lovely night.

"Fred, how have you been doing?" Maureen asked. He was one of the poorest residents, always broke, always a little hungry, something of an alien. But he had a quicksilver mind; if he found his niche in medicine, she thought, he'd be outstanding. Research was probably the answer for Fred. "Have you made plans for after graduation?"

"I'm still thinking about it. I was going to strike out for California . . ."

"Connecticut needs you more than California," Shulamit assured him. "We need warm bodies for support."

Fred scowled. "Who'd ever have thought I'd come to this?"

He cupped Shulamit's elbow in the palm of his hand and led her off. Maureen hoped Fred was serious about this one. He needed stability and security, the support that a loving young woman could supply. Solove, she thought. They were the people who owned all those supermarkets in Fairfield County.

Yes, this girl might be just right for Fred. Perhaps she would get him back on the track, neutralize his self-destructive urges. Maureen remembered the two residents who'd committed suicide the previous year. Odd, she thought, you never associated suicide with the medical profession. Yet a number of youngish physicians resorted to drugs or alcohol to counteract fatigue, long hours, the terminally ill patients, the wretched families left behind—oh, it got to be bad at times. Maureen had seen enough of their reactions to know how the death of a patient touched them, especially the men in their middle years. Whoever said they didn't care about their patients didn't know what she and other wives saw.

Silvie was having a ball tonight. Maureen saw her out on the deck, dancing with a new partner every five minutes, her frizzed red hair shining in the torchlight, her sequined evening pants suit clinging to her like black rubber diving gear. She and John Paul were doing a lively Charleston. After the song was over, Silvie looked around to the group watching them, held out her hands to Dr. Hilton to engage him in a dance. He put his arms around her and led her into a few slow steps, not the frenetic twists and kicks she'd been using. He danced in a quiet way but his movements were assured; he listened politely while she chattered, her face upraised to his. As they danced out of the spotlight, she rested her cheek on his shoulder.

Dr. Hilton saw Maureen through an opening on the dance floor and waved to her. She smiled and waved back. She was still smiling as she moved toward the kitchen to check on the food and drink situation. To her surprise, John Paul was there, at the little breakfast nook, and Karen Cole was with him. He was sipping Perrier from a tall frosted glass, and as Maureen neared them, she heard the girl ask, "Are you all right now, Dr. Macray?"

"Right as rain," he said, which didn't sound like him; he usually hated clichés. Was there a waxen quality to his sunburn? Maureen decided it was the bad overhead light and, without intruding, turned back to the waitresses who were now setting plates of Danish pastries and refilling the electric percolators.

It was nearly eleven o'clock. One of the senior doctors switched on the television set in the library. Several young couples had come in from the cooling night air; they were lounging, happy and relaxed, on the sofa and the large pillows scattered on the rug. They all look content, Maureen thought, it's a good party.

Karen left Dr. John Paul and found Peter out on the deck, overlooking the rock ledge and talking to Fred and Shulamit. Peter held out his arm, and she snuggled beside him, shivering slightly. He shrugged off his jacket and folded it around her.

"Do you want to go in?" he asked.

"No, I love it out here." She wanted no part of the late news. If the Third Network were on, she might hear Delos Burke's resonant voice commenting on whatever had happened in Washington today. She didn't want any reminders of him.

Listening to Shulamit and Fred argue with Peter about the promise —or threat—of national health care, she put her head on Peter's shoulder and felt his embrace tighten. Don't let me spoil it, she warned herself. He's every girl's dream . . . The boy next door . . .

But it reminded her suddenly of a conversation with Delos. It had taken place soon after they'd started sleeping together; they'd been lying together on the daybed after their third, or maybe fourth, tryst. Her head was on Delos's shoulder, her fingers pulling lightly at the thick curls of black hair on his chest.

"You're a dangerous woman, Karen," he said, stroking her hair idly.

She was taken aback; she knew she had been gifted with natural good looks, but she'd never thought of herself as a *femme fatale*.

"Who, me?" she had replied, her face turned toward his. "I'm the girl next door."

He looked at her quizzically, a lazy grin spreading across his face. "I know," he said, "that's what makes you so dangerous."

Danger-r-ous. She could almost hear his voice in her ear. Her thoughts and eyes drifted. Dr. Stone's wife was alternately dancing with Dr. Macray and Dr. Hilton, pressing her sinewy body against them in a suggestive way. But Silvie was not utterly preoccupied with the men. Mrs. Stone had been interested in Karen the entire evening. Interest wasn't exactly the word. Silvie's gaze had followed her throughout the evening, intense, probing, almost like an x-ray. Karen wondered if Mrs. Stone were one of those very proper ladies who disapproved of unmarried bedfellows. She didn't act that way; she was sending out sexy little signals to all the men present. And they stayed away from her mostly, Karen noticed, because of their casually watchful wives.

She had heard from Peter, Fred and even Mrs. Thalberg that medical men, more than the new breed of super-executives, successful artists and writers, were the most promiscuous group in affluent Belfort—the gynecologists and the psychiatrists, in particular.

She looked up at Peter who was listening to Shulamit describing the glories of Israel: He seemed so responsive to Shulamit's enthusiasm that Karen felt a pang akin to jealousy. And yet barely ten minutes before, her thoughts had been with Delos . . .

Was she counting too much on Peter's steadfast devotion? Perhaps he found Shulamit attractive too. Karen could understand it; next to the vibrant, articulate, sensual woman, Karen felt bleached out and inadequate. Shulamit was a fighter; the kind who would walk in picket lines, man telephones to collect help for the underprivileged. She was on a pro-abortion crusade now and she had even dared to tackle Dr. John Paul about the right-to-life issue. I'd like to be friends with her, Karen decided. I wish I could be as strong and decisive as she is.

Guests were leaving now and there was much intermingling, many lingering and indiscriminate kisses, promises to get together soon.

When Silvie and Malcolm were saying good-bye, Silvie turned to Karen, who was still beside Peter, with his arm encircling her shoulder. Her glance was sharp and critical.

"No man is safe with you around," she said coldly.

It was such a calculated insult that Malcolm flushed and immediately rushed in to smooth it over. "That's meant to be a compliment, Karen. In vino, veritas."

"Maybe what she meant," Shulamit suggested boldly, "was that Karen isn't safe with all these lechers around."

There was an embarrassed silence.

"Come, Sil, before you get into any more trouble," Malcolm urged.

Silvie hesitated for a moment. She peered at them, her eyes not entirely focused. She staggered a bit, Malcolm caught her by the arm. "Come along, Sil. Don't set a bad example for these young people."

She saluted them and allowed herself to be led away. They watched with conflicting emotions.

Shulamit said, "Mrs. Stone drinks a little?"

No one replied.

Dr. Hilton waited until the Stones left, then came over to their group. But Silvie spied him as she turned her back to the door and began to clamor for another drink.

"Join us," she called to him. "We're driving to New York. To a disco."

Malcolm shook his head. He was clearly on his way home to put her to bed.

Dr. Hilton spoke to them briefly, excused himself, kissing Maureen goodnight. This party was first rate, he thought. What a lovely woman Maureen was. She must be in her fifties but she had the sex appeal of a younger woman. Not like Silvie Stone, who was so blatant, whose every banal expression had said, "Do I turn you on?"

Maureen Macray had the true sensuality of a woman who had enjoyed the full scale of love as well as sex. John Paul was fortunate.

Hilton wondered fleetingly what it would be like to make love to Maureen, wondered if she'd ever been unfaithful to John Paul. It was odd, he thought, walking toward his car, how a night like this excited a man. He felt himself growing hard as he slid into the car seat. Odd, too, that the two women who were the most sexually attractive to him were Maureen and Peter Norris's companion, Karen. December and May. He suspected that Maureen had been like Karen in her youth and that Karen might resemble her as she grew older. What was that quality they shared? A nurturing spirit? Warmth?

He was suddenly very tired and he thought how nice it would be to come home to his wife. Oh, Esther, Esther . . .

CHAPTER XIV

The maids, waiters, bartenders had collected their fees, with a generous tip for their trouble. They had taken home the leftovers that Maureen gave them and had left the kitchen immaculate.

The big house was quiet now; the windows closed to the night; only the evening lamps cast a modest glow, and the burglar alarm system was turned on.

Maureen took a final glance downstairs. A perfect party; no one got sick in the bathroom. No one ground a lighted cigarette into the priceless Aubusson rug. Nothing was broken, even allowing for a Hora and the Charleston. And the air filters throughout the house left the air pure. The house was ready for the next party.

But she wondered if there would be another.

John Paul wasn't fooling her. There was something wrong with his breathing, though he refused to acknowledge it. He was a vital man, bursting with enthusiasm and energy. It wasn't likely there was anything seriously amiss. Except that his complexion was looking waxen at times. Well, he was nearly retirement age. His body was tired, though his spirit was invincible.

His term as chief of staff was nearing its end. She had an idea that he would become chief emeritus, if the board would create such a position. And probably Hilton and the board would choose whomever John Paul recommended as his successor.

During the summer months, she thought, they'll all start jockeying for his position. The ambitious physicians would begin a campaign that could turn as vicious and ruthless as any political one. She wished suddenly that John Paul was removed from all the infighting, it was such a drain on him. She wished they could go away together to some quiet place for the last third of their lives. She was suddenly very tired of the big establishment, the demands on their lifestyle, the requirements of his position. His former students, many of them now well-known surgeons, often returned to Belfort to visit him and pay him homage. And to be entertained.

John Paul was already in bed, covered only by a sheet. The lamps were pools of golden light, the FM radio was playing classical music.

She went over and knelt on the soft white rug beside their bed. She took his hand, so strong and flexible, and kissed the fingers with infinite tenderness.

"Our lives have gone by too quickly . . . I want to reach back . . . to recapture it all . . ."

He was smiling, the lines around his piercing eyes deep with suntan. "The good and the bad?"

"There's been very little bad."

They looked at each other, remembering the tragedy that remained hidden in the recesses of memory.

Maureen had panicked. She hadn't meant to sleep with John Paul until they were married. But he had said to her, "You are my wife already, Maureen, you know that," and she had felt it herself, with her whole body, and had yielded to the desire that had been plaguing them both for so long. And she had been punished; she was pregnant. If it were discovered, she'd be thrown out of nursing school. There were rigid behavior patterns in those days: no marriage for a nurse in training, and certainly no pregnancy.

John Paul told Maureen what he had heard from one of the other residents. There was a doctor in New Jersey—not a butcher, but a reputable physician whose only daughter had bled to death on the table of an unqualified abortionist and who had dedicated himself to saving other young women in trouble. His fee was only fifty dollars. John Paul had the name and a phone number . . . Maureen couldn't brave the disgrace, her nursing supervisors, her friends, her family, pious Irish Catholics from South Boston. She had to go through with it, even if it meant excommunication from the church. After two months of dreading and abstaining from communion she had come with John Paul to a liberal Greenwich Village church to learn her fate . . .

There was an awful silence, as she struggled for the words to tell the Confiteor . . .

After confessing, she had sat there waiting, the few seconds had seemed an eternity.

And then a voice, surprisingly benign. "My daughter, your sin is grave. But do you remember what our Lord said to the Magdalene?"

"Yes, Father." Where was the shock, the outrage, the dismay she had anticipated?

"My child, repeat them to me."

Her voice was low. "Go forth and sin no more."

"My daughter, are you truly penitent?"

What had followed was now blurred in her memory. She'd broken down, become hysterical, crying wildly that her sin was far worse than the Magdalene's, that God couldn't, and wouldn't forgive her. And that voice, so compassionate, so soothing, from behind the wall of the confessional, reminded her that there was but one sin that the Almighty could not forgive: despair of His mercy. Were not all men sinners, did the priest not say during Mass, "Look not on our sins but on the faith of your church . . . ?" He had assigned her a novena as a penance—given her absolution and said, "The Lord has freed you from your sins. Go in peace."

But peace had not come, not after thirty-five years. Not after the nine days of prayer nor the thousand private acts of sorrow she'd prescribed for herself since then. Not after countless hours of devotion to the community, to St. Mark's, not after four healthy sons and a lifetime with John Paul . . .

I want it back, she cried silently. I want to undo it . . .

Suddenly she felt the most painful constriction, but when the words came out, they were not what she meant to say, not really.

"John Paul, have you always been faithful?" She couldn't help remembering that vision in the kitchen, John Paul with Peter Norris's girlfriend.

He was laughing at her, that deep hearty laugh.

"Isn't it a little late in life for such a question?"

"It is. But I feel very vulnerable tonight. Maybe it was that lovely girl Karen—so young and fresh—as I was once . . ."

"What is this, a *Playboy* interview? To appreciate God's gift is one thing. To make love to a dear familiar mate is another. Come to bed, my girl. Right here. Beside me."

CHAPTER XV

On the drive home, through dark deserted country roads, Silvie sat close to Malcolm, who was at the wheel. He couldn't tell whether she was turned on or wrapped up asleep. He was sure, however, that she'd had too much to drink. During the last hour at the party, she had talked too much and laughed a lot at nothing in particular. When she was in that frame of mind, her straight lips had a way of moving and shaping sounds that could make almost any man imagine her working on him, sucking away. At such moments, she excited Malcolm, while at the same time, he wanted to smack her across the mouth. She could goad him into a fury that he would not have believed possible.

Men sensed her sexual powers all right; she was like a furry little animal in heat, coaxing, teasing, daring him to conquer her.

That was Silvie and he knew it when he married her. But he thought it was therapeutic then. He firmly believed it would work because he wanted it to work.

The lights were off in their house; they parked the car and walked in together. All was quiet, the children were asleep. They went into their bedroom and closed the door. Silvie pulled off her sequined overblouse and stepped out of her black silk pants. She was naked, her brown nipples prominent and firm. As he pulled her toward the bed, he was aware of her scent, perfume mingled with the smell of sex. She was ready for him.

As he mounted her, she was wet and loose but she began her muscle contractions—those damned sex exercises she practiced constantly —as soon as he entered her. Her flesh excited him, the body so lovingly anointed for sex; he dug his fingers into her flat belly and before he could stop himself, he came, with a low groan and a trembling of his whole body.

She sat up against the headboard, her face contorted with rage.

"Dammit, haven't I taught you *anything?*"

"I'm sorry, Sil . . . in the morning—"

"No. Now. Remember—we just touch each other, we just feel our bodies. We can use a rubber band to keep your control . . ."

He wanted desperately to go to sleep.

"You've got me turned on. What am I supposed to do?"

Malcolm had dozed off.

Silvie lay awake smoldering.

Nobody in Belfort ever suspected the skeletons in Silvie's closet. But if she ever feared her past would be uncovered, she didn't fret about it. She was adroit at getting out of unpleasant situations. As Malcolm Stone's wife, she carried some clout. Not seniority, of course. Nowhere near the level of Maureen Macray. But still, there were patients who adored Malcolm, and by osmosis transferred their awe and respect to his wife.

Silvie always implied that she was a child of the sixties. Not exactly a dropout or a hippie, but a rebel. On the state highway in West Virginia, there were any number of small towns like her birthplace. It was a once-rich mining town (at least for the mine owners), a railroad center, now sinking into obscurity. Vans, buses, trailer trucks had practically eliminated the freight yards. By the time her father would be ready for retirement from the railroad there would be damn little to feed his brood.

She was living in the too small bungalow, and yet was not a part of it. She didn't have much sympathy for her middle-aged mother sagging at forty, with kids still tumbling into the world—more kids than there was food or space for. She was nothing but a brood mare, Silvie thought with dispassionate scorn. At thirteen Silvie knew how not to have babies. She also knew that a valuable commodity rested between her thighs . . .

Silvie took the bus to school in the neighboring town. Her old man figured a high school education would help her support herself if she didn't get married right away as her mother had.

Silvie had other ideas. The mirror told her she was good-looking, and the whistles of the railroad men confirmed the image she saw there. Her skin was pale and porcelainlike, with a translucency that owed more to malnourishment than cosmetics. Silvie's mother was no cook.

School didn't appeal to Silvie; she had no intention of becoming a secretary. In spite of all the glossy romance magazines, there were few secretaries who married their bosses. Or even had long, meaningful affairs—meaning money.

She wasn't exactly greedy in her long-range plans. Not then. She just wanted to close the door on her family's way of life. She wanted to be rid of the whole scene—the overcrowded rooms, the noisy kids always fighting among themselves, the invisible smell of poverty.

She meant to be reborn. She would leave her family just as soon as she could. She knew that there was a world outside of her West Virginia village, a world just waiting for a clever girl to exploit it.

She began using her wits early. By the time she was out of high school, her sights were set. And her appetites were well developed—that is, the appetites that would help her achieve her goal. Sex was power—money would give her infinitely more power. She wanted everything that would put her at the top of the list. She had a right to expect a lot; her body was slender, with a flat stomach and a cute little ass. The jersey shifts she wore accentuated her figure. And it was all available for the right barter . . .

In Chicago, which was a stopover on her way to New York, she worked in a nursing home. But Silvie wasn't about to carry bedpans. She ran the office and dealt with guilt-ridden middle-aged children who were seeking a sanctuary for their parents, where they would be cared for and never trouble their kin again.

She stayed in Chicago less than a year, saving enough money to go to New York. In Chicago she was circumspect; the only sex she had was with the owner of the nursing home, and he, poor bastard, had more desire than stamina.

New York City, though, was something else. She had no trouble finding a job. She considered herself a nurse since she had nursing home experience. She knew how to take a patient's temperature, count a pulse, take a blood pressure, test urine for sugar; you needed only a few smarts to pick that up.

She answered an ad in the Sunday New York *Times* for a receptionist's job in a physician's office. He was on the west side of Manhattan, which she already knew was the wrong part of town. But considering the caliber of his patients, and his quietly thriving business giving them happy shots, he was better off in a brownstone with no nosy doorman to gossip.

There were never more than two patients in Dr. Felscher's waiting room, and they tended to be not only affluent but neurotic. He treated men with sexual problems, men who suffered from premature ejaculation or could not get an erection or simply could not function with the women in their lives. During the day Silvie was his receptionist.

Evenings, she moonlighted.

She was a sexual surrogate—one of the first. Her treatment for an impotent male usually allowed for ten sessions, each session lasting one evening. At Dr. Felscher's suggestion, she charged a thousand dollars for the series. Dr. Felscher gave his patients injections, a combination of procaine, hormones, vitamins and another drug, which she suspected was an amphetamine.

Dr. Felscher, a young, athletic-looking man, had spent his earlier years as a masseur in the reducing hideaways where rich women came to starve and be pounded into shape. He often told his wretched male patients that he was the best doctor in town; that he could sustain an erection indefinitely; that he could make a woman have multiple orgasms without losing his hard-on. He figured his patients would be affected by his candor; inspired. What he did for them filtered through their bodies, arousing an urge for sex that demanded satisfaction—if Silvie had anything to do with them.

In addition to the ten hundred-dollar sessions, the patient, naturally, took care of dinner, theater, dancing, whatever. Silvie usually chose a sexy play and dinner in a small, intimate restaurant. She made the evening memorable, for she was flashy, smartly dressed, and had the confidence of a woman men lust for.

Afterward, she took the patient back to his or her apartment, or to a hotel room. She was loving but not demanding. Her role was to be a coach—a sexy coach. Sometimes it took two or three sessions before they would disrobe and she would encourage her patient to pet her while she stroked him. She would try out various positions with him—never the missionary one, which was probably all he knew. She was creative, imaginative and when she finally allowed him to penetrate her, she became loving and caring. She didn't sigh or berate him if he came too quickly. She would simply begin again at the beginning—the important thing, Dr. Felscher had impressed on her, was to handle the men tactfully; they were uniformly oversensitive, easily hurt, terrified of rejection.

One of her most valued clients was a smart young politician who flew down from Washington on the shuttle for treatments. He had been having trouble making it since his Harvard days. Politically it was time for him to marry, so he needed her kind of treatment. The slow approach, the petting, all the foreplay that she had perfected didn't work with him. Finally, she went down on him, and as she nuzzled his flaccid penis, coaxing it into life, she murmured, "Can't you imagine I'm your boyfriend?" And finally he did.

Men came to her long after she had helped them to achieve normal sexual intercourse. I want to show you how good I am, thanks to you . . .

Malcolm Stone was still interning when she met him. He lived with his mother in Pittsburgh and was undecided where he would settle. He had made it to bed a few times, but was mostly unsuccessful in his shy courtships. When one generous nurse finally allowed him to make love to her and encountered his problem of premature ejaculation, he decided to seek out the doctor who restored manhood not only through his happy pills but through the services of a sexy young surrogate who practiced all the wiles of a little geisha.

He was so grateful to Silvie that he fell in love with her. All through his courtship, she had a throbbing young Baptist to sustain her sexually. When Malcolm asked her to marry him, she acted as though he was doing her a great favor. Which he was. But from what she'd heard, Jewish men made great husbands—even though they all had mothers.

Meanwhile, they lived in her apartment on the East Side. Silvie closed shop as a sex surrogate, except once in a while when Dr. Felscher asked her to help in a difficult case—something Malcolm knew nothing about. She loved New York, she loved the men friends she'd made. When Malcolm was off, they went to the theater, to concerts, to the ballet; by that time the patina of the fashionable woman glowed on her face.

The sixties were a time of flux but none of the headlines touched Silvie unless they had to do with fashion, new lifestyles, or making money.

During that time, she gave birth to Barbara and Norman. Not that she loved children, but she meant to insure Malcolm's ties to her, away from his mother. And then he decided to move to Connecticut. Doctors were finally beginning to make decent money. She had no ties with her family, who hadn't heard from her in years. And they lived, if not happily, at least neutrally, ever after.

Malcolm could function like a healthy male. Sometimes. And there was Jack Palfrey, his accountant. Jack was remarkably astute where income was involved, but a mere boy when it came to the intricacies of sex. She gave him head without the slightest concern; he was obviously a good husband who had never strayed before. He had been as innocent as a babe—before.

Palfrey's attachment to her could be milked in various ways. She suspected Malcolm was overly generous with his mother and her two aging sisters, but she had no way of checking on it. There was no reason for Malcolm to be so generous; the old biddies were probably eligible for Medicare and half a dozen other kinds of government help.

She hoped Malcolm was aware of his obligations to her and the kids. Security was her reason for getting married in the first place. Security was freedom—freedom from lack of money, background, ties. But money in the bank was not enough, nor was jewelry, or stocks and bonds; something deep within her craved the knowledge that she was in control. Security meant power.

She could manage Malcolm up to a point. No question that his pa-

tients came first with him—the heart patients first, his mother probably next.

After the children were born, there was a subtle change in Malcolm's sexuality. He was less interested; his patient load drained him.
He complained of a backache that seemed to have no physical origin.

She saw all her carefully cultivated talents from Dr. Felscher's
days wasting away. The sensual awareness, the touch of her delicate
fingers, her educated tongue, her educated pelvis . . . what was the
point?

She was irritated with Malcolm; her son and daughter were not
enough to keep her busy; so she set about a private course of sexual
self-fulfillment. Were there sexual pleasures she hadn't yet identified?
Flesh and mind were one; together they could transport you to a fan-
tastic high. Silvie read books by Colette, the Frenchwoman who
wrote so erotically about sensual pleasure.

Silvie bought fruit out of season, peaches, pears, melons, coming
from fruit-growers in Oregon. She would serve Malcolm ripe fruit,
with juices that enticed the taste buds: avocados with splashes of
lime; pears so ripe and succulent that you ate them with a spoon.
And her fragrance, rich, subtle, lingering. She watched her weight;
Audrey Hepburn was her model, spaghetti thin, erect in bearing, as
though she were always walking in the wind, a little breathless, with
chiffon floating from her shoulders.

She never ceased to work on the creation of herself; she always
had time for it, even while the kids were young. Her thin, graceful
figure, her spectacular red hair, the curious way she used her rather
thin lips in talking all created a magnet that drew men; there was a
promise of untold pleasures in the tilt of her face, in the way she allowed her upper lids to shadow her irises, and her wayward smile en-
hanced the promise. Malcolm was jealous of the attention men gave
her—when he was aware of it.

It wasn't as though she intended to turn her back on him. He was
her husband and she wanted the best for him, since it meant also the
best for her. If Malcolm reached the peak at Belfort Hospital, perhaps he'd forget his idiotic dreams of either teaching full-time at
Yale-New Haven or creating a rehabilitation center for heart patients.

She intended to be the second Maureen Macray of Fairfield County. Perhaps with the help of the new administrator of the hospital—Dr. Hilton was certainly a most attractive man—she'd be on her way. . . .

CHAPTER XVI

Peter left the car in the driveway and with his arm around Karen's waist, helped her up the steps to the porch. He nuzzled her neck, so soft and fragrant under the loose wisps of hair drifting from the top-knot. He was stirred by a fresh feeling, a sense of the most exquisite tenderness toward her. He was enormously grateful that the evening had gone so well. Karen was growing to trust him. It was, he felt, a significant step in their development. After the trauma of her affair with Delos Burke, she was naturally hesitant—he could understand it —but her faith and her heart seemed to be blossoming under his care. He longed to offer her his life, to cherish and protect her. Beneath the cool attitude that saved his emotions during his practice, there was a rich vein of emotion, previously held in check, because no love had tapped it. His feelings, his emotions, his body melded in an out-pouring of love deepened by a wild passion.

He was clumsy thrusting the key in the outside door. As they stepped inside, he held her until her breasts were flattened against his chest, until she too was growing breathless.

The brass lamp was burning in the hall. On the small table was a sheet of notepaper in Mrs. Thalberg's script.

Karen, you had a call from New York this evening. From a Mr Burke. He said he was a friend. He was anxious to get in touch with you. I told him to try again in the morning. I hope it's okay.

Karen's fingers were trembling as she held the paper. Dismay followed by a stab of fear banished the glorious feeling of a moment ago. She tried to keep the note from Peter, but he was reading it over her shoulder. He snatched it out of her hand, crumpled it and threw it in the wastebasket.

"Karen—"

"Yes, Peter?"

"Karen, are you still seeing him?"

She shook her head, bewildered by the abrupt change in his manner. "No, Peter. I haven't seen him since we broke up."

"Then why is he calling you?"

"I don't know."

His face grew stern, his eyes cold, his mouth set in a harsh line. "Are you going to return his call?"

Her impulse was to cry out, Of course not, I never want to speak to him, I never want to see him again. But Peter's harsh demand aroused a sudden childish willfulness. She hesitated. "I'll have to think about it."

He didn't touch her; that hurt her the most. Arms at his side, he stood there in furious judgment.

"Karen, are you playing games with me?"

"How can you say that? You know better—"

"You swore he was out of your life for good. Well, he wouldn't be after you without some encouragement—"

"Peter," she burst out, "you are one stupid male."

She could no longer contain the tears; they came in a rush. She stumbled toward the stairs, and holding on to the balustrade made her way toward their room. This was a Peter she'd never seen before. He was a demon, possessed by primitive fury. He followed her, trapped her in the bathroom where she was blotting her eyes with a tissue. He caught her in his arms. His hands were purposeful now, groping for the delicate fastener of her dress, pulling down the fragile straps, struggling with her until her dress lay in a white silk heap. He carried her to the bed; she lay on the coverlet too overwhelmed to move, while he managed to get clear of his clothes.

There was no tender prelude as he covered her naked body with his. His outrage, his fury fueled the fierce, rough demands that seemed to her alien to the man she thought she knew. His lips, his tongue, even his teeth claimed her throat, her upthrust nipples, the delicate concave belly and the soft triangle of blond hair.

Fury was an aphrodisiac they had not tasted before. Her response at first was timid, hesitant, but it grew in pace with his unleashed needs. She was now ready for him, matching him in his excesses, moving with him, finding within herself a wildness that surpassed anything she'd ever known. They came together splendidly and in the peak of their exultation she murmured, "Peter, oh Peter."

With a kind of sob, he answered, "Karen. Karen, my love."

Long after Karen drifted off to sleep, Peter lay awake. His thoughts weren't quite focused. He had lost count of the scotches he had consumed at the party and he wasn't accustomed to heavy drinking.

Does she love me? Or doesn't she? Maybe she's still hung up on that bastard.

But at the peak of their lovemaking she had said his name. She had been eager for him, not for Delos Burke. Through the fog in his mind, he could still recall that Karen had conquered her innate shyness and had reached a passion on a level with his own.

Why this reaction, he pondered. Was he being the old-style male, clinging to the double standard? Not so. He simply wanted more than a warm body; such offerings were available at the hospital. What he wanted was a commitment from Karen. I want her to love me. I want to share my life with her, unburden my heart to her. It sounded corny, yet this was his need.

He had taken such pride in her tonight; her poise and warmth had inspired admiration in all his friends. It was odd, he thought, that their backgrounds were so different. He was somewhat shy with her parents, who had the poise and self-assurance that came from generations of affluence and culture.

Yet class distinction meant nothing to him; his parents were admirable; his mother the classic country doctor's wife; his father had respect in the community, stature in the state medical society.

What am I trying to prove to myself? he wondered. Do I want to marry her? Does she want to marry me or does she still hope that guy will divorce his wife? He couldn't very well put the question of marriage to her until he was certain of her answer.

He rather envied Fred Farley's casual attitude toward women. Fred could sleep around with the Hispanic girls and then bring a nice Jewish girl to the Macray party.

But he wanted only Karen. In the cool wash of night, she lay curled on the bed, sleeping sweetly. He leaned over and with infinite tenderness touched his lips to her eyelids, her cheeks, her mouth.

"Mmmm," she murmured out of her sleep. "Mmmm, Peter."

She said it again, he thought. She said my name.

He cupped her breast with a gentle hand. She made a small sound of pleasure and curved her warm body closer to his.

Karen, he thought, what will happen to us?

The time Karen felt truly close to Peter was in the morning. She liked the way they always woke up, their bodies curled together and, still cuddling her in his arms, Peter complaining humorously that his arm had fallen asleep. And often, as they held each other in a snug fit, he grew hard again and they made love before he dashed off to the hospital. She'd never had the mornings with Delos . . .

This morning, as she recalled the forceful way he'd taken her, and remembered her own uninhibited response, she felt embarrassed. Peter was probably in the bathroom or on his way to the hospital, ashamed, no doubt, to face her.

But it was nothing like that. Opening her eyes, she found him lying next to her, his head on her shoulder, his arm across her chest cradling her, clinging to her.

She was afraid to stir; she wanted him to be close, attached, part of her.

His violent outburst last night—was it jealousy? Peter—jealous? She couldn't imagine it. He was so self-controlled. He wouldn't reveal himself that way . . .

She didn't feel much shame, though . . . In fact she felt a kind of pride. Two men wanted her, were in love with her. It gave her the most delicious sense of self. She couldn't believe it: Delos, who had had so many women; Peter, with the nurses and doctors' wives falling over themselves to talk to him. And both men wanted her, craved her. You're a dangerous woman, she said to herself, and barely stifled a giggle.

She wondered whether Peter might be ready to talk about marriage. She didn't know if she would say yes but she welcomed the thought of his wanting to marry her.

Her thoughts this glum spring morning were scattered. Why was Delos still pursuing her, she asked herself, was it because he was unaccustomed to being rejected? She had heard from several of her office friends at the Third Network that there was no new woman in his life. Did Delos miss her . . . or was he merely being faithful to his wife for a change?

And Peter . . . what did *his* new possessiveness mean? She decided to enjoy her role, to make the most of it. After all, it might not last . . .

What day was it—Sunday? Of course. Peter hadn't turned on the alarm clock because it was his day off. They would have a whole glorious day together away from the hospital with its antiseptic smells and its depressing, sick people.

The gray light washed away the darkness. A cool damp day was in the offing—the kind of gray day for which New England was justly famous—before May made her exit and June ushered in the golden summer.

Let it rain, she thought, we'll stay in bed all day. She'd make coffee and bring it up, and they'd huddle over the Sunday papers, reading, making love . . . They seldom had such a block of time together, an entire day, without interruption. How delicious, she thought.

The clock radio was going to come on. She wondered if she could reach over Peter and turn it off. He was sleeping so soundly. "My dearest," she murmured, and didn't care how the words sounded.

Before she could move, there was a rap on the door. Peter stirred, turned over and buried his face in his pillow.

Karen got out of bed carefully and pulled on her silk robe. No doubt it was Mrs. Thalberg. Damn!

Leaning against the door was Fred Farley. He looked terrible—his complexion was pale and there were dark circles under his eyes.

"Fred—what is it?" she whispered. "What's wrong?"

He stepped into the room. He wore pants and a T-shirt that looked as though he'd slept in them; maybe he had—she couldn't remember what he'd worn to the party.

Peter opened his eyes and sat up, instantly awake.

"What's up?" he asked. "Trouble at the hospital?"

"No, trouble with me." Fred approached the bed, looking, Karen thought, like a warmed-over cadaver.

"Peter, I'm on duty today—and I just can't handle it."

"What's wrong?"

"I don't know. Maybe I'm hung over. I'm not used to boozing like that."

"Where did you go after the Macrays' . . . ?"

Fred hesitated. "I took Shulamit home."

"And then . . . ?"

"Pete, what is this? The third degree?"

Karen watched them both, aware of a silent dialog going on between them. Why, she wondered, did Fred have to come in here and do this to them?

"Be a sport, Pete, help me out. I'd do the same for you."

"Watling will raise hell—"

"He's off today. I'll square it with him in the morning."

Peter hesitated. Karen was near tears. "But it's Peter's first day off in three weeks. And we've made plans . . ."

Fred ignored her. "Pete, I wouldn't ask if I thought I could do it. Believe me, I've got a problem . . ."

"Okay." Peter looked at Karen apprehensively.

"Thanks, man." Fred staggered slightly and left.

Karen closed the door after him, wishing she had slammed it. Their beautiful day together—sacrificed to Fred Farley's irresponsibility.

"Drugs?" she asked. "Is that what it is? That son of a bitch."

Peter shrugged. "I doubt it. Maybe he took some Quaaludes to help bring him down. He was pretty high last night." He put on his robe.

"You're sure he isn't on something?" Karen asked, trying to control her anger.

"The only thing he's addicted to is making money. As fast as he can."

"And *he's* taken the Hippocratic oath?"

Peter came to her and folded her into his arms. He smoothed her hair at the temples. "He shouldn't be around patients when he's like this. Everyone, even the older doctors, makes mistakes as it is. Why increase the chance of making a really bad one?" He looked at her. "Be patient, love, these are tough days. In another month, they'll be over with."

Karen looked up into his face. "But we were going to have the whole day together. I had it all planned out. We were going to make love and then read the papers . . . and make love again and—"

Peter interrupted her with a long kiss. "Mmm." He began to move his hands all over her back and down over her hips. Karen began to respond, making low sounds and clinging to him. The passion of their lovemaking last night had ignited a fire in her that was still smoldering.

Suddenly, remembering what had brought on their tumultuous lovemaking, she pulled back.

She touched the faint bruise on her neck.

"I'm sorry," Peter said, "I'm afraid I got carried away."

She smiled in spite of herself; good grief, she hadn't had a love bite since her prep school days, when all the gangling young fellows tried to leave hickeys to mark their territory, the idiots. She regarded him quizzically. "And it's not even the full moon."

"You're not angry?"

"I'll just wear a turtleneck for the next couple of days."

He laughed; he enjoyed her humor. "Come on," he begged, "help me take my shower."

After last night, she had no reticence. They turned on the full-flow force and ventured into the tub as though wading in surf. They soaped each other industriously, but their movements grew sly and sensuous as they explored the hidden places in their bodies. The full force of the shower head left them breathless; the mist enveloped them, and their bodies glided away from each other. "Karen," he said, when he caught his breath, "let's try something—" He positioned her against the tiled wall but they slipped in the barrage of water.

He shook the drops off his face. "We'll try it another time," he said.

"Try what—?"

"It'll be a surprise. All I need—" he said, his brows lifting comically, "are strong arms, good balance—and a non-skid mat."

They both recalled the scene in *The Godfather* and their laughter was hysterical. They finally compromised on the soft tufted rug near the basin. They were convulsed with laughter and their love came quickly and deliciously.

When Peter was shaving, Karen came in and sat on the edge of the tub removing the polish from her toenails and watching him.

"What're you going to do today, now that I've ruined it for you?" he asked.

"I'd hardly call our little joust ruining my day." Her look was forgiving.

"I'm serious. What's on your revised agenda?"

"Well, I could go over to the station and work. Or I might visit Mady Lukas."

"That girl sits around going nowhere—when she's not off to Europe."

"Mady's all right," Karen said. "She just needs a man. It's funny, it seems it's always the women like Mady—the ones whose whole purpose in life is to get married—who have the most trouble finding someone."

"It's no accident," Peter said. "Women like that give off a sort of scent of desperation. The men sense it and feel threatened."

"Now Shulamit is different. She is really committed. She has a cause. It's too bad she's attracted to Fred."

"I'd have to agree. Shulamit's too good for him. I take it you liked her?"

"I admire her." Karen threw away the used cotton pad and opened up a bottle of tomato red polish. She began stroking the polish onto her nails. "I enjoy my work at the station, but sometimes I wish it were more—I don't know—humanitarian. I mean, your work is more directly helpful to people. It must be a wonderful feeling, to know you've healed someone."

"It is," he said, "but don't forget, I can't heal them all. Take that poor girl, Jenny Emerson, the one who was gang-raped—"

"Isn't she okay now?" Karen stopped and looked up.

"No, it's gone from bad to worse."

"How so?"

Peter put down the razor and rinsed out the basin. "When Dr. Monroe treated her, he gave her a shot to prevent pregnancy and gonorrhea. Everything looked good, considering the trauma. He let her go home. Four days later she woke up with chills and a temperature of a hundred and four. She had to be readmitted."

"Oh, God."

"She had PID—pelvic inflammatory disease and it got worse. There were abscesses in the pelvis and the infection spread into her bloodstream . . ."

"Is she all right now?"

"More or less—thanks to Dr. Monroe. But he had to take out her uterus."

"Peter, how awful!" Karen fell back against the tub. "She's only a child."

Peter began combing his hair, blowing it dry.

"Well, physically she's going to be okay. Dr. Monroe is arranging for her to have some sessions with a psychiatrist."

"They've never tracked down the ones who did it?"

"They suspect it's a gang from Belfort High—they've got some wild kids there—they may even be from one of the private schools."

"Maybe I could do a story on it," she said thoughtfully, "for my radio show."

"But will they use it on the air?"

"If it's done in good taste, yes. Rape is a hot topic. I wonder if they have statistics."

"Probably, in the news department." He looked at the clock radio and hastily pulled on his pants. "Karen, I hate to run off like this . . ."

"It's okay, I can find plenty to do." She lifted up her arms for him to pull her up. They held each other for a minute.

"I feel guilty about it. But you understand, Karen. Or do you?"

"I have no choice, darling," she said, kissing him. "But I'll survive."

Somehow, Peter thought, she will survive. She has what it takes. Just, please God, let her do it with me.

CHAPTER XVII

Radio station WBLF, like the Belfort *Chronicle,* was owned by the Seaforths, a family that had been in Belfort for two hundred years. But Seaforth blood was running thin; the last two Seaforth brothers were now in their eighties, and their few descendants showed no interest in their acquisitions, preferring to build themselves a lifestyle in the southwest United States. In order to save their vast holdings—two banks, the *Chronicle* and its print shop, the radio station and the land on the Point—the two brothers had recently sold the newspaper to a forward-thinking western conglomerate and set up the Seaforth Trust to conserve their money.

Seaforth political influence was still strong but with the sale of the newspaper, the brothers had to forfeit some of it. Although the new mayor had Republican leanings, he had been elected on an Independent ticket. He was an honest, forceful man, who owed nothing to the old politicians or their purportedly unsavory affiliations in Manhattan.

Karen got her job at the radio station on her own, although her family's friends, the Lukases, had suggested it. When she filled out her job application she gave Mr. Lukas as a reference. She wasn't about to refer her prospective employers to Delos Burke.

As a full member of the staff, she was responsible for certain news reports and had a block of evening time for human interest stories. She couldn't decide whether it was manager Joe Garfield's way of testing her or whether he was actually impressed with her work.

If Peter thought the hospital had a problem with Dr. Watling, she thought, he should meet Joe Garfield. A heavyset, middle-aged man, with dark hair slicked down over his skull, a waxy complexion and a pugnacious jaw, Joe had started years ago as an office boy for the *Chronicle*. He was a perfect company man. To forestall the owners' complaints about rising telephone bills Joe eavesdropped on employees and forbade personal calls. If members of the staff had to make one, they had to put their money in a box on the front desk with a sign: *Personal calls: please drop dime in box. Local calls only.*

At Christmas, gifts sent to the staff by suppliers and salesmen were automatically put on Joe Garfield's desk and taken to his home off the Post Road near Noroton where he lived with his wife and his mother. Some of the crew who had been to the house reported that his cellar looked like a cache during Prohibition. There was liquor of every kind, most of it still in holiday wrappings from previous years.

He was rigid about business routine. There was no socializing during office hours. They were there to work, not play.

"What's he afraid of?" Steve Duncan, one of the newsmen, asked. "That we'll discover his latest 'deal'?"

They were a motley crew, Karen's colleagues. The cast changed frequently, since few employees remained long at the station. Either Joe Garfield's nitpicking annoyed them or, after a few months' experience, they went on to better jobs. When one of the newscasters, Eugene Carey, was offered a berth in the news department at CBS in New York, the others were happy for him—and sorry for themselves. Before leaving, Eugene took Karen to lunch and advised her to learn what she could and then get out.

She was astonished at how much she had learned from Delos. Not only from the responsibilities he had given her, but from observing how he himself did things. Too bad she hadn't confined the learning experience to working hours . . .

As the weeks went by she began to find her niche at the station. She was friendly with the staff and began to feel like a member of the family. There were only two females besides herself: the receptionist, Mary Lou, a handsome black woman with beautiful long legs, and Babe, who was divorced with two daughters and a dozen babysitters who were never available at the right time. As for the men there was Artie, the gangling twenty-five-year-old, who sold air time for the station and spent most of his free hours trying to seduce Mary Lou on the worn-down leather sofa in the reception room; and Bert, the easygoing newscaster who liked to mix with bookies and small-time gangsters but saved every Friday night for Sabbath dinner with his mother.

She grew fond of them all. They opened a new world for her; a world of daily anxieties about money, about their jobs, their families. When Babe ran out of sitters and brought her daughters to the office, admonishing them to be quiet, Karen took the girls to lunch and tried to imagine herself in the role of a mother. It was difficult, she decided, playing referee while Annie and Beth fought over a last spoonful of ice cream. No wonder Babe got cranky and threw things.

Yes, Karen soon learned all of their problems. Money and sex were at the center of them. Everyone was always talking about getting laid, about not getting laid . . . Or complaining that their salaries weren't keeping pace with inflation.

Money, Karen thought—Peter and I have never discussed money. Or how to share bills. She knew certain bills should be split down the middle, and other bills should be paid by each of them. She had resolved that first day to discuss these matters with Peter, but in the five weeks they had been living together, she hadn't given them another thought. Peter paid Mrs. Thalberg directly for their room and the meals they shared with her. Karen knew Mrs. Thalberg refused to accept any money for occasional snacks. So, without consulting Peter, she had gone to Tiffany's and bought her a delicate gold chain, set at intervals with tiny diamonds. Peter whistled when he saw it.

"How much did you spend?" he asked.

It wasn't disapproval in his voice, it was anxiety.

"Under five hundred dollars," she said.

"Good God, Karen! A hundred-dollar gift—even fifty—would have been plenty."

"You don't get much at Tiffany's for that," she said, "and this suits her so well. She loves chains, you know . . ."

He made no further comment, but asked for the bill.

"It won't come in until after the first of the month," she said.

"Okay. Be sure to give it to me then." His voice was grim.

She had bought the necklace impulsively, giving the salesclerk her mother's name—Tiffany's did not issue charge cards. She was accustomed to using her mother's charge accounts and it hadn't occurred to her that it might no longer be appropriate now that she was on her own and living with Peter.

At the end of the week, on payday, she decided to speak to Peter. Sharing, she hoped, would in some way cement their relationship, give it stability.

Peter had the afternoon and evening off. They went out for dinner, Peter at the wheel of her station wagon. Turning off the thruway, he headed for the shore. They had discovered a small seafood restaurant where the fish was fresh, the salad crisp and the desserts superb. Peter loved the house specialty, deep-dish apple pie with a hunk of cheddar cheese.

Karen kept her thoughts to herself all through dinner, and only when Peter had finished his second cup of coffee and sat back comfortably did she bring up what was on her mind.

"Peter, we've never talked about finances—" She was blushing in spite of her desire to be businesslike. "I mean—well, I hear so much about money at the radio station—everybody's short and worried about inflation and not earning enough to meet expenses . . ." She hesitated, then took the plunge. "Mrs. Thalberg once told me what your salary is—thirteen-five a year—and I earn two hundred a week. Now shouldn't we discuss our budget—you know, income versus expenses and all that?"

She was so earnest that he grinned. Although he had observed, from the beginning, her rich girl's naïveté about money, it was not until she had bought the necklace for Mrs. Thalberg that he'd realized just how mixed up she was about the value of a dollar. And now here she was, trying to show him how practical she could be.

"Sure, Karen," he said indulgently. "What would you like to know?"

"Well," she said, "can we make it, with our combined salaries?"

"It depends. If we continue living with Mrs. Thalberg, I think we probably could. If we decide to move—say we take an apartment—we won't find anything for less money. And then we'd have electricity, telephone and other expenses . . ."

"As well as an office for you—?"

"Right."

"Have you decided what you're going to do about your practice?"

"I'd like to stay in Belfort, at least for the first few years. I've gotten to like it here. How do you feel about it?"

"I like it, too." She really did. Her work at the radio station and participation in the hospital auxiliary gave her a sense of belonging to the community.

"Dr. Stone is renovating a house and turning it into a medical complex. I was thinking of taking one of the suites. The place isn't too far from the hospital."

"Will it be expensive to set up?"

"Yes. It would be a big investment."

"How will you manage?" An idea was forming in her mind.

"I'm not sure yet. My father will help if I need it—"

"Peter—" she broke in impulsively, "would you let me help? I mean, well—under the circumstances—" Her elbows were on the table, her face across from his, earnest, coaxing. "My grandfather left me some money that I've never used. I mean, it's just lying there, collecting dividends. It would be a privilege to do it—"

"Do you know what it takes to furnish an office?" He took her hands in his and by the pressure she knew he was deeply touched. "Let's not try to settle it all tonight, Karen. I'll manage.

"Meanwhile," he suggested, "let's keep on as before. I'll take care of the rent, and so forth. You can pay for your clothes, the car, books, records, whatever little luxuries you want."

Karen thought he sounded like a regular husband, and she was pleased. But then—she had doubts—maybe he didn't want to get further involved. Maybe he just didn't want to feel obligated to her financially, in case he should leave her.

Would she ever find out, she wondered, perplexed; what was really going on in the depths of his mind?

In what little time they had together, Karen and Peter found plenty to share, especially after she began preparing her weekly health care series for the radio station.

She found her work more absorbing as she realized how much there was to learn. With Peter's encouragement and instruction she tried to develop a program that not only enlightened listeners about recent discoveries in research, but also made people aware of the medical world from the viewpoint of the doctor and the hospital.

For example, patients took it for granted that everything that happened when they checked into a hospital was done automatically. But behind the scenes it was as structured as any production plant. And certainly it was cleaner. They also didn't know what stiff accreditation requirements hospitals had to meet and that hospitals had to maintain the highest of standards professionally, legally and ethically, in order to retain their accreditation. She wanted to make listeners aware of everything that went on in a hospital and give them medical advice in layman's terms. For example, few people knew the ugly facts about rape, she reflected. Before Peter had told her about Jenny Emerson she'd really had no idea . . . The victims and their families understandably shunned publicity and the most sordid details rarely appeared in the media. Perhaps if she did a series on the rape crisis center . . . Karen thought about it for a long time. Was she up to doing the research—learning about the grisly subject? She knew she would do it eventually, but decided to wait until her series was established and she had a loyal audience.

Whenever she thought of the challenges facing Peter she became more tolerant of his dedication, his anxieties, his respectful awe of the men in their fields.

There was little she could do now until his graduation except be loving and supportive. Then she'd see. . . .

CHAPTER XVIII

Karen's first show to be broadcast was a taped interview of Belfort's most respected physicians: Dr. Macray and Dr. Stone.

They sat around the long table in Studio A with microphones in front of them. The glass pane separated them from the announcer whom Karen watched intently. It wasn't live but she was nervous; so much depended on this effort. If she succeeded, it meant the station would commit itself to the series, every Wednesday evening. But if the pilot bombed, the series would be killed.

She played with the clipboard beside her and rifled through her notes. She looked at Dr. Macray and Dr. Stone, who seemed relaxed and comfortable.

Peter had primed her on questions. "Won't they resent them?" she had asked him anxiously.

"Dr. Macray is blunt and outspoken. So is Dr. Stone, provided you ask the right questions. When he first came here about seven or eight years ago, he aroused a lot of antagonism from the profession because he was so candid and knew so much about cardiology. Don't worry about them. I think you can get a good dialog going."

Peter supported her; he was enormously pleased she had found work that interested her. The staff at the radio station was impressed with her initiative. She had already planned a number of informal, behind-the-scenes kind of interviews, focusing primarily on medicine.

Dr. Macray sat opposite her. He was an eminence, she thought, even though he was wearing slacks and a sweater. That thick shock of white hair, falling over his forehead, gave him the look of an eagle. If he were ten years younger, she thought, I could really fall for him . . .

Dr. Stone was more dressed up than Dr. Macray. He wore a white shirt with a starched collar and a red and blue rep-striped tie carefully knotted under a Calvin Klein jacket that set off his spare frame. He was probably twenty years younger than Dr. John Paul; his smooth-shaven face was mildly attractive, his smile ingratiating. Peter said he was a brilliant cardiologist; he'd performed angiograms on a number of outstanding business and political leaders.

If only they'll both speak frankly, she prayed. It was going to be up to her to keep the dialog flowing.

The engineer motioned to her that the tape was rolling. After the introduction, she began: "Why are people mad at doctors?"

Dr. Macray's bright blue eyes were amused. "Because they think we make too much money."

"That's true," said Dr. Stone. "People used to have tremendous respect for their physicians. Now, many are upset by what they consider medicine's mercenary attitude. They'd like the good father image back again, the bedside comforter who charges five bucks a house call."

"Is there any way that image can be restored?" Leery of sounding too solemn she added, "Not the five-dollar house call, of course, but the rest of it."

The ploy worked; Dr. Stone chuckled. "I'm afraid not," he said. "Times have changed. And the money factor is at the root of the problem. People get mad when they read that today physicians have the highest income in the country."

Dr. John Paul rubbed his sunburned cheek. "Come to think of it, I don't blame them."

"I've talked to a few people," Karen said. "What seems to bother them most is the lack of communication between them and their doctors. One woman said that her doctor didn't listen to her problems, he was too busy. There was an office full of patients waiting and telephones were ringing. She said that during the fifteen minutes allotted to her, he wasn't paying attention to her. She thought that since he wasn't listening, his treatment might be ineffective—"

"Karen," Dr. Macray said patiently, "doctors, especially the older ones, are not necessarily equipped to do the counseling some patients require. Many patients come in for reassurance rather than purely physical problems."

Dr. Stone leaned forward. "A successful physician sees between twenty-five and thirty patients a day. His average day, not counting hospital rounds and nursing home visits, stretches to twelve hours, sometimes longer if there is an emergency—and there are plenty of them. He studies the x-rays with the radiologist. He waits for the report of the pathologist—"

Dr. Macray piped in. "It's true that he spends less time with the patients but with the development of so many new tests, he takes much better care of them."

"I understand the surgeon gets the most respect," Karen said. "There's something magical about the surgeon.

"Of course," she went on, "there are more procedures in surgery than in general practice—" she hesitated, wondering if she were treading on sensitive ground—"so naturally surgeons make a great deal more money in less time."

"Except for the time they give the clinics," Dr. Macray chided her.

"Right. But would you agree that medicine is big business today?"

Dr. Stone said flatly, "There are no physicians listed on the New York stock exchange."

"But physicians are heavy investors in those stocks." That comment had come from Fred Farley, who had goaded her into asking some prickly questions. "What do you think will happen if we have national health?"

"The same thing that happened in England," Dr. Stone said dryly. "The doctors will charge less and the patient will get less for his money."

Two days later, on the Thursday before Memorial Day, Karen got a telephone call from her father. He was back from London; his reports had been delivered to Washington and he was free for several days. He invited Karen to come into the city for lunch.

"I'd love to," she replied. "I'll arrange for someone at the station to cover for me."

When she heard his voice, patient and precise, she realized how much she had missed him in spite of the excitement and exhilaration of living with Peter.

She expected to meet him at home, but he suggested his club, which was near the Museum of Modern Art. She was surprised but not uneasy. Perhaps he was planning something special for her mother's birthday in two weeks. They had such a good marriage; no wonder he wanted as much for their only child.

She left her car in the Belfort train station parking lot and caught an express to Grand Central, then dashed uptown ten blocks. Her father was waiting for her in the lounge.

"Daddy!" There was such joy in her voice. Wasn't it strange that since she had moved in with Peter, she was more relaxed with her father, less on the defensive, less apprehensive of his rare criticism. "It's so good to see you."

Although they were almost the same height, there was an aura of stature and authority about her father. His thick hair reminded her of Dr. Macray's, except that his was gray. He gave Karen a quick peck on the cheek; his expression was solemn. There's nothing to worry about, she told herself, he just wants to see me because it's been so long . . .

"You're looking well, Karen."

"I'm very happy, dad."

They followed the maître d' to a secluded banquette; Karen sat next to her father so they could talk more easily. She noted gratefully that his face had a healthy glow instead of the red flush that had bothered him last year. She knew her mother was concerned about his blood pressure, but she decided not to ask him about it.

"You look fit," she said. "You've trimmed down."

"Yes. I made a point of walking every day between meetings."

"I hope everything went well."

She could see him flush under his tan. "There was a lot of talk and many problems but no solutions." He shook off the suggestion of anxiety. "Your mother says you haven't been in town very much."

"No, I have a job. It's demanding, but I love it." She described her duties and her friends on the staff, exaggerating their eccentricities to amuse him. She added that she kept in touch with her mother and with her grandmother by telephone. Although Grandmother Wickersham still knew nothing of the arrangement, she did know that Karen was living and working in Belfort and dating a young physician there.

"Grandmother has asked us up to the country several times. But Peter can never get the time off. It'll be easier when . . ." she was floundering, "he graduates. He'll have some time while he's setting up his practice, and we'll definitely drive down to see her."

He kept their talk light until she finished her salad and the waiter cleared the table.

"Honey, are you really happy?"

"Very, dad."

"You look happy—but I was afraid you were looking that way just for me."

"No. As a matter of fact, I'm happier—or shall I say more content —every day."

"Have you and Peter talked about marriage?"

She laughed. "Daddy, isn't the bride the last to know?" Then she shrugged. "Sorry, I was trying to be funny. No matter what happens to Peter and me, it's been good, and I'll always be grateful to him. He came into my life when I needed someone like him. He's good for me . . ."

Her father covered her hand with his and she was aware of his affection, even his support, which, she suspected, was hard for him to offer her under the circumstances.

"Well, Karen, your mother and I respect your feelings, even though they cause us concern. But there are practical matters that have to be taken care of. Your grandfather left you provided for— and you will have more after your grandmother's death. Her will gives you the country house, her town apartment, a trust fund. We can't afford to be casual about your link with Peter Norris. We've got to avoid any legal problems."

She looked down, too troubled to meet his gaze. He was thinking of her welfare, of her future, but she hated it. Their discussion of money seemed sordid—like those dreadful Hollywood separations in which the unmarried woman asked for a split in community property.

"If my bluntness offends you, Karen, look at it this way: the whole business of living together without legal ties is so recent that the laws are open to all kinds of interpretations. You shouldn't have anything in joint ownership that might later cause disputes. It is especially true in the case of a doctor. If he's sued for malpractice and your funds are tied up with his, you're apt to lose a good deal of money if he loses the case. And malpractice suits aren't small potatoes these days—they run into millions."

He was talking sense but she found his words distasteful and knew she couldn't possibly discuss it with Peter.

"There are certain things you must do . . . Are you planning to buy a house?"

"We hadn't thought of it," she said. "But I suppose it might be a good idea."

"Before you buy any property, let our lawyers check every detail. I am very serious about this, Karen. Don't co-sign any notes. Don't file your income tax together, file a separate return. Keep a record of what he buys and what belongs to you—"

"It sounds so—so mercenary . . ."

"It's for your own good. Peter seems like a decent young man, his intentions may be the very best, but, honey, listen to your father: a young lady in your position—especially with your financial expectations—can't be too careful."

Listlessly she stirred her coffee. It was all so degrading. She knew it would be simpler to get married. Would she be able to discuss *that* with Peter?

CHAPTER XIX

As her health care series flourished and as she felt herself drawn more and more into the medical community through her participation in the auxiliary, Karen felt the bond between herself and Peter become tighter, closer. But as she listened to Maureen Macray reminisce about her experiences as John Paul's office nurse—experiences they shared together—Karen thought wistfully, I wish Peter and I could take part in each other's lives like that. Not that she wanted to be Peter's office nurse—or a nurse at all, for that matter—but if only occasionally she and Peter could move in the same orbit, not merely being together but working in the same channel, toward a common goal . . . She wanted her own career but she wanted, too, to have some overlap between her sphere and Peter's, a common ground to meet on and look back on together . . .

One Tuesday, in early June, Karen had just that opportunity. Peter had the afternoon and evening off and suggested they have dinner in a small family-style restaurant just beyond the newly revitalized main section of town. It had been recommended to him by one of the other residents.

They had chicken salad, perfect for the hot steamy night. As they left the restaurant, Peter told her about another young doctor's discovery—George's Confectionery Shop—an old-fashioned ice cream parlor that had homemade ice cream.

A frozen yogurt was enough for her, but she enjoyed watching Peter dig into his elaborate sundae. Watching Peter now, she thought, he doesn't let death and disease get to him, he still has the zest for life and its small pleasures. She felt a gentle warmth radiate through her body.

Before he paid the check, he ordered a pint of chocolate ice cream to take out. "You're planning on seconds?" Karen teased.

He said they were going to visit someone; he hoped she wouldn't mind. In the soft pale glow of the street lamps, he guided her away from the modern buildings to an ill-lit quiet street of old houses.

They stopped in front of a shingle house that looked shabby and unkempt. Peter wanted to visit the elderly woman who lived there, because he was worried about her. She'd been treated for a fractured wrist and was discharged before she could take care of herself; the Medicare people weren't paying her for any more hospital days. Presumably the woman's needs were being taken care of. The hospital and the health agencies worked with a patient to see that he or she had post-hospital care and wasn't sent home without some provision for additional care. But it didn't always work.

"I just want to make sure there's somebody looking after her," Peter told Karen. He'd been here before.

They climbed the high steps to the porch and he looked at the names on the bell. When he found Mrs. Brand's, Peter rang and the door clicked and released its lock. Then he knocked on the first upstairs door and said, "Mrs. Brand, it's Dr. Norris . . ." After a moment, the door opened.

She was small and wrinkled, her hair in two white braids, an Indian blanket over her shoulders; her left arm fitted into the sleeve of her dress but her right arm was in a sling.

"Oh, Dr. Norris . . ."

"How are you feeling?" he asked.

"Better, thanks, better. The pain pills are helping." She didn't know whether to ask them in or not. Peter introduced Karen. "This is my Karen," he said, which Karen thought was both graceful and sweet. She would have to remember it when they finally got up to see Grandmother Wickersham.

"We brought you some dessert." Peter held out the package.

The lines on the woman's cheeks creased with pleasure. She stood back to let them enter. It was a small room filled with bric-a-brac—figurines, pill boxes, bud vases—the things that mattered to her. Her bed, by the window, was unmade, and in the small sink, dishes were stacked. Peter walked over to the pine cupboard, took out a soup plate, scooped out the ice cream and brought it over to her. She was still standing by the door as if she were surprised by the visit, perhaps afraid to show her gratitude. Or reluctant to reveal her poverty to strangers.

"Sit down, Mrs. Brand." Peter arranged the Morris chair with a pillow but she shook her head.

"I can't get out of it with one hand," she explained, easing herself into a straightbacked chair.

Peter asked if anyone had been in to see her. She was puzzled, since she didn't expect anyone.

"How will you manage with food?" he asked.

She nodded to a box of crackers and a container of milk by the sink. "My landlord brought me a few things today."

"What about Meals-on-Wheels?" Peter asked.

"I can't afford to pay for them, and I won't take them without paying . . ."

"But there's a sliding scale so you just pay what you can afford."

She shook her head, cradling the soup dish in her lap as she licked her spoon. Karen thought, shocked, she's probably starved. We should have brought something more nourishing.

Mrs. Brand seemed a little startled by their visit, but became more animated after finishing the ice cream. She said that she'd try to manage but was clumsy with one hand doing the work of two.

"What can we do to help?" Karen said. "How would it be if I came by tomorrow and did some shopping for you?"

"Oh, I don't want to bother you. The doctor was so kind to me at the hospital . . ."

"Tell me what you need," Karen said. "I'll pick it up at the market first thing in the morning."

She took down a list despite Mrs. Brand's reluctance, and when the woman offered her money, Karen said, "Let's see how much it will cost."

Once they were out on the street again and walking back to the parking lot, Karen said, "Peter, it's unbelievable. It's inhuman. She shouldn't be allowed to stay in that hole. She needs to be looked after."

Peter shook his head; Karen apparently thought Mrs. Brand was an isolated case. "Karen," he said, "there are hundreds like her, old and poor, even in affluent towns like Belfort. The hospital is too crowded. The social services are too busy and the government agencies are swamped. It's an enormous problem."

"We've got to do something. Can't we talk to Sheila Ryan when we get home?"

Her magnanimous feelings had dimmed. As Peter drove home, Karen sat beside him frowning, chewing on the nail of her forefinger.

She's learning how the other half lives, Peter thought, and it's painful. But he loved her all the more for her willingness to face it.

He swung the car into the driveway, parked it in the rear and switched off the motor. In the backyard, Sheila and Fred were sitting in chairs, having a late evening talk. Morning glories and ivy climbed on the lamp posts and torches were burning to keep the bugs away. The faint scent of citronella mingled with the flowering bushes to give the air a sweet smell. On the round iron table nearby was a pitcher filled with iced tea.

Mrs. Thalberg was coming out of the kitchen, carrying a plate of sandwiches and cakes covered with a cheesecloth protector.

"We're just having a snack. Come, join us."

Karen and Peter walked up toward the group; Peter pulled a couple of wicker chairs from the shadows for Mrs. Thalberg and Karen, and he sat down on the mat beside Fred. In her T-shirt and shorts, her face scrubbed and moist with the humidity, Sheila looked younger than she did when she was on duty. She had a youthful Irish face, a pert uptilted nose and a small mouth. Stretched out on the chaise longue, she looked more like a coed relaxing on a college vacation than a social worker who daily faced what Peter had called a tidal wave of misery.

Peter told them what they had just done. Fred sat up. Except for khaki shorts and running shoes, he was naked. Karen's glance took in his strong wiry body, his darkly hairy chest. She thought, surprised, he's got a good physique—it's only his posture that gives him that sort of misshapen look.

"So Peter gave you a view of how America lives," he said sardonically. "How did you like it, Karen?"

"It was appalling." Karen turned to Sheila. She had not taken any particular interest in Sheila before. But now she recalled Peter's respect for her ability as a social worker. She also remembered Peter's saying that Sheila, although about five years older than Fred, was a good influence on him. He listened to her.

"That poor old woman should not be left alone," Karen appealed to Sheila. "You should have seen how she ate the ice cream we brought—as though it would be her last meal for days. And her arm in a sling . . . Can't you do anything?"

Sheila said patiently that she'd tried to place Mrs. Brand in a convalescent home until her wrist healed, but there simply were no beds. They couldn't keep her in the hospital because Medicare didn't think she needed that level of care.

Karen pursued it: wasn't there some church group that could help?

Sheila said that she had contacted the home care agency and in a couple of days, a nurse from there would be sent to evaluate Mrs. Brand's condition.

"And what happens to the poor woman tomorrow?" Karen asked.

"Tell Karen what the home care agency is," Fred suggested. "Before she gets on her soapbox."

Sheila explained that the home care agency employed people with certain skills. There were nurses where professional nursing was required. There were homemakers who took care of a family if the mother was ill. And there were handymen to do the heavier chores. The agency was especially sensitive to the indigent patient who might be deprived of care for lack of money.

"United Way allocations provide some of the support," Sheila said.

"You have to understand," Fred put in, "that the home care people are already swamped with cases . . ."

"Too many needy people, not enough people to help out," Mrs. Thalberg said, remembering how often her late husband had fought with Medicare for better coverage. "And if the hospital keeps a patient past the discharge date Medicare fines them."

"And most of the time, we have no place to send them," Sheila added. "It's a sad fact of life."

Karen was silent, remembering how Mrs. Thalberg had spoken to her of the plight of widows like Mrs. Brand the day she had moved in with Peter. How callow, how self-righteous she must have sounded just now—pleading with people who knew the situation only too well and had been trying to rectify it long before she had come on the scene. Well, from now on she would do something too.

Karen asked no more questions. The following morning, however, before going to work, she asked Mrs. Thalberg about which were the best supermarkets to go to and what foods were easy to prepare.

Then she went shopping for foods that Mrs. Brand could prepare single-handedly: cottage cheese, yogurt, whole wheat bread, orange juice, eggs. She went on to the radio station and put them in the refrigerator.

Once she finished writing her nightly report, she carried the armload of groceries out to her car, drove to a bookstore that carried a book about nutrition for the handicapped and then on to Mrs. Brand's house. The elderly woman was waiting for her. "You didn't forget," she said, almost unbelieving.

"Of course not." Karen bustled around, feeling useful and enjoying the woman's appreciative comments.

"Look, Mrs. Brand," she said, "this is how to make one hand do all the work." She showed her how to open a carton of milk, by using the fork in one hand to pry up the flaps and pull out the center spout. How to light the gas range by striking a match on a piece of sandpaper stuck to the back wall, then laying the match against the burner and turning on the gas. How to slice meat and vegetables by covering the underside of a cutting board with hobnail rubber to keep it steady. The book was full of helpful hints: Karen spent another hour explaining how to survive until home care took over.

Then Karen helped Mrs. Brand get ready for bed, brushing and rebraiding the once thick and lovely white hair. After washing herself, with Karen's help, Mrs. Brand eased herself onto her narrow bed and lay there, as Karen tucked in the sheets, with pillows piled high against her shoulders. Karen washed the plate, mug and saucer and stopped there. "You think you can manage until Miss Ryan gets someone to look after you?" Karen asked.

"Yes, yes . . . and bless you for your kindness."

Karen left, feeling great. When Peter came home, she reported to him that their patient was doing well. He leaned down and kissed her.

"My own lady bountiful," he said. "Or is it lady beautiful?"

Karen stuck out her tongue; he reached out and pulled her hair lightly, which started a playful wrestling match that ended on the bed.

She's learning about my world, Peter thought as Karen nestled against his chest. She's trying to put down roots here.

Did that mean that she had recovered from Delos Burke?

The next day the news director of the radio station reminded Karen about her broadcast on rape.

"I'm working on it," she said vaguely and offered no more information.

The truth was that she was squeamish about the project. She had visited the rape crisis center and had talked to the director, Miss Sandowsky, who had offered to arrange for Karen to interview some rape victims, but after reading the case histories, Karen had backed off. Wasn't it bad enough, she told herself, that these women had been physically violated. How could she violate their privacy as well, forcing up painful memories? But as she looked over her notes, she realized she needed the kind of immediacy that could only be obtained by talking to the rape victims. Maybe she couldn't help these women, but didn't she owe it to other women to publicize the issue?

Finally, in June, just before the family practice residents graduated, Karen made another appointment with Miss Sandowsky. The office was located in a small building adjacent to the social security offices. It was a service funded by the U.S. Department of Justice and provided a 24-hour-a-day hot line. Several women were working in the small office, with a few desks, chairs and filing cabinets and a stack of rape warning posters waiting to be distributed. The director, a stocky middle-aged woman in a dark pants suit and a white blouse, came to meet Karen. Her gray hair, sprinkled with the remains of a frosting job, was brushed off her round pleasant features, made even more anonymous by her gilt-rimmed glasses.

She explained, as Karen took the seat beside her desk, that the staff provided emotional and legal counseling to rape victims.

"Not enough come to us," she added. "They've been brainwashed that assault is an embarrassment to their family and friends rather than a crushing outrage.

"We have women counselors to help victims who are mature women, child psychologists to counsel the very young victims and male counselors to advise husbands, fathers, boyfriends of victims. And we help in medical and legal procedures."

Miss Sandowsky went on, explaining that most rape victims were young women ranging in age from sixteen to twenty-four. That the most dangerous hours for a woman alone were between six P.M. and midnight, when most rapists wander through streets or parking lots or parks looking for a potential victim.

Then Miss Sandowsky led Karen to a small private office where one of the victims who had volunteered to talk to Karen was waiting. The rape had occurred six months ago, Miss Sandowsky explained, but the girl was still in therapy, working out the feelings of humiliation, anger and fear brought on by the assault.

The young girl who was introduced to Karen as Jane Smith was seventeen years old. She worked alone in a coffee shop from six P.M. until midnight, when her father picked her up and drove her home. She wasn't afraid because there was an all-night gas station open across the street. At eleven-thirty one Thursday night in May, two young fellows came in and ordered donuts and coffee to go. They looked pleasant, clean-cut, in T-shirts and jeans. When she handed them their order, they grabbed her arm and forced her outside into their car. When she struggled, they slapped her into silence. They had her wedged between them on the front seat and both took turns mauling her with their hands, as they sped toward the New York border. Since it was late there was little traffic. They reached a valley just before the curving road climbed and dipped, then turned off and parked off the road in a hollow beneath sloping hills. They dragged her out of the car, warning her to be quiet or they'd gag her, made obscene gestures to show her what they'd gag her with. Then they dropped an old blanket on the rough ground, stripped her of her apron, her yellow uniform, her panties and bra. They repeatedly raped her and beat her until she was nearly unconscious. Then she heard them discuss how to get rid of her . . . whether to abandon her there in the woods or drop her on the road. She blacked out then. When she came to, she realized they had thrown her on the floor of the back seat. At the outskirts of Belfort, they stopped the car on a lonely stretch of highway, dumped her out and threatened to come back to the donut shop and kill her if she ever told. She was damn lucky, they said, that they were good guys.

A police car patrolling the highway an hour later found her, mute and comatose, and took her to the hospital. Her father had come for her at midnight, and when he couldn't find her and saw the open door of the shop, he called the police. They didn't take the complaint seriously until they found her, bruised, bleeding and in a state of shock.

Now she sat opposite Karen, a thin teenager, her brown hair pulled back in a pony tail fastened by a rubber band; her plain young face robbed of its freshness. It was a haunted face, torn by grief and cold, maniacal anger.

"When he saw me in the hospital, my own father read the riot act to me," she said tonelessly. "He said if I hadn't teased the fellows, it wouldn't have happened. He said I deserved it; he said all girls were cockteasers."

Karen was shocked. She couldn't bear to interview any more of the victims; she was nauseous, overcome by revulsion and a sense of ineffective empathy. Miss Sandowsky understood her reaction. It was what they all experienced, she said.

"Any woman who has gone through this shattering experience," Miss Sandowsky added, "needs immediate psychological counseling. Because the injury she's suffered bodily strikes deep into her emotions, she often becomes disorganized and goes into shock. Her feelings may include fear, guilt, self-pity and a deep-rooted anger. Before she comes to terms with what happened to her, she may become acutely depressed, with periods of extreme withdrawal.

"The trauma may be compounded by the way she's treated by the police, the doctor, even her family. It can affect the rest of her life . . ."

She told Karen of several more instances but when it came to stories of young children who were victims of molesters—often men within their own family—Karen found she could bear no more.

She wrote the script for her broadcast when she was alone at home, while Peter was on duty at the hospital.

She didn't have any guests on the program; not even physicians or members of the crisis center staff. She used a case-history approach, then she ended with a summary she'd developed after she had talked with Dr. Monroe, the gynecologist.

"It's a misconception to think that rape is primarily for sexual gratification," she said. "The offender uses it to gratify other needs. He uses sex to punish women in general, for the women who have offended, rejected or humiliated him.

"He has a vicious need to wound his victim so he lets out his rage at the woman on hand.

"Sometimes he wants to tie up the victim, to control her. This makes him feel virile and powerful. When he assaults his victim, he feels he is proving his manhood."

When she got off the air, she wept with relief and with exhaustion. She had spent so much time on the project and had relived so many victims' experiences with them.

The broadcast generated calls of praise and calls of outrage. And obscene letters to Karen, most of them unsigned.

Women in politics thanked her; Sheila Ryan commented that the program should be helpful, since it also included suggestions on how to avoid rape.

The rape crisis center announced the sponsorship of a clinic to teach women self-defense and the town of Belfort began making plans for a rape awareness week.

Yet when it was over, all Karen could think of was the voice of a victim who'd called her anonymously to thank her, adding, "I wish I could kill him! I hate all men! I don't feel safe with them anymore!"

But in the end, Karen felt a sense of accomplishment, not entirely because Peter was so proud.

CHAPTER XX

The Stone family was gathering for breakfast in the modern kitchen that was Silvie's joy, second only to her elegant bathroom. The gathering of the clan was in itself unusual, for the Stones seldom ate together as a family. Since Silvie no longer prepared even toast and coffee for Malcolm, he usually had breakfast in the hospital cafeteria. Besides, the women behind the counters were solid, motherly types who loved to pamper the physicians. Whenever Malcolm passed through the line, ready to settle for juice, a muffin and coffee, the good ladies looked upset. "Is that all, doctor? A poached egg, maybe? Some crisp bacon?" So he often expanded the order and carried a full tray, under their benevolent eyes, to the cashier. The odd thing was that even though his appetite was dull in the morning, he ate the food and enjoyed it. He reflected that he liked being pampered and coddled. That he needed the stroking he sometimes withheld from his patients.

This morning, however, it was Silvie who had prepared ham

(which she knew he didn't like), eggs, toast and coffee. After serving him and the children she moved around the kitchen in her flowered housecoat searching for fingerprints on the stove and the refrigerator, attacking the smudges with cleanser and a damp sponge. Silvie was a compulsive housekeeper, but she was proud of it. From what she had cautiously revealed about her childhood, Malcolm gathered that her mother had been a poor housekeeper.

"Barbara," he ventured, turning to his daughter, "when is your graduation?"

"Oh, in about ten days."

"Are you excited about it?" Try to communicate with her, Malcolm thought, these moments are rare. "About graduation week and all that?"

"It's a lot of shit," Barbara replied, her voice filled with disgust. "There's the father-daughter baseball game, then the trustees' dinner for the seniors, then the class play, the picnic supper, you name it. Count me out!"

Silvie put the sponge down. She wiped her hands and came over and stood between her daughter and Norman, who was busy eating his breakfast and deliberately abstaining from the incipient explosion. Silvie glared at her husband and daughter. You see what being even half Jewish has done to Barbara. She doesn't belong—outcasts always rebel and make fun of the things they'd like to participate in.

None of Silvie's efforts to erase the Jewish part of her daughter's pedigree had been effective. High Episcopalian church services, confirmation classes, none of it had helped. It would be easier for Norman, with his fair coloring, his narrow bones and his quiet manners. He would make it in the world Silvie had chosen for him. Girls were a drain on the market, but a young man like Norman, with a prep school background and a good college—Silvie would settle for Princeton or Brown if he were turned down by Harvard and Yale—why, the world of power and influence would be within his grasp. If only he were a bit more aggressive . . .

"What are your plans for the future?" Malcolm directed himself at Barbara but looked at his wife. He had heard Silvie's complaints about how prejudiced the Locust Ryse teachers were; they had done nothing to help Barbara get into a good college. Silvie was disenchanted with them, particularly the headmistress, who was a double-edged snob if ever Silvie saw one. On the other hand, Silvie was quick to cut Malcolm with her insistence that Barbara be sent to secretarial school.

"Tell your father your plans," Silvie mocked her daughter, "that's why I asked him to stay and have breakfast with you. That's more time than he's given you in the four years you've been at Locust Ryse. I don't expect him to play in the father-daughter baseball game at commencement. Not when he has so many hearts to heal. But now that your future is upon us, Barbara, tell him what you'd like to do. Go on, *tell him*."

"I'd like to be a model," Barbara said. Her dark smoldering eyes defied them to laugh at her.

"A model!" her mother said. "With your figure, your face?" Silvie's brittle laughter filled the room.

"She could lose weight." Malcolm was trying to be circumspect. He did not want to demolish Barbara's fantasies but he did not want to give her false hopes. Even he, her father, realized what an unrealistic career she had chosen. Silvie should have taken charge of her diet and exercise long before this. Whatever he said would only set up another barrage of recriminations. He felt his way cautiously, "Are there any schools for models?"

"Do you want her to be the laughing stock of Belfort? Even after a year of courses, they'd still use her 'after' picture as the 'before' one."

"Silvie!" Malcolm countered.

Barbara, usually quick to meet her mother's attacks with defiance or truculent silence, blanched at her mother's barb. Her young face crumpled with pain; Malcolm could see the tears welling in her eyes as she pressed her lips together stoically.

It's my fault, he thought, stricken with guilt. If I hadn't copped out on her so many times, Silvie wouldn't be so shrewish. This child, with her deep dark eyes, her dark curly hair, her plump curves that would, one day, be seductive—was his daughter. It wasn't that he'd meant to treat her shabbily. He just had no time to spend with her; he was expanding his profession, and all of his thoughts went to his peers, to the older physicians who were his idols, and to his patients.

Not that he had given Norman more, but somehow he was less

worried about his son. A boy can always make his way in life. And a rich father helps.

"We'll talk about your plans this weekend," he promised Barbara, who excused herself and walked out of the kitchen. Malcolm looked to Norman, who was concentrating on a schoolbook. Too bad he wore glasses; Malcolm wondered if contact lenses were the answer. Perhaps then the kid would be more athletic.

"What about you, Norman?"

Before the boy could answer, Silvie said, "I told you, Mal. He's going to stay here all summer. A group of the Regent boys are staying home. They'll swim and picnic at each other's houses, go on one-day field trips, see some of the sights . . ."

Norman seemed content to let her answer for him. With a nervous gesture, he pushed the rim of his glasses up on the bridge of his small blunt nose. He is handsome, Malcolm thought. Nobody would take me for his father.

Norman excused himself and disappeared. Silvie looked at his retreating figure with deep affection.

"I'm glad you did your duty for a change," she said. "Now you see what I'm up against."

"Be patient with her, she'll grow out of it. Your taunts don't help any, Sil."

Silvie snorted with anger. Malcolm decided not to tell her that his reason for staying home had nothing to do with the kids. He was keyed up, bursting with anticipation, the way he used to feel when he was living at home and going to medical school. Whenever something big happened to him, he had to share it with his mother. He imagined her standing beside him in the big sunny kitchen, her head cocked, nodding approval even before he finished talking. She had such faith in him; even before he had finished medical school she had had faith.

Silvie was talking to him about a house she wanted to buy. It was to be remodeled and would be designated a landmark.

"Well, what do you say, Malcolm? Will you give me the money? I've checked with Jack and he thinks it's a great investment . . ."

He wasn't listening, but he agreed just to get her off his back. Maybe she'd be more amenable . . .

He was still far away. He was sorely tempted to call his mother.

But if he varied from his weekly Sunday morning call she might think there was a crisis . . .

"Whatever you do, don't for Pete's sake ask your mother," Silvie said. God, Malcolm thought, her instincts were really uncanny. Maybe there was something to her claim of ESP.

She poured herself a cup of coffee and sat down opposite him. She looked as modern as everything else in her kitchen. Why she had gone in for that frizzy hairstyle he couldn't fathom. It might have come out of *Vogue,* but it looked like hell. As she reached for the cream, her housecoat opened and he saw her small uptilted breasts. Her breasts had attracted and intrigued him from the first; she wore neither girdle nor bra, and she rouged her nipples. Which made him horny as hell.

"Mal, do you have some time for me at noon?" she asked, her voice suddenly gentle, with the sudden switch of mood so characteristic of her.

"I'll make time. What'd you want to do?"

"Bloomingdale's has one of those modular pit sofas reduced. Maybe if we showed interest, they'd reduce it more . . ."

"What color is it?" he tried to sound interested.

"Well, it's gray velvet. Kind of a light gray, smoke, they call it."

"Where would you put it?"

"In the livingroom. We could move the old sofa down to the family room. You know, I need a diversion."

"I'll give you a diversion."

"Don't be funny."

Ah, we are not amused. Wait until you hear this . . .

"I'm doing a catheterization at noon. And I can't just do it and run—not with him—"

"Not with whom?"

He waited until she looked at him, her lynx's eyes suddenly suspicious.

"John Paul."

"John Paul Macray?"

"That's right."

"Oh, my God. Is it serious?"

He answered in his most authoritative voice. "It's hard to diagnose now. After the cath we'll know more."

"Oh, come on. Mal—"

"He may have a small blockage."

"Is his blood pressure high?"

"Way up."

"You know, I thought there was something funny about him the night of their party. He was spending so much time with Peter Norris's girl."

"He's a good host, he likes to make his guests feel at home."

"At home! He looked like he was ready to go to bed with her. You'd think Maureen would notice it. But she's so oblivious; she likes her."

"Why not? Karen is an exceedingly attractive young woman. And very pleasant."

"You've noticed that, too. I suspect every man will be after her."

He was enjoying this; after all, it wasn't often that he held the ace. "She's the best of the lot. An old-fashioned pretty girl. Most of the residents seem to be tied up with women's libbers."

"Can you blame them . . . you doctors have a corner on wives."

He had diverted her from a discussion of John Paul. "Peter Norris is an able young physician. He'll do all right," he said.

"I suppose John Paul will have to resign as chief of staff," she said.

"It's too early to tell."

"Don't quibble. You know perfectly well he's a candidate for heart trouble. He's overweight, he travels too much, he has high blood pressure." She pointed her long red-tipped finger at him. "Malcolm, when he resigns, you are his logical successor, his own choice for the job . . ."

Malcolm could not count on it, though; it was too early and there were too many obstacles ahead. But Silvie's premonitions were usually right.

"The new administrator thinks a lot of Virginia Carruthers."

"Well, Virginia is okay. But since when has a pediatrician been chief of staff? And a woman, yet?"

"I have competition," he reminded her. "There are more WASPs and Catholics on the board than Jews."

"If you have a lemon," her voice was mocking yet determined, "make lemonade. Don't give up in advance, Mal." Wishing will make it so, she implied.

Malcolm was uneasy. Whenever Silvie took a hand in his affairs, it usually ended in disaster.

Dr. Macray was stripped to the waist, and waiting for an x-ray in the special procedures room.

He was calm, exuding the aura of control that was characteristic of him, particularly in an operating room.

But this morning, he wasn't scrubbing. He wasn't the surgeon but the patient.

Dr. Stone was going to take pictures of his heart—an angiogram. It would be done by passing a catheter tube through the blood vessels and into the chamber of the heart.

Earlier a nurse had given Dr. Macray a tranquilizer, which he swallowed without fuss. He was cooperating because he knew the importance of the procedure and because he didn't want to embarrass anyone. He knew the staff was a bit uneasy around him; they didn't quite know how to treat him. He smiled, that warm, gracious smile that always struck a responsive chord.

The nurse nodded toward the examination table in the center of the room and Dr. Macray approached it. He looked at the cradle-shaped device resting on the table, then stepped on a footstool and lay back against the cradle while the nurse strapped him in.

Then Peter Norris attached leads to his arms and legs. "Place your right arm here, sir," Peter said, nodding toward a board set perpendicular to the cradle. Dr. Macray's right hand had to be held stationary so Dr. Stone could work on it. Dr. Stone did not prepare for it the way he would if he were performing surgery; instead he used an antiseptic wash and wore a scrub suit with a lead apron and sterile gloves. He also wore a film dosimiter badge that registered the amount of radiation he was being exposed to. Since he performed catheterizations nearly every day he had to protect himself.

The syringe had been filled with dye that would be injected and sent to the heart. It was placed in a special barrel holder for Dr. Stone's index and middle fingers, to be used after he had located the catheter in the blood vessels of the heart.

Everything was ready now. Peter, Dr. Stone, the nurse and the technician who would control the electrical equipment were in position.

Dr. Macray closed his eyes. He felt the tingle of antiseptic in the crook of his right elbow, then the needle's prick and the slight burning sensation as the anesthetic went to work in his arm. He knew how the catheterization was done, but Dr. Stone had gone over the process with him. It was important to feel relaxed. They both knew the danger involved in handling a tense patient; too much adrenalin could cause blood vessel spasms or heart beat irregularities.

Dr. Macray felt a faint electric shock run down his arm. He knew Dr. Stone had opened a blood vessel and that they were ready to insert the catheter.

The nurse wiped Dr. Macray's face with a damp towel. He was deliberately keeping his mind blank, not allowing emotions to interfere with the operation. He dared not think of Maureen and how he would break the news to her. He dared not think of the future. Blank, John Paul, keep your mind blank . . .

"Take a deep breath, John Paul. Hollld it," Dr. Stone said. "Cough, please. A deep cough. . . . Good."

The cradle was turning now, so they could photograph the heart from different angles. He took another deep breath and coughed as the camera made a buzzing sound. After several repetitions, Dr. Stone asked for the lights to be turned on.

Malcolm tried not to think of who his patient was in order to remain steady. He had already injected some dye in order to look at the blood vessels and he was about to inject more to see the main pumping chamber, the left ventricle, of John Paul's heart.

"John Paul, you're about to have a hot flash," he said. "It won't hurt, but you will experience palpitations."

He asked for lights out again.

"Once more, John Paul, take a deep breath and hold it . . ." He turned to the nurse. "Fire," he ordered. The dye entered the blood vessel.

Dr. Stone was coordinating the injection system as well as a set of foot pedals. He was alert to the fluoroscope, the camera and the monitoring equipment. One pedal helped him follow the dye passing through the blood vessels. The other triggered the shutter when he wanted to take a picture, which was to be studied later as an aid to establishing a diagnosis and performing surgery, if surgery was warranted.

The procedure was finished. As Malcolm slid the catheter out of John Paul's arm, he sewed a small thread around the opening in the blood vessel and pulled it tight, like a purse string, to keep it from bleeding. Then the skin incision was closed. The procedure had taken less than an hour.

"I'm much obliged to you, my friend," John Paul said as the nurse walked him back and forth to restore his balance. Dr. Stone suggested that in a half hour he start exercising his arm.

"When will we go over the test?" John Paul asked.

"Sometime tomorrow," Malcolm said.

They smiled at each other and at Peter, who stood silently in the background.

John Paul returned to his office, relieved to have it over with, but concerned about how to tell Maureen.

Every hospital has its cache of secrets that, if fed into a computer, might reveal information that would destroy reputations, create scandals. Information that might make the hospital and certain physicians vulnerable to malpractice suits.

The patient's right to privacy and the public's right to know were often in conflict when a famous public figure checked into the hospital. The more the hospital put a muffler on official information, the wilder the speculation. Whenever Dr. Macray operated on one government official, the efforts to hush the surgery resulted in unfavorable press, anger from secret service men and hourly calls from Washington.

As a result of his travels throughout the United States and Europe Dr. Macray's name and reputation were familiar to the public. The news of his angiogram was common knowledge in the radiology department before the procedure was over, and the radiology department secretary reported to Dr. Hilton's secretary that their adored chief had a serious problem.

By the time Dr. Hilton telephoned cardiology, Malcolm Stone had already left for the day. His secretary reported that he was somewhere in Belfort and would check in with her later.

"Have him call Dr. Hilton," the secretary said. "It's urgent."

The administrator didn't think it was wise to closet Dr. Macray in his office. Aware of his own anxiety and speculation, Dr. Hilton had a sandwich and coffee at his desk. His mind was absorbed with this new contingency, and he tried to analyze it and put it in perspective.

The new wing of the hospital had been made possible by Dr. Macray's influence. His reputation was such that when the former development director had sent out letters all over the country and abroad—to Dr. Macray's former patients, to schools where the doctor had lectured, to the heads of the Fortune 500 companies (who surely appreciated the value of having Dr. Macray nearby in a hospital in Belfort)—generous donations flowed in. At first, it had even seemed likely that the donations would cover the initial cost of the wing. But with the final touches, the addition of new equipment, the expansion of the emergency department and the inflationary spiral, the costs topped the original estimates.

All hospitals were working under a deficit, Dr. Hilton knew, but ours only more so. And we ought to redo the operating room and recovery room. The auxiliary—bless those women—were taking on the cost of renovating the pediatrics floor and incorporating an adolescent and young people's section. They had completed payments for a new generator, which was needed in case of a power failure. With all the new equipment drawing so heavily on electricity, the old generator was not sufficient. Now if Belfort had a bad storm and the hospital had to go onto its own generator, there was enough power to keep surgery and delivery and other units where seriously ill patients relied on electricity to keep them alive, all functioning.

But the hospital's deficit was appalling. There were weeks when Dr. Hilton and the comptroller were seriously worried about meeting the next hospital payroll, and when suppliers were beginning to press delicately for payments past due. Medicare and Medicaid were behind in *their* payments and recently they had slashed their allowances to the hospital; apparently, they too had a cash flow problem.

Dr. Hilton felt that they could surmount the difficulties only if Dr. Macray would stay on as chief of staff. When Dr. Hilton had first arrived in Belfort and gauged the medical staff—in stature, knowledge, reputation, board certification, teaching appointments—he had immediately identified John Paul as the symbol of the hospital and the guarantor of its future.

During Dr. Hilton's first week in Belfort, Dr. Macray had performed one of his miracles, a mastectomy on a movie superstar whose breasts were as important to her image as her extraordinary voice. Without doing a radical, Dr. Macray had got out all the malignant cells, and had caught the cancer early enough that it had not spread to the lymph nodes. The star's chest was barely scarred, and in her next film she wore her usual revealing décolletage. Her press agent exploited her surgery, bringing it to her public's attention, and Dr. Macray was in the limelight again.

"I'm surprised that the new wing wasn't named after him," Dr. Hilton said to Dr. Stone over coffee one day. "He certainly deserves it."

"The Board offered it, but John Paul refused. In many ways he's a shy person. Fame has been forced on him."

Now Dr. Hilton wondered what would happen. Would Dr. Macray have heart surgery and retire? He *couldn't* retire! The new wing was built around him. Without him to shore up the medical structure, to lend not only his good name but his wisdom and reason, the hospital would be in serious trouble. Even at the cost of a threat to his health, Dr. Macray has to stay, Dr. Hilton decided. If there were people in the hospital who opposed him or whose value he doubted, they would be asked to resign.

In his mind Dr. Hilton began to evaluate the current staff members. Dr. Macray was pleased with the graduating residents in family practice, so they were clear. And he liked the first and second year residents. He was obviously fond of Malcolm Stone, since Malcolm was his doctor in this catheterization matter. He got along well with the rest of the medical staff, with the nurses, with the technicians and other employees. As long as they did their work in a first-rate way, he was friendly with them.

Wilbur Watling was another story. Watling created an atmosphere of tension and distrust. Dr. Hilton recalled that the graduating residents had complained of his lack of supervision. If it had not been for the help of the attending physician they wouldn't have done so well in their examinations. Yet Watling had taught at a well-known university and its affiliated hospitals. His credentials were solid and impressive, but the man's personality . . .

What disturbed Dr. Hilton the most was Watling's deep-seated anger against the world, except for a few of his favorites like Fred Farley. The hospital was stuck with him; his contract had another two years to run. Hilton wondered dispassionately how much dissension the man could cause in that time . . .

CHAPTER XXI

Maureen Macray had been unanimously elected president of the auxiliary eighteen months ago. Her term of office would not be up until October but already there was talk among the members that she should be reelected for another term.

Most of the officers were devoted to the hospital. With them backing her up, Maureen had expanded the interests of the auxiliary as a whole. Under her guidance, it had earned a great deal of money for the hospital, increased its membership, and broadened its reputation.

When Dr. Hilton congratulated Maureen on the way the annual ball was taking shape, she replied with her warm quick smile, "I've got a dedicated committee. Every one of these ladies would make a first-rate executive."

"Good leadership is what counts," Dr. Hilton agreed. He looked a bit wistful, Maureen thought, as though he wished he were as fortunate with his board of directors. What disturbed Maureen was that most of the new members of the board were executives of the Fortune 500 corporations whose headquarters were in the greater Belfort area. Although they were good businessmen, they knew nothing of the town or the hospital.

As a former auxiliary president, Eve Rothschild was automatically on the board of directors. Eve was garrulous but she often misinterpreted what she heard. Maureen knew, for instance, that the board was disappointed in Roscoe Osgood, the director of development and public relations. Without consulting anyone, Eve had taken it on herself to confer privately with Osgood and give him some advice.

When Maureen told John Paul about it, his tanned face flushed with anger. "Sure Osgood's a problem. But who the hell is she to reprimand him? That's Hilton's job."

One of Maureen's recent projects met with John Paul's enthusiastic approval: she planned to hold seminars for a health and education series. She had persuaded a number of doctors to donate their time, giving presentations on problems that many people faced daily: nutrition, exercise and retirement, how to cope with a handicap, and the like.

One of the gynecologists suggested a seminar on family planning, which she was sure would meet with Dr. Hilton's approval; but when it came to abortion, she hesitated.

"The right-to-life people are likely to come down on us," she told Dr. Hilton.

He agreed that since some board members were Catholic—including her own husband—it might cause a problem. "Right now I am reluctant to provoke controversy. The residents are quiet. We're paying decent wages." He put his hand on her arm. "I'll support you in whatever you want to do. But I'd advise you to take it easy until after the residents graduate and we have a new group checked in."

She was aware of his hand through her silk shirt and she felt an urge of desire course through her body. How ridiculous, she told herself after he left the coffee shop, where they'd met to talk. She had an aesthetic appreciation for attractive men, but up to now she had never felt any personal involvement. Yet here she was, responding physically to what she was certain was only friendly pressure. Hilton's brief gesture had aroused her sexually. Absurd, ridiculous, she told herself. Remember, you are about to become a grandmother.

She spent the rest of the morning in the hospital, attending to her projects. Dr. Monroe's nurse dropped off a video tape on breast examination, which they would run next week for the auxiliary. I hope we get a good attendance, Maureen thought, impressed by the simplicity of the film, with its emphasis on education rather than the triggering of fear.

Another project close to her heart was a plan for monitoring elderly people who lived alone, which meant calling them on the telephone, visiting them, and shopping at the supermarkets. She persuaded the Solove supermarkets to give them a ten-percent discount on their bills; the Soloves even arranged for a private bus to pick them up and take them to the store.

The gift shop in the Pavilion took up a great deal of her time. It was a bright, attractive spot and its merchandise was colorfully displayed. There was everything from cards and books to nightgowns and robes, toddlers' outfits, perfumes, candy and costume jewelry; and because it was a nonprofit enterprise, there was no sales tax.

The gift shop's sales were constantly increasing. So were the sales at the thrift shop downtown. The inner city residents flocked to its racks and counters piled high with clothing and to the back room filled with used furniture. The property of estates was often willed to the hospital, and when the saleswomen couldn't get the price suggested by the appraiser, they cut the prices. Auxiliary members tipped their friends to these bargains, and they snapped them up before regular customers got a chance to see them.

Earlier this morning, Maureen had been up in the attic of her own home, cleaning out her sons' athletic gear, leftovers from prep school and college days. She unearthed boxes of porcelain, fragile and exquisite bits of Staffordshire that she had packed away while the boys were toddlers, pretty little figurines of English country folk delicately tinted in the pastel blue, yellow and heather of the lake country, and small houses, with roofs that could be lifted off. How she had loved them. These precious bibelots had been the sole decorative items in the first apartment she'd shared with John Paul. She'd bought them at Macy's, after scrimping to save up for them. Macy's had been the store for people like her and John Paul who were just starting out. They had to pinch pennies but they didn't really mind it too much. They had each other . . .

Now, whenever she drove in to have lunch at the Plaza, she would shop at Henri Bendel and Cartier. John Paul had instinctive taste and he knew what she liked; the small wall-safe in their bedroom was filled with expensive jewelry, diamonds as well as the more colorful semi-precious stones she favored, particularly turquoise.

What she really should do was clean out the black velvet box that was filled with costume jewelry she'd bought over the years. Yet she clung to it for purely sentimental reasons, each piece carried memories—like the lovely cameo, so beautifully carved, that they had found in the Greenwich Village shop so long ago—after that trauma that had nearly broken them up . . .

She tried to bring her thoughts back to the present but she fell into a reverie. To the world and to her admiring friends she looked the perfect feminine role model; a slender, attractive woman, wearing a Geoffrey Beene shirt and a matching peach flannel skirt, cut just below the knees. Her blonde hair was artfully combed off her forehead; she looked poised and elegant.

Inside there was a sense of anxiety, a hollow feeling in the pit of her stomach. Why should she be suffering an anxiety attack now, for heaven's sake, when all was right with her world? It was the trip to the attic that had upset her. The memories, the poignant scenes and painful ones as well . . .

What in the world, she reflected, had triggered these gloomy thoughts? It was the same feeling that she had felt the day of the party several weeks ago. After they all left and John Paul was finally asleep, she had gone back downstairs and wandered through the deserted rooms into the kitchen. She went to the bar in the butler's pantry and poured herself a shot of cognac. Why the blues after such a happy evening?

She didn't need answers from a Ouija board. She knew. She closed her eyes and the images returned: John Paul was smiling at Karen, and she—that lovely golden girl—was looking at him with awe, with respect, perhaps with something more?

Maureen was too much of a realist—even at her age—to ignore the effect of a young, beautiful and vivacious woman on a man who had always had a healthy appreciation for the female body, even if he saw women's bodies every day. She tried to calm down and stop feeling so insecure. She knew John Paul loved her very much, but for some odd reason she felt desperate to spend as much time with him as she could from now on. They were not getting any younger.

It was almost noon and Pamela Shaw was to meet her for lunch to discuss the upcoming ball, to report on ticket sales and ads for the souvenir booklet. The ball was the auxiliary's most important function as far as money-raising was concerned and it would be taking place in only a few weeks. If I had one or two more like Pam, Maureen thought affectionately, we would fulfill our pledge to the new pediatric and adolescent wing in no time.

In the coffee shop there was a message for her. Pamela Shaw was in the radiology department, picking up some x-rays of her young daughter, who'd recently broken her wrist. Maureen decided to meet her; she was fond of the new team of radiology experts, who had recently come here from Sloan-Kettering Hospital in Manhattan.

She walked through the corridor aware of how quiet it was; the new wing was busy, and yet there was no sense of crowding; there was ample space and a sense of peace.

Outside the Cath Lab, she saw Dr. Malcolm Stone. He was in a scrub suit and seemed somewhat distracted.

Speechless, she stared, stunned, as she looked beyond him into the special procedures room. Her husband was lying on the table.

Dear God, she thought, what is wrong? John Paul! She turned and walked briskly away down the corridor. She found a waiting room and fell onto a sofa, her head in her hands.

The only logical procedure for a heart as badly damaged as John Paul's was open heart surgery.

"I'm considered a high risk," John Paul told Maureen. "One coronary artery is completely blocked. Malcolm thinks I'll need at least two by-passes."

They were sitting in their spacious sun-drenched bedroom, its windows open to the gentle breeze from the Sound. Maureen had brought up a tray of freshly squeezed orange juice, coffee and melba toast. Dressed in a Victorian robe of white eyelet, her blonde hair pulled back off her face, Maureen looked fresh and serene. Under no circumstances would she allow John Paul to suspect that she had already known about his condition before he confided the news to her.

"Does he feel it's necessary?" she asked. "Should you get another opinion?"

"I saw the films and the results of the tests. They verified my own suspicions," he said. He ignored the breakfast tray and walked back and forth, clenching and unclenching his fists. She wondered whether the pain on his face was physical or emotional.

"You mean you suspected something was wrong with your heart?"

He nodded. "Nothing definite. Just a feeling."

Maureen regarded him gravely. He was the right build, she thought, and right age for a massive heart attack. He worked hard; he played hard. He hadn't slowed down with the years; in surgery he often operated all day. When he went hiking on vacation, he kept up with the young guides. He loved life, he challenged life, he infused friends and patients with his joy in living. Even his sons adored him, and that was unusual considering how little time he'd been able to give them. He had lived a forthright, decent and blameless life.

Somehow, Maureen felt she was being punished. John Paul was going to be taken from her slowly, painfully. God still had not forgiven her for having had the abortion so many years ago. What if it had been a girl? She adored their four sons, she considered herself fortunate, but a daughter, a little girl . . .

This was no form of retribution to heap on his head. This weakening heart was punishment for her transgression. It must be faced bravely.

"Where will you go for surgery?"

"Malcolm suggests New York—St. Luke's."

"When?"

"Next week, if we can get a bed."

"So soon?"

He nodded. "Mal says I'm sitting on a powder keg."

She summoned all her strength. "Of course, we must listen to him. I'll make plans . . ." She held out her hands and he took them and pulled her up to him. He gave her a hug that left her breathless. "I'll be home for a while afterwards. Will that please you?"

"Under any circumstances . . . yes, yes. It's been so long since we've had time together . . ."

After he left, Maureen went to her desk in the small room she used as an office. It meant, she knew, a complete change in their way of life.

If the surgery were successful, John Paul could return to work. Perhaps. What was it Malcolm had told her? "We've had patients with severe angina who have carried on for years. And sometimes a patient for whom we have great hopes may have a heart attack or die suddenly without warning."

Well, John Paul would live. And they would arrange their life around him, around his needs. She hoped he could find new interests, new enthusiasms to keep him functioning.

Feeling somewhat in better spirits, she made concrete plans for the coming weeks. She needed someone to take her place in running the auxiliary ball. So many details remained to be solved. Whom could she ask? Pamela Shaw, certainly; and to assist her . . . Karen Cole.

Later in the day, after lunch, she placed calls to her sons on the west coast. John Jr. was instantly supportive, as were Bruce and Lynden. They offered to fly out to be with her, but she wouldn't allow it. She insisted that even the youngest, twenty-one-year-old Pauley, remain at the Vermont college where he was working on an independent honors project.

She promised to stay in touch with them, that their father would appreciate their visits more after surgery. And then they would decide what to do about the house. It was their pride and joy but the upkeep was costly. If John Paul's income was sharply reduced, they couldn't afford to keep it.

After she had spoken to her sons, she sat down at her desk, figured out their daily expenses and how they could be cut. Again the telephone rang.

"Maureen? This is Clemmie Watling. My dear, I just heard . . ."

CHAPTER XXII

Jedd Cramer was a junior partner in the old respected Belfort law firm of Davidson, Haskins and Gilbert.

Last January first, one of the only living senior partners, Luther Haskins, had allowed Jedd to buy out the firm, with the rather sweeping proviso that Jedd preserve its dignity and integrity. After all, the firm had a reputation to uphold and its list of older clients read like a page out of *Who's Who*. Mr. Haskins came to the office once a week to discuss various cases with Jedd, but otherwise did not interfere with Jedd's interpretation of the law, except to chide him once in a while about his fees. Two hundred dollars an hour seemed high for a firm that had once charged forty dollars to draw up a will. Still, Mr. Haskins admired Jedd's agile mind.

To keep his hand in the practice, Mr. Haskins gave women—elderly widows or unmarried ladies—advice on how to manage their money, including their husbands' estates and investment portfolios.

Jedd had come to Belfort from a law firm in Washington; although he was not connected to Richard Nixon, his future had come to an end in the aftermath of Watergate. The clients of the firm he worked for there dropped by half when Gerald Ford became president, and Jedd, having been the last associate hired, was the first to be fired.

His beginnings had been modest. His father operated a liquor store in Norwood, New York, not far from Syracuse. Jedd was the first person in his family—and that included a dozen cousins—to attend college. No one in Norwood had ever gone to an Ivy League school, so Jedd Cramer went to the state university. After four years at the grindstone—with few girlfriends and little booze—he had an academic record he hoped would get him into Harvard Law School. The Harvard Law graduates were the country's elite. Harvard lawyers practically ran Washington, visibly and behind the scenes.

In the end, Jedd was forced to settle for Columbia Law School, which wasn't bad at all, considering the reputation of its graduates. But he never forgave Harvard for rejecting him. He did well in law school. He was brash, brilliant, aggressive and ambitious. He also had an inborn radar that directed him to the people who could help him.

Between his second and third year of law school, he accepted a summer law clerking job with a distinguished New York firm. The senior partners who interviewed him saw potential in the serious young man. They offered him $200 a week and it was well worth it. Jedd blended in well with the associates in the firm, he was innovative and persistent; and when it came to dealing with a case, he had endless patience.

He was very impressed by the retainers that poured into the law offices, and he began to realize that it wasn't the type of law that mattered, it was who you knew.

Before he graduated the next year, he received an offer from a Washington law firm that represented a large number of powerful lobbies. It was an opportunity to learn Washington politics. Nevertheless he had been last to be hired, first to be fired. Still, with so much going for him, he thought he would land another job reasonably soon. But he discovered that the firms were not absorbing that many graduates, even from the most prestigious law schools. Where he had previously been courted by the law firms, he was now being ignored. There was a glut of young lawyers on the market. Even the

New York firm where he clerked the previous summer had more than enough bright young lawyers. Was there no place, he wondered angrily, for the full use of his talents?

It was through a family friend Paul Rieber that he finally established himself in Belfort. Paul Rieber had gone to Harvard Law School with Luther Haskins, and Haskins's firm was looking for a young lawyer to take charge of the office.

Jedd hated to leave Washington; for a few more weeks he clung to the hope that somewhere among private companies, the federal government, public interest firms and trade associations he would land a job. But after two weeks of indecision he joined Haskins's firm.

Jedd soon discovered that his work at Davidson, Haskins and Gilbert was limited. He had had enough disappointment in Washington and he knew his future here would depend on how solid the foundations of this firm were.

He set to work finding new clients among community services groups. He cultivated administrators at the hospital, health agencies, mental health centers, family and children's centers, the voluntary action center, and the rape crisis center. In each case, he impressed the staff with his desire to work with the underprivileged, those who had nobody to defend them.

Within a year he had become the best negligence lawyer in Fairfield County.

"Aren't you close to becoming an ambulance chaser?" Haskins asked, his voice tremulous with anxiety.

"This town needs a new kind of public defender," Jedd answered, "especially in the field of medicine, where people are being exploited by physicians, hospitals, even nursing homes. I'd like to speak for them." He was his own version of the great Clarence Darrow, his idol.

He quickly found a kindred soul in Fred Farley. He shrewdly estimated the extent of Fred's greed, and without actually discussing it with him, he was soon reaping the benefit of Fred's affiliations with the hospital. Whenever Emergency treated a battered wife or a rape victim who needed legal help, Fred would tip Jedd off. In such cases, Jedd would take one third of whatever his client was awarded if it was settled out of court; half if the case went to trial. Then Jedd would quietly give Fred ten percent of his share. It worked out well. Everybody made money. Even the victims.

Bribes, kickbacks, payoffs and double dealing were never linked to Jedd by fact, only by insinuation. He was fiercely loyal to his clients; the prosecuting attorney was the enemy, and there was none of the after-trial friendliness that was characteristic of most counselors.

Shulamit Solove had been his receptionist and legal secretary for two years. After Karen had delivered her broadcast on rape, Jedd asked Shulamit if she knew her.

"Yes, she's called here several times to check the facts on some of your cases for the legal aid society."

"Next time she calls, set up a lunch date for me and include yourself."

Jedd knew how to get the best results from his small but effective staff. In addition to Shulamit there was another secretary and two law clerks. He was generous with them, handing out bonuses whenever he won a case they had all worked hard on. He appreciated the team effort and they liked working for him; it was a highly charged office, in contrast to the days when Haskins was running it. In time, Jedd bought out the partners and the law practice was his.

Jedd gradually became more involved in the burgeoning field of malpractice. Some of the physicians knew his reputation and were rather leery of him. They recognized the stiletto behind the smile and the soft words. Cramer sued at the drop of a hat.

"Wouldn't you like to come to court and see him in action?" Shulamit asked Karen. "Even if there's no story in it for you, I'm sure you'd enjoy it."

Karen, always on the lookout for fresh material, said it sounded like a good idea. But when she mentioned his name to Peter, his face froze.

"Lawyers like him are the reason behind the increase in malpractice suits. Doctors are having to shell out as much as fifteen thousand a year on their insurance premiums."

That remark piqued Karen's interest even more.

When Karen and Shulamit walked into the courthouse a few days later, Jedd was in the hall talking to a group of young lawyers. When he saw the two women he came forward with a warm smile on his face. Karen thought he was definitely more interesting looking than the other young lawyers standing there. His face was craggy, with a large nose and long chin. He had thick sandy hair and gray eyes and looked a little like a young Spencer Tracy. He was wearing a dark blue suit and was carrying his raincoat and briefcase in one hand.

Shulamit made the introductions, and Jedd led them into the courtroom and found seats for them. He directed himself to Karen and his voice was gentle. "The case today involves a couple of high school seniors who were high on drugs, came charging down Belfort Avenue one morning and hit a car with two elderly people—a husband and wife—who were hospitalized for weeks and are still recovering."

Although his voice was soft then, it later changed in timbre, when he was addressing the jury:

"You good people, who have your limbs, your bodies—who can walk and run and play, who have your eyes to see the world—do you understand what it means when young addicts with no respect for human life rob a man and his wife of their limbs and their organs . . . ?" He paced back and forth in front of the jury.

"Do you realize what it is like to depend on strangers for your most intimate needs, to be helpless in a wheelchair because your back is broken? Broken by a couple of kids who were high on drugs?" He stopped and stared at the defendants. "My clients used to have full control of their bodies and faculties. Look at them now, the husband in a wheelchair, his spine crushed—and the loving wife whose pelvis was broken and her bladder so badly injured that she must wear a catheter at all times . . .

"These gentle people are prisoners in their own bodies. Think of the humiliation and pain they have gone through. Think of what it means to have to have an enema every day. Think of what it means to be immobilized, and have your arms and legs rubbed to keep the circulation going, so you won't get bed sores. Think of it."

His voice was impassioned, his eyes wide with anger.

"The young lawyers all come to listen to him," Shulamit whispered to Karen. "He's the Barrymore of the legal profession."

Karen was enthralled by Jedd's performance. She was sure he would win a huge settlement for his clients. And he did. Nine hundred thousand dollars.

Later, when she described the scene to Peter and Fred, Peter said, disgusted, "It's guys like him who give his profession a bad name."

Fred added, "He's the Robin Hood of Fairfield County."

But Karen was haunted by the plight of the couple sitting there in the courtroom. "Just remember," she said, "all of the money in the world will not bring them back to normal again. Their lives will never be the same." It frightened her to think that in seconds, a person's life could be drastically and irrevocably altered.

CHAPTER XXIII

Whenever her boys, as Mrs. Thalberg called Peter and Fred, had an evening off, she prepared dinner for them and the girls—Karen, Sheila and Shulamit, who seemed to be spending much more time with Fred nowadays. It was like a family.

Mrs. Thalberg had known Shulamit since she was a child, before she'd gone to work on a kibbutz in Israel, adopted her Hebrew name, and developed into a political activist. Shulamit was, Mrs. Thalberg suspected, something of a disappointment to her mother. When she was at Radcliffe, her mother used to call her every Sunday night to get a rundown of the men she had gone out with that week and which one was showing serious interest in her.

Shulamit was indeed an attractive, sensuous young woman. If she had been born a generation or two earlier, no doubt her family's orthodox ancestors would have shaved her head of its short, glossy purple-black locks, so she would not be a sexual temptation to either her young husband or his Talmudic brethren. Her eyes were widely spaced, as black as ripe olives; her lips were full and her teeth were straight. Her breasts had developed early; at the age of ten, a B-cup. Whenever she inspected herself at night after her bath, she knew she was what men called "stacked."

Physically, Shulamit was a striking contrast to Karen. Perhaps instinctively they became friends, knowing each complemented the other. Karen was amused and impressed by her new friend's outspoken ways. Shulamit talked back to everybody, including her family, her friends and those who interfered with her plans to change the world.

This particular Tuesday evening was the only free night Fred and Peter would have until after graduation. Karen was busy, too; besides her radio job, she was working closely with Maureen Macray and Pamela Shaw on the auxiliary ball; checking on reservations that weren't coming in as quickly as they'd hoped; selling advertising space in the souvenir booklet to various merchants in town.

Mrs. Thalberg had set the diningroom table with ecru-embroidered linen place mats and napkins she'd bought in Madeira and seldom used anymore. Her sense of well-being was strengthened by the presence of the young people. She was humming to herself as she tore the Boston lettuce and escarole into bite-size morsels.

She often thought of her late husband when she was with these bright young people. Her son and daughter had pulled up roots in Connecticut and gone to California; they never invited her to visit. She sometimes wondered if they had appreciated their father.

Well, the Belfort Hospital executives remembered him. Last night had commemorated the first of the Henry Thalberg Memorial Lectures, and all of them, Peter, Karen, Fred and Sheila, had attended.

Karen opened the tarnish-proof box that held the heavy silver flatware and said, "You must have been so proud last night."

"Wasn't it a beautiful tribute to my husband?"

Karen took out the service plates and set them on the mats. She had been impressed by the new wing. They had moved through the spacious reception room and gone directly to the corridor, which was hung with photographs of deceased physicians who had made a significant contribution to the hospital. Karen and Mrs. Thalberg went straight to Harry Thalberg's photograph. He had a gentle, compassionate face, with a touch of humor in the eyes and a quizzical set to his eyebrows. Mrs. Thalberg touched Karen's arm and paused, as though she were in communication with him. Then they waited at the bank of elevators, where a group of the late doctor's contemporaries greeted them and Dr. Monroe, Dr. Stone and a group of residents, still in their baggy green scrub suits, joined them. John Paul and Maureen arrived, having brought the guest speaker with them. Dr. James Weldon, Maureen told the group, had been at Johns Hopkins ahead of John Paul.

Karen thought Dr. Macray looked well, though his normal high color was gone because he had not been out in the sun in the past ten days. Dr. Stone had asked him to rest, but did not want to make an invalid of him. The trouble with John Paul, Maureen confided in an undertone to Karen, was that he never relaxed. He was a Type-A personality.

"What did Maureen mean by a Type-A personality?" Karen asked Peter as they took their seats in the air-cooled auditorium.

"Someone who's active, ambitious, aggressive, impatient. Always on the run, doing more than he should. Successful. Excels in his work. But at a cost. The perpetual drive often creates stress and makes him prone to heart problems. He's compulsive in his work—in his demands on himself and others."

"And that describes Dr. Macray?" she asked.

Peter nodded. "To a T."

They were seated in the front row. The auditorium was nearly full. At the last minute Dr. Carruthers hurried in, looking like a college girl in her blue linen dress and white sweater.

Dr. Monroe introduced the guest speaker; his name was well known in the medical profession. Dr. Weldon was a slender man in his early sixties, slimmed down since his own coronary a year ago.

The speaker began quietly. Karen looked sideways at Peter. He was leaning forward, mesmerized, as though he expected great wisdom to pour out of Dr. Weldon's mouth.

Dr. Weldon spoke about the great changes in medicine over the last fifty years. "In 1927, at Gaylord," he said, mentioning a Connecticut sanitarium, "they were treating tuberculosis patients with three months of complete bed rest. They also thought keeping a sack of birdseed on his chest would help him get well."

He spoke of the innovations that had come about with the advent of the space age. Research into space flight had given fresh insight and impetus to the future of medicine.

"And," he added, "with computers and other modern methods, medicine will make even greater strides in the next ten years."

Karen noticed the respectful attitude of the middle-aged physicians and the look of awe and worship on the faces of Peter, Fred and other residents.

Dr. Weldon took no credit for the breakthrough in the profession during his active years. Before him came the pioneers, the physicians who had developed the principles by which later doctors had succeeded. "We stood on the shoulders of giants and looked into the future . . ."

Peter was inspired by Dr. Weldon's lecture. All the way home he talked about the progress that had been made. And now, with microsurgery, surgeons could perform miracles—as in the case of the Manhattan girl who had lost her hand to the subway train's wheels, and then—through this technique—had the hand restored to the stump of her arm in an eight-hour operation, slowly, painstakingly, sewing together the ends of blood vessels and muscles. . . .

Even Fred had enjoyed the lecture, which wasn't like him. He was usually negative about everything, scornful toward the older physicians. But tonight, as they all sat around Mrs. Thalberg's dining table, he seemed in unusually high spirits.

Although Fred still lived at Mrs. Thalberg's, Karen saw little of him. She had put a stop to his barging in with one request or another. She was still annoyed because he took advantage of Peter's good nature, but she sensed recently a change in Fred.

Now, sitting across the table from him as they sipped Mrs. Thalberg's delicious sorrel soup, Karen took a long look at him. His beard was heavy; no matter how much he shaved each morning a faint blue shadow deepened on his cheeks and chin by noon. When he smoked, the cigarette hung carelessly at the corner of his mouth. Off duty, he wore his shirts open, revealing the thick, dark, matted chest hairs and his pants were always too snug. Altogether, he looked like a hero in a grade-B movie. His fingers were long and flexible. He was, Karen realized, an immensely attractive man.

As Karen got used to Fred, the disturbing side of his character seemed less offensive to her. Once she began to feel a little sympathy for him, she accepted the dark, brooding streak in his nature. Every three weeks or so, he would become despondent. He would attend patients and make rounds, but he was silent, his face shadowed, his slouch more obvious than usual.

Fred had decided to remain in Belfort after they graduated, contrary to his earlier plans to take off for the southwest. Dr. Watling had offered Fred a post as staff physician in Emergency. Karen realized Fred's decision to stay, his despondency, probably had something to do with Shulamit, but she did not ask, of course.

Mrs. Thalberg and Sheila wheeled the serving cart into the dining-room. She served roast brisket on a bed of onions, carrots and celery, seasoned with garlic, onion soup and ketchup, the way her mother used to make it. And there were thin, crisp potato pancakes with warm homemade applesauce.

Having just finished a three-day hunger strike, to enlist sympathizers for the Equal Rights Amendment, Shulamit ate more than Peter or Fred. In between mouthfuls she told them about her experiences with the right-to-life committee.

"I even asked some of the women on the auxiliary to march with us. But they refused. You'd think older women would be more sympathetic, considering what they used to go through in order to get an abortion."

"Who did you call?" Fred asked.

"I started with Maureen Macray. She has a lot of influence on the women in this town . . ."

"She turned you down," Fred said.

"How did you know?"

Fred scowled. "Why didn't you use your head? The Macrays are devout Catholics. Especially Mrs. Macray."

Crestfallen, Shulamit murmured, "Belfort needs more Jews."

"What Belfort needs," suggested Karen, blotting her lips with her napkin, "is a medical clearing house. I have received a lot of requests for information—"

"Because of your rape broadcast?" Shulamit asked. "Our chaste little town was finally confronted with the ugly reality."

"What do they want?" Peter asked Karen.

"Oh, they ask all sorts of questions. Most of them I can't answer, so I tell them to call the hospital or the medical society."

"Anything juicy?" Fred asked.

"Depends how you look at it. One woman called me yesterday with a real problem. She's wise to a doctor who's selling her 17-year-old son prescriptions for uppers and downers—"

"Who's the doctor?" Fred asked.

"She wouldn't tell me. She only wanted to talk about her son. Evidently he was hooked on drugs but has been clean for two years. Now she's terrified he's starting up again. When her son tried angel dust, he went crazy, tore off all his clothes, and went screaming into the night that he was one of God's angels and that the world was coming to an end in twelve hours."

"Did she give you any leads on the doctor?" Fred persisted.

"Only that he's from out of town. He slims people down. I think he's been selling prescriptions to the kids. She said she'd gone through her son's belongings and she found a couple of prescriptions —one for a hundred Quaaludes."

"Sounds like her son is a pusher," Peter suggested.

"That's what she finally admitted. Her son gets drugs, then he sells them on the street and splits the take with the doctor."

"What's he selling," Sheila wanted to know, "besides Quaaludes?"

"Amphetamines. And the drugs that athletes take to build up muscle and strength."

"Anabolic steroids," Fred guessed.

"She said some of the high school athletes are taking steroids."

"They're used in Europe," Peter said. "They're given to young kids to build them up for the Olympics before they even reach their teens."

"The problem is, the athletes given these steroids aren't as potent as they should be," Fred said. "Their sperm count is lower than the normal male's—"

"And there are rumors of kidney cancer in weight lifters who take abnormally large amounts of them," Peter added.

"But what do I tell her when she calls again? Who should she report this doctor to?"

"There's the county medical society, the state medical society, and the state licensing board . . ."

"I'd refer her to the Connecticut examining board," Sheila suggested.

"Do you think there's a story in these steroids?"

"I wouldn't touch it." Peter's voice was grim. "Legal problems may develop."

"Okay, boss . . ." Karen said. "I'll do as you say, but I think that doctor should have his license taken away."

It was a stimulating evening; good food, good company, good talk. Fred began to open up. For the first time he related some stories about medical school, about Mexico. He talked about how undernourished but happy the children were. He described how the doctors tried to teach the natives about contraception—a futile effort. Peter added that he'd had the same experience in Africa, when he was working on a pilot project there. Karen looked surprised. "You never told me that," she said.

Fred winked broadly, "I'll bet he hasn't told you a lot of things about himself."

"Don't worry, Karen." Peter patted her knee. "You'll have plenty of time to find out more."

Karen beamed, wondering if that meant he was planning to marry her. Would he never propose?

When it was time to leave, Fred walked Shulamit to the car, and they discovered that her battery was dead. She had neglected to turn off the headlights when she arrived earlier. Fred wondered if she had done so deliberately. He instinctively questioned people's motives, especially those of the women he was involved with.

"Could you borrow Karen's car and drive me home?" she asked him. "It's too late to call a service station."

Her suggestion, Fred thought, smiling, harmonized perfectly with his own plans. Shulamit was smarter than she realized.

He asked Karen if he could use the station wagon. There was no problem. Thinking ahead now, he went up to his room, picked up his jacket, stuffed the pockets and returned downstairs. Shulamit kissed Mrs. Thalberg. "It's been a marvelous evening. Thanks again." And to Karen, "Don't forget now, Jedd expects you for lunch soon. You name the day. Right?"

"Right," Karen said, giving Fred her car keys.

Fred pulled out of the driveway. The food and wine had been delicious, but what he had paid the most attention to was Karen—her beauty and her growing friendliness were both seductive and threatening. He felt desire spreading through his groin. Suddenly, he felt annoyed with Shulamit and she seemed to sense it as they sped through the empty streets. "What's the matter, Fred?"

He said thinly, "What's the idea of bringing Jedd and Karen together?"

"What's wrong with that? She's looking for material for her broadcasts."

"She won't use what she gets from him. He's nothing but an ambulance chaser."

"I thought you were friends!"

He couldn't say what he was thinking. Business associates; what else could you call his relationship with Jedd Cramer? They had met for the first time when Jedd was at the hospital visiting a patient, an elderly Italian with a pacemaker in his chest. The following day Jedd called Fred and suggested they meet for a drink—he needed some information and he'd be grateful if Fred could supply it.

With the information Fred gave him Jedd sued the company that had manufactured the pacemaker. The mechanism was faulty, and rather than get involved in a lawsuit with consequent bad publicity, the manufacturer settled out of court. Which was good for the patient, who had been living on social security; good for Jedd, who had taken a chance and won; and good for Fred, who had deposited a couple of hundred dollars in his safety deposit box.

"Fred—?" Shulamit's voice was tentative, coaxing; her feminist tone had all but disappeared.

They were driving along the Point now, past the Macrays' toward the end where the Soloves' house sat on a rocky rise like a magnificent lighthouse.

It was always damp here, especially on cool nights. Shulamit's hair seemed to get curlier at times like this. Her perfume was subtle, unlike the acrid scent of the girls on Jackson Hill.

Karen had been warmer toward him tonight than she'd ever been. Karen was the archetypal dream girl; the golden-haired ideal with money in her voice. And her body, which he had glimpsed only in a bathing suit or shorts, appealed to him with its promise of soft, ripe flesh, full, molded breasts and shapely calves. Age wouldn't affect her the way it would the Hispanic and black women on Jackson Hill.

Karen was certainly different from Shulamit. Perhaps not as brilliant—Shulamit challenged him with her bright sharp wit and intelligence, while Karen mesmerized him with the promise of a gentle complaisance . . .

With Shulamit, he decided, you had to be very *macho*.

"Fred—?" She turned her face toward him. He drove erratically, hunched down in the seat, trying to peer through the fog on the dark road.

"Why are you so quiet?"

He shrugged. He was moody; you could never tell what would send him into his shell and make him uncommunicative.

"It was a nice evening, don't you think?" she asked cheerfully, hoping to get a response. "With all the exposure Karen's getting, she won't be just a rich girl any longer."

"You'll never make an activist out of her," Fred joked.

Shulamit frowned at his negative way of looking at things.

He guided the station wagon through the iron gates, where soft lights on brick columns lighted the entrance to the courtyard. The Solove families lived in a compound. Shulamit's parents owned the largest of the three houses. The other Solove brothers and their families lived in two more modest houses. Their mother had a spacious bedroom in each of her son's homes and stayed with them whenever she felt like it. She was still the matriarch—ancient, tough, unyielding—the power of wisdom and money.

Fred pulled in beside some flowering bushes, switching off the lights and motor of the station wagon. In the dark she could barely see the expression on his face, but she touched his full, sensuous lips with her fingers and traced their curve.

"Come here," he said, scooping her into his arms and holding her with rare gentleness.

"I came prepared tonight," she whispered. "I have my diaphragm in."

He grinned to himself but said, "Shulamit, we're not going to do anything—except kiss goodnight."

"What do you mean?" She was puzzled and a little hurt; his display of self-control seemed uncharacteristic to her. She had always had a hunch that when Fred finally made love to her, he would be greedy. The last time they had gone out, he had wanted to make love but she had held back. Only because she couldn't take the Pill; she reacted badly to it, and she didn't have a diaphragm then. She had been fitted for a new one only a few days ago.

Because she was upset by what he had just told her, she didn't hear precisely what Fred had just said. Something about the fact that he didn't want her to be just another fuck for him. "I'm getting serious about you . . . and I don't know how to handle it. I've never felt like this before . . ." He drew his hands away from their embrace. "I think we should wait . . ."

She tried not to burst with happiness, but it was hard to read his tone.

"Freddie, are you serious?" Slightly coy.

"I'm serious, kid."

"Why—" she choked, emotion tightening her throat, "that's the loveliest thing I've ever heard."

"I'm not committing myself right now." He sounded so solemn. "But it may work out for us. And if it does, I want it to be right. I want to be able to look your folks in the face and—don't ask me to explain. I can't even explain it to myself."

"Freddie, I never guessed . . . I had no idea you were so—so straight."

"I never was before." He kissed her lightly on the cheek and opened the door on her side of the car, to let her out. "Goodnight, Shulamit."

"Goodnight." She blew him a kiss and trotted up the walk. He waited until the front door opened and disappeared from sight, then started the engine and drove away from the Point. At the lower intersection, instead of turning toward the Thalberg house, he swung left for Jackson Hill. He just couldn't bring himself to tell Shulamit that he couldn't make love with her for a while . . . that he had a venereal disease. If he gave it to her, she would never forgive him. And he couldn't afford to lose her.

CHAPTER XXIV

Fred Farley was a complex young man. Beneath his physical good looks, intelligence and confidence was a restless man whose faults the hospital staff had yet to discover. He had a way of seeming to pay attention that was reassuring. The way he walked in a slouch, head bent, the wire-rimmed glasses always slipping off his nose suggested a professional tone and devotion to healing. Sometimes he wondered if the attendings or his fellow residents could see through him. Fortunately, Dr. Watling was on his side, which counted.

But Dr. Watling, in spite of his sound medical background, was a bad influence. No man his age could be respected for his temper. The other residents had visible contempt for him. He demanded respect and did little to earn it. A couple of newspaper articles about his background were not a passport to earning esteem, either as a teacher or as a man.

Yet if Watling could make it in medicine, Fred figured that he, too, could make it.

Being a doctor was a status symbol nowadays; it didn't matter how much patients resented them—for their outrageous fees, for their indifference to pain and suffering—the fact was that a physician could manipulate his patient, body and soul. Perhaps that fact had originally appealed to Fred on an unconscious level. To be in control, to exert power, to influence. In a way, he had to show people that he was worthwhile after all.

He recalled a recent case in the delivery room. One of the new obstetricians had delivered a breech baby that died. Fred had scrubbed for him and it was bloody. Afterwards, when the mother lay in the recovery room, the obstetrician had walked in to check on her. Fred and the nurse were nearby.

The new mother, young, attractive, in her mid-thirties, slowly opened her eyes as the anesthesia wore off.

"You're looking pretty good," the doctor said. "It's too bad the baby didn't survive."

Fred had seen the shock and anger on the nurse's face as the obstetrician strode out. Fortunately, the mother was still under sedation. Fred wondered how he would have handled the case. Warned the woman's husband and family that there was a problem, that it might end in a choice between saving the mother or the child? Found out if there were other children, or if this was the first?

Dr. Macray and Dr. Stone and Dr. Monroe took extra time with their patients. Fred had seen evidence of their healing powers in the way they handled their patients, always sensing their needs. That was also the kind of attitude Fred admired and longed to emulate. Despite his aloofness, he was not callous. It was part of protecting his ego.

As a family doctor, you had to develop a close relationship with every specialist whose treatment you wanted your patients to have. The patient looked to his family doctor as his counselor, his confidant and sometimes even his God.

Dr. Watling felt that a patient should listen to his physician and keep his mouth shut, without asking any questions. But that was an outdated concept. When Dr. Macray lectured the residents, he reminded them that the little time the doctor and patient had together was a two-way exchange. The doctor who was rude, impatient, and unsympathetic was violating his Hippocratic oath.

Fred understood the oath without actually subscribing to it. He was willing to take care of patients—up to a certain point. If they began to control his life, forget it. He had built a wall of cool aloofness around him. He knew damn well that if he ever weakened, if he ever let his feelings take over, there would be an explosion. And maybe the wrong people would get hurt. . . .

When it came to his personal life, Fred was extremely calculating and looked out for his own interests. He did his work when it came to important decisions. He had done the necessary research on Shulamit's family by making some discreet inquiries.

The Soloves were a nouveau-riche family who owned a series of supermarkets in Belfort, Stamford, Darien and Norwalk. Their first operation had been a mom and pop grocery store in the south end. The three sons came home after school and worked in the store, which was patronized mostly by blacks and Hispanics. They had put roots down in Belfort just before World War Two. And now they were rich and daily growing richer.

As the sons and daughters grew up and went off to college—mostly prestigious eastern colleges—the pressure to succeed in other endeavors mounted. The natural choice for Shulamit was to marry a doctor, if not a rabbi. Privately she confided to friends and lovers, including Fred, that all she wanted was to get her family off her back. But if she broke with them, they might disinherit her, which would put the kibosh on her grandiose political plans. She felt no guilt about her family's rapidly increasing fortunes. Indeed, she merely meant to use her share to further the feminist aims that were dear to her heart.

She was sharp, Fred acknowledged, though extreme; honest if misguided. He hadn't met many like her. Nor many families as wealthy as hers . . .

Would his being a doctor make up for whatever objections her parents had about his not being Jewish?

But then, Fred thought, as he drove up to Jackson Hill, who was to know whether he was a Jew or a Christian, or, for that matter, a Moslem. He wasn't circumcised. His natural mother probably didn't know about such things.

Jackson Hill was a blot on the inner city. Neither the wrecker's ball nor rehabilitation had touched its streets. Here, in old brick rowhouses with their white stoops, lived the welfare people, whole families that lived in one room and shared a communal toilet with their neighbors. Many families had been evicted from their homes in the urban renewal section, without new ones being built for them. They were herded together like refugees, compressed into surroundings that were even more filthy and demoralizing than their former homes.

In Jackson Hill the music was a little too loud and the narrow streets and alleys were a trap to the unwary. All the young people in Belfort got their kicks here, the rich kids from Greenwich and Stamford and New Canaan had discovered Jackson Hill too. No sense driving to Manhattan, where you had to bribe your way into places like Studio 54. The kids came to Jackson Hill to get amphetamines; they were not into hard drugs like LSD or heroin.

As Fred looked for a parking spot, he decided that first he would visit Joey's. Not exactly a disco, not much of anything except for the proprietor's reputation as a stud; but the joint was heavily patronized by prosties and their pimps. Not all black or Hispanic; there were white chicks, too, those who weren't working the interstate out of Darien, where, nightly, there were plenty of pickups as the big trailer trucks stopped for a cup of coffee, and . . . The women who worked the thruway maintained a certain illusion of respectability, of gentility even; they were not pros, but were simply working for a little extra change to help the family budget.

The pool hall next to Joey's was busy at all hours, a kind of meeting place for the johns and hookers. Behind the next wooden building was a Greek restaurant with good takeout food. In the rear was the big abandoned storehouse that originally belonged to the clockworks that dominated Belfort a couple of decades before, when it was more of a manufacturing town. Now that the clockworks had been phased out, the warehouse had a stockpile of typewriters, radios, television sets—all stolen goods that the fences sold to customers at cut-rate prices.

Wandering idly from one storefront to another, Fred saw the usual crowd: young dropouts, offspring of welfare families, mostly Belfort-bred. Their grandmas scoured and cleaned and ironed for the rich ladies of Belfort Hills. At the end of the day, they rode home to Jackson Hill on the bus, sitting in groups, surrounded by paper bags filled with leftovers, talking about their mistresses. Their grandsons scorned the leftover food, hand-me-down clothes. They hated the rich whites in their fancy houses. They knew where to get fancy clothes on their own. There wasn't a john who came around to Joey's or the adjacent pool hall in smarter clothes. They were young, but they knew what styles were in at the big Harlem clubs.

Jackson Hill was high tonight, though it was all behind closed doors. If a police car drove up the hill, there was nothing to make the cops suspicious.

Fred wondered if Jedd Cramer would be around. Jedd could dismiss it as an investigation of illegal activities, but Fred was wise to him. They both shared a compelling curiosity about the underbelly of Jackson Hill. To meet its characters and to see the world through their distorted eyes made their adrenalin flow.

Sometimes Fred wondered what made him court danger, respond to it. Was it genetic? Had his parents come from this same nether world, or one like it? Or was it the result of his unhappy childhood and adolescence, when taking risks was his only chance for survival.

Watching the young prostitutes and their pimps, Fred speculated on his own mother—funny, he couldn't use the word *mother*. He had no memory of her, although once in a while he was tempted to try sodium pentothal to see if clawing back in the darkness of post-birth, he could call up some image of her. The only one he could entrust to supervise such a session was Peter Norris. Though Peter's straightness sometimes annoyed Fred, he trusted Peter, knew he could count on his integrity under any circumstances.

Thinking of Peter evoked the image of Karen in Fred's mind. She would never go for *him*. But knowing her had dampened his enthusiasm for the chicks he met on Jackson Hill. Even Shulamit couldn't compare with Karen.

Certainly the Hispanic women here could not compare with either one of them, in spite of their hot-blooded ways. And that included Juanita, whom he'd met when she had been brought into Emergency, after a fight with her pimp. They had to take a hundred stitches in her face and because she was disfigured Juanita now worked as a waitress in Joey's, and solicited only after hours.

Fred wasn't in a Juanita-mood tonight. She was a professional who knew how to use her natural gifts: her well-trained tongue and her slender hands. When he climaxed with her, it felt like he was on speed. Speed appealed to him; but he was too smart to use it. Some instinct told him that if he did, he'd be hooked. No, the stuff he carried in the pockets of his jacket was strictly business.

Most hospital crash carts were equipped with drugs. Doses for patients were measured out and the rest was kept under lock and key. In Emergency, when the nurse was filling a syringe with Demerol and was called away to help out in a crisis, it was easy to replace the Demerol with water and put the drug in a vial. Everyone was too busy to notice if a drug was missing, and so some poor soul received water instead of his painkiller. Fred tried not to think of the effects of his petty larcenies on the patients.

He preferred working Emergency to any other department because it was easier to help himself to the drugs. He got Quaaludes, amphetamines, codeine and other uppers and downers from drug salesmen and from the assistant in the hospital pharmacy. He always showed his appreciation to them by giving them a percentage of his take on Jackson Hill. His best customer was Carmen. Early in their friendship, when she questioned how many drugs he had ordered, instead of sending them back, he kept them. Of course, Carmen was wise to him, but she played along for her own ends.

He had discovered an outlet for his wares on his first visit to Jackson Hill and unloading his merchandise was no problem. Joey and the disco managers paid him in cash; it was a smooth operation now. He usually stashed his take in a money belt that he had bought in Mexico and put it in his safe deposit box at the bank the next morning. He was saving to buy gold. He often heard the doctors discuss investments, but stocks and bonds were like so much confetti to him. Gold was real, like land . . .

Juanita was a great help to him. Whenever he was on a thirty-six-hour tour of duty and he wanted to get rid of his cache, she would come to the hospital, pick up the stuff and deliver it to the right places. He was partial to Hispanic girls, particularly the virgins, who were always torn between desire and fear. There was something about their bodies, the curves that would turn to fat but were so sweet now. He enjoyed teasing them, holding back when they were ready to go into orbit. He sometimes wondered if there were an ethnic bond between him and Hispanics. His almost primal experiences with them left him more relaxed than those with fair-skinned, fair-haired girls.

Yet tonight, he had no desire for Juanita; tonight he needed someone new to awaken senses dulled by anxiety, self-pity, whatever. He took a cigarette from the pack in his shirt pocket, lit it and inhaled deeply, feeling the smoke burning the membranes of his nostrils. When he was like this, self-absorbed, he loved to make the scene. It took him away . . .

He wandered into the first disco, three doors away from Joey's bar. The exteriors were all shabby and needed paint. But inside the walls were brightly painted, in wild colors intensified by flashing lights. The crowd that danced to the recorded music was dedicated to satisfying its own urges and needs, which were magnified by the music and the whirling bodies around them. The sound throbbed, finding no outlet beyond the soundproof ceilings, and turning in on itself and its habituées.

There were kids in outlandish outfits; a boy in a black leather jacket with girl's ruffled panties; others in costumes that seemed to be copied from Kiss and other rock groups. They looked dirty and smelled faintly of underarm sweat and cheap perfume. They looked like rejects from Manhattan's East Village. Fred watched silently as they gyrated out of rhythm, but it didn't matter, since each couple was lost in itself. It was difficult to make out faces; the only thing that was clear were the sounds of voices above the music, punctuated by manic laughter.

It was, Fred thought, a form of primal therapy, which had been touted a decade ago for releasing tension. A frizzy-haired creature—he couldn't identify the sex—was shrieking, marking time to its own beat and accentuating it with a series of shrill wails.

Fred was suddenly repulsed by the scene. He decided to split—once he got rid of his merchandise. He went back to Joey's, unloaded the Quaaludes and the codeine and got his money. He knew Juanita must be looking for him, but he wouldn't feel right about infecting her either, even if penicillin was easy to get.

As he left the third disco, he noticed a handsome blond boy in a Nazi stormtrooper uniform, his chest decked out with fake medals. His helmet was too big for his head; it kept slipping off, pushing his glasses down on his nose. The girl with him, in a kind of gypsy tea-room outfit, was dark-haired with large eyes. The boy was hand-some; the girl was sexy, though not very appealing. They looked fa-miliar.

Of course. He had met them in the hospital cafeteria one Saturday with their father. They were Malcolm Stone's son and daughter.

He debated whether to approach them. Then he walked over to a dark corner where they were standing and asked jovially, "Having fun?" They turned to look at him, alarmed, not old enough to flaunt their independence. Fred could tell that they had no idea who he was. Well, that might just turn out to be an advantage for him . . .

"You need a lift home?"

They were holding glasses filled with colorless liquid, sipping them as though they were ice cream sodas. They were high on pot and beer and his invitation sounded good.

"You going up to North Belfort?" the boy asked, sticking out his chest with the ridiculous iron cross and other medals.

"It's not out of my way," Fred said.

"Well—we live—" the girl began.

"I know where you live," Fred said. "Come along. You better get home . . ."

"Our parents are out," the boy said.

"Good, then you'll get home before they do. Come on, let's split."

They followed him meekly, taking their glasses with them, won-dering about accepting a ride from a stranger. Fred led them outside.

They had just driven out of the parking lot when a police officer with a flashlight motioned Fred to stop. He felt his heart skip a beat; he made a mental inspection of the car.

Fred took out his California driver's license. The officer, now joined by another, searched him thoroughly. Thank God, he was clean, he thought. They asked him what he was doing here.

"I'm taking these kids home," he said. "It's not Halloween, you know."

"Who are they?"

"They're Dr. Malcolm Stone's kids—you know, the cardiologist. He had to go out tonight on a case and he asked me to pick them up."

"You mean he knew they were here—in these joints?"

"Better here, where we can keep an eye on them, than in Harlem."
He sounded like a big brother, and the cop allowed him to drive on.
The kids seemed glad to be going home.

He dropped them off at their driveway. The outside lights were on,
so evidently their parents were still out. Fred looked at his watch; it
was nearly two. He watched them trudge up to the house, and then
backed the wagon down and around. He felt good about acting like a
Dutch uncle, but at the same time wondered if he could use it to his
advantage someday . . .

CHAPTER XXV

"Peter, what do you know about Southrock Village?" Karen asked.

"Southrock?" Peter had bathed and changed into clean chinos and a fresh shirt. His hair was still dark-wheat damp but the shower had revived him, and he was looking forward to the evening. They were going out to dinner and the movies. Just like an old married couple, Karen thought to herself, pleased. She sat on the bed in her favorite position, legs crossed, heels locked over her knees, hands clasped in her lap with the palms together. She looked freshly scrubbed, her apricot tan had a sheen to it. Her dress was a Liberty of London print, with a full flared skirt and spaghetti shoulder straps.

"The Million Dollar Slum? It's a bad neighborhood," Peter said. "Why do you ask?"

"I spent the morning there." She added quickly, "Oh, I didn't go alone."

"I should hope not. You wouldn't visit Harlem alone."

"Of course not. But this is different. Besides, I had two men there to protect me . . ."

"Who?"

"A couple of boys from the studio. One was armed—" She grinned, very pleased with Peter's concern for her safety. "He was carrying a knife in his pants leg."

His sandy eyebrows came together and his mouth creased in a firm line. "Karen, who gave you this bright idea?"

"Eve Rothschild. She's a volunteer in the school system. They need someone to teach remedial reading."

"I take it she didn't volunteer for the job herself?"

"Don't be cross, Peter. It's going to be interesting."

"Karen, listen—" He came over and sat down beside her on the bed. "That housing project is a *mess!* There are gangs, brawls, drugs —you name it, they've got it plus abused kids and battered wives."

"But if my broadcasts are going to matter, I should be reporting on places like the Million Dollar Slum. Human interest."

"Your audience can get along without a broadcast like that. I don't want you going there—even with protection. It's dangerous!"

"Oh, Peter, don't be so arbitrary! I'll be perfectly safe . . ."

"If you want material on the slum, just read the daily police blotter."

She didn't insist; she didn't want to ruin the evening with a quarrel. They had plans to see an early movie, and afterwards they were to meet Dr. Malcolm Stone to inspect the suite Peter would be leasing. Dr. Stone had said he would be free at ten P.M., which would be perfect.

Karen and Peter rarely had an evening together because of Peter's schedule. But, fortunately, Karen loved her job. Besides her interviews, she often did the evening news whenever one of the regular newscasters was off. And there was always research. Peter had told her that the Belfort medical society liked her interviews because her material was well researched.

Often, after finishing a stint, she and Mrs. Thalberg went for an evening walk. Or they sat in the livingroom, watching television, while Mrs. Thalberg worked on her needlepoint. "It was such a comfort to me after Harry died. I'd work on a canvas for hours, completely absorbed . . ."

Mrs. Thalberg returned home one afternoon with a plastic bag full of canvases. She took out two of the canvases and gave them to

Karen. "I thought you'd like to make pillows for Peter's office," she said.

One canvas was of a tape of an EKG, showing the hills and valleys of an electrocardiogram. The other was of a more domestic nature—a pair of Siamese kittens. For the future, Mrs. Thalberg suggested, when Karen and Peter had their own home.

Mrs. Thalberg was delighted with the gold chain Karen and Peter had given her, but she could tell that it was terribly expensive. Karen had hoped Peter would forget about the bill, which was just what happened; in the last-minute rush before graduation his mind was completely absorbed in his work.

More and more he was sharing with her the details of his daily work, and would explain the fine points of a case. She was excited by the new knowledge she was acquiring.

She listened to Peter with greater concentration than she had ever given her professors at college. Her questions showed she was absorbing the material, and even at the end of a long and tiring day, Peter found it stimulating to talk to her about his patients.

Their evenings together were rare and therefore precious. They were loath to share their time with others, even with Mrs. Thalberg. Without being consciously aware of it, they were growing more dependent on each other.

For Karen, her relationship with Peter had given her a new understanding of sex. Initially she had been hesitant and tentative about exploring his body. With Delos she had always played a passive role. But now her fingertips roamed boldly over the curves and crevices of his flesh, seeking the sensitive areas. When his tongue hungrily sought her mouth, she responded with equal hunger, sucking and pulling him in deeper, licking his tongue with hers or putting her own tongue into his mouth. She liked the weight of his body on hers, his male hardness and strength excited her. Most of all she liked the passion with which he made love to her—the health and vitality of it. Sex was still a new world for him—he had not slept around enough to become blasé or debauched. And she responded to him with unselfconscious passion. They were supremely compatible.

The relationship had changed Peter's feelings about sex too. How different this was from his casual affairs where always, instinctively, he would turn from the woman after he withdrew, rolling as far away from her as he could. After making love to Karen he had no desire to shower quickly and leave. When they were both sated he would snuggle close to her, holding her lightly and savoring her exquisite body, with its sheen of perspiration.

In the morning, he was always tender, even if he was late getting to the hospital. When he kissed her, there was something about his manner that suggested she was special to him. He expressed what he was unable to verbalize in a kind of body language that calmed her fears. She was learning to trust a man again, in a stronger, more positive manner. They expressed their intense feelings with their bodies, which impelled them finally to experiment with new forms of pleasure and new positions.

"Does doing this make you happy, darling?" she would whisper, lightly stroking his scrotum at the crease or tenderly caressing his balls. And he would raise his face from her breasts and murmur, "You'll never know how much."

But through their sheer physical rapture she did know.

Once, after making love, she whispered, "Peter, I'm afraid."

"Of what, Karen? What are you afraid of?"

In the dark nest of their bed she could speak honestly, "That it won't last . . . that in time we'll just go through the motions and it won't mean anything."

Peter reassured her. He had thought about it too but he said fiercely that nothing could weaken their attachment, though it might undergo a change with time . . . But by then they would have formed a more enduring relationship.

It was the first time he had talked about the distant future; she felt his desire was not just physical. It was as though he were reaching for a state of rapture they had not dared to imagine, one that would merge them—body and soul—into a permanent oneness. She completely surrendered to him during their lovemaking, certain that he wouldn't take advantage of her vulnerability the way Delos had. Peter was neither selfish nor greedy. Her awareness of his good qualities would help her forget Delos. Peter was forthright and completely honest. He was reasonable and dependable. She felt very comfortable with him.

Still, *forever* was such a difficult notion to accept. When she visualized life with Delos Burke ten years hence, the image would not take shape. But with Peter, it came into sharp focus.

How would it feel to be a doctor's wife? She had talked to a number of young women who were married to physicians. They had managed to create lives for themselves outside the home. Once the children were out of diapers, the mothers arranged for sitters or ran babysitting pools. They were all, Karen realized, remarkably supportive of one another. Women who had left college to go to work to support their husbands were returning to classes. Many were getting their master's degrees, some even Ph.D.s.

Some women were committed to their own careers and were already in control of their futures. To them marriage was a sharing experience. They expected their husbands to carry a fair amount of the responsibility for the house and eventually the children.

"Those are the smart wives," Mrs. Thalberg told Karen wistfully. "They run little risk of feeling lonely. They love their husbands but they're absorbed in their careers and command equal respect."

"And do they get it?" Karen asked.

"In many cases, yes. Unless the women have the misfortune of choosing men whose mothers waited on them hand and foot and want their wives to do the same for them. But somehow they're managing. It's hard on these new super-women—running the home and having careers. Still—" Mrs. Thalberg hesitated, fingering the chain around her neck, "I envy them."

Aroused from her reverie, Karen moved off the bed and opened a bureau drawer to get out a sweater. She followed Peter downstairs. Mrs. Thalberg was watching television in the livingroom and waved. Karen was tempted to ask her to join them—she looked so lonely. Karen had never thought about being lonely herself; she had many friends and relatives, a wide range of interests and enough money not to worry about her old age. She thought of Mrs. Brand, infirm and poor. And Mrs. Thalberg, with a modest income, and clinging valiantly to the memory of her husband. Suddenly she found herself blinking away tears . . . all the money in the world would not prevent her from someday being lonely, especially if she were to lose Peter.

As Peter opened the car door for her he caught a glimpse of her face in the soft evening glow. "Karen—what's wrong?"

"I don't know . . . I feel so—I don't know—sad, I guess. I thought of Mrs. Brand and the other women like her . . . so many . . ."

"You're afraid—" He pulled her to him.

"Peter, we have to make the most of every day—" The words came honestly, from the deep spring of her feelings.

"We will, Karen—we'll cherish what we have."

She wanted so much to believe him. She had suffered a momentary feeling of isolation, a fear of loneliness that she had never felt before.

There were so many new feelings, some of them troubling, others confusing; some she could not sort out. She sat close to Peter. She wondered if it was being in love that made her sad and vulnerable. Or just maturity . . .

They had dinner at The Clam Box, then went to the seven o'clock showing of a French film. They sat close together, holding hands. She couldn't shake her mood; in fact, the film, with its permissive attitude toward love and sex, only intensified her angst. After Peter graduated he would set up his own office and have his own patients. The move made her feel uneasy. She would have to make her own life work, too. It was a frightening thought.

Her school friend, Mady Lukas, was leading an entirely different way of life. She was restless this summer and was thinking of taking classes at the Sorbonne in the fall. When Karen had lunch with her recently at Emily Shaw's, Mady had told her about some of the men she was crazy about. She had met a few of the younger sons of the ruling sheiks of the Arabian nations; they were self-centered and childish, with an overbearing arrogance where women were concerned—and she found them utterly irresistible. Karen had looked at Mady, so blonde, so physically Aryan, and thought she should meet Fred Farley. He had that same appeal.

Shulamit, unlike Mady, seemed so independent, so impatient of the conventional manners of courtship that you could not tell how she felt about Fred. She would probably end up heading a center for battered wives and mistreated children, running the rape crisis center or working for passage of the ERA. Karen still admired Shulamit, but she had an uneasy feeling that the future would be difficult for her. Shulamit was too independent to attract most men. They would be afraid of her aggressive behavior.

Driving now to their meeting with Dr. Malcolm Stone, she sat close to Peter, grateful for his nearness, finding comfort in it.

CHAPTER XXVI

The house Malcolm Stone bought in Skytop Woods gave the impression of age rather than neglect. It had actually been built around the turn of the century; it was an imposing house with a mansard roof and long French windows on the main floor. Malcolm had some ideas for restoring it once he got the zoning board's approval to convert it into offices for nonresiding physicians. Current zoning regulations only permitted one single family home to a half acre. At first the neighbors banded together to protest the conversion, but Nona Lish did a persuasive public relations job on them.

Nona Lish, thin, elegant, and persuasive, was the wife of a nose and throat physician who earned more than a quarter of a million dollars a year. When her children went off to college, Nona was at odds with herself, her marriage and the world. She thought about doing volunteer work at the hospital, but that was an unattractive prospect to her. She could be a secretary, but Nona did not relish the prospect of earning two hundred dollars a week. She finally found her niche in real estate.

She sold the house to Malcolm and wasn't the least disturbed by the neighbors' protests. They would be simple to override, she had assured Malcolm. Zoning laws were made, Nona Lish suggested, to keep out undesirables. What could be better for this restricted neighborhood than a house given over to a group of outstanding physicians? More doctors would mean more protection for the neighborhood. Fairfield County was known for its consumption of alcohol. And since most of the men who lived there were of an age when heart and arteries were under the greatest stress, it would be good to have a cardiologist nearby. They would make provision for off-street parking, so that the streets were not congested.

The renovations were nearly complete. The house was painted a soft gray, the shutters white, the heavy front door lacquered red, with a brass knocker.

As they drove up to the house, Karen and Peter saw the Stones' Cadillac parked in the driveway. Bright lights shone in the windows. The grounds had been resodded and the shrubs had been put around the house and around the garage and parking area.

"How do you like it?" Peter asked Karen.

"It's beautiful."

"Wait till you see the inside." He sounded boyish and excited, as he led her up the brick walk and opened the red door. Dr. Stone and Silvie were examining the paint on the hall woodwork. Silvie was pointing out spots that had been ignored or painted carelessly.

"I'll talk to the painters tomorrow," Malcolm promised.

He greeted Peter and Karen warmly, his eyes taking in Karen. She had slipped the white sweater over her shoulders, but even its loose cut did not hide the lines of her breasts and flat stomach.

Silvie walked across the floor, avoiding the paintcloths the workmen had left. Her hair was growing out and she had brushed it up to create a Grecian effect that was startling. She wore narrow designer jeans and a loose purple knit top with batwing sleeves. Her eyelids had been carefully made up with a dark shadow and above the creases in them was a pale pink rouge. She was even thinner than Karen recalled and she did not say hello.

"Have you seen Peter's offices?" she asked Karen.

Karen looked toward Peter but he was deep in talk with Malcolm.

The door to an examining room was open and Malcolm was pointing to the new equipment.

"He bought the most modern equipment there is," Silvie said sourly, "and it cost an arm and a leg." She opened the gate of the small elevator that went to the second and third floors. "No wonder patients are always griping about bills."

On the second floor, they stepped off the elevator into a reception room. The wing on the right would be Peter's. Karen felt a tightening in her stomach. She knew how much this meant to Peter. He had gone to the bank for a loan to buy his equipment; when Karen offered him money (Very well, consider it a *loan!*) he refused. His father had co-signed the note and had told Peter to order everything he needed to make his office functional. Malcolm had told him that Dr. Crowley, a senior practitioner, was retiring. He had been practicing in Belfort for fifty years and the Belfort Medical Society was about to give a dinner in his honor. Peter went to see Dr. Crowley and arranged to buy some of his office equipment: an old rolltop desk, which was a museum piece; the cabinets, the examination table. Then Peter ordered the latest in technical equipment. Between loans from the Belfort Bank, where Dr. Macray was on the board of directors, and his own father, Peter would have enough money to pay for whatever he needed.

Karen wanted to do more than make the needlepoint pillows for his office, but she was afraid to offend him. She realized that for all his support of women's lib, he still believed men were the breadwinners and women were the wives. At least it was true in Wisconsin and true of his two older brothers' marriages.

While Malcolm and Peter measured the windows in what would be Peter's reception room, Silvie turned to Karen.

"Have you talked to Maureen Macray about the auxiliary ball?"

"Yes. I've talked with her and so has Pamela Shaw," Karen replied.

"That's interesting." Silvie was miffed that Maureen had not asked for her help. "Is Pam on her committee?"

"Unofficially. We'll be working together on the last minute details."

"Have you any idea of what's involved in organizing a charity ball?"

"Not directly, but my mother is often involved in big affairs in the city. And I've heard her discuss them."

"That's not exactly working at it. I've had some practical experience, of course, and I told Maureen to call on me. But I haven't heard from her."

"Dr. Macray is taking up a lot of her time. He's not an easy patient, I'm sure."

"She knows how to manage him." Silvie nodded her head. "When are they due at St. Luke's?"

"Next Monday, I believe."

"I must send flowers. And where will Maureen be, do you know?"

"She's going to stay with my parents." In reply to Silvie's shocked look, Karen elaborated. "I told my mother about Maureen, and she called her to invite her to stay at our house while Dr. Macray is in the hospital."

"Well, that was a gracious gesture. Perhaps I should make arrangements to drive them to the hospital. She may be too nervous to drive in New York traffic."

"Pam is driving them."

Silvie managed an abrupt laugh. "Of course! Why should they ride in a Cadillac when a Rolls will do."

"It isn't anything like that." Karen found herself defensive for she was genuinely fond of Maureen Macray. "Pam Shaw's been very helpful. She's made arrangements for all the ads in the souvenir booklet. She's got all kinds of super gifts for the raffle. The business establishment has been very generous to her."

"Why not? With all the money the Shaws spend! Now what about Teresita?"

"Maureen and I drove over to Sunset Hill to see her."

"When was that?"

"The middle of last week."

"Would they let you see her?"

"Oh, yes. She's about to be discharged."

"Did she agree to make an appearance at the ball?"

"Well, she was very pleasant. But she's uncertain of her plans. I'm driving over tomorrow to tape an interview with her." She added, "She'll let me know then."

"Look, would you mind if I went with you?" Silvie was looking at

Karen, intent, determined. "We can tell her I'm doing the publicity for the ball and need some material about her. She's thinking about making a comeback, I read about it in *People*. She'll jump at the chance for publicity." Silvie was planning out loud now, her eyes glittering with excitement. "We could say Teresita is making her first appearance since her breakdown. We could call the press and have photographers cover the event. It could be a real break for us."

Silvie knew about show business personalities; how they were made and how the hangers-on benefited from their fame. She read every gossip column, every personality sketch, the titillating behind-the-scenes comments in *New York* magazine and *Women's Wear Daily*.

It was taking her too long even in Belfort to achieve her dream of upward mobility, but she knew Maureen Macray was part of her goal. Any physician's wife who had Maureen's approval and support could go far in Belfort. Silvie had plans and they were shaping up properly. However, she did not intend to lose the foothold she had gained at the auxiliary.

"Will you call me, Karen, when you drive out to see Teresita?" she said.

Karen hesitated; she realized Silvie was prying and she was annoyed with herself for letting her do it.

"On the way there," Silvie persisted, "I'd like to show you a little cottage by the Rippowam River . . ." At Karen's look of surprise, she added, "You didn't know I've gone into real estate? I'm studying to get my license."

"We're not in the market for a house," Karen said.

"Why not? Peter is opening an office here. He means to stay, I gather. You can't live at Mrs. Thalberg's forever. It's not in keeping with Peter's position. You know," she added sagely, "people expect a doctor to live well. They feel if he lives modestly he's not a good doctor." She put her arm around Karen's waist. "You're such an innocent, my dear. Someday I'll give you the anatomy of a physician's wife, in five not-so-easy lessons. Meanwhile, *please* look at the cottage—it's simply divine—I *know* you'll love it." There was no way to evade Silvie.

When the men were finished talking they all left to get in their cars. Silvie leaned over and kissed Karen on the cheek. "I'm glad we've had a chance to meet again and really talk. I'll call you in the morning."

Driving home, Karen leaned her head against Peter's shoulder; he took his right hand from the wheel and touched her face lovingly.

"What was that bitch saying to you?" he asked.

"She wants to sell us a house."

"Hers?"

"Oh, no. She's into real estate. She has just the right cottage for us —a dream cottage."

"You might take a look," Peter said.

What did he mean by that? Karen looked at him with wonder. If they bought a house they would surely get married.

CHAPTER XXVII

Peter was excited about his new office. While he was waiting for the arrival of equipment, he devoted his time to the hospital's clinic and the drug rehabilitation group that was set up at the Unitarian church. He also found time for the rape crisis center and served with a group of physicians and psychiatrists who were counseling battered wives and abused children. Dr. Virginia Carruthers was active in this group, which Peter found rather surprising, since her primary interest was in small children. But when she spoke of the harm inflicted on the children of battered wives, Peter was impressed by her awareness and her willingness to speak out. He thought Dr. Carruthers and Shulamit should know each other. He knew that Shulamit had been after Karen to do a tape on abortion, but Joe Garfield, the station manager, had ruled it out. They had too many Catholic listeners, including the right-to-life group. They'd be swamped with protests. Their advertisers would cancel business, which would be disastrous.

"I know how my father and brothers feel about abortion—" Peter said to Karen as they got ready for bed.

"They're for it?"

"Yes, if the mother's life is in jeopardy."

"I'm surprised," she said. "I can understand about your father. But your brothers . . ."

"They're products of a midwestern medical school . . ."

"What does that mean?" Karen had wrapped herself in a ter-rycloth robe after her shower. The room was fragrant with her bath lotion.

Peter was surprised at her challenge. "Karen, my family is totally different from yours."

"How do you mean?" She was puzzled.

"Well, they're really conservative. My grandfather was a horse-and-buggy doctor in Wisconsin. My father, when he came out of medical school, had a Model-T Ford to make his rounds. He was a father to all of his patients—I guess he still is. The stuff that seems outdated today—integrity, honor, loyalty—well, that's what he was brought up on—and what he gave us in turn."

"He sounds like a fine man," Karen said.

"You've no idea what he's like—wait till you meet him."

"Will I?"

"Oh, definitely. He and mom will be here for graduation."

"And how will you introduce me?" Karen smiled.

Was she teasing him, he wondered. Or was she concerned that his old-fashioned parents would regard their arrangement with disapproval?

"I've thought about it."

"Well . . . ?"

There was a challenge in her voice. He said soberly, "We'll just have to play it by ear."

"Do you want me to go to New York while they're here?"

"I wouldn't like that at all, and you know it, Karen. I'm eager for them to meet you. But I've got to figure out how to do it without offending them or outraging their feelings."

Suddenly she shed her robe and moved over to her side of the wide bed, covering her body with the sheet. The air was fragrant with the lotion that coated her skin like silk and the sweet clean smell of her hair that was skewered on top of her head with tortoise shell combs. Her eyes were closed and the solitary lamp on the night table lavished pale gold light on her face. He turned from the window to look at her, wishing she would make it easier for him. But she was mute. And hurt, no doubt. His rational mind suggested she was right; his answer had been pretty cowardly.

He slid into bed beside her. Was she deliberately hugging her side of the bed? He knew it was important to clarify his thoughts and his position; otherwise this situation could lead to misunderstanding, maybe even a break.

"I can't confess to them that we're living together without marriage. He wouldn't say anything, but he'd be shocked, disapproving. I also couldn't explain to them that you were jilted by someone."

"Do you have to bring that up?" Her voice was filled with tension. "What would they think? That I'm promiscuous, floating from one affair to another, I'm not the right woman for their adored son . . ."

"Don't, Karen. You know who you sound like? Shulamit."

He hoped the mention of Shulamit would bring on laughter. Instead, she said coldly, "Maybe she has the right idea . . ."

"Oh, come off it, Karen—you're not being yourself . . ." With an impatient gesture, he turned on his side, away from her. There was enough space between them for another body. They both felt outraged. The night was interminable. It was their first argument, blown way out of proportion, because of the resentment that had been building up, slowly, in Karen.

She decided, still huffy, not to touch him tonight, and kept the resolve while she was awake. But toward dawn, when she finally fell asleep, she moved toward him and her fingers curled around him . . .

"Let's never have a night like that," she cried in the morning. Her cheek was against his chest; the blond hair tickled her skin. She knew without knowing how or why that being angry with one another would make her life untenable. Whatever her feelings were, she knew that sleeping in his embrace, waking to his love, thinking of him while she worked, eager to earn his respect as well as his love constituted happiness.

Don't be angry with me, Peter, she thought. She was falling into a groove, a trap. And she was idiotically happy about it.

Peter was relieved that she seemed to have forgotten her outburst. He was gentle and tender with her, yet even as she responded a warning flashed in her mind. She was being too grateful for his gentleness. Her desire to please him bothered her. Was she being old-fashioned?

Did it have to be that way? Did the balance of power always swing toward the man? In a relationship it should be evenly divided, like a seesaw, with each partner carrying equal weight. It was a seesaw, all right. She felt uneasy, confused, vulnerable . . . just balancing there.

CHAPTER XXVIII

The following morning Karen talked to the program director at the station about her project at the Million Dollar Slum. She wanted to interview its social service director, Alva Britton.

It was midmorning as she drove toward the thruway. The exhaust of the trucks and automobiles, combined with the heat and humidity of the summer morning, was almost unbearable. The air-conditioning of her car made it livable, and Karen looked cool in her white pants and a striped blue and white knit shirt. Beside her a white linen blazer lay on the seat next to her white canvas shoulder bag.

She was ambivalent about today's trip. If Peter knew, he would be furious. He'd think she was defying his, well . . . orders. His concern was endearing but she was irritated because he was telling her what to do. There was a great potential in the human interest stories in the Million Dollar Slum. She cared enough about her job to do a good job. She had confided in Shulamit, who thought it was a super idea. Shulamit said she would tell the chairman of this year's United

Way fund drive; perhaps they could use some of Karen's material at one of the fund dinners.

Karen drove under the railroad viaduct and beyond it, passing factories and warehouses until she came to the right turnoff. The mid-morning sun glared down on the yellow brick buildings with their tiers of outside walkways, like black horizontal ladders; some were adorned with pots of green, others with bedding that was being aired. The deterioration was visible. There were broken windows in the ground floor apartments, broken swings that had been left to rot, and old newspapers swept into a yellowing sodden mass. The grassless yards contained empty soft drink cans and beer bottles, dog droppings. There were kids playing and running around in the courtyard, which was parallel with the thruway, but protected from traffic by a wire fence. They descended on Karen's station wagon in a flock and watched her with interest. At one end of the buildings was a patch of dirt set with picnic tables and chairs, an inducement for the residents. The wooden furniture, like the buildings, was ramshackle and showed lack of care. A group of teenage blacks and Hispanics were lounging around, their sex indeterminate in their jeans and T-shirts. They watched Karen lock her car and walk across the sticky pavement to the room on the ground floor that was used by Social Services. This was her first visit here alone.

Mrs. Britton had told her it was the hanging around, the *waiting*, that got to the kids. It inoculated them with a kind of anxiety that could take a vicious turn.

Mrs. Britton opened the door a trifle in answer to Karen's knock. There was a chain latch on it so she could inspect her visitors before she let them in.

"Karen, how nice of you to come." She sounded surprised, as though she had not expected Karen to keep her promise. Karen smiled and deposited her bag, which held her tape recorder, on the table where Mrs. Britton had been sorting reports. She was a small delicate woman in her fifties. Short curly gray hair outlined her youthful face and her lively brown eyes smiled even when her mouth showed disapproval or disappointment, as it did a dozen times a day. A seersucker shirtwaist dress clung to her meager frame.

There was no air-conditioning; an electric fan set on a chair whirled ineffectually in the moist heat. On the wall facing the courtyard were the bookcases built by young men of the junior chamber of commerce; the books were donated by several big companies in Stamford that were involved in the Reading Is Fundamental program; Xerox had been especially generous and had donated many classics for young people. It was in this room that Karen had helped some of the teenagers with their reading last Thursday evening. It had been difficult; concentration seemed to be an unknown skill here. The girls had stared at her with open envy; the boys had made nuisances of themselves in spite of Mrs. Britton's orders. Karen was too naïve to be uneasy. Besides, the men from the radio station were sitting at the other end of the room, watching to make sure the students didn't get out of hand.

It had been a rewarding experience but Karen realized that the job to be done with these kids wasn't helping them with their schoolwork.

"Most of my families are in the lowest income group," Mrs. Britton had said, after the students left the room. "When a family moves in here, it is a step up for them, since they usually come from a slum worse than this. To rehabilitate them—to educate them—is a job in itself. They have no respect for property, for their neighbors, or for themselves, even."

Mrs. Britton was going over some cards, making out forms that would enable the kids to go to the nearby beaches during the summer. The service clubs even donated camp money as well. But to take the youngsters on an outing meant booking the bus and asking a company to pay for it; arranging for a picnic; and making sure the kids had bathing suits and towels and someone to watch them.

Mrs. Britton pushed her hair off her forehead in frustration. "We're so handicapped by lack of money . . ."

"Doesn't United Way help?"

"Yes, but it's not enough. I could do more if we had leaders the kids would respect."

"Aren't there some older boys who would do it?"

Mrs. Britton smiled thinly and cocked her head like a bird.

"Let me tell you my experience with local boys as leaders. I chose one—or maybe he chose me. He was a big fellow, a good basketball player, but a brute and a bully otherwise. I persuaded him to help

240

start a ball team for the younger kids. He agreed, but I didn't believe him. One morning a police car drove up and took him away.

"The kids applauded him like crazy. They thought he was the hero and the police were bandits."

Karen listened, dumbfounded. It was the kind of story Peter told when a slum child or adult was brought into the emergency room. She mentioned that Peter thought the children were ill-nourished. Cokes and potato chips were their usual morning meal.

"They suffer from malnutrition all their lives," Mrs. Britton said. Her voice was level, but Karen sensed the anguish, the hopelessness of this woman.

"The families are so big that the older children have the care of the younger ones. At least the older girls develop a sense of responsibility to the younger children.

"But at fifteen, these girls are already worn out simply by trying to stay alive. At sixteen, they marry or have a boyfriend, usually another sixteen-year-old, who's dropped out of school. He has no skills, so he has to take the lowest paying job—if he can find one. They start having babies right away and the girl is doomed."

Karen had the tape recorder on and Mrs. Britton unburdened herself. The girls loved Girl Scouts and being members of the girls' club because they learned to cook and could bring home whatever they made. They were very devoted to their younger brothers and sisters, marvelous with children. "We had several girls who were unmarried and pregnant who worked in the homes of the Belfort Hills families, helping with the children."

"What happens when they get pregnant?"

"They don't understand sex, but they often want babies. Many are Catholics and won't use contraceptives. And they're always surprised when they get pregnant. Fortunately, there are nuns who run a shelter for unwed mothers."

An idea was taking shape in Karen's mind. Dr. Leela Rajan, the young physician from India, would be marvelous with the young girls. According to Peter, she was not only warm and kind but a brilliant doctor. They would not feel with her the way they would in the presence of a white male doctor. There must be some positive way to help these people. She would speak to Peter tonight; yes, even if she had to confess that she had come here again, she would get him interested. And was there someone who could speak to the United Way and get more money for Mrs. Britton's project? Maybe they could use some of Karen's information when they submitted next year's budget; maybe it would increase the allocation.

She could give some money herself. If Peter wouldn't take her money, maybe some charity would. Daddy couldn't fuss about a contribution here.

She was smiling as she walked to the car. A small-fry who had been sitting on the hood slid off and ran away. She looked at the teenagers lolling around in the blazing sun. Somehow it reminded her of something in her childhood . . . when Grandmother Wickersham had taken her South . . .

She did not know it, but she was taking the first step toward being a liberal, like her grandmother. She was not obliged to tell Peter everything. Or heed his stern warning against going near the place.

Three days later, she returned in response to a call from Mrs. Britton, who was eager to give Karen good news.

"You remember—I talked about getting a youth counselor to help the teenagers? Well, you'll never guess . . ."

"You found one?"

"I did! Come take a look—" She led Karen out to the playground. Teenage boys and girls who had been lolling around during Karen's last visit, were cleaning up the playground. They weren't moving fast, but then the morning sun was furnace-hot.

A portable radio was bleating out rock music. The cleaning squad swung to its beat. They were picking up Coke bottles, soft drink cans, empty bags from fast-food spots and piling them into trash barrels. The young fellow supervising the cleanup was goading his crew like a coach with a laggard team. He was a mixture of black and Hispanic and wore patched jeans and a T-shirt. There was something about him, a kind of lazy unspoken authority that marked him as the leader.

"That's Raoul," Mrs. Britton said. "His family lives here—at least his mother does. He's been in and out of trouble, though never seriously. He's smart—all of them are smart—and he's tough. He was arrested recently for stealing hubcaps. But the judge is trying to rehabilitate boys like Raoul. Instead of sentencing him, he assigned Raoul to work as a youth counselor for the rest of the summer. I'll be working with him, of course. Perhaps they'll listen to me, now that he's the boss."

"I would like to tape this," Karen said.

"That's why I called you. The *Chronicle* is interested, too. They're sending a photographer over at one o'clock."

Karen watched, fascinated. The kids were having fun, evidenced by their rowdy laughter as they tossed the junk in the trash barrels. Raoul was very *macho;* the boys were proud to be his soldiers; the girls were bewitched. They preened, their movements openly inviting, seeking his approval; they were innocent but direct in their wiles. He could try to make out with the whole line of girls, Karen thought, and none would refuse him.

He knew Karen and Mrs. Britton were watching him but he ignored them. When the photographer arrived, Raoul told him what pictures to take, but the photographer ignored him and took what he wanted. Karen was in some of the pictures, talking to Raoul and Mrs. Britton.

After she got home, it occurred to Karen it wasn't such a good idea —the photograph with Raoul. But she was reluctant to call the *Chronicle* and ask that it not be used. Well, perhaps no harm could come of it. Peter would hear of it eventually. Besides, the more people she knew who saw her picture, the more publicity—and donations —the slum would get.

CHAPTER XXIX

If it had not been for Fred there might not have been a pre-graduation bash. The other residents knew that Fred had the makings of an authentic wheeler-dealer and more or less expected him to organize it; he could cope with the medical establishment better than they could.

Fred reserved a small suite at the Continental Hotel near Stamford for Friday, the night before graduation. The next day they would scatter in all directions, taking off for the cities where they planned to establish their practices.

Fred wasn't all that friendly with most of the group. It was difficult for him to be close to anyone, even women he was sleeping with. In three years he had made some casual ties, but still was somewhat paranoid about people's motives.

"This is strictly stag," he reminded three of the residents during the afternoon coffee break.

"What about our wives?" It was Leo, a Swiss with the body of a burgher and ruddy coloring. He had recently married a new member of the physical medicine department and when they were together even briefly in the cafeteria or in the halls, sexual energy emanated from them like Fourth of July sparklers.

"Let the wives and girlfriends get together. They can go to Greenwich for dinner and an X-rated movie."

"A bash without girls?" asked another young doctor out of Brooklyn and, next to Peter, the most brilliant of the group. For three years he had protected himself from the nurses by announcing he was engaged to marry a girl in Flatbush. Now he was woman-starved. "What kinda party is that?"

"Oh, we'll have girls. More than you'll need." Fred was smiling, at least with his mouth; his eyes, as usual, were hidden behind his dark glasses—his way, the fellows thought, of protecting his innermost feelings. He used that smile in dealing with Dr. Watling. Fred disliked the bastard more fiercely than the rest of them did, but controlled himself when he was in Watling's presence. The director might yell at the others but he was civil, even affable to Fred. He overlooked Fred's misdemeanors and absences. He even praised Fred at the same time he was criticizing the rest of the group, particularly the female residents and medical students. But, then, Fred manipulated him like he did everyone else.

"What girls are coming?" another resident persisted.

"We're raiding Jackson Hill," Fred replied.

The group knew all about Jackson Hill; they had heard Fred talk of the pleasures to be enjoyed there.

"And—?" Two of the men spoke in unison.

Fred lowered his head until his chin nearly rested on his lab coat. "We'll have enough women," he promised. He had been hoarding the amphetamines, marijuana and cocaine for this event.

"What about Watling?"

Fred actually grinned at Leo. "It's all taken care of," he said smoothly.

Fred had also managed a surprise guest and he wasn't about to leak it before the actual event.

He knew how the fellows felt about the director. Three years of outrage against his injustices, his temper, his unfair and self-serving behavior.

As a group, the residents got along well with the attending physicians and after three years of constant work with them, were shrewd in their character assessments. They knew who was superior, who was ordinary, and who incompetent. They knew who showed off, who played to the gallery. They knew which of the men were also decent human beings and didn't confuse their great medical stature with their sense of values.

Dr. John Paul was still their role model.

Dr. Malcolm Stone knew cardiology and was also a great man, ready to help the residents, and devoted to his patients.

Among the newer, younger physicians a few were found wanting. They were superficial—always comparing the quality of cars, whether a Cadillac or Mercedes was better; whether a Land Rover was a good second car in winter storms. They were always annoyed with patients who protested their fees and were reluctant to accept anyone on Medicaid. Fortunately, there were few elderly poor people in North Belfort. And the ones who lived in the Million Dollar Slum went to clinics.

Most physicians were decent about their fees. They welcomed a patient's inquiries and often arranged a sliding scale to accommodate those who couldn't afford the standard fee.

By now they knew all about stress; the pressures, the demands, the jealousies, the aggravations, the ungodly hours. They knew which physicians resorted to liquor to keep going and which combined drink and drugs.

The hospital was a nest of gossip and speculation. For example, the residents were the first to learn about a mysterious patient who had been brought into Emergency late one night with a drug overdose. Fred and Peter pumped his stomach. Then the patient—with a fake name for the admitting office and the chart—was deposited in a call room. One of the residents was to stay with him. Before the night had ended, they learned he was one of the state's most outstanding gastroenterologists. His wife had recently sued for divorce and for custody of their children. He agreed to her wishes, gave her and the children money, rearranged his will and then came home to the now empty house, swallowed a bottle of pills, washed down with scotch and soda. Fred, always the realist, wondered if they had done the right thing by saving him.

The residents acknowledged the hazards of their profession. True, some of them resorted to amphetamines during the grueling 36-hour duty, but only in an emergency; and using caution.

Most of the married residents had working wives, who planned to continue working even after their husbands set up their practice. Otherwise, they were likely to feed on their husbands' careers and glory in the perks that went with them. That was an obsolete concept of marriage.

None of the residents, not even the married ones, were very savvy when it came to women in general; they were too immersed in learning and working too long hours to have much time or energy for women. Their experience was extremely limited. Their sex lives were insulated, divided between wives or nurses. They knew about some of the physicians' affairs, the gynecologists in particular. But even during their third year, the residents had little time to arrange anything but hasty coupling.

They were anticipating a big night. Tensions, anxieties, exhaustion had ground them down after three long years and gave them little time for a rousing good time with no holds barred.

Fred had laid the groundwork for a bash that they would not forget.

The weather in late June was seriously compromised by the pollution drifting over from New York and Long Island. There had been a series of humid days and the air seemed unfit to breathe. In the midst of a hectic afternoon at the hospital, the air-conditioning broke down and the patients sweltered.

Fred gave them the address of the hotel and the suite number, and then he took off for Jackson Hill to lay in his special supply of females. He had dispensed with the two women residents by explaining to them that this was a stag party, so why didn't they join the wives and girlfriends heading for Manero's.

Peter was his great disappointment. He had counted on Peter to be part of the bash, because after a couple of drinks, Peter was funny and made people laugh. Besides, he wanted Peter to see what a great job he had done on the party. But Peter was driving into Kennedy Airport to pick up his parents, who were attending the graduation ceremony tomorrow. "I'll look in if it's not too late," Peter promised.

"It won't be too late." Fred was jaunty. "It'll go on all night."

By seven o'clock one whole section of the hotel parking lot was filled. Except for Peter, all the members of the graduating class, the first and second year residents, the clinical clerks and the third and fourth year medical students had arrived. The hotel was only half full because most of its business clientele had departed for the weekend. Fred was able to reserve a large suite on the second floor at the rear of the building. He had advised the guests to be discreet, especially the men who were bringing Resusci-Annie.

When the two residents arrived with the bundle, discreetly covered by a clean shroud, their entrance was hailed with loud hurrahs. Earlier that day, they had sneaked into the in-service education storeroom, where all the audio-visual and other teaching equipment was stored and chose a mannequin from the half dozen Resusci-Annies.

The draperies in the hotel room were drawn against the sticky twilight and the air-conditioner was doing a fairly good job of cleaning the room of the odor of marijuana. The desk, converted into a bar, held bottles of scotch, bourbon, vodka and gin; a basin of ice cubes, paper cups. The talk was general, relaxed, as the young men discussed the last three years. Then Fred took the mannequin's shroud off and stood her up for general inspection.

"Gentlemen, our sage, our inspiration, the one and only . . . Weird Willie Watling."

The mannequin was dressed in a blue jogging suit, outlined with white trim, with a zipper down the front of the jacket.

"Wait, fellas—" Fred went into the bathroom and returned accompanied by a white rooster with magnificent plumage and a fierce red comb, which he held by a length of twine fastened to its yellow foot. With help, he unzipped the front of the jogging suit, inserted the rooster, so that its head and cockade emerged obscenely out of the pants. The rooster protested, there was a flurry of his white feathers to the amusement of the guests.

"Now—" Fred said, "we have asked Weird Willie to make an appearance here—this is not an inquisition—not a Kangaroo Court—we just want the gentleman to answer the questions that have been constipating us for three years . . ."

He looked around the room; the chairs and sofas were occupied, but several fellows had brought out pillows from the bedroom and were lounging on the rug, heads on the foam rubber. The radio was turned to a Manhattan rock station, but the music was low, so they could hold court.

Fred took a seat behind the bleached oak desk; hunched shoulders, scowling expression on his face, he looked like a stern judge.

"The men who are about to leave this sanctum, after three lousy years, have a beef against you, Doctor Watling. Their major complaint—"

"Total lack of supervision!" one of the residents, a pleasant cherubic fellow spoke up. "The last two years—more than that—maybe nearly all three years, you haven't made rounds with us *once*. What'd you say to that . . . ?"

The paramedic who was holding Resusci-Annie guided her head so she appeared to be looking at them all. A crown of leaves, which they had made of discarded leaves from the florist's shop at the hospital, tilted over the mannequin's face, giving it a naughty leer.

"Our mighty mentor has nothing to say to that," Fred concluded. "But let us be fair. Maybe there's a reason for his lack of supervision. Gentlemen, do you recall an incident that happened in our first year—when we got wise to Weird Willie and decided to sabotage him?"

"We remember, we remember!" they announced in a chorus, like the audience in a participation television game show.

Fred remembered it best. It happened about a month after they appeared at the hospital to begin their first year's residency. Dr. Watling, who was considered an authority on family medicine, was sounding off, giving them insight into how he practiced medicine. The odd thing was that he had written books on general medicine and was reputed to be an excellent physician. But it was all by rote; he could rattle off incredible mathematical calculations but was helpless in one-to-one relationships. The residents—the dozen young men— decided almost by unspoken directions to play games with him. When they made the rounds with him, they each made a diagnosis of a certain patient; and they all agreed on it; they sounded so sure of themselves that Dr. Watling, without checking the patient, agreed with them.

Their diagnosis was deliberately incorrect, and Dr. Watling was embarrassed for agreeing with them. He didn't criticize them immediately. He took his time about meting out punishment. But he never forgave them, and never made rounds with them again.

Weird Willie hung his head in remorse. The rooster struggled, shedding more feathers, his scarlet cockade rising and falling, while the men howled with laughter.

"What's our next gripe, fellas?" Fred asked.

"Temper tantrums . . . failure to set a good example," Leo said.

"Never showing up to advise us—unless there was a photographer present—"

"Being vain and pompous—and keeping all his press clippings like some damned movie star."

"Yelling at the girls."

"Speaking of girls—" someone shouted, "where are they?"

"Bring on the girls!"

"Wait—hold it."

"Are we through with the Kangaroo Court? What's the verdict?"

"Let's nominate him as the Captain Queeg of the medical world."

"Captain who . . . ?" a South American asked.

"Captain Queeg—the tyrant of the navy . . ."

No further explanation was needed, for there was a knocking on the door and they all brightened. Fred walked to the door, opened it with a flourish, and the cream of Jackson Hill's hookers entered, not warily, but with some hesitation. Though Fred had a reputation on Jackson Hill, they didn't quite know what to expect from his bash.

They soon discovered. For the next couple of hours, they gave the young residents an outlet for all the frustrations they had felt for three years. The drugs released their inhibitions and tensions, the girls were happy to participate in the orgy, which ended in a kind of musical chairs game of oral sex. The girls were adept. Not many of the fellows had ever participated in group sex. Weird Willie had fallen on an otherwise unoccupied sofa and rolled to the floor. Out popped the rooster, who strutted about, bewildered, pecking about at clothes on the floor.

It had been a long time since the young doctors had laughed so uproariously; and a long time since they had been so drunk. Maybe this kind of sex was available in Belfort, but they had had no taste of it.

The girls were eager, even greedy. Some were experimenting, taking cocaine and dousing it on erect throbbing penises. They knew how it helped sustain an erection. The rock music was drowned out by laughter, by squeals of delight and of pain.

Fred sprawled in an easy chair, getting his kicks by watching them all. The pain in his penis had lessened, but there was still the burning, the sense that something awful was eating away at him. He decided that once the infection was cleared up, he would get a preventive shot of penicillin before he went out whoring again. Not that he could trust some of the recently arrived nurses. He was probably safe with Shulamit. She was too obsessive to pick up a lousy dose of this stubborn strain of gonorrhea. Maybe the bugs wouldn't dare attack her; she was such an independent lady.

When there was a lull the fellows returned to Resusci-Annie.

"What about Weird Willie?" Leo demanded, shoving a pretty little Hispanic girl from his lap. "What's the verdict?"

"Hanging . . ."

"Hanging's too good for him."

"What'd you suggest?"

"Okay. I got it. Let's burn the ole bastard in effigy . . ."

"Got it." One of the girls, anxious to show her cooperation, slithered across the rug to the mannequin, which was lying on its side. The rooster had given up its struggle and sat near it, momentarily quiet. She pulled the rooster away from his nest and threw it across the room, while the men ducked to avoid him. The girl took a folder of matches from a tray on the side table, lit a match and torched Weird Willie's clothes. The flame flickered, died out, was revived. A smell of smoke overpowered the sweetish smell of pot.

"Hey, watch it!" Fred was suddenly alert. "Put it out before the smoke detectors pick it up—"

"Burn the weirdo!" Leo chanted.

The flame was creeping up the mannequin's trousers; the smell of smoke drifted toward the ceiling.

The telephone rang. The boys were suddenly yanked from their drugged oblivion and brought back to reality. Like small boys caught with their hands in the cookie jar, their sense of guilt emerged and reduced them to silence.

"You take it," they said to Fred.

He was nearest to the telephone. "Hello? No, this is not Dr. Watling. He stepped out for a moment—care to leave a message?"

He hung up. "Somebody's complained. We're having too much fun."

"Why did they ask for Dr. Watling?" Leo asked, the most nervous of the group.

"Well," Fred said, "I reserved the suite in his name."

"Oh, boy. Wait'll he hears about it."

"Wait'll he gets the bill," Fred said coolly.

His casual announcement triggered a round of applause. That they had been censured appealed to them. There was more laughter, more squeals, more screams.

"Turn up the music . . ."

Resusci-Annie's garments were still smoking. Fred went over and doused it completely. "Let's not overdo it," he suggested.

Unlike the others, he had smoked only one joint. His instincts warned him it was time for a break.

Before he could quiet them, there was a knock at the door, steady, insistent. The girls looked frightened; without a word they ran into the bedroom and closed the door.

Fred looked around; the men were at ease, lounging on chairs and sofas, a few on pillows on the floor. But it looked like an innocent scene, except for the odor of pot that was being wafted away by the air-conditioners.

Two policemen accompanied by the hotel's night manager blocked the doorway.

"Dr. Watling—?" the manager looked around at the slack faces.

"He's not here yet," Leo said.

But the manager singled out Fred. "You're Dr. Watling."

"No, sir. I'm not."

"You said you were Dr. Watling when you made the reservation."

Fred looked pained; chin resting near his chest, he met the manager's glance. "You're mistaken, sir. I didn't say I was Dr. Watling. I just made the reservation in his name."

The police officers were of the new breed in Belfort; shrewd and knowledgeable, with education in handling situations like this. They knew most of the young doctors; they had often worked with them in the emergency room. What the hell; these guys sweated it out in the hospital; they were entitled to break loose on their last day . . .

"Listen, fellas, quiet down, will you," they suggested. "This is a public place—and you're making a nuisance of yourselves."

"I don't want any trouble," the night manager said, moistening his dry lips. "Get them out of here . . ."

"We've paid for this suite; it is ours for twenty-four hours," said Fred. "You're trespassing. Get out—unless, of course, you'd like to join our celebration . . ."

"Loook, why don't you guys just relax and go home . . ."

But the sight of police officers seemed to strike a bad chord in the young men. Perhaps it was the result of three years of tedious, unrelenting subservience to the strict rules of conduct foisted on them. They had swallowed so much criticism, so many snide insults, that, fortified by the drugs, they were ready to make a stand. Arrest us, throw us in the slammer, punish us . . . but how the hell can you? We're free, we're no longer under the petty rule, we are free men now, not slaves . . .

Something in the air warned the officers. They called headquarters and explained the problem to their sergeant. They held on while the sergeant got Dr. Hilton through the hospital tie-line. They listened in silence. The bedroom was quiet, all lights off.

The sergeant came on the line. "I've talked to Dr. Hilton. Bring them to the hospital . . . to the administrative conference room. He'll be waiting."

It couldn't be discounted as a mere prank; not with the pot, the little bowl of cocaine they hadn't had time to hide, not with the bennies and Quaaludes.

They were obliged to wait quietly while the officers called for the police van. The night manager was worried about how to sneak the residents out of the hotel. Before they left, however, the police checked the bedroom, where the sounds of a toilet being flushed had attracted their attention. The girls were sitting around on the beds and furniture chewing gum and watching television. There was no sign of drugs around. The police knew the girls; they were frequent visitors to the hotel during week nights. There was no reason to arrest them.

One of the paramedics was carrying Resusci-Annie over his

shoulder when they ran into two elderly women in the hall. The paramedic explained gravely that the lady on his shoulder was being taken to the morgue. The women turned pale and ran to their room before they fainted.

Resusci-Annie sat in the front seat with the policeman.

"Where's the rooster?" The paramedic slapped his forehead in shock. "What's happened to the rooster?"

The rooster was attached by its narrow rope to Fred, who was inside the van. Fred thought about letting him loose in Mrs. Thalberg's garden.

Fred was coming back to reality and he did not like what lay ahead for them. What can they do to us? he asked himself. We can't be fined; we can't be campused; we can't lose privileges. If Watling blows his top, he may have a hemorrhage. But we're free, dammit, we're free!

But the years of discipline had left a mark and Fred was scared.

Dr. Hilton had returned to the hospital after dinner and he was mending fences. He was thoroughly disenchanted with Roscoe Osgood; the man was bumbling and pious, which was a fatal combination for one whose job was to present the hospital in a favorable light. The sight of the *Chronicle* clippings on his desk renewed his sense of frustration. He dialed Osgood's number and waited for the man's unctuous voice.

"Osgood, where the devil did the *Chronicle* get that photograph of the kid who was brought in last night?"

"Through me," Roscoe Osgood replied, sounding bright and chipper. "I let him take the pictures. He's going to give me some, too."

"Osgood, that's a battered child . . ."

"I know. Her bruises showed up on all the pictures."

"Osgood, that's a child abuse case. Her parents are being arraigned for nearly killing her . . ."

"True. But the public's right to know—"

"Osgood, for God's sake," Dr. Hilton snapped, "the public's right to know stops at the patient's right to privacy. This can end up in a lawsuit against the hospital." All they needed was for Jedd Cramer to latch onto it . . .

He would have to spell out again for Roscoe Osgood what could be disseminated and what should be kept confidential. It was a problem that should be handled very delicately. Release any information other than the routine reply—the patient is in fair condition, his vital signs are stable—and you were letting yourself in for a lawsuit. Everybody was malpractice-happy these days. Sue the physicians, sue the hospitals. All the young lawyers were eager to test their skills.

The problems at hand, however, caused him even more concern. There was so much pilfering. Some department heads, he suspected, were stealing the place blind. Getting bolder, too. Why should a Resusci-Annie be spirited out of the supply room? What could you do with a dummy used to teach cardiopulmonary resuscitation?

And the drugs. The security chief thought he had the culprit tagged; one of the paramedics, he suspected, was managing it, perhaps with either the help or the carelessness of a nurse. The head nurse? All things were possible. He suspected that both the residents and the nurses turned to amphetamines to get them through long tours of duty. But the amount being pilfered was more than an occasional staff member could use. Was somebody selling it?

Or could it be a physician, who was trying to avoid writing prescriptions for himself? The pharmacies were more careful these days; they kept records of the drugs a physician prescribed. It was easy to check up. Even Valium, the pacifier of half the wives in Fairfield County with their chronic fatigue, severe depression, too much alcohol, too many uppers and downers—was hard to get. Jackson Hill was the source of drugs; you only needed to drive around the hill in your car and before long, you'd get what you needed. At least none of the young addicts were brought in with infected heart valves, the result of careless sharing of needles.

He called for a meeting with the executive committee of the medical staff the next morning. He had received a number of patient complaints about a physician who was reducing his patients' weight by the use of liquid protein and amphetamines. He had privileges at the hospital. It worried Dr. Hilton.

And again and again—what to do with Wilbur Watling? A number of out-of-state doctors, fresh out of medical school, had applied for the family practice residency program here, but had changed their minds after meeting Dr. Watling and talking to some of the residents who would be graduating tomorrow.

Dr. Hilton hesitated to confront Watling. The man looked as though his blood pressure was sending danger signals to his brain. Was there any way to distract him from his obsessive-compulsive pursuit of showing his residents what a genius he was? Dr. Hilton felt that the man was heading for a stroke. Perhaps he had already suffered a few small ones. There was no way to save him from himself.

When the telephone rang, his spirits lifted. Maybe it was Esther; perhaps the house was sold and his family was on its way east. Perhaps his enforced bachelor days were ended.

"Dr. Hilton? Police Sergeant Snyder. We have a little problem here."

"What's the trouble?"

"Well, it's this little shindig that Dr.—what's his name—Dr. Watling—ran for your boys, the ones who're graduating tomorrow. It got a little out of hand and the manager of the hotel complained."

"How many men?"

"Quite a few, sir. They say they're graduating tomorrow."

"What do you plan to do? Take them into headquarters?"

"I called the captain, sir, and he said to contact you first. It might be just high spirits—but, well you know—they were letting off steam . . ."

"Can you bring them here?"

"Sure, that's the best way. One thing, sir . . ."

"Yes?"

"What should we do with the mannequin?"

"Resusci-Annie?"

The sergeant turned away from the telephone for a moment. "Yes, sir, that's it."

"Bring it along. And be sure Dr. Watling comes—"

"Just a minute, sir—" And the sergeant's voice came back on the line. "He's not here, sir. The—uh—doctors say he took off before we got to the hotel."

Watling. He couldn't believe it. Perhaps this was the opening he needed to fire the man. No, he couldn't fire him. He had signed a firm contract. Well, he would have the switchboard call Wilbur at home. Tell him to get his ass over here and tell Osgood to make sure none of *this* hit the press. He hoped that the policemen had not transmitted the call over the police radio, and that the news desk at the radio station was not monitoring it.

The public's right to know . . .

Dr. Hilton pushed back his chair, got up and stretched.

He couldn't stay angry with the residents; they had worked damned hard, under brutal pressure. They were entitled . . .

But what got him was Wilbur Watling. Was he among the merrymakers? Wilbur, so proper, such a fussbudget about the length of the nurses' uniforms!

When explanations came later, the group of chastened young men listened to Dr. Hilton's censure. Wilbur Watling threatened dire deeds because they had used his name. They were down from their highs but were grumpy and restless. It would be overlooked somehow—every graduating class did it.

"Go home and get some sleep," Dr. Hilton suggested, "and for God's sake, be on time for tomorrow's ceremonies."

After they left, and the rooster had been dispatched to the kitchen, Dr. Hilton called the sergeant into his office, opened his petty cash drawer, filled an envelope and said it was the hospital's contribution to the police association.

Then he took a cold shower and went to bed. He dreamed of Carmen and Silvie and when he awoke, he wondered what in the world those two had in common.

CHAPTER XXX

The fortnight between the 15th of June and the 30th had been hectic. Dr. Hilton felt as though he were inundated by problems, large and small. The hospital census was down; there were too many empty beds.

The big corporations who were usually so generous with contributions to the hospitals were again demanding a cut in the duplication of services. They thought having obstetrics in each of three hospitals was superfluous. Belfort, for instance, had less than three hundred births a year, a census very low in the government's estimation. There was a need for a unit for alcohol detoxification, but the final decision on which hospital would have that service was still being debated.

The problem was that the hospitals were treating a large number of patients who could not pay for their own care. Neither Medicare nor Medicaid covered all of the expenses incurred for these patients' bills, which meant each hospital was obliged to shoulder the burden.

We will have to devise new ways of dealing with the problem without making the indigent patient pay, Dr. Hilton reflected. But how do we go about it? Hospitals in the big cities had similar problems; many were close to bankruptcy. He had not anticipated such a financial mess in Belfort.

The people of Belfort did not want to consolidate services of several hospitals into one. They attended meetings of the health systems agency and made a strong showing at forums, where the hospital staff spoke out, determined to retain all of its services. Their patients would not want to travel to Greenwich, Norwalk or Stamford. They would prefer to be with their own physicians, in their own hospital.

Dr. Hilton, in a carefully researched position paper, expressed himself vigorously on the government's lack of direction, its insensitive approach to the people's needs.

While Dr. Hilton was grappling with the problem of government intervention, he was also seeking to firm up his relationship with the staff. Early on, he was aware of Dr. Watling's power plays. Watling was evidently nervous about his position in the hospital, perhaps afraid that Dr. Hilton would in some way demean him. The board of directors thought well of Watling, perhaps because the search committee was so enthusiastic about him. Well, Hilton was obliged to live with Watling; no sense in letting the fellow get under his skin.

It did not ease his mind any to turn from serious problems to the residents' pranks last night. Not that he considered their behavior tolerable. But he could understand, even sympathize. The making of a physician had not changed much in decades. It was still an ordeal, a test, no less exhausting than the training of Olympic champions. And not all residents made it. Although none of them flunked out, a misfit was encouraged to drop out. Sometimes Dr. Hilton wondered who among them was better suited to a research lab than to treating patients. He was sensitive to the fact that some of the young physicians were not prepared to deal with patients on a psychological level. They had need of psychiatric help themselves. Even so, they were now ready to treat the sick of the community.

Dr. Hilton looked at the clock. It was nearly eleven A.M. Time for him to join the people moving into Kennedy Auditorium, where graduation was scheduled to take place. Chairs and tables had been brought up from the cafeteria for the buffet lunch to be served here. The erratic June weather had let up for a few hours; a touch of blue shone through the heavy storm clouds and promised an end to the threat of rain.

The residents and their guests were seated in the front rows of chairs. Dr. Hilton noticed Peter Norris's parents whom he'd met the previous evening. Peter, Dr. Hilton saw, took after his father in stature and bone structure, but his sunbleached hair, his high coloring seemed to come from his mother. Dr. Hilton suffered a pang of longing for his family, even to the point of wondering whether his move had been wise. Yet all hospitals were much the same today; all faced with insurmountable problems. And Esther did love the northeast . . .

We will survive, he thought, watching the guests file in.

Dr. Hilton finally went to the lectern, where Dr. Watling joined him. The ceremonies were brief enough. The residents and guests sat strained but polite, listening to Dr. Watling describe the first graduating class in the family practice residency program. He spoke rather haltingly at first, as though conscious of the cool critical glances of the young men who had been under his thumb for three years. Then he seemed to forget about them as he launched into the importance of the primary physician.

He held onto the lectern as he spoke. Without his long white coat, he looked monumental, even impressive in a dark suit, white shirt, knitted black tie. It was, Dr. Hilton reflected, as though he were another person, not the man full of anxieties, accusations and generally irrational behavior. When he chose, Watling could be outwardly pleasant, even effective. Surely it was this quality that had beguiled the search committee into recommending him to the Board.

John Paul Macray was to have addressed the graduates, but he was not present. On Dr. Malcolm Stone's orders, he was waiting for the summons from St. Luke's in Manhattan. Dr. Stone didn't want him to become too stimulated; a day like this would have undoubtedly reminded him of his own graduation, and memories were apt to raise his blood pressure.

Dr. Hilton and Dr. Monroe handed out the parchments.

Peter was given the Tunkell Outstanding Award for aptitude. It was a complete surprise to him and his parents, and Karen beamed with pride.

Malcolm Stone was singled out by the graduates for the attending physician teaching award. He had shared most generously his knowledge of the art and science of medicine. When he got up to accept the honor, he looked so pleased with the recognition that the graduates applauded even louder. As he returned to his seat, Silvie, beside him in beige silk, took his hand, smiled dramatically with pride, and gave him a kiss.

Dr. Hilton concluded the ceremonies by assuring his audience that in spite of the problems inherent in the delivery of health care, Belfort Hospital would continue to meet its responsibility, providing community services wherever they were needed.

The luncheon was presented with all the French chef's skill. Silvie and Malcolm sat at the table with Dr. Hilton, Dr. Watling and his wife. The women were talking about the auxiliary ball which was slated for the July Fourth weekend; the event had been booked a year in advance. The waitresses served the chef's special chicken in champagne sauce and wild rice. Silvie turned to Dr. Hilton, on her left.

"When is your family due here?"

"Reasonably soon, I expect. But there is no definite date."

"It must be lonely for you."

"Well—it is. But I keep busy."

"Dr. Hilton, you should come and have a swim and dinner with us." And aware of his reluctance, she smiled and added lightly, "Suppose I check with your secretary about your first free night."

He nodded his thanks. At the table next to them were Mrs. Thalberg, Fred Farley, Peter Norris, Karen, and his parents. There was such a warm feeling about them. They looked happy, he thought; even Fred Farley had removed the perpetual scowl from his face.

Dr. Hilton thought of another problem. Perhaps Fred could give him a lead on this drug business. Fred was an odd one; he was the type to go into research rather than active practice.

He listened to Silvie's light voice.

"Teresita *is* coming to the ball," she assured Clemmie Watling. "She's as good as promised she'd be there."

Dr. Watling turned to her, "Who're you talking about?"

"Teresita."

"Teresita—the movie star?" His eyes lit up.

"The movie star—the one who married that English lord."

"And where's she going to be?"

"At our ball. She's the guest of honor."

"How do you know she'll come?" Dr. Watling demanded. "Did you call her in Hollywood?"

"Didn't have to," Silvie said. "She's been drying out at Sunset Hill . . ."

"Teresita." Dr. Watling was clearly awed. "Here?"

"Didn't I tell you," Clemmie said. "She's his secret passion."

"I guess she was every man's secret love," Dr. Hilton remarked. "I used to see her in Beverly Hills. She was a beautiful woman."

"Not anymore," Silvie said. "She needs magic—and I don't mean only exercise, I mean a face lift."

"How do you know?" Dr. Watling asked, enthralled by memories.

"Karen was going to Sunset Hill to tape an interview with her for the radio, and she invited me to come along. We both talked to her and she agreed to come to the ball. I suspect she was delighted to come out of hiding. We'll get a great press . . ."

"How does she look?" Dr. Watling persisted. Her films had captivated his heart.

"I hate to disillusion you, Wilbur," Silvie said, "but she looks like a beat-up ex-lush of fifty."

Dr. Watling had so few dreams left from his adolescence; he didn't enjoy the feeling of having this one crushed. He excused himself, got up and moved over to the next table.

"Dr. Norris—" he said, holding out his hand to Peter's father, "you must be very proud of your son."

Claiborne Norris smiled; the sunburst of lines around his eyes were like his son's; his face too was open and disarming, as though he trusted everyone. His wife, who was seated facing Karen, said, "We're so proud of Peter. He's always been outstanding . . ."

Peter flushed. He was wearing a dark suit, a white shirt and dark tie, which gave him an air of maturity. Karen, in a white silk dress, smiled at him. Dr. Watling continued, "It's a pity he isn't going back to Wisconsin with you . . ."

"Dad's already got my two brothers with him," Peter said. "I figured it could be too much of a good thing."

His mother said softly, "Perhaps the time will come—"

For Karen, the encounter with Peter's parents was enlightening. They were both so warm. His father was rather reserved after the ceremonies, as though he did not want to detract from his son's moment of glory. Peter's mother was a singularly beautiful woman; age had touched her lightly; her figure was still excellent, her bearing upright. Her wheat-blonde hair, faintly graying at the temples, was simply coifed, combed back over her high square forehead and knotted at the nape of her neck. Her print dress, a white background sprigged with bluebells, was immensely flattering.

Karen thought: in ten years, when Peter looks in the mirror, he will see his father staring back at him.

They were both generous people; it was evident in their reactions to the other graduates and to the staff. Karen could tell that Dr. Hilton was impressed with Peter's father. He had read some of his papers on the thyroid gland in medical journals. Dr. Norris was pleased.

While the men talked to one another, Mrs. Norris turned to Karen. She asked about Karen's work, evidently thinking Karen was on the hospital staff. It suggested to Karen that Peter had mentioned little about her in his letters home.

Karen explained her job and because she loved it, her expression was vivid. She was now involved in serving on some of the boards of the voluntary agencies. She described the Million Dollar Slum and added that she had recommended to Mrs. Thalberg, the physician's widow, that she hire one of the young fellows to do some work around her house.

When lunch was over, Peter suggested to Karen that his parents might enjoy a drive around North Belfort. From here, they could return to the parkway and head for Kennedy Airport for their six o'clock flight. Karen drove; Peter sat next to her, but at an angle, so he could include her in the conversation with his parents, who were in the rear seat.

As they drove up the state road beyond the Merritt Parkway, the Norrises were impressed by the attractive landscaping and the scattering of new, modern houses. Peter inquired about the clinic. Peter's mother explained that the older boys now took a heavy load from his father. The new clinic, his father elaborated, was equipped for minor surgery and there was a new and modern laboratory. No problem recruiting nurses. Many of the retired ones were coming back.

"We're emphasizing preventive medicine," he said.

What he didn't add was that perfect health had ended early for him. Peter inquired about his recent blood tests and his father admitted to having a bit of a problem with high blood sugar. "My patients have been too generous with me," he added. "I'm expected to have a snack at every home I stop at. And you know how partial I am to apple pie and cheddar cheese."

"I was considering making up a little sign to put around Clay's neck," Mrs. Norris said to Karen, "saying, 'Please don't feed the doctor'."

"Dad, are you still making house calls?" Peter asked.

"Only to a few older patients who can't get to the clinic easily. Most patients manage, although your brothers can't understand why they refuse to come in for their appointments. When I go home for lunch, I keep the police radio on in case of any emergencies."

"The boys gave Clay a beeper and he loves it," Mrs. Norris said. "Only problem is that it usually goes off when he's taking a nap."

"It keeps me active," Dr. Norris said, "and on my toes. We will all have to be alert if the government takes over medicine. Nothing in the government works, not even the government."

Mrs. Norris said, "That Mrs. Thalberg is a charming lady. How is she connected with the hospital?"

"She's the widow of a very fine internist," Peter said, "and she's our landlady."

"Oh." It was a polite comment without emphasis. Yet Karen knew instantly that Peter's mother was not surprised. Karen looked at Peter. You said it, she thought. I didn't.

She was certain of her hunch when they left the elder couple at the airport. Mrs. Norris kissed her warmly with a gentle knowing smile. It made Karen feel relaxed for the first time all week.

CHAPTER XXXI

Maureen's senses were alert, finely tuned tonight, in spite of the Valium and hot milk. She heard John Paul turning in his bed, next to hers. He had become a restless sleeper in the last ten years. Except for the vacations in Maine, when he fished on the boat all day and returned to camp burned by the sun and wind, pleasantly beat. And did he sleep then.

But it was five years since he had taken a fishing trip and his sleep had been fitful ever since. When he operated on patients where the chance of recovery was doubtful, he did not sleep well.

Tonight, Maureen was tense. She had spoken to their sons on the coast and played down the seriousness of John Paul's surgery tomorrow. They were concerned but she convinced them that they didn't have to be at their father's bedside. If they could arrange to fly east, once he was home again . . .

This was a matter for her and John Paul to face together. Dear God, she thought, give him strength—and give me the strength to support him.

She remembered the first room where they had slept, where she and John Paul had come together in the tumult and passion of young lovers. He would fall asleep with his head on her breast, his arm flung across her stomach, and she often stayed awake, listening to the rise and fall of his chest, feeling the slow steady pulse and breathing in the male scent that she found so exciting. She was aware of him, first as lover, then as husband, every day when she was on nursing duty; and when they were married, she never lost touch with the wonder and miracle of his love. There were many times when she could not wait to get off duty and rush home to their first apartment. If he were late, fear would gnaw at her insides. Something dreadful has happened to him. It was too good to last. I don't deserve him.

Then, the sound of his footsteps, the movement of the key in the door—and she was there before he had time to open it, the door flung wide, her arms outstretched. Oh, my darling John Paul. Thank heaven, you're here. I'm always so nervous when you are delayed. I'm afraid God will rob me of my good fortune. . . .

Over the years she grew less anxious. If John Paul was delayed at the hospital, one of the residents or a nurse would call her. He flew all over the country and to Europe. It was as though the pilots knew they were carrying a man who was a healer; there was never an accident. By now she was accustomed to the demands of his work. She knew how much faith he had in the future of medicine. And he loved his work, which would certainly be a strong factor in his recovery . . .

But a triple by-pass?

Oh, she knew the details. She'd found a book in the hospital library that gave her a graphic description of open heart surgery.

She wasn't present when Malcolm Stone first spelled out the risks and the advantages of this surgery, and it was John Paul's hope to spare her the details. "This operation will make your life better," Malcolm had said to John Paul—as though he did not know it already.

The surgeons would cut open his sternum. It would be pulled apart, the heart-lung machine would be connected and would take over while the surgeons worked on his coronary arteries. They would take a vein from his leg and suture a segment of it to the coronary artery, beyond the site of the obstruction. The other end

of the vein would be sutured to the aorta. Since there were three con-
strictions in John Paul's heart, the surgeon would use the vein for a
bypass in three different places where the coronary arteries in the
heart were blocked by a wax-light buildup—blockages that might
have caused a massive heart attack.

During the surgery blood would be taken from the veins, diverted
to a pump to be oxygenated and then returned to the arteries to
nourish the brain and other vital organs of the body.

Once surgery was completed, once John Paul's own heart was
working again, the tubes would be removed. His blood would be
circulating on its own again.

Throughout surgery his brain function would be monitored by
electrodes on his scalp. And his other vital signs would be monitored,
too.

When he saw Maureen alone in the hospital coffee shop, Malcolm
sat down and talked to her. "The operation will relieve the pain he's
had; the pain that he finally admitted to. It will postpone further
damage from the disease. But there are no miracles . . ."

Then, aware of the anguish in Maureen's eyes and the corners of
her mouth, Malcolm put his hand over hers. It was a caring gesture.
It brought tears to her eyes.

"We doctors don't talk about it. But none of us underestimates the
curative power of the will to live. John Paul has seen it help his patients a thousand times. Now it's his turn."

Please God, Maureen thought, holding the pillow to her face in
order to muffle the sounds of her crying. It is his turn now.

She wanted to get out of bed and go to the bathroom and wash her
face. But her movements might awaken him. Holding her breath, she
strained to listen for his breathing. Years of medical school, internship and residency had trained him to sleep lightly. Recently, she
knew he was taking sleeping pills; she could not find the capsules in
the medicine chest and she had too much respect for his privacy to
go through his pockets. She wondered if he had had pains and was
medicating himself for that, too.

We've always been so close, she thought. Why has he kept this
pain and suffering from me? I want to share in all of his needs, his
fears. Now that our sons are grown, I want to return to the one-to-
one relationship we cherished in our early years.

The sky was buttermilk white when she was awakened by his presence. John Paul had come to her bed cautiously, so as not to awaken her. He lay close to her, their bodies touching. He had covered her with a light blanket, because she was shivering. He held her, his arms strong as always, but his hands clutched her in a kind of desperation so unlike him.

His chest was bare, since he slept only in pajama bottoms. He was stroking her cheek, gently, almost she thought as though he were trying to absorb her through his fingertips. She was quiet, silent; there was nothing sexual about his embrace. It was somehow an expression of vitality, an ache that penetrated her body, a kind of communication beyond words; a renewal of commitment that had bound them together all these years. If this is to be the end, remember what we have had together, and remember that the end is the beginning for us, as Catholics. He didn't attend Mass or Communion as she so faithfully did, but the faith of a true believer had never left him.

"John Paul," she whispered.

He was quiet, his hands touching her face again, so gentle she scarcely felt his skin.

"John Paul, there is still so much to share—so much to see and experience . . ." She couldn't express it the way she wanted to. Don't leave me, my dearest. I have no life but in you. The boys are on their own now, and our best days are just beginning. Live, my darling, for me, John Paul, for us. If anything happens to you . . .

Don't show him your anguish, she counseled herself. It will only make it worse for him. Let him go into this strong and free, unafraid, confident, so that his frame of mind—the will to live—gives him added strength.

"Time to get up," he said. "We don't want to rush."

"Let's have breakfast on the deck," she suggested. There was something about the water that John Paul always said gave him a curious lift. The source of life. If he can smile, so can I. . . .

As she was preparing toast and coffee he slapped her lightly on the fanny.

It was an old familiar love pat. She wheeled around and came into his arms, and they stood there, while she shed her tears. He rocked her gently as though she were a lost child.

Pamela Shaw turned the white Rolls-Royce into the Macrays' crushed stone driveway, with Karen Cole in the seat beside her. Both young women stepped out of the car and waved to Maureen and John Paul, who were waiting on the expanse of rich green that led toward the dock.

"I'm glad you're coming with us," Pamela had said to Karen on the way over. "I was rather dreading the drive to Manhattan. I mean, what do you talk about . . ."

"They may be comfortable just being quiet together," Karen suggested. She had arranged for the station to run one of her tapes while she took the day off. They walked across the lawn, looking fresh and crisp in their summer suits and silk shirts, like two college girls.

John Paul and Maureen greeted them warmly, kissing them and murmuring thanks. He looked no different, Karen thought, except that his face was pale. Under the gray summer suit, his body was erect, shoulders thrown back, spine straight. But his posture was forced, tense. Maureen's too. They both wore their dark glasses although the sun was showing only briefly between the clouds. They were keeping very much in control.

The drive into Manhattan seemed interminable to Maureen and she dreaded arriving at the hospital. John Paul was asking Pamela about the Rolls, making an effort to be interested. When there was a moment of silence, Maureen asked Karen about the auxiliary ball.

Maureen nodded absently and said little. She felt a haze in her head during the whole drive to Manhattan. Pamela seemed to need no directions from John Paul and drove skillfully through the traffic. She said something, as they reached 113th Street between Amsterdam and Morningside Drive, about this neighborhood no longer being safe, and she warned Maureen against taking a walk here, even during the day.

With every minute, we are closer to John Paul's death. What a frightening, foolish thought. I am having an anxiety attack. Where is my faith, where are the prayers I have offered . . . if they are tinged with fear, their strength is weakened . . . I may leave here a widow.

Pamela shut off the engine and they got out. I must be strong for him, Maureen resolved.

They all walked to the main entrance, Karen carrying the small bag, John Paul holding the folders with tests and x-rays. Outwardly they looked composed. On the steps to the entrance, Karen and Pamela said good-bye. Maureen kissed them and Dr. Macray shook hands with them. Impulsively, Karen raised her head and touched his rough cheek with her lips. He pressed her to him, reaching out to capture some of her vitality. Maureen was only dimly aware of it through her anxiety.

Karen took her hand. "Mother is expecting you tonight. Whenever you're ready, call her and Otto will come to pick you up."

"Thank you, my dear." Maureen watched them leave and then turned to her husband. "Well, let's go, darling."

She followed him to the security guard at the entrance. A young man walked toward them. He was sandyhaired and wore glasses; a white physician's coat flapped open, showing levis and sneakers.

"Doctor Macray . . . Mrs. Macray . . . ?" He was Dr. Prichard Saunders, a member of the surgery team, and would show them to their room. They were in the building that housed the main administrative offices.

They followed him to the admitting office, a spacious open room of desks and chairs where women were taking information and filling out forms. John Paul was handled immediately and the process went quickly enough. Then he and Maureen followed Dr. Saunders through the solarium to where John Paul's room faced Morningside Park. Maureen helped him settle in. A nurse unpacked his bag, hung up his robe and sweater, and put his shaving kit in the bathroom.

He was in pajamas when one of the cardiac surgery residents took his medical history and did the physical examination. He drew blood, did an electrocardiogram, then took him down for a chest x-ray. Maureen waited in the solarium until the workup was completed.

Then the surgeon who was to operate on John Paul stopped in to see him. He showed him where they would perform surgery and give him post-operative care.

John Paul was ambivalent about what he was seeing, fascinated as a medical man, yet fearful as a person about to bare himself, body and soul, to a knife.

Although he was familiar with coronary care and ICU, which were awesome in themselves, the open heart surgery recovery room was an

overwhelming experience to John Paul. It was, he reflected, straight
out of a Stanley Kubrick film.

The dim lights were tinged an icy blue. The lights on the monitors
were flickering, and the instruments attached to patients whose hearts
had been mended and who lay inert, were bleeping. Various tubes
and wires fed and guarded their vital signs. He felt his body protest-
ing. So many of his friends and fellow physicians had offered their
hearts to these magicians. He knew what an ordeal surgery was and
the risks involved. And now it was he who was about to face it—the
pain, the recovery process, the waiting.

Back in his room, he thanked the surgeon and said, "I feel like the
tin man in *The Wizard of Oz* who was looking for a heart."

Maureen had sat quietly while nurses and technicians moved in
and out of the room. Her rosary was in her bag and she was tempted
to lift it out. But she hesitated, thinking it might make John Paul
think she was panic-stricken. She remembered when she used to pray
to St. Jude, the patron saint of lost causes, to find her a husband.
And then she met John Paul, and always in her heart she was grateful to St. Jude, as if he had answered her prayers.

John Paul was resting quietly in bed. She thought he might be doz-
ing. She wanted to reach out to him, to sit on his bed and hold him
tenderly in reassurance, as she had held their sons when they were
children. But something cautioned her. Be stoic. Don't let him know
how frightened you are. It might weaken him and open a dam of
fears.

He was aware of her gaze; he opened his eyes. "What time is it?"

"About one o'clock."

"Have you eaten?"

She shook her head.

"Why don't you go down to the coffee shop," and as she hesitated,
he said with a quizzical smile, "I'll be here when you get back."

She wanted to say, be strong. These years we've had together
have been wonderful but they are only the beginning. I have shared
you with everyone who has turned to you for help. Now I want you
to myself.

She went to the coffee shop and had some strong black coffee.
When she returned John Paul had fallen asleep reading, his book and
glasses resting on the bed. She left and went out into the solarium

and then slowly, scarcely aware of her purpose, retraced her steps to the old building toward the chapel. The sound of organ music beckoned her; a man was at the keyboard of the organ in the chapel, which was two stories high. The music filled the room—Bach, the noble Toccata and Fugue. The organist was communing with his Savior.

There was peace here. Maureen knelt and prayed silently. Surely, she thought, He must heed . . .

It was nearly six in the evening when the telephone rang in John Paul's room.

"Mrs. Macray? Hello, this is Eleanor Cole . . ." The inflection of the voice, Maureen thought, was much like Karen's. "We are hoping you will join us for dinner."

Maureen hesitated, then softly said that would be lovely. No, it wasn't necessary for Otto to pick her up; she would take a cab.

She went to the closet for the bag containing her overnight things. Then she paused at the foot of the bed. John Paul was propped up on pillows, the small television turned to the nightly news. He looked rested; better than he had recently. She said, "Darling . . . I'm leaving now."

He managed a smile that deepened the creases around his mouth. "Goodnight, Maureen." He held out his hand.

"Goodnight. I'll be back tomorrow." She bent to kiss him.

With a final glance, she backed out into the corridor. Her eyes were glistening but she controlled the outburst of tears that was waiting to happen.

CHAPTER XXXII

There were two Rolls-Royces in Belfort. The black one belonged to a high-fashion photographer recently exiled from London and the company of royalty. The other was a white Rolls that Dale Shaw had brought over from England as a gift for his wife, Pamela. Dale, a rather shy but attractive man in his early forties, was in the computer business which made it necessary for him to travel a good deal.

Pamela had no problems with servants; their housekeeping couple was steadfast and competent. The big rambling Victorian house at the Point was perfectly run. Now that her children were off in preparatory schools in Virginia, she devoted herself to volunteer work at the hospital. After all, she told Maureen Macray when she first came on the board, I'd like my husband to know how his money is being used.

When Maureen's two-year term as president of the auxiliary was up, Pamela Shaw would be the next head of the organization despite Silvie Stone's efforts to step into the position. Silvie tried too hard,

Maureen sometimes confided to Pamela, even if she does have her goals set. She was ambitious, and Maureen reluctantly admired her, even though she was uncomfortable around her.

Silvie had a formidable opponent in Pamela Shaw, just as her husband would have formidable opponents to face when the board of directors replaced Dr. Macray when he retired.

Maureen often said that if she had more women like Pamela Shaw and Karen Cole to help her, she'd be more effective in helping Dr. Hilton achieve his goal. She knew that he and John Paul often had discussed the hospital's future and that Hilton had the courage to plan ahead, forging reality with a kind of idealism seldom seen these days.

Dale and Pamela Shaw would stand by; they could be counted on, a fact that made Maureen feel that in an emergency the auxiliary would have good leadership.

"The auxiliary ball has to be a success for everybody's sake," Pamela Shaw said. "Particularly Maureen's."

She and Karen had met several times to go over last minute details; the ball was only two weeks away. Usually they had lunch at the confectionery shop—tuna fish on rye, coffee and the marvelous homemade ice cream to bolster their energy. They were good friends and shared mutual feelings of admiration and confidence. In spite of the difference in their ages, they worked well together.

Karen admired Pamela's glowing beauty. She was small-boned and slender, of medium height, with dark slanting eyes and perfect creamy skin that she protected from the sun with large-brimmed hats. Her thick dark hair fell to the nape of her neck and had a premature scattering of gray, which she refused to touch up. Her exotic appearance, helped by the sports clothes Dale brought her from Beverly Hills boutiques, was a contrast to her practical nature.

When Karen suggested to Pam that there was a career woman's sense about her, Pamela shook her head. "I know my priorities and I have no interest in working for a living."

Karen had worked with her on the publicity for the ball, which included writing radio announcements and sending press releases to the health care writer at the *Chronicle*. They tried to stress some of the future plans that Dr. Hilton and the board had for the expansion of the hospital, including the mammography room, among others. They did an excellent job and often managed to outshine Roscoe Osgood, who seemed to flounder in their midst.

The last-minute publicity focusing on Teresita was in Karen's hands. Through her work at the radio station, she'd made good contacts with the local press, who were intrigued by the fact that Teresita would be the guest of honor. Her press shots were stills from her Hollywood days. Teresita had asked the *Chronicle*'s photographer not to use recent photos. They were not flattering. Dr. Watling idolized her in her early years; how would he react to her changed appearance now?

Teresita was staying at a motel, and since she had dried out, she could again fit into her 'forties evening gowns that the studios had let her keep. She'd always carried one of them in a dress bag for memory's sake. Pamela saw to it that it was pressed and in perfect shape for the ball—even if they had to sew her into it.

"Shouldn't somebody stay with her Monday and Tuesday?" Pamela asked. "She seems fine, but you never know . . ."

Silvie Stone almost got the pleasure of keeping their star attraction company. Silvie offered to let Teresita stay at her house, but the actress insisted on staying at the motel. Pamela and Karen both were a bit uneasy about her. Suppose she went off the wagon and made a disgrace of herself . . .

They were concerned about it Monday morning, when they drove John Paul and Maureen into St. Luke's Hospital. But they decided not to bother Maureen with it. She had enough to think about.

There should be a cloudless sky, pure blue and the sun in full splendor and family picnics on the beach and Sousa and "Stars and Stripes Forever", as well as Rodgers and Hammerstein and at dusk fireworks shooting diamonds toward the sky.

That's what July Fourth should be, even in quasi-sophisticated Belfort.

"Peter—" Karen whispered, scarcely out of her dream, "how's the weather?"

"Cloudy at the moment."

"Is it going to rain?"

"Well . . ." he was reluctant to upset her.

"Rain . . ." she was awake now, apprehensive.

"Not yet. But threatening."

"Damn!" She sat up in bed, against the pillows, naked, shivering. He wrapped the blanket around her shoulders. "They can't *do* this to us!"

"Who can't?" he asked.

"The weatherman."

"You'll get last-minute reservations." Peter comforted her. "With lousy weather, the outdoor sports will be cancelled and everyone will come inside. You'll end up a sellout."

"The manager of the club may not be so accommodating." She swung her legs off the bed, reached for a terry robe on the nearby chair. "Is it too early to call St. Luke's?"

"I already have . . . and I checked with Malcolm."

"And . . . ?"

"Dr. Macray is doing fine. He'll be in special recovery for twenty-four hours. Then he'll be returned to his own room."

"Will he recover . . . fully?"

"Let's say the quality of his life will be greatly improved. Perhaps not the length of the life. But the quality."

"Poor Maureen. This has been rough on her."

"She'll bear up. She's a gutsy lady."

After Karen bathed and dressed in jeans and a knit shirt, she made coffee on the hotplate in the bathroom.

"What's your day going to be like?" she asked, sipping the hot strong brew.

"Busy." Peter was covering for two doctors who were off. Since his office wasn't ready, he was using a small space at the hospital thanks to Dr. Hilton. If they needed him, he would assist in Emergency. And in his spare time, he would study for his family medicine boards, which were coming up soon. They sat close together, Peter on the armchair, Karen on the needlepoint-covered footstool beside him. Today would be a long one, but this brief time together was precious. They had so little time to spend together.

"When are you due at the yacht club?" he asked.

"Before noon. I'm going to help Pamela with last-minute details. I really like working with her. In fact I like all the women in the auxiliary."

Peter drained his coffee and stood up. "It's mutual. The doctors are impressed with your interviews. Malcolm Stone told me the other day that you're the only reporter around here who does any research."

"Thanks." She was pleased. "I'm glad you have faith in me. It's more than I have. . . ."

He tousled her hair, loosening the thick topknot she wore at night. The fine golden hairs on her forehead curled in tendrils. In the morning, when she had neither her glasses nor her lenses on, her eyes had a misty quality; the whites were dazzling.

"It'll come with experience. You're getting better all the time."

She grinned. "I didn't realize you'd noticed."

"Karen, I notice a lot about you. I guess I just don't have time to talk about it."

"Peter, that's what bothers me, our lack of time together. It'd be so marvelous if we could be together more—even a little more."

"Karen, look, we've got to be realistic. It afflicts every doctor in the world. I'm afraid I'll always be rushed, that meals will be interrupted, that I may be late for parties . . ."

"I know your work has priority," she said, "but—"

"That's why it's important for you to have a life of your own."

She felt a tightness in her chest. Was he implying they would have a future? Was it perhaps his subtle way of suggesting that she have something to fall back on when they broke up?

She banished it from her mind, thinking that your fears become your realities.

"Are you going to have any free time tomorrow morning? I'd like you to see that river cottage—remember I told you about it? Silvie took me to see it. She's not the agent for it, Norma Liss is . . ."

"Dr. Liss's wife?"

"Yes. She's doing spectacularly well in real estate. She's got Eve Rothschild interested and Silvie Stone—they're all going to earn scads of money."

He shrugged. "It'll keep them out of mischief, I suppose."

"About the cottage on the river—it's not really a well-built house, but the setting is so romantic."

Peter leaned down and kissed her. "It's a date."

CHAPTER XXXIII

The Coles' townhouse was on a street given over to private houses centuries old, carefully preserved and attended. Even if she was distracted, Maureen was aware of the dignity and architectural charm of the Cole house. She carried her overnight bag to the front door and rang the bell.

Otto, the middle-aged, heavyset houseman, appeared. Behind him came a stunning woman with dark glossy hair like an open fan above her angular, distinguished face. She was wearing a simple gray tussah silk suit with a jacket outlined in red and black braid. She held out her hand, "You must be Maureen Macray. Do come in, I'm Karen's mother—"

The houseman waited deferentially as Maureen entered the hall, then took her bag and deposited it on the dark carpet. Maureen was aware of the quiet elegance of the spacious hall; the red damask walls, the selection of English hunting prints. And the fresh greens and summer flowers banked against the stairwell.

"My mother is so eager to meet you," Eleanor Cole said. "Karen has told us so much about you."

She led the way into the library, a small booklined room with oak paneling, comfortable chairs and a green and white striped cotton sofa. Sarah Wickersham was standing against the bookshelves. She was tall and beautiful, erect for a woman in her mid-seventies. Her white hair, silken soft, was piled in a topknot above her tranquil, lined face. There was no suggestion of a double chin; indeed, her flesh was smooth and taut. The blue and white diamond print silk dress, with its long sleeves and full skirt, the white shoes on her long slim feet, the triple row of matched pearls, bespoke elegance and taste.

She took Maureen's hand in both of hers. "My dear, you must be tired. Will you have something to drink? Scotch? Sherry?"

"Sherry will be fine," Maureen said. For all her experience and cultivation, she felt in awe of Mrs. Wickersham.

"Do sit here." Sarah Wickersham nodded toward the love seat in front of the bookcase. "Is your husband ready for tomorrow?"

"Yes, the surgeon and the anesthesiologist are going to look in on him tonight."

"He is comfortable?" Eleanor Cole asked.

"Yes, under the circumstances. I suppose the surgical procedure is so interesting to him that he doesn't think about the discomfort."

The women seemed hesitant to ask many questions; they drew the delicate line between courtesy and curiosity and for that she was grateful. When Eleanor had asked if she would like to freshen up, she thanked her and refused, although it was the proper gesture. She needed to be near them this evening, these warm gracious women, so she would not feel totally alone. John Paul would receive a sedative to see him through the night, while she would face it alone, without even an aspirin. She had resolutely ignored the bottle of Valium. She didn't want her senses dulled. If sleep deserted her, she would simply spend the hours praying for him.

Eleanor apologized for her husband's absence. "Phipps is in Washington so often these days. He goes from one committee to another—without accomplishing much, he says."

Otto came in to announce dinner.

"We're eating outside," Eleanor said, leading the way. Sarah

Wickersham took Maureen by the hand. "Careful for the step here—" she said, as they walked through the dining room, whose French doors opened onto a flagstone terrace bordered by ribbons of perennials and edged with sweet alyssum.

Maureen acknowledged its stunning beauty and Mrs. Wickersham said, "It's Eleanor's handiwork. She could have been a fine landscape artist."

Mother and daughter smiled at each other.

Unlike the house, where the rooms had furniture of museum caliber, summer pieces were stark modern, the heavy glass square surrounded by chairs of steel and beige leather. Candles flickered in the hurricane lamps, the dishes were old Majolica, the centerpiece of fine gold mesh was heaped with peaches and apricots and splashed with the pale green and deep purple of ripe grapes.

Maureen ate the delicious meal, a chicken and shrimp curry, and crisp salad, without really tasting it. She joined in the small talk simply to keep her mind off John Paul. They asked her about Karen, and her success with her radio program. They wanted to know about the hospital, carefully avoiding the subject of Peter Norris. Maureen responded warmly, suspecting they were thinking of Karen's future.

"Loneliness used to plague doctors' wives," she added, "but most of the young girls married to doctors today have their own interests— and their own careers. They manage very well. Karen's radio program has been wonderful for her. She has a bright future ahead of her."

Eleanor Cole was pleased, but suggested that perhaps Maureen would like to turn in early, since she wanted to get to the hospital before John Paul was taken into surgery.

"I won't be able to see him, of course—"

"But you'll feel more comfortable being there," Sarah Wickersham said. "Will there be someone with you tomorrow?"

"No, but my sons are going to fly in as soon as they're needed. I can manage."

"You will be alone tomorrow?" Eleanor persisted.

"Well, yes . . ."

"I'll come with you, Maureen," Sarah Wickersham said quietly.

"Mother, what about your appointment in Seal Harbor?"

"It's not that important," Sarah said matter-of-factly. "I'll call in the morning and arrange for another flight."

How kind they were, Maureen thought as she prepared for bed. The bed was a four poster, draped in a soft cerulean blue pattern fabric that was repeated on the deep easy chair by the windows. There was a bowl of roses on the table beside the chair and on the nightstand was a basket of fruit—tangerines, peaches and plums, with a plate and pearl-handled fruit knife next to it. There were two novels and a carafe of water as well. The bed was turned down, her nightgown and robe laid out. The air-conditioner had cooled the room to a comfortable temperature.

Before getting into bed Maureen sat in the deep armchair, relaxed by the tranquility of the room with its soft light and fragrance. She thought of her own house. Although it was spacious and beautiful, there was a difference. These people were born to wealth and elegance. She and John Paul had to struggle years for it. Was she content now? She wasn't sure—right now she felt very troubled.

There was aspirin in the bathroom cabinet and she swallowed a couple after she bathed and brushed her teeth. She slid into the bed, which was remarkably comfortable—it had the kind of firm mattress she was accustomed to. For a while she lay quietly, thinking of her husband, offering a prayer for him. She was not ready to be a widow like Sarah Wickersham, because she had not spent enough time with John Paul. She was still hungry to be with him, to share much more of his life.

What a deep satisfaction it must give Eleanor Cole to have a daughter like Karen. Maureen considered her sons a source of comfort, but having a daughter was different. The ties were closer.

Lying quietly in the dark, touched only by the glow of the small night light, she found herself drifting off, not into sleep, but into a kind of trance. She saw herself in a golden stretch of sand, against a rose-streaked skyline. She was seated in a rocking chair, waiting . . . waiting expectantly . . . and the little girl emerged, fashioned out of color and light, a lovely child, an exquisite child, with pert Irish features, Maureen's features. Maureen held out her arms and the child came close, not shy, but aloof, as though hurt. Maureen cried, Come to me, but the creature moved back, her baby face suddenly fierce with hate. Maureen, feeling her nearness, wanted to hold her, to touch the child's flesh and soothe her cries, and begged, Come to me, what do you want—

And then she knew why the little one was angry, she grasped the meaning without hearing the words: His life for my life—

John Paul's life.

She awakened with a muffled cry. There would be no more sleep for her tonight; she lay trembling under the light covers, in the depth of anguish. Her Irish melancholy was eating away at her, brought on by John Paul's surgery. Knowing him as well as she did now, she realized they would have married each other no matter what. The priest had forgiven her; she had offered reparations by giving unselfishly to the community. We were so young, she thought, and we were only human. But the sense of guilt over having the abortion had never left her, and she still expected to be punished for it.

Don't take John Paul from me, she prayed.

CHAPTER XXXIV

"The great beauties of our age are not beautiful at all, except to the camera eye. They acquire presence and the superficial gloss that creates an aura of beauty, thanks to the skills of their beauticians, speech teachers, coaches and Svengalis, but these fragile women, products of the Hollywood legend, love their pets more than their men. They are mostly frigid and they end up, not exactly like the star of *Sunset Boulevard,* but close enough. They become part of a new California religious sect: they seduce young boys and become slaves to liquor and drugs.

"Teresita is no exception, but—she is a woman of dazzling contradictions."

She kept the newspaper clipping—the only one she had ever kept—in her appointment book because it was a kind of self-fulfilling prophecy. The man who wrote it was not one of her lovers, even though she had slept with many of the men who wrote about her. She thought doing it would help them realize she was really a nice human being with a sensuous body.

Her designer friend Bob Maltbie said she was elusive, somehow unattainable. Unattainable was okay for Garbo, a great actress, but not for Teresita, who counted on her blatantly sexy look for success. It was her essence: chin raised, dark glossy hair flying around her head, the eyes, dark and mysterious, the nose, perfect.

Make love to the camera, make love to the director, make love to the exhibitors who recently voted you the sexiest star in films, the producers said to the Pinup Girl of 1944.

Teresita stood before the mirror over the sink in the bathroom of her motel on U.S. 1 in Darien and thought it a damn shame the way these places arranged electric lights for the convenience of men, not women. She was accustomed to mirrors outlined by bands of electric bulbs, so she could cover every flaw with makeup. She was skilled at it. When she first began dancing at the small clubs with Maxim and they were bloody broke, she learned how to apply the liner to her eyes, make hollows in her cheeks that men loved to kiss, apply vaseline to the full lower lip. Promising so much to the patrons of the smoky clubs. Their eyes would follow the flow of her luxurious black hair down to bare arms that swung to reveal the full, round Italian breasts, the flat belly, the long slender thighs and the full calves.

She narrowed her eyes to catch the reflection in the mirror. She saw her mother's face, then shook her head hard to blot out the image. "All girls end up looking like their mothers after a while. I hope it never happens to me." That was her daughter, Daphne Fellowes. Teresita heard that clipped upper-class English accent and saw the cool contempt in her face, so much like her father's, an English face with perfect bone structure and the fairest of colorings.

But now as she looked again, Teresita still saw her own mother in the mirror. Why did she shudder at the sight? She loved her mother; she was highly emotional about mama. Mama in her youth had been beautiful, but she was a good wife, a good mother, she knew her place. She believed that her children should marry within their class and have babies like everyone else.

Mama had died at Teresita's present age, fifty-two, of a series of small strokes, the result of a size 44 body and high blood pressure. The family turned against Teresita when she came to the funeral because she arrived at the last moment. She was making a film and had to leave immediately afterwards, or else be fined or put on suspension. The relatives behaved as though she were a fallen daughter and made her feel guilty for not coming to visit mama more often. God will punish you for this, they said; a daughter who abandons her dying mother. But I didn't abandon her. I always sent her money, sometimes a little, sometimes a lot. More than any of you. . . .

It was crazy to think of that now, she thought as she applied her makeup. She put the mascara wand on the basin. Her hand was shaking. She opened the medicine cabinet and took out ten milligrams of Valium. Her first mistake had been to combine the tranquilizer with scotch, a habit she learned from husband number three—or was it number four?—Nigel Fellowes. But now that she was weaned from alcohol, the Valium was safe. She was not apt to end up in an emergency room with her stomach being pumped, as she had once. When was it? she wondered, groping in a fog of recollections. When the Fellowes' lawyer suggested it would be better for Daphne to live with her father's family in Sussex?

One of the psychiatrists at Sunset Hill had tried to explore her feelings about growing up as a nice, quiet Italian girl from a lower middle-class family and becoming a movie idol. She knew she had always listened to men. In her youth, papa was the one who gave the commands. Later it was men who got things from her without giving her anything in return. Gentle, soft, hiding the hurt and the shame, she let men use her.

Husband number one, Maxim, was one of the owners of a small, successful dance studio. He was gentle and romantic. He loved her big, generous, emotional family. He was ambitious for her, which was unusual for a man before World War II. She learned to dance well because she had a natural grace, and even in the most sensuous tangos her face remained tranquil and soft. She and Maxim danced in seedy little nightclubs on U.S. 1 on the way to Florida.

It was through Maxim that she got her first screen test; he sent photographs of her to Fox, MGM, Warners—all the important studios—and Warners offered her a screen test.

Maxim was ecstatic. He had discovered talent. He felt a little guilty about promoting her, aware of her family's reaction, but something in him saw Teresita's potential.

She wasn't Teresita then. Teresita was his name for her; a good name for a dancer who was destined for fame. The name suggested a golden Spanish background, Andalusian perhaps; anything but Italian.

The screen test was made in New York City. The big-shots who saw it shrugged, saying her forehead is too low, she needs plastic surgery to make her chin more pronounced. She needs, she needs . . .

When she received the offer of a six-month contract with Warners, Maxim told her parents he was going to open a dance studio in Hollywood; their daughter would, naturally, go with him.

Husband number two was an intellectual. And why not—Rita Cansino had her Orson Welles; Marilyn Monroe her Arthur Miller. Why shouldn't an intellectual, an idealist, a liberal fall in love with one of Warners' starlets? Being docile, Teresita allowed the studio to transform her. Her forehead was raised by electrolysis, giving her a widow's peak. She had plastic surgery on her chin, and while they were at it, they put a dimple in. She had a natural overbite so her lips didn't quite meet and she often licked them when they were dry, in an unconscious sexual come-on. They didn't need to touch her body.

Away from the strict Catholic influence of her family, she blossomed. The California sun sent its magic through her pores, giving her a light Tahitian tan that contrasted with the flashing whites of her eyes and even more the dazzling white of her newly capped teeth.

Number two was a failed young novelist who hoped to make a comeback as a film writer, with Teresita's help. By this time she was screwing one of the producers.

Number three was a U.S. Army major whom she met while entertaining the troops overseas. He was from a socially prominent San Francisco family that went back to the gold rush days. By the time they were married, she was already a full-blown star, along with Betty Grable, Rita Hayworth, Frances Langford and others. She commuted to San Francisco on weekends. Warners had loaned her to MGM at the time, and while the major's family thought it amusing to have a pinup in the family, they were not very happy about it. After Teresita's first postwar flop, when a new director ignored her dancing, her body and her face, and put her in an O'Neill drama, she stopped commuting and began to worry about the future. She also began to drink.

Stardom did that. Soft quiet girls who listened to the men around them often became rag dolls to their ambitions and somehow a little drink now and then helped them to relax when they were feeling tense.

She didn't worry for long. It was natural for her to be acquiescent, to drift along with almost catatonic sweetness in the role established for her. She was mild and compliant, in bed and out. Finally MGM decided she needed a change of scenery, which meant she was fired. Teresita never really knew how it happened; she had not objected to the films they assigned her. But the lawyer suggested she was tired and a little stale and wouldn't she like a trip around the world; they would underwrite it and even send a companion with her. She got as far as London, where she met Nigel Fellowes.

The Englishmen knew how to treat a woman. Teresita was enchanted by Fellowes's charm, breeding and charisma. He was a gentle lover and when she discovered she was pregnant, he saw no need to get an abortion. They were married at the Fellowes's country estate, with its crenellated turrets, small-paned windows and massive fireplaces. They had the flat in Chelsea and spent weekends at the family house in Sussex.

Nigel was what—number three or four? Teresita couldn't quite recall. There had been so many. Teresita now knew better than to believe a man's declaration of love, sweet love before he screwed her. It didn't last. Nothing lasted.

She turned away from the unfriendly mirror. Lighting a cigarette, she looked through her makeup case—a Victorian leather box lined with satin and filled with several beautiful gold and mother-of-pearl boxes. When Nigel's mother gave it to Teresita, she said one of the English royalty had given it to her grandmother, who was a precious beauty with an indelicate reputation. Teresita had the impression that Lady Fellowes linked her with her dashing but disreputable grandmother, and was rather glad to be rid of the tainted case.

She obliged the Felloweses by returning to Hollywood in the summer of 1970, without her daughter Daphne and without alimony. "Terry, you'll make more money from one film than I can make in a decade," Nigel had said, "so why don't we just say farewell." So she did.

She was offered a cameo role in a film by a young director she had never heard of, one of the new breed who considered themselves the lords of creation. The wild sixties were long gone, dismissed as a twentieth-century children's crusade, so it looked like a new beginning, particularly for Teresita. She agreed to take the part. But the change in Hollywood shattered her.

When she arrived in Los Angeles, she had been stricken with a wave of terror. There were such crowds, so many people, all in a rush, not caring whom they elbowed. There was no one to meet her; no chauffeur and limousine, no photographers, no press agents, no officials from the companies for whom she'd once earned millions. Hollywood Boulevard had turned into a sordid extension of Manhattan's 42nd Street. Teenage prostitutes and homosexuals paraded before the tawdry boutiques, the army and navy stores, the cut-rate drugstores and the pornography outlets.

Teresita was scared; she was about to embark on part two of her life, but what life was there for an ex-beauty who was over forty and broke?

Her young director, a Brooklyn youth with talent refined by the film courses at NYU's Washington Square division, saw her as a symbol. He was doing a war film; he superimposed the reality of war —bloody soldiers and bewildered refugees—with shots of Teresita in a tight little dress with spaghetti-thin straps, her breasts spilling out as she sang to the boys. Teresita represented all that was artificial and pseudosexual in Hollywood. Her cameo was good, as a matter of fact, but it didn't evoke sentimental memories from the audiences or kind words from the critics. She waited and languished and drank.

She had few possessions with her and soon had to pawn them to help meet her living expenses and buy her booze. She clung to an old appointment book, beautifully bound in Moroccan leather, the year of "peace at last" 1945, the year she was at her peak, when there was only one way to go and that was down.

She did a television game show, but she just didn't think quickly enough; she was not staying in touch with current events and new attitudes, and alcohol was beginning to take her mind apart.

She was bewildered by the hippie culture with its contempt for convention, for makeup, for the gloss that producers had demanded of stars in Teresita's time. The new breed wanted realism: show life as it is. In the late forties, she had had a bungalow at the Beverly Hills Hotel; now when she appeared for lunch at the Polo Bar, nobody recognized her. They were too busy making deals, out-maneuvering their buddies and knifing the competition.

So she spent a decade on the dark side of Beverly Hills; her agent, a has-been like herself, got her an occasional job. But through an appearance as a hostess in a commercial, filmed for a Detroit motor company, she met several new sources of income: top automobile executives who remembered Teresita when she was a pinup. It was one of them who finally arranged for her to enter Sunset Hill for treatment of her acute alcoholism. She was overweight, her face and body bloated with liquor; her voice was husky, a whisky- and cigarette-coarsened voice that had no charm, no sex appeal. She needed someone to take care of her affairs, to conserve what small income she had. When the psychiatrist at Sunset Hill asked her what she wanted to do, she told him that she wanted to die, quickly and painlessly. Because she couldn't have what she really wanted, which was to be loved and worshiped *again;* to be the darling of men who wanted her even though she didn't want them, she wanted her youth back; she would sell her soul for a second chance.

But even St. Jude couldn't help her this time. She was beyond help.

CHAPTER XXXV

The women in charge of the auxiliary ball did not have to worry after all.

Even though it was raining heavily, it was a beautiful night inside the Yacht Club. The party was so crowded that people without tickets were being turned away. Six hundred guests! The chef frantically ordered additional supplies; the manager called for extra kitchen help and waiters.

Fairfield County had come to see Teresita. They wanted to see the woman who had so many men, so many affairs. All the middle-aged wives, themselves betrayed by their hormones, were eager to inspect her in the cruel light of today. To see, to just see, if Sunset Hill had really treated her alcoholism, her drug problems and her depression successfully.

Pamela Shaw and Jedd Cramer went to pick up Teresita, while Peter went to get Mady Lukas, who was home for a week and who practically invited herself to the ball in order to see Teresita. Besides, Mady had confessed, she was just getting over her last affair. She needed a diversion.

Karen thought Jedd Cramer would be suitable for her, at least for the evening. She telephoned Jedd and described Mady, emphasizing her family background. It sounded like a good opportunity, Jedd calculated to himself.

Karen was in her favorite draped white chiffon, her thick fair hair coiled on her head with tiny gold wisps curling around her face. As she entered the ballroom she smiled, relieved and delighted. She and Pam had labored all afternoon to achieve the effect—from flower arrangements to the exquisite little gazebo behind the tables assigned to the officers and board members. Teresita would stand there, flanked by the important medical couples, for the photographers. Karen had arranged a table for members of the press, including the society editor and photographer of the *Chronicle*.

The guests started pouring in early—earlier than the committee had anticipated. The presence of the notorious movie star had changed their plans. Everyone wanted to arrive early. The crush was not unlike that premiere night of one of Teresita's films.

And there they all were, the auxiliary board and its members, physicians and their wives, contributors to the hospital fund, businessmen, political figures, including the mayor, and many members of the hospital staff: supervisors and nurses, young women and matrons all transformed in their pretty evening dresses.

Pamela Shaw, slight and graceful in her white silk dress with scarlet poppies, moved among the round tables surrounding the dance floor. The room was colorful with bright balloons that floated toward the ceiling, bouquets of mixed flowers at every table, carafes of red and white wine. The first course—scooped-out pineapple halves spilling over with fresh strawberries and melon balls—was ready to be served.

As Jedd Cramer escorted Teresita to her table, not even the more restrained guests tried to hide their curiosity. Teresita wore black taffeta with an off-the-shoulder neckline, puffed short sleeves and a snug skirt slit alluringly to the knee. It was a Charles James design, which seemed faintly familiar to the older guests. Teresita had worn it when she was on the cover of *Life* magazine, which had sold as many copies as Marilyn Monroe's calendar nude or Betty Grable's pinup.

Jedd, looking impressive in his white dinner jacket, black trousers and cummerbund, introduced Teresita to the group—Karen and Pamela, whom she knew; Fred, Peter, Shulamit and Mady Lukas, who were strangers to her. Teresita smiled and nodded graciously, making eye contact with each person.

She had just sat down when Dr. Watling approached their table. Even he looked handsome in his dark dinner clothes. His awe of Teresita deterred him from making any derogatory remarks. He told Teresita that she had always been his number one favorite—a sincere compliment. It was true; Watling had long adored her, ever since the forties. Meeting her was a dream come true.

As the dinner courses were served, Teresita kept the people at her table fascinated by her stories of Hollywood in the forties. The group was fascinated and Teresita was flattered by their attention. She felt her spirits renewed as though it were with an electrical charge. She regressed to the girl of the war years; the musical comedy princess, the goddess, object of every G.I.'s dreams.

The musicians were aware of her; they played songs that were popular in the forties and fifties—Rodgers and Hammerstein, Cole Porter, and the song that had become her theme: "The Lady Is a Tramp."

There was dancing between courses; Jedd turned and held out his hand to Teresita. "May I have the pleasure—?" Encouraged by her languid smile, he led her on to the floor, confidently aware of everyone watching him. His face was level with Teresita's, and he was aware of her perfume, her swelling breasts under the black taffeta, the suggestion of a belly, that nonetheless took away none of her grace. Jedd found it pleasurable to hold her in his arms, to touch the flesh so many men had coveted. As he pressed her close, he knew she was aware of his hard-on but it didn't seem to bother her. In fact, she grew more animated and her smile flashed with a neon radiance, her dimpled chin upraised, a pose that surely her fans would recognize. He knew they were attracting the attention of the other dancers, as well as those seated at the tables. He knew how to play to an audience, the way he played to a jury. He would treasure the moment forever, poignant because it was brief and would lead to nothing more.

"You dance well." She was breathless.

"You make it possible," he said, "usually I am two left feet."

"You remind me of a young Spencer Tracy. Did you ever see his films?"

"Only his last ones."

"When he was young, he had a special quality, a kind of rough-neck but gentle. I was in one of his early films."

"Are you going to do any more films or television work?"

"No. I couldn't allow myself to be seen . . . all this weight, and my face—" There was a suggestion of a double chin, drooping lines around her mouth, circles under her eyes that makeup couldn't blot out. "I should go back to the coast and have a plastic surgeon take a few tucks first."

"Why not do it right here?" Jedd had an idea. "We have some of the world's best plastic surgeons at the hospital."

"Well, it's something to think about. I would if I could just collect the money that's owed to me . . ."

"Perhaps I can take care of that for you," he said casually. "I happen to be a lawyer."

They were suddenly aware that the music had stopped. The other couples had returned to their tables and they were the only people on the floor. Teresita did not seem to mind; she smiled and nodded at the crowd. Then Jedd returned her to their table. He whispered in her ear that he would telephone her in the morning so they could talk about her plans for the future.

Flushed, really radiant now, Teresita sampled the fresh fruit before her. She played with the melon balls, savoring their soft texture. If she ate carefully, there would be no problem. Her blood sugar would stay level.

Karen and Peter were dancing; they looked like a dream couple, she thought. When Peter brought Karen back to the table, he asked Teresita to dance and she was delighted. She took his hand and allowed him to lead her to the dance floor. Unlike Jedd, resplendent in dinner clothes, Peter wore a dark suit, white shirt and small patterned tie. His natural vitality put Jedd Cramer's calculated polish in the shadows. She wondered how Peter was in bed. She became fluid in his arms and regarded him with a suggestive look. To achieve her best closeup shots, she would imagine herself in bed with a stud like this; her sleepy glance and her moist parted lips were sexual invitation, an aphrodisiac more potent than anything a doctor could prescribe. She tried it on Peter.

Then she noticed Karen. She had a certain style that Teresita envied; she carried herself as though success were her birthright. She wore no jewelry except a flat gold band around her neck. Teresita didn't always practice elegance and taste, but her experience as Nigel Fellowes's wife had helped her recognize the good taste in simplicity and understatement. She wondered if her black taffeta was out of season; most of the women tonight were in pastels . . .

The next man to ask her to dance was Dr. Watling, that giant of a man whose beady eyes behind the glasses, loose moist lips, and too tight dinner jacket reminded her of a Hollywood producer—the combination of predator and admirer: Stick with me, baby, and the world is yours, his expression said.

He was a top doctor at the local hospital, he mentioned casually as they danced. He was clumsy and apologized, which surprised her. Holding her in his arms was simply overwhelming, he said. Never before had he felt so giddy. Meeting her meant more to him than anything ever had in his entire life. He had never dreamed of actually dancing with her.

Was he disappointed? she asked. She was flirtatious, but also searching. Dr. Watling seemed to totally accept her—the scarred, bloated woman who was regarding him with her lustrous eyes. He wasn't as bad as he originally appeared to be. When she approached him with the subject of plastic surgery, he was tactful. The march of time, he suggested, was particularly cruel from the camera's angle. But it could be easily corrected, if she thought it were really necessary. He said he thought she looked fine the way she was.

Did he think so? she countered, mentioning that the young lawyer —was it Cramer—Jedd Cramer—knew of several highly competent plastic surgeons.

Dr. Watling agreed; one in particular, who divided his time between the east and west coast, often brought his New York patients— film stars, society women, a number of career women—to Belfort. The hospital handled such cases with tact and finesse. The nurses were discreet; everything was absolutely hush-hush. As Teresita perked up and showed interest, Dr. Watling said maybe she should give cosmetic surgery serious consideration.

Dr. Watling had given her confidence, which added to the good vibrations that surrounded her tonight. Men were her lifeline to sanity, to a comeback. She felt frantic and isolated without a man. The last decade had been such a failure. The search for a man who cared left her wasted and scarred.

Like her friend, Judy Garland, she needed to be in love. She needed a man to boost her ego, to keep her from shattering into a thousand pieces. One of her early lovers suggested that her fear of loneliness was not all that bad, that the anguish of a long, empty night added a dimension to her personality and made her a better actress. But the fear of losing one love without finding an instant replacement stalked her constantly.

What keeps a man committed to a woman, she had asked Nigel. He had shrugged, lean and eloquent. It was the initial spark, the first glittering allure, like the first glass of champagne. The rest he left unsaid, but she knew, how *well* she knew. The girls men bed are not the girls men wed. Englishmen had their showgirls and their lower-class mistresses but they married in their own class. Women like Teresita were not meant for a permanent alliance.

Yet she longed for permanence and stability. If Maxim had not entered her life, she would have become like her mother and married to a man with no ambition.

At Sunset Hill, the doctors had come to the conclusion that in spite of her suicide attempts, she had inner strength and resilience. She was a survivor, and coming here tonight was a good sign. Her luck was changing. She dared to think about the future. Someone among these handsome men would decide her destiny. It would be nice if it could be someone as young as Peter Norris. He was certainly the most attractive. But anyone would do. She could even see herself succumbing to Dr. Watling's desires. A woman could create a whole new life by choosing the right man. . . .

She moved happily from one partner to another until, still smiling, she had to take a break. Fred Farley offered her some champagne. But she shook her head and sat down in her chair. The young doctor knelt beside her; he removed her fragile slipper and rubbed her toes.

Her foot was exquisite, long and narrow, barely confined by the black satin straps. Smiling, she told him it felt good. She felt as if she were flying.

Still, she turned down Dr. Stone when he asked for a second dance. Her smile was there but her feet were burning.

Soon she was back in control of herself. Masculine attention was the best antidote for low blood sugar. The attractive young *Chronicle* photographer asked her to stand beside the flowers surrounding the lattice of the gazebo. Give me that famous pose, he begged.

Dr. Watling was at the adjacent table, positioned so he could watch Teresita without being obvious about it. Not that it mattered; all eyes —even his wife's—were on her. He was dazzled by the possibilities. She wanted him to help her. If she got back her stardom, she would be everlastingly grateful to him. A physician like him would be of greater value to her than a mere lawyer like Jedd Cramer. It would be a dream come true.

Silvie and Malcolm Stone were at his table, as well as Harlow Hilton. And at the last minute, Carmen and two of the older floor supervisors were assigned to their table. Silvie thought it rather presumptuous; after all, these women weren't on their social level at all. Still, she was surprised at how stunning Carmen looked in a green silk jumpsuit that contrasted with her auburn hair. When she danced with Fred Farley, the curves of her neat little body, outlined by the soft green silk, were downright indecent, Silvie thought. Carmen wasn't wearing anything underneath. No wonder all the men asked her to dance. Even Malcolm.

When she suggested to Malcolm that that little creature was flagrantly on the make, Malcolm replied that Carmen had done him many favors. She was the best nurse he had. When Carmen called him at home or office about a patient, it was never an idle call. There was a problem needing his attention.

When he danced with Carmen he felt relaxed, almost content. He looked down into her face and their eyes met in a kind of communication that aroused him; his hand quivered against the warmth of her back. Abruptly he cut the dance short; he did not want to upset Silvie. He felt guilty.

The tempo of the party was accelerating. Teresita had brought Hollywood to Fairfield County.

Fred turned to Shulamit, who was squinting through the smoke of a Tiparillo cigar. She looked cute and a little boyish in her dinner jacket and slim trousers, with the fine linen shirt and its tucks that accented the swell of her breasts. By all rights, he should be annoyed with her for dressing like that. He had had dinner with her family twice in the last two weeks and they liked him. He could tell by their warmth, by the way Mrs. Solove said, "Fred, I can't get anywhere with my daughter. You talk to her. She'll listen to you." As if he were part of the family. It would be no sacrifice for him to marry Shulamit. Everything was on the right side of the ledger. He could do anything he pleased professionally. They would help him; he could write his own ticket. He would have money and family and a beautiful wife. She was probably lively in bed, judging from the way she behaved when they made out on the blanket on the beach. She may have screwed plenty in Israel, but to him she was a virgin and that was the way he wanted it; at least that was what he told her.

But still he was confused. To become part of a large, gregarious family appealed to him, as it would to anyone who was an orphan. The evenings he spent with her family touched some deep recesses in him, warming him so that he began to want more of it. It was a need that had been too long ignored. To feel accepted was foreign to him. He knew he was afraid of it.

Shulamit had excused herself from the table. He thought she was on her way to the ladies' room, but she had stopped at the table where the right-to-life group was seated together, as though gaining strength from each other. They were bright, attractive women in the years when the abortion laws would affect them. Would she ever settle down to be a, well, just a wife? Fred wondered. He didn't know what he really wanted in a woman. Was Shulamit, with her sassy mouth, her independence, her lack of tact—the kind of woman he wanted to marry?

Why couldn't she be like Karen Cole?

It seemed natural to break in on Karen and Peter, dancing cheek to cheek. It was his only opportunity to hold Karen in his arms, and he took full advantage of it, enjoying her nearness, her soft fragrance, her gracious smile. He told her he had seen the photograph of her in the *Chronicle* with that black dude from the slums.

"Don't mention it to Peter," she said nervously. "He doesn't like my going out there."

"I don't blame him, but I'll keep quiet." He made her feel there was a secret understanding between them, and she did not like it.

She suggested again that he talk with Mady Lukas. "She's interesting and great fun."

This time, Jedd Cramer cut in. He was in great form tonight; evidently something had sparked his enthusiasm. He was not nearly as personable as Peter, Karen reflected, but he already had the trappings of power. Somehow she compared him with Fred. She had no reason for this feeling; it was just an instinct, and she felt Peter should not be too friendly with him.

Malcolm Stone was dancing with Carmen again and Silvie had Dr. Hilton on the floor. Karen noticed that Teresita was in Peter's arms again and seemed to be enjoying it.

The party was at its peak. Teresita's presence seemed to have a leavening effect. Karen, sitting out a dance, leaned over toward Pamela. "I think we did a good job," she said. Palmela nodded, pleased that they would have a good report to give Maureen Macray. The dancers formed a conga line and snaked their way around the dance floor, out the door and around the terrace. The spattering of raindrops did not stop them.

Silvie Stone was part of the tail end of the line, just behind Dr. Hilton. She was clutching him, laughing, breathless. When the rest of the dancers went back inside, she pulled him to a stop, saying she could not catch her breath.

Dr. Hilton waited politely, watching the rest of the dancers scurry out of the rain, while he and Silvie stayed behind, protected by the awning flapping in the wind. Silvie shivered; she caught his arm and somehow coaxed his arm around her. She whispered an appeal: hold me, I'm frozen. His next move, an embrace, would be inevitable. Then her hips would move close to his groin, her lips would reach for his. It was a classic come-on and she wanted results. And she got them, but not what she expected. Dr. Hilton disengaged himself. He said, coolly, "It isn't necessary to exercise your very considerable charms on me, Mrs. Stone. Your husband's future in the hospital will be decided in the board room, not the bedroom . . . Shall we go in?"

Silvie walked back into the music and the crowds, but did not see them. Dr. Hilton left her at her table and seemed to take all of her sexual appeal with him. She shook her head to clear it. Was it possible she was losing her beauty, that a man who had been separated from his wife for months could still reject her offer? She finished someone's drink. Malcolm was approaching the table. She got up unsteadily. "Dance with me," she commanded.

They moved well together. She rubbed against him, looking at him seductively through half-closed eyes, full of promises. How he wished he could respond properly—that he could focus on the passion rather than letting reason get in the way. We can't go back, he thought, we must simply accept it as a fact of life. At least we have a semblance of a marriage. The kids have turned out well. He was surprised at how calmly Barbara had reacted to Silvie's edict that she go to secretarial school. And Norman, God love him, was never any problem.

It was after midnight. The party was beginning to lose steam when one of the assistant managers came to his table. Malcolm's answering service was on the phone. He was to call police headquarters.

Puzzled, Malcolm dialed the number. As soon as he mentioned his name, he was transferred to the chief.

"Dr. Stone—you'd better come down here. We have a boy who says he's Norman Stone . . . your son."

Malcolm was visibly upset and worried. He whispered to Silvie and they made a fast but gracious exit. They were in their car before anyone noticed they were gone.

As the crowd thinned out, fewer and fewer couples were on the dance floor. They had all been drinking and dancing for hours and those few left did not want the night to end. Some of them started chanting a square dance routine. Everyone joined in, and those seated at the tables stood up, laughing and clapping a rhythm and singing, "Swing your partner . . ."

"Never have I seen anything like this," said Mrs. Thalberg, who was seated at a table with the older physicians and wives. "Not in all my years . . ."

Watching Peter dancing with Teresita again, Karen was getting upset. Shouldn't there be a limitation set on how many times these two should dance together? Teresita seemed to single out Peter to be her only partner. Fred had noticed it earlier and teased Peter about it. Maybe she thought some of his vitality will rub off on her.

But it wasn't just Teresita. The hospital nurses were taken with Peter, too. Why else would they be begging him to dance? Karen thought he should have come to get *her* for this dance. He didn't seem to notice that she was sitting alone at the table with Mady. At the occasional parties her mother persuaded her to attend, Karen always had two devoted young men at her side. They wouldn't dream of leaving her to dance with other girls.

What had begun as a slight touch of irritation was developing into a blaze of outright anger. Good Lord, Karen, you sound jealous. She suddenly understood what the wives meant when they complained their husbands had second homes at the hospital. The nurses were their handmaidens; they worshiped and flattered them. "Every damned doctor is a bigamist," Silvie had said earlier in the evening. "They should all be Mormons."

Karen faced a new truth. Her emotions weren't sublime. They were down to earth and ugly and she felt ashamed of herself. She was jealous. She wanted Peter to herself. She wanted him to ignore all the females who were hanging onto him. She wanted to yell, Leave him alone; he's mine.

But he wasn't. Not really. Peter was free to do as he pleased. There were no legal ties, no commitments. She should keep her primal urges to herself. If she complained, Peter could very easily remind her that there was no reason why she should demand a one-to-one relationship, with no outside interests.

How to keep him to herself. Karen thought so intensely about it that her head began to ache. Odd, she never felt like this with Delos. She was shaken by her feelings; she could not handle them.

She wondered abruptly if the tyranny of love was any different today than in her mother's generation.

CHAPTER XXXVI

Malcolm and Silvie slipped out of the Yacht Club without attracting attention.

The sky was clearing, clouds were drifting, the alabaster moon was riding high through a scattering of brilliant stars. The breeze cooled Silvie's overheated cheeks but not her temper. She ignored the parking valet and cut across the lawn to her car. Malcolm cautioned her to watch it but she ignored him. He did not exist where she was concerned. Her mind was reeling with the brief but shocking news Malcolm had told her.

Their son, Norman, was at police headquarters. The chief wanted to talk to the parents.

No, Malcolm did not know what the problem was.

"He's been in an accident—" Silvie cried. He reassured her: if Norman were hurt, the call would have come from the hospital. It was probably nothing serious. Silvie glared at him. *Of course* it was serious; the police had never called them before. Norman was not wild like other boys his age. He was a decent kid, he was never in trouble . . . .

Norman was slumped in a chair, his T-shirt rumpled, faded jeans stained. His head was down and his glasses hid his eyes. He smelled of beer.

Malcolm had met the police chief at various civic functions: a handshake, a few polite phrases, that was it. The chief was a balding, compact man with a round face and shrewd eyes; he was trained to keep his thoughts to himself.

He said a police car had noticed a station wagon with a half dozen boys in it near the bathhouses at the Point. The boy at the wheel was driving in an erratic manner. He was fifteen, he admitted, and he had no driver's license. None of the boys had one; the station wagon belonged to one of their families. He was allowed to use the car with the understanding that one of his friends with a license would drive. Tonight they were all high on booze and pot.

And Norman was the driver.

A search of the station wagon had produced two six-packs of beer and a bottle of J&B scotch, obviously borrowed from someone's parents' liquor cabinet; some grass, and deep in the corner of the back seat, a pair of glasses, which were Norman's. He said he'd lost them a couple—maybe three—months ago. He didn't know how they got in the car.

"That's true," Silvie said, "he lost his glasses sometime in April."

The chief asked him how his glasses got into the station wagon and Norman shook his head vaguely. He didn't know anything about it; he couldn't remember where he lost them—

"He's always losing his glasses," Silvie offered helpfully.

Malcolm was shaken; he couldn't believe his son would do this. Silvie often said Malcolm didn't know what went on around him. Well, he certainly didn't know what his son was doing. The problem of teenage drinking and drugs seemed outside his circle. Yet here it was, his son was involved, he thought grimly. The booze somehow seemed less difficult to accept.

Silvie spoke to the chief. She was visibly disturbed, but articulate and obviously in control. They had taught their son to respect the law. But once a child was with his peers, he often behaved in a manner unlike his usual self. She and Malcolm promised the chief it would never happen again. They would ground him; they would do whatever he suggested—

He nodded. Then he turned to Norman; his words, spoken in a low voice, were nevertheless direct and effective. He described some of the grisly accidents he had seen that were a result of drinking and drugs.

When they left the station Silvie and Malcolm guided Norman toward the Cadillac. As they reached it, Norman broke away and was sick to his stomach. Silvie turned away in disgust; Malcolm wiped the boy's face and led him into the car, covering him with his dinner jacket. They sat in the back seat; Silvie drove at a furious speed until Malcolm said sharply, "Watch it, we don't want Norman to get picked up twice in one night—"

She turned on the air conditioner, sickened by the ripe smell of beer and whiskey. It took a lot to unsettle her; she had seen people in pretty degrading situations, but tonight she had suffered a severe blow. If this ever got out, and it was certain to, the gossip would explode. It wouldn't touch Malcolm—he was too entrenched—but what it might do to her—the women would certainly pounce on it, shredding her to pieces—

If that wasn't enough, there was that bastard, Hilton. The insolence in his manner. Had she lost her appeal? She must have, if a man who probably hadn't been laid in months had rejected her.

The hell with him. Malcolm still stood a chance, even if he was Jewish. There was talk about Virginia Carruthers being considered, but the board would never make a woman chief of staff, no matter how talented she was.

And as much as she loved her own son, she was obliged to be firm, even unreasonable, for the boy's good. How long had he been drinking? Did he use marijuana? Would he confess if she questioned him? Should she leave it to Malcolm? How to manage. . . .

They brought him into the house and led him into the kitchen. She would not allow him out of her sight, so Malcolm brought down his pajamas and robe. She told Norman to toss his stinking shirt and jeans in the garbage.

Then she brewed coffee and poured them each a cup. She said, "Norman, talk—out with it. Tell me about your drinking."

She sat on a kitchen chair opposite her son; Malcolm stood by the cabinet. After a while, Norman sobered up; at least, he could talk.

He drank beer mostly, sometimes vodka; he smoked pot only on the weekends—a couple of joints when they went to the beach, or after church, or at Jackson Hill—

What did he know about Jackson Hill? Who had introduced him to Jackson Hill?

Some of his school buddies who knew where to get the grass . . . and dealt it—

"Norman," said Silvie, "I thought you had more—more pride than to hurt yourself—and us—you've hurt me, Norman. I've never wanted to send you away to school—even though your father wanted to—but you may force me to agree with him."

"How long have you been going out with those kids?" Malcolm asked.

"Since spring, I guess—"

"Lucky you haven't got into worse trouble—"

Abruptly the boy broke, his sensitive face contorted with fear. "I never touched that girl—the others did—but I didn't! Honest mom—I never did—"

"What girl?" Malcolm demanded, a sinking feeling in his stomach.

"Leave him alone," Silvie said. "Go to your room, Norman. We'll talk again—if you need help, we'll see that you get it. And if Regent's isn't the right school for you, we'll find another."

There was damn well not going to be any scandal while Malcolm's future at the hospital was being decided, she decided, forgetting her previous uncertainties.

As an afterthought, she walked down the hall and quietly opened the door to Barbara's room. The night lamp was on; Barbara was terrified of the dark. The small gray kitten was curled in a soft ball next to her head; Barbara's hand gently rested on its silken fur.

After Malcolm made rounds the following day, he stopped in the doctors' lounge for a cup of coffee. The cup was shaking in his hand—hell of a reaction for a doctor who did catheterizations. He debated whether to go up to the intensive care unit; he rather enjoyed being there when Carmen was on duty.

Before he could decide, Fred Farley walked into the lounge. "Join me for coffee?" Malcolm asked. Fred seemed down this morning, his forelock almost hiding his bespectacled eyes, his mouth set, his shoulders hunched.

He filled a cup from the electric coffeepot, added plenty of sugar and cream, came over and sat beside Malcolm.

"Fred, do you know anything about the drug situation around Belfort?"

Fred looked at him sharply. "What do you mean?"

"Do you know anything about the drug and liquor problems with schoolkids?"

"We see some of them in Emergency, but there aren't many hard drug cases. Plenty of pot, though. They start early these days—in grade school. They get high or drunk—spaced out—" Suddenly he put down his coffee cup. "Dr. Stone, I was listening to the police radio last night. A group of kids was picked up—was your son among them by any chance?"

"He was."

"Gee, that's too bad. I thought maybe he learned his lesson—"

"What do you mean?"

"Well, I was out at Jackson Hill one night—must have been about ten days ago—I saw a couple of kids in a discotheque where they had no business—"

"And he was there?"

"Both of your kids. I remembered them from the time you had them in for lunch on a Saturday in the cafeteria. So I took them home."

Malcolm was stunned. It looked as though he knew nothing about his kids' behavior; Fred seemed to know more than he did.

"The cops were out that night. I guess they always patrol Jackson Hill. I figured your kids shouldn't be there."

"Thanks, Fred."

"Forget it."

"Anything I can do for you—any time—"

"Yeah," there was a cynical smile on the younger man's brooding face. "No sweat."

CHAPTER XXXVII

Four days after John Paul Macray's surgery, Peter and Karen drove into Manhattan, hoping to be allowed to visit him briefly. They made good time on the Merritt Parkway, since it was Friday and most of the traffic was heading toward them out of the city. The day was cool, with enough sunlight to give the landscape sharp clear colors, with all variations of green, from the flowering bushes to the massive clumps of evergreens. It was tranquil and Karen felt deliciously at peace.

On the way they decided to take a look at the river cottage that Mrs. Liss had suggested for them. They took the turnoff that led them to a main highway for a quarter of a mile. Then, swinging to the left, they found the narrow country road that ended at the water. The riverbank was once a hunting ground for the Rippowan Indian tribe. Now the banks of the river, tumbling over old dams that created natural pools, was occupied by a half dozen houses, homes of artists, writers, actors—people who used their excess creativity to shape their environment. The one Karen and Peter were to inspect had belonged to a New York interior decorator, a woman of great taste, who used it as a hideaway. It was low and sprawling; the garage and guest rooms on the north end were an afterthought; the eagle's nest at the south reserved for weekend guests.

Since the owner had moved to Arizona for her health, the house was vacant. Karen had the key, and when she walked through the doorway that opened on the spacious livingroom, she turned breathlessly to Peter. "This is beautiful."

Most of the space was devoted to the livingroom; the bedrooms were small and intimate, the kitchen, old-fashioned yet compact and efficient. A terrace bordered the riverbed but was situated well above it and served as a breakfront in case of spring flooding. The soil was rich with natural compost, oak leaves from the two-hundred-year-old trees. The shrubbery around the house, particularly in the verdant banks by the terrace, added to the natural beauty. It reminded Karen of an English cottage, with the bend in the river softened by the willows. Along the faded brick wall, protecting the lawn from the river were green patches of summer annuals and perennials. It was a house of real individuality.

Karen thought, I love it, I must have it! But she was hesitant about expressing her enthusiasm, feeling it was up to Peter. He seemed to agree with her. The house was attractive, more than mere living space. They decided to look into the mortgage market and try to buy it. She was too tactful to suggest using her trust fund again. But privately she thought, if we can't manage it any other way, Peter will have to let me . . .

Driving into the city now, her thoughts began to gel. For the first time since they were together, she was certain that to be married was the best way to live. It was something she had grappled with ever since the night of the auxiliary ball. That evening she had seen Peter in a new light, surrounded by young attractive women, she realized that she was wildly jealous. Jealous of Sheila and Carmen and other nurses. If she and Peter were married, would she have been as jealous?

There was something infinitely solid in a deep and durable attachment between a man and a woman. Her sympathies lay in that direction. Her parents had been married a quarter of a century; they were totally different personalities yet devoted to one another. They admired each other. Was that an important factor? She wondered if her mother, so poised and self-confident, so respectable, was ever jealous of her father, who surely came up against temptation in his travels.

She had heard a great deal about doctors' private lives; their indiscretions, their infidelities. She questioned her own strength. Once Peter was in practice, would she be jealous of him, knowing how vulnerable women were to their doctors?

How did a wife deal with jealousy? Was it a normal reaction or a weakness born of insecurity? When Peter had first suggested their arrangement, she never anticipated that her feelings would be so strong, even primitive. But now she admitted: *I want Peter all to myself*. She did not want to share him with any of his patients no matter how old. She suspected Sheila Ryan had a crush on him. For the first time she let herself wonder if they had ever had an affair.

One of the physicians she had interviewed said that when a woman went to her doctor, it was with the same feeling of total trust that she felt for her father when she was a child. "It's quite natural for a sick person to feel like a child," he said. "We know the doctor will make us well."

Other physicians said that some female patients offered to sleep with their doctors. And others had such a crush on their doctor that they would not tell him how sick they felt for fear of repelling him.

How did doctors' wives manage? They learned to cope.

I can learn to cope, she resolved.

It was important for their relationship, she decided, to find something permanent. Living at Mrs. Thalberg's perpetuated the feeling that it was a temporary relationship. They needed roots; a house, a nest of their own.

The river house was the answer.

When they arrived at the hospital, Maureen was in the solarium, pacing up and down. Her usual elegant composure was gone.

Karen ran to her. Maureen embraced her as though body contact might ease her fear. Her short blonde hair, usually so beautifully coiffed, was tousled. She had chewed the lipstick off her mouth.

"He's running a fever," she said. "The doctors don't seem to be worried, but I am."

The surgeon had just been in and had reassured her that everything was normal. She looked to Peter for encouragement and his voice was low and soothing.

"It is a trauma to the body, Maureen. John Paul, being a surgeon, knows what happens in these cases." He reminded her that Malcolm Stone had placed John Paul on a cautious exercise program and had prepared him for the surgery.

What he did not tell her was that there was always a danger of a lack of oxygen, which could lead to brain damage. It happened rarely. But the possibility was always there. Some patients become disoriented, others even needed psychiatric help.

Maureen tried to change the subject.

"Your grandmother is so gracious," Maureen said to Karen. "The day John Paul had his surgery, she came and stayed with me all day. I'll never forget her kindness."

Maureen became lost in thought then as she relived that black Tuesday. The wait had been interminable. Sarah Wickersham had sat quietly with her in the waiting room. She brought endless containers of coffee and did nothing but pay attention to Maureen in devoted silence. Several times, early in the morning, they went to the chapel.

By noon he had been in surgery five hours. At two o'clock, it was seven hours. Each minute dragged. Maureen's fear was almost physical, but Sarah's attention and sympathy calmed her.

About that time Eleanor Cole appeared. She looked at her mother as though waiting for a signal. Sarah shrugged eloquently. Eleanor sat down beside Maureen and took her hand. Maureen responded with a wan smile of gratitude and thanked her for coming. Wasn't it wonderful that these two strangers would come here to support her?

At three o'clock, the surgeon arrived. He told her all had gone well and described the highlights of the operation. She tried to listen but was distracted, waiting until John Paul would be wheeled into the recovery room. Even then she would not be able to see him.

As she waited by the door, she saw them wheeling the stretcher, bottles surrounding him, the intravenous lines carrying needed fluids. There was an endotracheal tube in his mouth connected to a respirator and his face looked pale. She had been warned that he would feel dreadful for a couple of days, that the first few days were crucial. He had round-the-clock nurses and the team would watch him carefully.

They would have to make sure that his lungs did not become congested and that blood clots did not form in them. Each breath would hurt because of the deep incision in the chest. Meanwhile, the Intermittent Positive Pressure Breathing machine would be helping him to get oxygen in his lungs.

Karen and Peter tried to reassure her; and Karen asked if she would like to come back to her parents' house with them; then they would bring her back when Dr. Macray was out of the recovery room. She refused and thanked them graciously and resumed her vigil.

They left her with misgivings.

"I didn't know what bad condition his heart was in until I saw the results of the catheterization," Peter said as they drove down to the east side of Manhattan.

Karen became disturbed to know that about Dr. Macray. "Is heart disease peculiar to doctors?"

"Above average."

"Isn't there some way to prevent it?"

"Diet, exercise, stop smoking—whatever he tells his patients applies to him."

"I think we should start jogging."

He looked at her; she was earnest, determined to preserve his health. "I love you, baby."

CHAPTER XXXVIII

The tall rangy man with a classic Grecian head walked back and forth along the conference table, staring at the mass of clippings, photographs, and articles from *Time* and *Newsweek* that his secretary had borrowed from the network morgue.

He was in jeans and a white knit shirt, his bare feet in polished loafers. The weather was muggy with the promise of more rain for the weekend. Rainy weekends in Southampton were a bore and he always came back to the city hung over. It was simpler to stay in his apartment or office and work.

He sorted the batch of information, pushed some aside and paused at a full page clipped from a fashion magazine known for its elegance and taste. It was a portrait of three women, of various ages, but linked by blood: the distinguished Sarah Wickersham; her daughter, Eleanor Wickersham Cole; and her granddaughter, Karen Wickersham Cole. He looked at them a long time; Sarah, with her topknot of silky white hair, her small bones that made her look taller than she actually must be; the straightforward, serene smile; a single strand of pearls around her faintly wrinkled neck and the simple black dress. Eleanor was in black and white tweed, not as delicately boned as her mother, but with a certain stark beauty; she looked pleased and at ease with her world. And Karen, beautiful Karen . . . with her long straight golden hair. Only she, with her features, could compete in looks with two such stunning women. They were three generations of distinguished and beautiful American women, all right.

Why had he not thought of a documentary of Karen and her family when she worked here? He had missed the opportunity then, but it was not too late. He had had more than second thoughts about her, although another private secretary had taken her place. He kept thinking about her because she had left him flat, with not even a kiss and tears to show her anguish. Recalling the expression on her face when she had faced his wife, he thought, dammit, that was unnecessary! His wife was back at the Hartford retreat and he was free to do as he pleased. But he didn't like it much.

A documentary on the three women wouldn't be out of place. Nobody could suggest he was susceptible to pressure, although come to think of it, the grandmother was on various boards of directors with Mr. Lukas, the network owner. It was legitimate and would make a fine documentary—different from a typical women's lib report, which he detested.

Sarah Wickersham worked for civil rights and prison reform, and was a trustee of two black colleges. She was helping the American Indians before Marlon Brando was born. And she believed in equal rights and equal pay for equal work. She was seventy-five years old and still a political activist.

Her daughter, Eleanor—had been quoted as saying that her mother had always marched to a different drummer—and that sometimes he was playing a tango. "Mother," she said, "is totally unpredictable. I suspect my daughter will take after her. Karen has inherited mother's feeling for justice." She is strongwilled, Delos reflected—coming from a family of strongwilled women, how could she be otherwise? He had handled the whole affair badly.

He summoned his secretary. "Take a letter, to Mrs. Sarah Wickersham; you'll find her address either in the phone book or the Social Register . . ."

Sarah Wickersham was in her apartment Friday morning, calling her friend Beulah Parsons, who was recuperating in Seal Harbor after surgery and a series of chemotherapy treatments.

"I'll leave for Maine tomorrow morning," Sarah promised. "Definitely." They would discuss plans for a benefit for a new children's center and Sarah hoped the prospect would ease the gloom for Beulah.

It was important for Sarah to be at Eleanor's for lunch today. I must see Karen, she thought. I'll see for myself whether she is happy or has made a mistake. She won't confide in her mother, or in me, but once I see her with the boy I'll know.

Sarah was more concerned about her granddaughter's welfare than she would admit. She was aware of Karen's sensitive nature and hoped life would not cause her too much pain and sorrow. Karen had the potential for being a real individual. The intellectual climate was better for her than it had been for Sarah.

Sarah had been independent when it wasn't acceptable for a young girl to be that way. The choices between speaking out against what was wrong and keeping silent, because women were supposed to keep silent on affairs outside the hearth and bed, had always tormented her. Although she tried to be a good daughter and wife, much of her early life was in conflict with her inner dreams.

Her daughter Eleanor was just the opposite. She graciously carried out the rituals of womanhood, but there was a barrier, a no-trespassing signal between her and Sarah. They finally had something in common when Karen was born. They were friendly now, their reluctant admiration had finally settled into mutual affection.

Sarah was immensely pleased with what Maureen had told her about Karen's job, that her radio broadcasts often showed a deep concern for underprivileged and disadvantaged people. It made her proud. She was using her talents, not just letting them go to waste.

Sarah left her apartment for Eleanor's townhouse; in spite of the humidity, she walked briskly and people glanced at her with more than casual interest. She waited patiently for the traffic light, thinking about Delos Burke, the man from the Third Network who was to be

Eleanor's guest at lunch. She had a vague recollection of hearing his name, not only on his broadcasts, but from Karen. Had she not worked for him briefly last year?

He was in the library with Eleanor when Sarah arrived. "You don't know me at all," Sarah said, accepting his hand, "but I feel as though I've known you for years. Do all your fans feel the same way?"

"It would be nice if they did," Delos Burke said, holding her hand a moment, patting it, "but I get hate mail, too."

"You don't let that stop you, I hope."

"No, the network is liberal—"

"That's Arnold Lukas's philosophy."

"Right you are."

They were having drinks in the small library, with its rich background of rare books, when the doorbell rang and Otto showed Karen and Peter into the room.

Delos stood up, smiling, his hand outstretched.

For a moment Karen was in shock. What was *he* doing here? She wanted to turn and run. She looked at Peter, then at Delos. Help me, she begged of herself, help me handle this.

"Delos, I never expected to see you—"

"Mr. Burke thought it would be a nice surprise, since—"

Karen didn't wait for her mother to finish. She turned to Peter, who was beside her, linked her arm with his, moistened her lips. "Peter, this is Delos Burke, my old boss. Delos, Dr. Peter Norris."

Were all of them aware of her tension? she wondered. Her mother and grandmother had no idea what kind of influence Delos had had on her life. She had certainly not talked about him once they had become lovers. She was aware of him staring at her; she had to be careful. Peter knew who he was even though he had never met him. Foolishly, stupidly, she had confided to Peter, had even wept during her confidences. What must he think? That Delos had planned this? That her family was trying to break them up? Whatever the reason, the harm was done. She could tell by the way Peter was hiding his own shock with the distant look on his face, the way a doctor looked when he learned a patient had a fatal disease.

She looked at her grandmother frantically; no, it was not her family's doing, but Delos's. He could manipulate, she recalled; he was proud of the way he manipulated people.

"Mr. Burke wants to discuss doing a documentary about the three of us—your grandmother, myself . . . and you," Eleanor said. "We can talk about it at lunch."

"Oh, I'm sorry, mother. We can't stay. We just dropped by to—"

"This is important, Karen," her mother said firmly, "your father thinks it's important enough for him to take the shuttle back from Washington. He can't make it for lunch, but he'll be here later."

"Peter has to get back to the hospital—"

Peter looked at Karen. He didn't look like a doctor today. He looked more like a young broker on his way to the Hamptons for a weekend. He said, "I have time—" His blue eyes surveyed them and finally came to her, "Lunch would be fine."

Karen, furious with Peter, followed them out to the walled garden. As Peter drew out the chair for her, she glared at him, but his face was noncommittal.

Otto served salade Niçoise, crisp wheat wafers and tall glasses of iced tea. Karen picked at her food, feeling frantic over Delos's presence. She heard snatches of his plans for the documentary: He wanted to focus on the continuity of the family, the commitment of one generation to another, the grandmother who at seventy-five was still active and had broad interests; the daughter who sat on boards and committees and had done so much to help make Manhattan beautiful; and the third generation, the woman of the eighties serving the community through the media of television and radio—

"What do you think, Karen?" Sarah asked. Her eyes read her granddaughter's expression. Something wasn't quite right here. Peter had been silent for most of the meal, listening courteously. Delos Burke had enchanted them with his foresight and awareness. Then, suddenly, he asked Sarah: "How does the new morality strike you? Arrangements. Live-ins, without license. The permissive attitude toward sex." Karen froze at his deliberately pointed question.

Sarah shrugged. "A half century ago, a judge—I believe it was Judge Ben Lindsay—came out for trial marriages. About the same time a writer, Fannie Hurst, married, but she and her husband maintained separate apartments. If two responsible young people—"

"Mother, I hope you don't express your liberal opinions too freely during the interview—it would be bad for your image." Eleanor put down her napkin and put her hands on the table.

"Betty Ford spoke out freely and it didn't hurt her image—or Gerald Ford's, for that matter."

"Mother, you're outrageous," Eleanor said with a helpless shrug.

"Peter—" Sarah turned to the young doctor sitting opposite her, "how does Delos's idea strike you?" Without waiting for his reply, she added, "Do you think it will interest television audiences?"

"I think people who watch public television would enjoy it," he said carefully. "Especially Karen's segment. She's been helping the social director of one of our slums—a housing project—and reporting the progress on her radio program. She's doing a great job."

"We could film her segment there." Delos showed enthusiasm. "It would be a great contrast between Karen and Mrs. Cole—whom we could photograph at the New York Botanical Gardens, and we could do Mrs. Wickersham at her home in Rhinebeck and in her New York apartment—maybe having a dinner for her friends at the U.N."

"I think Phipps will approve of it, Eleanor," Sarah said.

"Certainly. Karen, can you arrange for time off—"

"Karen hasn't agreed as yet," Sarah said, looking shrewdly at her granddaughter. "What do you think, my dear?"

Karen raised her hands, palms out, a helpless uncertain gesture. "I don't know. I think the people I've met at the station and the auxiliary would feel a little betrayed. They might not feel as comfortable being around me as they do now."

"That's a good point," Peter said, looking directly at her with the objective expression she suddenly detested. "Why don't you think it over, Karen?"

"Peter's right, Karen," her grandmother agreed. "Sleep on it—"

"Well, I can't imagine anyone turning it down," Delos said. He was looking at Karen, his chin lowered, his dark thick brows protecting his eyes, giving his face an intense look.

They finished lunch and Karen stood up abruptly, "We have to go."

"Karen, I don't mean to pressure you," her mother said, "but it does sound like something special. You might regret not doing it."

"Eleanor," Sarah suggested mildly, "why don't we let Karen decide for herself." She could see what was happening.

Karen kissed her mother and grandmother. Delos held out his hand. "It was good seeing you," he said, with the sexy smile that had devastated her not so long ago. "You'll let us know soon?"

She nodded. He looked so sure of himself; he must have forgotten that she had walked out on him.

The East River Drive was thick with cars pouring out of the city for the weekend. They had left the townhouse before Karen's father arrived from Washington. Karen had thought it wise to leave; certainly the situation could not get any worse. Delos had been at his best: warm, persuasive, charming her mother and grandmother, who were both obviously impressed by the idea of the piece.

Peter's hands gripped the steering wheel, his eyes hidden by sunglasses, his mouth set in a grim line.

She held her hands together to control their trembling. She moistened her lips. "Peter—"

"Yes?"

"I hope you understand . . . I didn't know *anything* about this . . . it came as a complete surprise—"

"That's a lot of coverage he'll be giving—"

"Look, Peter, he's not doing it just because of me. Mother and grandmother are important women—and it *is* a great idea. You don't find that many families—"

"So do it."

"Peter, you don't want me to—"

"Do whatever you want, Karen—" He kept his eye on the traffic.

"Peter, don't be angry at me—" She was shaking, bewildered by the turn of events. After all, they had looked at the river house this morning. She started to cry.

"That was a pretty bad scene," he said.

"I know. I'm sorry it happened—"

"For God's sake, don't cry . . . I can't cope with tears."

"You're being unreasonable, Peter."

"The way he looked at you . . . Jesus, have you seen him lately?"

"Since we've been living together?"

He nodded.

"How could I—I don't keep things from you—" She was beginning to feel defensive.

"You didn't tell me you went back to the slum—"

"I knew it would upset you, but it was important for me—"

"What's his claim on you—?"

He was being thickheaded. She was torn between wanting to scream at him and pleading with him to understand.

"No claim, none whatsoever." She was suddenly steaming. "Except that I could probably get him to propose—which is more than you've done lately."

"How do you expect me to take you seriously with him still around? Why do you think I suggested this arrangement?"

"I'm *over* him!" His remark cut to the quick. Was he still living in the past?

"You were trembling when he looked at you—"

"I was upset for *you*—wondering what *you'd* think. And it came out just the way I was afraid it would—" Her voice broke with fury, "I could kill him for this. I could kill *you* for wanting to stay!"

"God, it's obvious you've still got some feelings about him. Violent or otherwise—"

They were driving along the Merritt Parkway now, exceeding the speed limit and screaming at each other.

"I don't, he means nothing to me—unless you drive me to him—which you seem perfectly content to do."

"Don't start that up—"

"For a doctor, you've got about as much understanding as a—a—butcher. Don't you have any feelings? No wonder they say doctors have no feelings!"

"Cut it out, you idiot. I love you. I want to make certain you can love me—there's no sense getting into marriage if you cry every time you see him on the boob tube—"

"Oh, be quiet! You have to go and spoil it just as we're getting so —so adjusted to each other—"

"*I* spoiled it?"

"You're jealous," she said with sudden insight, "Peter, my darling, you're jealous—you know something? I can understand that. I was jealous the night of the ball—wildly jealous of all the girls making passes at you—"

They passed the turnoff to the river cottage. "Peter, let's go to the river house—everything was so nice there—"

"Forget the house. We're hardly ready for it."

"You'd be kinder to me if I were one of your patients."

"I don't have to spend the rest of my life with my patients."

Have to, that's what he'd said. She was silent now, anger churning in her, anger having built up over the uncertainties, the insecurities of the relationship.

She did not understand how they could live in harmony and understanding, for all their differences.

"Oh, the hell with this. I'm moving back to New York."

"The hell you are. I have no right to stop you from doing that interview, or whatever it is. But I want you to know I love you. And I won't take less from you—" They had arrived home in Mrs. Thalberg's driveway. He pulled off his dark glasses and turned to her, gripping her by the arms. "Dammit, we can make it—"

When he blotted her tears, telling her she looked a mess, he could hardly see through his own.

The house was deserted this afternoon, and when they made love it was with a fury they had not felt for a while. Afterwards, he kissed her and told her she was wonderful.

Later, when he was back at the hospital covering for one of the doctors, she had a call from New York.

"Karen." It was grandmother. "I've given Mr. Burke's idea considerable thought. I have decided I cannot undertake it. It would quite likely undo whatever public good I have managed to do. In a way I'd be exploiting other people, and that would be rather shameless, don't you think?"

"Mother will be disappointed."

"I've already discussed it with her. And now I've discussed it with you. I'm going to call Mr. Burke."

Her darling, darling grandmother. How adroit she was in easing Karen off the hook. Suddenly Karen was filled with the most glorious relief. She couldn't wait for Peter to get home.

CHAPTER XXXIX

Wilbur Watling was really a dreamer, only the lean heroic figure striving to break out of his gross body was securely hidden. Nobody suspected his innate vulnerability. As he grew up, heavy and thick in a family obsessed with physical beauty and discipline, he did all he could just to survive. Survival meant making the most of the intellectual ability passed on to him by his brilliant parents. When you are in doubt, pretend you know what you are doing. Hit first, while your enemy is gathering his forces. Make noise if you need to; intimidation often leads to victory.

It worked with his older patients, who thought of him as the deity. It worked with Clemmie, who was afraid to complain about him to her own family. It even worked with his two daughters until they moved to California, far from the family hearth.

But now, abruptly, the rigid personality traits were melting away like ice under a furnace blast.

What's with him? His secretary wondered silently, grateful for the change.

Even the new group of residents and interns thought he was mellowing, different from the man they had met when they arrived for inspections and interviews earlier in the year. He was courteous, attentive, helpful.

The metamorphosis had taken place shortly after the auxiliary ball . . . .

Monday morning he arrived in his office, his bulk disguised in a dark, somewhat dated, silk Italian suit that the salesman in a men's shop on Belfort Street had sold him. He had added a cream-colored shirt, open at the throat, and polished moccasins. His dark thinning hair was parted low on the right side and carefully brushed over the bald spot. The gleam in his eyes behind their glasses was softer that day, more human.

All morning he dealt with matters unrelated to the family practice program. He had Fred Farley in for a closed door consultation and took a couple of calls from Jedd Cramer. Later, he telephoned his wife to say he would not be home for dinner because he would be tied up most of the evening. He had no idea when he would be home.

At four in the afternoon, he left the hospital.

Teresita was waiting for him in the secluded motel that had been home for her since she had left Sunset Hill. She opened the door wide in a welcoming gesture. She wore a Chinese silk tunic embroidered with dragons and exotic flowers that strained slightly over her bosom and stomach. The pipestem satin pants fitted her thin legs beautifully.

"I've been looking forward to this—" she said, gesturing toward one of the armchairs. "How nice you look!"

He reddened with pleasure and thanked her. He was already in love with her like a schoolboy, embarrassed and enchanted. He watched her sit down—right leg over left, her body turned slightly the opposite way, which gave her neckline length and beauty. His breath quickened at it.

"I didn't know what you would want to drink," she said. "There's Perrier and iced tea—"

"Perrier is fine," he said. "How was your weekend?"

Smiling, she said, "I did what you told me. I walked. I even tried jogging, but I'm out of condition—Whew!" She touched her bosom with the palm of her hand.

Dr. Watling had told her before that walking was as good as jogging, especially for someone who wasn't in good condition. He thought she would have little trouble getting into shape for the operation. After all, she was a dancer—

"But I've been, well, lazy for a long time—"

He stressed how important it was for her to get back into shape before she had any corrective surgery. He had brought her a small container of vitamins.

Jedd Cramer arrived shortly before six. He wore jeans and a knitted Lacoste shirt. He was carrying his briefcase jauntily as if it were a tennis racket. He looked tanned, fit and ready for his future as Teresita's agent. He had begun to realize that a number of lawyers were becoming theatrical or literary agents. Even though his law practice was doing well he suspected time was running out for malpractice suits. No one knew what national health insurance would do to the picture—and national health was coming.

He had talked to several television producers about Teresita making a comeback, but their lack of interest didn't bother him. Once she was back on her feet they would find a writer and put a package deal together.

He had already contacted the people who owed her money; it might take time, he said. Dr. Watling, however, volunteered to pay for the hospital and surgery. It would give him a great deal of pleasure and besides, he thought to himself, it would bind her to him. Anyway, he had enough money to swing it. Jedd brought some papers for her to sign and they spoke of setting up a corporation. "Just leave it to me," he said to Teresita. He was full of energy and enthusiasm. Once her face was healed, he would fly out to the coast with her. Not to worry, he said, kissing her palm. She would be better than ever.

After Jedd left, Wilbur assured her Jedd was a top lawyer. Jedd would arrange for her to meet the right people—not the has-beens, but the new television producers. He would get backing, too. He knew people with money who were always looking for tax shelters and loved the idea of being involved in the field of entertainment, as if they were stars themselves.

Wilbur had decided that Dr. Ezra Smith, the plastic surgeon who had a summer home in Fairfield, would be the best choice for her. Dr. Smith was middle-aged, a gentle man with a head of thick white hair, a sensitive face and extraordinarily skilled hands. His specialty was reconstructive surgery, especially on children who were born with facial deformities. To bring natural harmony where nature and genetics had failed was his first consideration. He also operated on breasts and buttocks of women who wanted to look more youthful.

When Dr. Smith went over the photographs of the Teresita of the 1940s, he saw that the eyelids, the cheeks, the jowls would need the most work . . . .

Wilbur Watling spent considerable time with Teresita for the next two weeks. On his lunch hour, they took long walks and sat in the fresh air. Teresita was happy; now that she had a reason for living, her need for liquor was less insistent. She was taking injections of the B vitamins. Wilbur was in control of her life and was going to save her. After her surgery, there would be time to consider their future together. Now he was grateful just to be near her.

His enthusiasm and devotion made her feel uneasy. Why is he doing so much for me, why is he helping me? she wondered. Men who had helped her before had always expected something in return. And because she always paid her dues, she went to bed with him.

But for Wilbur it was different from sex with Clemmie. She was so passive that he never enjoyed having sex with her. For years he had left Clemmie alone. He had resigned himself to a future of nothingness. But Teresita was a wild one and she even admired his body. She let him suck her nipples greedily, she purred and coaxed and spoke gently, lovingly. The big hulk of a man who had been put down by his peers and by women all his life was suddenly experiencing exhilaration. The beautiful creature was responding to him because she understood his needs and was restoring the pieces of his bruised, abandoned ego.

At lunchtime the day before Teresita was scheduled to have her surgery, she checked into the hospital.

Wilbur came to get her in the admitting office and escorted her to her room. It was in the old section of the hospital, but it was clean and pleasant and looked out on the lawn adjacent to the cafeteria.

"Dr. Farley will arrange for your tests," Wilbur said, hovering over her. "You remember him from the auxiliary ball?"

Teresita remembered him. He was a good dancer, surprisingly agile. Wilbur remained in her room while the nurse hung up the satin robe, put the lingerie in the chest of drawers, and set the white kid slippers by the bed.

Teresita moved in an aura of perfume. She slid the gay Pucci scarf off her head and shook out her thick hair. She would have to wash it later with a disinfectant soap. The unflagging care she had given herself in the past weeks had already produced results—and would help safeguard her recovery.

Wilbur Watling thought a face lift was necessary only because of her profession. If she were only a middle-aged wife and mother, she could achieve the same results by dieting and exercising and staying away from liquor and pills.

But Teresita insisted that surgery was her passport to the future. Even Jedd Cramer agreed.

Wilbur left the room when Fred Farley came in to arrange for her tests. Dr. Farley explained the procedure and stayed close by during the tests, a courtesy she was most appreciative of. She had confidence in Wilbur Watling and faith in Dr. Smith's magical fingers. She was entrusting her life to them.

Fred was in the nurses' station, going over Teresita's chart when Peter Norris stepped off the elevator. Fred motioned for him to come over and look at her chart. The patient's name was Mrs. Nigel Fellowes and she was scheduled for surgery in the morning.

"Teresita?" Peter asked.

Fred nodded, and Peter scanned the chart he was holding. The tests were all within a normal range; her blood pressure was a bit high, but it was still normal.

"What drugs did they give her at Sunset Hill?" Peter asked.

Fred shrugged. It didn't matter; a month had elapsed since she left the sanitarium; there was no problem there. Dr. Watling had assured him she was in good shape, and Dr. Smith would be here early in the morning to operate.

Peter nodded and went down the corridor to check on an elderly man's condition. Something about Teresita's chart nagged at him, and he didn't know what it was. The vibes weren't right. Was she ready for the rigors of surgery so soon after getting out of Sunset Hill? What medicine had the psychiatrists prescribed for her? Sedatives? Antidepressants? She had complained of a sudden weight gain.

He remembered dancing with her at the ball, and she had stopped for a few minutes to complain about a cramp in her leg. The cause, she thought, was probably due to dancing in those three-inch heels.

Peter returned to the nurses' station to change the medications on the elderly man's chart. He asked Fred's permission to look at the chart again and jotted down some data on the cards he always carried with him.

That afternoon, he put in a call to the chief of surgery in a hospital at the Connecticut-New York state line. Then he drove down the thruway to the hospital, which was larger than Belfort's and had some new equipment.

The chief surgeon, who had taught at Yale Medical School when Peter was there, was waiting in his office and greeted Peter warmly. He was a thin man with a gray crewcut that was in keeping with his stern features and shrewd eyes.

Peter explained his concern about Teresita, and the chief understood. He led Peter into a room where their newest computer was hooked up. He said they were fortunate to have this machine. It was a physiologic profile and there were fewer than thirty of them in the country.

Data fed into this small computer, he added, came up with answers that might not give certain danger signals in routine tests and it could, with reasonable certainty, predict the outcome of the patient's surgery.

Basic information about Teresita such as height, weight, age, blood pressure, heart rate and breathing rate, was fed into the computer, as well as her complete blood count, temperature and kinds of more technical readings and symptoms. The computer processed the information and, two minutes later, ejected the printout.

Thanking the chief surgeon, Peter raced down the hall to call Belfort Hospital. Fred was on duty and he answered his page.

Peter told him the results of the profile.

"Get hold of Watling, Fred. And have him call Dr. Smith. Don't let them operate. She's likely to die on the operating table."

Unfortunately, Dr. Watling had left for the day, so Fred called his home. He asked Clemmie to make certain Dr. Watling called him—no matter how late he came in.

Clemmie had a headache—not a migraine, but a tension headache. She scribbled the message but instead of putting it on the telephone table where Wilbur picked up his messages, she carried it upstairs and left it on the table between their beds. By the time her husband got home she was sound asleep. He got into his bed without turning on the lamp, and in the morning he left before she woke up. He wanted to be with Teresita before she went upstairs to surgery.

"Good morning. Time to get up," one of the voices said.

"Rise and shine!"

Teresita made an effort to open her eyes. She blinked but couldn't see. She must be hung over, she thought, but it wasn't quite the same feeling.

Two nurses had brought the gown and cap she was to wear in surgery. They had wanted to meet her, having seen her old films on the late late show and read plenty about her in the tabloids. What juicy stories they would have for their families and friends, even though they were supposed to keep mum whenever a celebrity came into the hospital.

The dark-haired nurse with the Dorothy Hamill haircut shook her shoulder gently. She was waiting to give Teresita her shot.

"Good morning," she said again. "We're going to get you ready to go upstairs."

But they had trouble rousing her. When she finally opened her eyes, she just stared. She didn't look right.

They spoke again; this time their voices were louder. There was no response. When the dark-haired nurse picked up her left hand it fell limp and inert.

"Get the doctor—" she told the blonde nurse, "quick."

For the next few minutes doctors and nurses rushed in and out of the room. Meanwhile, the dark-haired nurse got to the public telephone booth and called her husband, who worked for the local radio station.

Five minutes later, he called Roscoe Osgood.

"Yes, it's true—" Roscoe said with authority. "We do have a Mrs.

Nigel Fellowes here . . . yes, Teresita, the movie star. She was due for plastic surgery this morning, but it's been cancelled. . . . She has suffered a stroke . . . Her condition? Critical, I'm afraid."

Jedd Cramer took charge, after a conference with Dr. Watling. He faced the press. He put in a call to London and spoke to Teresita's daughter, who sounded very British, very polite, and totally without sympathy. She did agree, however, to send her mother a check to cover her hospital expenses. But that wasn't what Jedd wanted.

So he had a talk with Dr. Hilton. He emphasized that the privacy of the patient had been violated. If Osgood had kept quiet, nobody would have known about her stroke until she was willing to release the information herself. Consider what it would do to her image. He assured Dr. Hilton there would be an invasion of privacy suit if the hospital asked her to pay her bills, no matter how high they ran.

In the end, Jedd's personal plans for using Teresita's comeback as his ploy for entrance into the entertainment field were anything but demolished. He was too conscious of the quirks of fate to accept her present situation as final.

Tonight, the third Monday in September, the executive committee of the medical staff was scheduled to meet in the board room at six-thirty in the evening.

None of the doctors would make it on time. Many couldn't break away from office hours; nearly all of them had telephone messages to return, and there was always a last-minute emergency to attend to. The meeting was never called to order until seven P.M.

Dr. Watling glanced at his watch. It was an Omega that Clemmie had bought for him in Curaçao, but whenever a patient admired it, he implied that it was a gift from a grateful patient. It was four o'clock. If he slipped out now, he would have three beautiful hours.

Too keyed up to wait for the elevators, he took the stairs at a fast pace. His new relationship had had an effect on his appearance. Without much of an actual weight loss, he looked healthier. His clothes hung better on his bulk; the new brown and white checked wool jacket, the fawn colored slacks added a certain style.

He cut through the back corridor to the parking lot. The weather had at last cooled down. September was the perfect month. The air was clear and sparkling. In the small atrium, dahlias and chrysan-themums in varied hues of bronze, yellow, taupe and purple made a pleasing mélange of color against the greens of the hedges. He was aware of the freshness of the air, the beauty of the colors, the onset of a rich burgeoning autumn. His senses were splendidly alive.

The drive to New Canaan took less than a half hour. Once he was off Route 123, he turned toward the lane that led to the rehabil-itation hospital, at one time a rich man's mansion replete with panels, stained glass, turrets, parquet floors, marble fireplaces and thirty bedrooms, each with its own bath. The hospital was a pri-vately owned extended care facility, dedicated to the complete reha-bilitation of patients who in an earlier era might have been doomed to a lifetime as invalids.

Teresita's room was on the first floor of West One, where the rich afternoon sunshine layered the furniture and paintings, all light, all cheerful like the tropical flower patterned draperies.

Teresita was resting in bed, which had been jacked up so she could half sit, half lie, without putting a strain on her muscles. Her dark hair was cut boyishly short, with wisps over her forehead and on her cheeks. The white threads in her hair gave her a comfortable middle-aged beauty. The nurse had put lipstick on her mouth. Except for the faint droop on the left side of her face, she seemed quite normal . . . until one saw that her expression was fixed, an odd touch of placidity in her face. Her left arm hung close to her side, her hand on the bed-spread.

Dr. Watling reached down to the helpless hand, raised it, and kissed the palm. Finally, he kissed her on each cheek, and brushed the hair off her forehead.

"How are you today?" His voice was cheerful, optimistic, unlike the one he used at the hospital.

Her smile was tilted. "Thank you. Thank you." They were the only words she could say. How typical, he thought, how gracious she is, how much she feels and cannot show! The neurologist wasn't sure how much she understood, but Dr. Watling knew she understood ev-erything. He was her friend, her protector. Nothing could harm her while he was watching over her.

He sat down on the easy chair beside her bed. "I have some more letters for you—all sorts of mail is coming in from your fans. It's amazing. They haven't forgotten you, Teresita. Everyone is praying for you."

She leaned forward a bit, trying to understand. He opened his briefcase and took out a bundle of mail, spreading the letters like a fan across her bedspread. The flowers he had sent this morning were in a glass container on the chest of drawers. Tea roses, expensive but worth it. He had paid cash for them so Clemmie would not see a bill.

She fixed him with an intense look of appeal. Love had always been tragic for her. But he was confident that Teresita's spirit was alive, wanting to live, to feel, to love. And he intended to give it all to her.

He read some of the letters aloud; he could tell she understood. He told her that he and Jedd were making plans to transfer her to Tufts-New England Medical Center's Rehabilitation Institute. He was optimistic about her eventual recovery. She would have distinguished predecessors: Patricia Neal, the actress; Pat Nixon, the ex-president's wife—and so many others . . . She listened to his pep talk.

When the supper tray came in, the nurse who was trained to help the stroke patients to eat arrived with it. The effort of eating tired Teresita, so they had put her on six small meals a day instead of three large ones. The fish on her plate was poached, moist, easily flaked. The applesauce was pureed, fragrant with cinnamon. The milk shake with essential nutrients that she would have before bedtime was placed in the small refrigerator on the other side of the room.

When she grew tired of eating and began to choke, Dr. Watling said to the nurse, "Why don't I take over for a while?"

He moved the straight chair closer to the bed; he dipped the spoon into the applesauce and brought it up to her mouth. "*Good*," he said, his voice soft and coaxing. Somehow it reminded him of his children when they were sick. "A little more—good—try to swallow, you'll feel better, you're doing better every day."

Coaxing, pleading, questioning, "Is your mouth dry, my dear one, would you like some fresh lemonade or a lime drink?"

It was the threat of choking that worried him most. Suppose it happened when he wasn't there—what if a nurse in a hurry persuaded her to swallow a piece of food before she had chewed it. Yes, the nurses were trained, but suppose she were alone in her room . . .

He wanted to take her home; put her in the downstairs den, which could be fitted with a hospital bed, and have 24-hour duty nurses so he could feel secure. But it was a pipedream. Clemmie had behaved so badly when he wanted to put Fred Farley up for a while. And if Clemmie had any idea how he really felt about this woman . . .

Teresita finished what she could; the nurse removed the tray and wiped her mouth with a damp serviette, fluffed her hair and sprayed her neck and hands with cologne. Except for the odd droop to her mouth, she looked normal. Wilbur could scarcely restrain himself from touching her cheeks, giving her little pats of affection. She closed her eyes and relaxed, he was convinced, because of his presence.

Always before, he had believed it was better to be feared than to be loved. Now he realized what a fallacy that was. All these years he had been deprived of what he now knew was the most vital force in a man's life.

No woman had ever really responded to him, not even Clemmie. She put up with the nonsense he foisted on her—sometimes deliberately, to see how much she would take—because she got what she wanted: stature in the community and plenty of money to enjoy it. She had been bugging him recently for a Rolls-Royce; probably as a weapon to show Pamela Shaw she herself was just as rich. He imagined Clemmie in a Rolls; the little short-necked pigeon Clemmie, boobs and belly blurred together as the estrogen was leaking out of her body—

He had been inordinately nice to her lately, but he had avoided her as much as possible. Fortunately she kept busy in the auxiliary thrift shop, since Maureen Macray couldn't find any place else for her to work.

He glanced at his Omega; he had better leave if he expected to show up on time for the meeting. Yet he was reluctant to go. Everytime he left Teresita he worried whether she would be okay. And he was worried about all the problems she would have in the future. They seemed insurmountable right now.

If she remained helpless, became a permanent invalid, his

influence on her would grow even stronger—he would act as a father and be a devoted friend, even an undemanding lover . . . .

If she were completely healed, and there was always that chance, what would happen? It was a testament to his newfound capacity for love that he wanted her made whole again—whatever it cost him, either financially or where Clemmie was concerned.

In the doctors' parking lot, Dr. Watling ran into Roscoe Osgood, who was just getting into his car. Roscoe looked more rumpled than usual. His nearsighted eyes swam behind his steel-rimmed spectacles. Before Dr. Watling had time to say hello, he began to chatter about Teresita.

"The way I see it, I did Teresita a good turn. I mean, by confirming the story to the wires. She's been in all the papers, on radio, even TV—pretty good for a has-been, I'd say. But all that sob Hilton keeps prattling about is the patient's right to privacy—"

"He's right, Roscoe. If she kicks up a fuss, it might make trouble for you—Jedd Cramer's her lawyer."

"I'm already in trouble," Osgood said bitterly. "Hilton just fired me." And with that he got in his car and drove away.

CHAPTER XL

Carmen flopped down on a chair in the nurses' lounge and took a deep breath.

Who said nurses married either doctors or policemen? Right now she would entertain a proposal from the next man who walked through the door, even if he were on welfare.

She had had it with the intensive care unit. Working in the coronary care unit required doing a fast dance, with a brain and eyes that were alert to everything going on in the lives of half a dozen very sick people. She had given every ounce of herself, using up even her second wind. There was one serious heart patient after another.

Malcolm Stone was in the unit most of the time; they worked well together. He knew he could count on her; that when she telephoned him about the condition of a patient, he could rely on her judgment. He knew she never complained.

But then he set a towering example for the staff. Two weeks ago, when he was doing a heart catheterization, he slashed his own thumb and it began to bleed badly. But he finished the catheterization and made sure the patient was in good shape, then went up to the operating suite and had it sewn up.

Dr. Stone had a great deal of respect for the cardiac nurses. He counted on them to manage the patient as a whole and he considered the nurse as a guidance counselor to the patient. Three or four days after a heart attack, when the patient's condition was stable, the nurse was the one who sat down to talk with the family. Carmen always gave the patient the bright side of their future. Yes, there are certain risks, but if you take care of yourself, there's a good chance you can return to a fairly normal life. Carmen always cited examples and conveyed tremendous enthusiasm to the patients and their families.

Carmen had a hunch Malcolm appreciated a lot about her but was too reticent to compliment her. They worked superbly together. As tired as she was, she would always look back at the long, grueling night with a certain satisfaction.

She heard the telephone in the nurses' station but ignored it, until the unit secretary said, "It's for you, Carmen."

"Carmen—" It was Malcolm. "I tried your apartment—"

"I slept here. I was too beat to move."

"It's a pity to waste your time off. Could you eat some lunch?"

"Is that an offer?" She was cautious, aware of what everyone would say if they knew who she was talking to.

"Sure. How about sandwiches?"

"Fine."

"What kind?"

"Oh, I don't know," she thought a second. "Corned beef on rye, lots of mustard, sour pickles, cheesecake and Dr. Pepper . . ."

"That was decisive. We'll have a picnic. I'll pick you up in a half hour."

"Where shall we meet?"

"In the doctors' parking lot. I have something to talk to you about."

The picnic was in his new offices. They weren't completely furnished yet, but some of the signs were already hanging from a post on the lawn: Malcolm Stone, M.D.; Peter Norris, M.D.; Charles Stengel, D.D.S.

Malcolm helped Carmen out of the Stingray; then he picked up the brown bag from Harry and David's delicatessen and carried it into the office. He was in jeans and a red and blue striped jersey; he looked boyish and eager.

He spread a clean towel on the desk, took out the food and brought in papercups for their drinks. He waited for her approval of the sandwich.

"Oh—" she rolled her eyes heavenward.

He grinned, pleased. They ate in silence, but it was a friendly sharing silence. When they finished the first course, he offered her tongue and turkey and probably the best cole slaw she had ever eaten.

They decided to wait for dessert. Carmen walked around the suite, going from one room to another, squinting in the sunlight. Everything was so new and modern; it was the best.

"What a pleasure it would be to work in an office like this!" she exclaimed.

"You think so?"

She looked at him, alert to the change in his voice.

"That's what I wanted to talk to you about. If you're serious," he added, "the job is yours."

He told her about his other plans. The big corporations were becoming health conscious, eager to preserve the health of their employees—from the chief executive officer on down. He was negotiating for the purchase of an estate near Fairfield to remodel into a prevention and rehabilitation center. It would require a lot of his time in the beginning, but eventually he would hire a medical director, and she, Carmen, would serve as nursing administrator.

"How does that strike you?" he asked.

"I'm . . . flabbergasted. It's as though—" she shook her head, awed, "I'm walking through a rainbow."

"You've been on my mind for a long time. You're too good to lose, Carmen."

We'll make a good team, she thought silently, and it was a promise.

"So, it's settled." He gathered the wrappings, folded them and stuffed them into the brown paper bag. "I have to get ready for to-night's meeting."

"I forgot. This should be a great day for you. The talk in the hospital is—"

"That I'll be chief? I don't know. We have good people on staff."

"The odds are on you, Dr. Stone."

He shrugged. "I suppose the donation from my patient, Leo Shumasky, helped."

"Was it a big donation?"

"Enough to buy the physiologic profile computer Pete Norris has been begging for."

"Jesus, those are expensive."

They walked out together.

"By the way, will you help with the cardiology symposium in October? October third, I think. It's going to be one of the Harry Thalberg Memorial Lectures."

"Of course, it'll be my pleasure."

"Are you ever free evenings? In case we have to work on the project?"

"My time is yours, doctor," she said, but her smile had been answer enough.

Silvie's experience with men had given her the ability to deal with her son's problems without cracking up. She decided Norman was probably like most boys and decided just because they drank beer didn't mean they were alcoholics. Sure, the kids drink. But better that than drugs.

Malcolm said military school was wrong for Norman, but Silvie was going to have her way on this. She said, "Let's try it for a year. If it doesn't work out, we can try another school. I know Maureen Macray's younger boy went to Putney and loved it."

Why did she want him out of the house, Malcolm wondered, knowing she had motives behind motives. Was there any threat of the truth about that rape case—that poor retarded girl—coming out? Malcolm wanted to believe his son's innocence. But he knew he would never be sure of it—

He regretted that he had never been able to take a long vacation. He would have liked to take the boy on a trip west, riding the rapids in one of the rivers, something daring and adventuresome—like the Kennedys, who were always piling their big families into those rubber rafts and challenging nature. But he wasn't a Kennedy, exposed from childhood on to games and athletic challenges. He was a nice Jewish boy from the inner city who, to this day, was not comfortable with dogs or horses. He often criticized Silvie because she was so self-centered, but was he any better?

It was nearly six by the time he turned into the driveway. Silvie's white Caddy was in the garage and the door was open, which suggested she would be going out to show some houses in the evening or do some work in the real estate office with Mrs. Liss and Mrs. Rothschild, who were as intense about their new selling jobs as they once were about bridge, backgammon and golf.

He went around the side, hearing sounds in the pool. Silvie was doing her ten laps; exercise and drinking that liquid protein glop had reduced her body to a rail, which she thought was marvelous. Barbara was sitting on the deck in white shorts and a halter, playing with her kitten.

Silvie reached the steps leading out of the water, pulled off her lavender swimming cap and unfastened the top of her brilliant green swimsuit. The new diet had reduced her boobs to saucers, he thought, trying to remember what they were like when they had appealed to him.

Barbara gave him a weak smile. Silvie, drying herself, said, "You'd better hurry; you'll be late for the board meeting—"

"I have plenty of time," he said.

She followed him through the kitchen and upstairs. "Any news about who will win?"

"Not that I know of."

"Eve Rothschild says Virginia Carruthers has a lot going for her."

"So do a few others. But the board won't have a woman chief. They're too traditional."

She dropped her suit, padded over to him, put her bony hands on his shoulders and stared him in the face.

"Malcolm, according to the grapevine, the job is yours." Her fingers dug into his shoulders. He had the feeling she was hypnotizing him; that in some way her wanting it so badly would cement his success. That because she wanted more than anything to prove she was just as good as everyone else, everything would fall into place, and she would be the wife of the chief of staff of what was destined to become the finest hospital in the northeast.

What would happen to her if he was not selected, he wondered. He knew privately that he couldn't step into John Paul's shoes. Leave it to executive stress tests, he thought to himself, feeling he had gone as far as he could. I'm content to live in my narrow world—if only Silvie would stop bugging me.

Dr. Monroe deserves to be chief of staff, he decided, and Dr. Virginia his deputy chief. But he didn't want Silvie to start thinking he wasn't interested in the position.

To forestall that he said, "Jack Palfrey called me this morning."

"Yes?"

"He thinks the Winterhaven Street properties are a good investment. He's drawing up the papers."

She favored him with a wide smile. "Great! I'll remodel them and convert them to condominiums." She put on a silk robe a shade lighter than her red hair. "It is a terrific investment. They'll make tons of money—" And if he ever tried to divorce her, she would be well protected. No accountant could do more for her than she could herself. Malcolm, poor guy, felt so guilty about making money, he was always finding ways to lose it. Not her. With Jack Palfrey's help, she would end up being rich, securely, imperturbably, gloriously rich. . . .

Malcolm showered and shaved and got into a gray silk Italian suit; the medical staff dressed formally for board meetings. Before he was ready to go, Silvie was leaving. She knew Jack approved of Malcolm's negotiations for the Fairfield estate; what annoyed her was that here he was buying a half million dollar property without giving her the chance to sell him one herself. He could just as well have bought a place she was representing.

Malcolm looked into the bedroom, but Barbara was nowhere in sight. He found her in the kitchen pouring milk for her kitten.

"Barbie—" he came over and put his arm around her.

"Mom said that was champagne and caviar in the kitchen—what's it for?"

"To celebrate."

"To celebrate what?"

"She thinks I'm going to be made chief of staff tonight."

"Are you?"

"I don't think so."

Barbara was silent for a long time. Then: "Will you be sad if you don't get it?"

"Maybe for a little while. But we don't always get what we want." He rubbed her bare back. "I understand you don't like secretarial school?"

"Nope."

"Pity you couldn't get into Katharine Gibbs. What's wrong with this one?"

She shrugged. "It's tacky."

"Your mother didn't think it was bad."

Her eyes didn't look away from his. "Mom's tacky."

"Barbara, you don't like it here, do you?"

"I hate it. Sometimes I wish I could run away—I almost did—with Al."

"Al who?"

"This kid from high school. But he joined up with this creepy group—"

"A cult?"

"Yeah—Father something or other."

Oh, my God, he thought, it's all my fault. He forgot about the meeting. He needed to make sure his child was not going off the deep end.

"Barbie, tell me what you want."

But first she told him what she didn't like: the church Mom sent her to; the dancing class, the fact that they did not belong to the right club.

Finally she told him what she wanted. "I want to be Jewish," she said. "Jewish kids have more fun. Their mothers always drive them everywhere and they have the best food to eat—and their mothers treat them like little princesses . . ."

"Barbie—" Malcolm said, scarcely hiding his joy. "How would you like to live with your Jewish grandmother for a while?"

"Gee, I'd love it."

"I'll call her the first thing in the morning."

338

Silvie couldn't say no. He would remind her of the law in California that allowed a teenager to be independent, to live away from her parents if the court decided it was in her best interests. Besides, she would be eighteen soon and could vote and make her own decisions. . . . Mama and Barbie. Bless them. . . .

CHAPTER XLI

The telephone rang as Mrs. Thalberg and Karen were arranging the final details of the luncheon they were giving for Shulamit.

"It's for you, Karen," Mrs. Thalberg said, handing her the phone. "It's Fred."

Wouldn't you know, Karen thought, stifling her impatience, that he would call at the worst possible time. It's about Shulamit again, no doubt; for the last week he had been on the telephone to her constantly, in long drawn-out conversations that were rambling and tedious, all about Shulamit's treatment of him. It certainly was a role reversal, Karen thought, for Shulamit to decide *he* wasn't good enough.

Her family likes me, Fred had told her at least a half dozen times over the telephone. They want to set me up in my own office. They want to send Shulamit and me to Europe or Israel for our honeymoon. I'll go to Israel if she wants.

The spot Shulamit wanted to visit, Karen thought to herself, was Egypt.

Shulamit was preparing for a visit to Egypt, where she would be hosted by an organization of Egyptian women ready for sexual liberation and information about the newest contraceptives. Planned Parenthood had virtually no foothold in Egypt, but Shulamit was determined to do whatever she could to help educate the Moslem women who had been too locked in *purdah* to realize that their bodies belonged to themselves, and were now, in ever greater numbers, beginning to see that they no longer needed to be second-class citizens.

"Hi," Fred said when Karen came on the line. "I'm getting off duty in about an hour. Tell Shulamit to stick around . . ."

Shulamit finished her chef's salad and said, "I'll remember this meal—when I'm mouldering in some ghastly Egyptian jail, waiting for the American Embassy to rescue me."

"Contraceptives are safer than hash," Mady Lucas said. "Only a mechanic would know what an IUD is."

Karen had invited Mady because she had introduced Shulamit to her at the auxiliary ball. Besides, it would be her own last chance to see Mady for a while, since the Lukases would soon be flying to London, where her grandfather was having a week of executive meetings with the managers of his diversified companies. Maureen looked more stunning than usual, she had gained some weight and looked more statuesque than ever.

"Will you girls do me a favor?" Shulamit asked, including Mrs. Thalberg with her conspiratorial smile. "Can you keep Freddie occupied for a couple of days—just until I take off?"

"Aren't you being a little unkind to him?" Mrs. Thalberg said.

"I guess I am. But I feel like I have to, the way my family 'approves' of him."

"Oh, I'll take him on," Mady Lukas said.

By the time Fred arrived home from the hospital, Shulamit was gone. She had planned it that way. But Mady was there, helping Karen pack. Even though he was depressed, he drove to Karen's new house. For two days, Mady could handle anything. . . .

Dr. Hilton had a clear desk before he went into the executive committee meeting this evening. He placed a call to his wife before going into the board room. Esther was accustomed to his uncertain hours;

but at the moment, she didn't mind, since it took most of her energy and time to get their new house in order.

"Harlow, let me know who they pick as soon as it's over."

He put on his suit jacket, tightened the knot of his tie, and smoothed back his dark straight hair. He walked toward the board room where the executive committee was already gathered. It was going on seven o'clock, and the last slanting rays of sun were soft and gold through the window panes. The small buffet under the clock was set with cold cuts, rolls, salad, miniature pastries and urns of coffee and tea.

The chairs around the board table were occupied by the heads of each department: Dr. Stone, from cardiology; Dr. Monroe, obstetrics and gynecology; Dr. Carruthers, pediatrics; Dr. Watling, family practice, as well as the other departmental chiefs, the deputy chief, the secretary and the delegate-at-large—all M.D.s.

On the table before each of them lay a folder containing the agenda and backup material for the meeting, as well as pads, pencils, glasses and pitchers of ice water.

They were strained and uncomfortable as they looked at each other, wondering. They would have to discuss the physician who would replace Dr. Macray as chief of the medical staff and fill out his unexpired term. But who, they wondered, could really fill his place?

The deputy chief touched the gavel lightly to the wood. They were all staring at the empty place.

"The meeting will come to order."

At that moment there was a sound at the door. Dr. Macray strode in looking lean, rugged, tanned and radiating energy. He walked down the length of the room to the chair at the head of the table, and pulled it out. The people at the table gasped in surprise. Dr. Macray had made a spectacular recovery.

"Well, doctors," he said with a triumphant smile, "shall we begin?"

When Peter left his office, he went home to Mrs. Thalberg's for the last time. But she told him that Karen had left earlier.

"Mady Lukas and Fred helped her move. They should all be at the river house by now. Karen left the station wagon for you."

He thanked her and went upstairs to get his belongings; there weren't many boxes, mostly his medical books and his notebooks. When he was loading the car, Mrs. Thalberg came out with a small hamper. "You won't have time to go out for dinner—I fixed a little something for you . . ."

He turned to her. "What a nice lady you are." She came close to him, her dark eyes shining. She placed her hands on his shoulders and kissed him on the cheek.

"Be happy, Peter."

"Thanks, Mrs. Thalberg. Thanks—thanks for everything."

"My pleasure; I've gotten more out of it than you'll know. And don't be strangers."

"We won't."

"And Peter—don't be mad at Karen for making the payment on the house. Be glad she could do it."

He smiled. They certainly kept no secrets from Mrs. Thalberg. But he didn't feel right about it, even though Karen had been so sure. He had never seen her so determined.

"My father is having the trust take care of everything," she had said. "If I alone have to see that we have a roof over our heads and a bed of our own, I'll do it."

He had been torn between love and shame. "You're bold, you're brazen. I know you used me to get over your first love affair. But I'm hooked. What can I say?"

"Play along," she had teased. "Like the song says—'help me make it through the night'—the day *and* the night . . ."

He cut through the back roads to the river house. Mady's Mercedes was gone, and so was Fred. But Karen was there, dressed in shorts and a halter, her hair in braids. She was helping a young man wash the windows.

She is crazy, he thought, that's Raoul—he's a rough customer.

He parked the car, half anticipating trouble. But Raoul stood grinning, holding the window mop, while Karen raced out to greet Peter.

"What's he doing here?" Fear always made him seem gruff.

"Don't be stuffy. He's helping me get the place in order. And tomorrow, he's going to bring some of his friends. We'll have our own WPA."

"You don't listen to me, do you?"

"Sometimes, but only when you're right. Your mother says you are pig-headed like your father and your brothers." She snuggled up to him, coyly. "I sent her a photograph of the house. She wrote me the nicest letter."

"Did she, now? And what did she say?"

"She suggested we get married before the cold weather sets in. Otherwise she'll have to send us a bundling board."

"She thinks we should be married?"

"No, it's what *you* told *her* when you took them to the airport this summer. You can't back out now, buster!"

So they were married in her parents' townhouse and spent their honeymoon in her grandmother Wickersham's place in Rhinebeck.

I'm one hell of a lucky guy, Peter thought, lying in the double bed and listening to the river gurgling with the early autumn rains. Karen lay close to him, her body conforming to his, the fragrance of her hair and skin stirring his senses.

He was in the right place at the right time, he reflected . . . with all the promises for the future falling into shape. Technology that opened the path to the moon had given his profession new weapons. Within the next decade, the medical workup of every patient would be detailed by computer and presented to him. Already, high-powered microscopes allowed for delicate operations that had been impossible a few years earlier. Severed arms and legs had been reattached and ultrasound waves had given new clarity to images of the body's interior. The CAT scanner had revolutionized diagnostic techniques. It was a time for change, a time for growth.

The streak of moonlight stretched along the lawn, silvering patches of the lawn, making the shrubs a dark, mysterious sculpture. He stretched and Karen stirred lightly, murmuring something in her sleep—

The telephone's ring was muted; its summons soft but urgent. It was the nurse from Kennedy Four, the respiratory care floor; one of his elderly patients was having a pulmonary problem. He gave the nurse instructions, lay quiet for a moment, then got up and dressed.

He knew the man would receive the proper care but he would not feel right until he saw him personally. The commitment between him and those in his care went beyond technology, maybe even beyond—

He looked over at Karen. *No,* he thought, *she's part of it now.*

He walked out into the moonlight and got into the station wagon. And made what would be the beginning of new tracks, from the river house to the hospital.